JUST DESSERTS

Married with four sons, Sue Welfare is the author of
A Few Little Lies and also of eight erotic novels.
Born on the edge of the Fens, she is perfectly placed
to write about the vagaries of life in East Anglia.
Sue Welfare was runner-up in the *Mail on Sunday*
novel competition in 1995, and winner of the Wyrd
Short Story prize in the same year.
Just Desserts is her second mainstream novel.

SUE WELFARE

Just Desserts

HarperCollins*Publishers*

HarperCollins*Publishers*
77–85 Fulham Palace Road,
Hammersmith, London W6 8JB

A Paperback Original 1999
5 7 9 8 6 4

Copyright © Sue Welfare 1999

The Author asserts the moral right to
be identified as the author of this work

A catalogue record for this book
is available from the British Library

ISBN 0 00 649993 7

Set in Sabon by
Rowland Phototypesetting Ltd,
Bury St Edmunds, Suffolk

Printed and bound in Great Britain by
Caledonian International Book Manufacturing Ltd,
Glasgow

For Tom, Ben, James, Joe and Sam, who – fuelled
by the kind of faith that can only be sustained by
those who love you best – have wisely ignored
all my hopes and fears

Chapter One

'Telling lies is a fault in a boy, an art in a lover, an
    accomplishment in a bachelor, and second-nature
    in a married man.'
Helen Rowland (1875–1950). *A Guide to Men*, 'Syn-
    copations' (1922).

Murder, thought Katherine Bourne, picking at her teeth
with the vegetable knife, was a possible solution. It wasn't
the first time she'd considered it. Of course, there was no
such thing as the perfect murder. The only certain way of
avoiding prison was suicide, though Katherine considered
being married to Harry Bourne for twenty-five years just
about as much suicide as one woman could take in a
lifetime.

Perhaps she should have been more assertive, less com-
pliant, embraced that empowerment thing.

Under the work-top the dishwasher hissed malevolently
while Katherine skilfully disembowelled a beef tomato. She
couldn't claim ignorance of the feminist movement. She'd
read all the books. The thing was, somehow she knew that
it didn't fit. She had liked being at home when the children
were small, liked gardening and baking and running the
house. How could you throw yourself whole-heartedly into
the cause if you were constantly worried about what the
baby-sitter might be doing in your absence? Besides, her
hips were too big for boiler-suits and maybe she was just
too old now.

'Kitty-Kat?' Harry's 'Oh dear, oh dear' voice from the
kitchen door reprieved an innocent tomato.

He stepped into the kitchen wearing an immaculately pressed, pristine white shirt that she had recently hung amongst a dozen identical ones. She looked up, knife in hand, fingers slick with tomato pulp. Did he flinch or did she imagine it?

'Yes, darling,' she said pleasantly, sliding the knife down alongside the chopping board.

He looked heavenwards. 'Too much starch again, Kitty-Kat.' He ran a finger around his reddening turkey neck. 'Anyone would think you wanted to cut my throat.' He laughed nervously and undid the buttons with a certain flirtatiousness, as if there was some possibility she might still be intrigued by the fish-white belly that lurked beneath.

'Are they all the same?' he said, discarding the clean white shirt casually on the kitchen floor.

Katherine Bourne wiped her hands and stooped to retrieve it. 'Your others are hanging in the wardrobe.'

He sighed theatrically. 'I'm going to be late.' His voice lifted towards the end of the sentence; the implication was that it was her fault – again. She rinsed her hands in the nifty little half sink she'd had put in the new kitchen and hurried upstairs.

'While you're up there . . .' his voice pursued her up the stairs. 'Do you think you could bring down my suit jacket and my brief-case?'

Noisily Katherine opened and shut the wardrobe door and then carried the same shirt she had just rescued back down to him.

He slipped it on and smiled.

'That's much better,' he said, running a finger around the collar. 'Might be better if you rinsed those other ones again.'

Katherine nodded.

When he kissed her goodbye and whispered, 'Miss you, Kitty-Kat. Remember I won't be home until late Monday night. Don't wait up,' she actually shuddered. His touch was just another obligation.

He lifted his hand in salute and was gone.

She waved, watching his slick anonymous grey company car glide out of the drive.

'Goodbye, you miserable little bastard,' she said, smiling as she did.

Carol Ackerman picked up the phone and pressed the button to take her call. Her new office at Lactons was like a damned fish tank; glass walls, glass door. She peered into the reception area. Outside she could see her secretary, Jeanette, smirking.

'Hello, Carol Ackerman?'

'Hello, darling. It's me.'

Carol swung her chair round so that she was looking out over the Thames.

'Hello, Harry. How are you?' she purred.

In the reception area Jeanette had given herself an unofficial nail file break.

The girl at the desk opposite nodded towards Carol's office. 'Lover-boy again?'

Jeanette rolled her eyes and then glanced at the clear plastic clock standing beside her keyboard. It always disturbed her to see its innards like that, all throbbing and glistening. She nodded, sliding the file in a flawless arc around her index finger.

'Friday afternoon, two forty-five. Phone call from Harry Bourne? I smell a dirty weekend in the offing.'

The other girl grinned. 'A "Hold my calls, I've got to go out and see an important client" sort of Friday?'

'An "Oh, and I may be late in Monday morning" sort of weekend,' Jeanette continued in an exaggerated impression of Carol's cultured voice. 'Do you reckon she's planning to sleep her way into a promotion as well?'

3

The girl grinned. 'She'd have to be dedicated to sleep with old Collingwood. I dunno about promotion, I'd need an anaesthetic.'

Jeanette snorted.

They both turned to look into the fish bowl office. Carol Ackerman was stretching out her long black-stockinged legs like a sleek cat. She tossed her head back and ran one hand through her lush dark hair. As if sensing she was being watched, she swung round a little further, arching back in her chair, carmine lips drawn back in a throaty laugh.

'Must be somewhere good,' said the girl at the other desk, enviously.

After a few more seconds the buzzer on Jeanette's desk flashed like a winking eye. Jeanette tucked the phone onto her shoulder and carried on filing. 'Yes, Ms Ackerman.'

'I'm afraid I have to go out. Can you hold my calls, if anyone asks I've had to go to a meeting –' Carol hesitated.

'And?' prompted Jeanette.

'It must have slipped my mind. I may be late in on Monday morning. One of our Japanese clients is flying back first thing.'

Jeanette nodded. 'And it's important you see him off.'

'Well, of course,' said Carol.

As Carol spoke, Jeanette dropped a slow conspiratorial wink to the girl on the desk opposite.

Back at Harry's country house, Katherine was busy in the kitchen when the phone rang.

'May I speak to Mrs Katherine Bourne?'

She was just dropping the last of the vegetables into freezer bags. Bright, electric-green peas and beans, fresh from their trip through boiling water, glistened under the misty polythene.

'Speaking.'

4

'Hi, my name is Hope Laughton, I'm from Quirners?' The woman's soft transatlantic lilt added a question that wasn't really there.

'Uh huh,' said Katherine, tipping more peas through a fat-necked funnel. She nipped the phone tight between her chin and shoulder. 'I'm afraid you have me at a disadvantage. You're not selling anything are you?'

The woman laughed. 'No, sorry, and I'm not in time-share either.'

Katherine smiled. She liked the sound of the woman's voice. 'Damn,' she said, with a grin, 'so you won't be tempting me with a wonderful mystery free gift?'

Hope Laughton guffawed. 'Naw, 'fraid not. I work for a television locations company. We've been spying out the land for a new TV drama series in your area. I was hoping I might persuade you to let us use your house. Just the exterior. Shouldn't take more than a day or two.'

Katherine squeezed the breath from the polythene bag and twisted the metal tie into a garrotte. 'I'm not sure that I understand exactly what you mean.'

'Not a problem,' countered Hope. 'Look, I'm just down the road from you. I know it's short notice, but how about if I drop by and explain? No strings, promise.'

Katherine glanced round the kitchen. It was littered with the signs of good harvest.

'Yes,' she said cheerfully. 'Why not? I was about to put the kettle on.'

'Great, I can be with you in about ten minutes.'

Katherine plugged in the kettle and then returned to ripping nubile young beans from their fur-trimmed cradles.

Hope Laughton had curled up on the sofa under the picture window in Katherine's kitchen. Harry had always thought soft furnishings in the kitchen were some sort of joke. Katherine almost wished he was here so that she could prove him wrong. Hope Laughton, in her chic little grey

5

suit, was made for that sofa. Katherine carried the tea tray over to the kitchen table.

Hope slipped off her elegant court shoes as if she'd come home.

'Shit, I really hate high heels,' she said, wriggling her long toes as she took the cup and saucer. 'I'm really glad you said you'd see me. I was beginning to think I'd never find the right place.' She sipped the tea gratefully and purred her approval.

Katherine pulled out a chair at the table. 'How did you decide on our house?'

'I'm staying in a little guest house on the outskirts of Huntingdon. I must have driven past about twenty times. Every time I think, wow, that's the sort of place I'm looking for. I'll just go down here another mile or so and see if I can find anything better. Well, I've been down here a week now and I haven't.' She leant forward and took a biscuit off the tray. 'It's a really great house.' She looked around the low cool summer kitchen. 'I'd love a place like this.'

Katherine stirred her tea thoughtfully. She loved it too. It was like another child. She'd tended it, nursing it gently but firmly into maturity, despite Harry's initial objections to it being so far away from London, chosen every piece of furniture, every yard of fabric, built the garden. It was one of the few remaining reasons she couldn't quite bring herself to murder Harry. After all, who could she trust to look after the house while she was in Holloway? She realised she had said nothing. The American woman was watching her with interest.

'So sorry. I was miles away. Tell me what you have in mind.'

'Would it be too pushy to ask for more tea?'

Katherine shook her head smiling. 'No, not pushy at all. Have you eaten? I was just going to make myself a sandwich when you rang.' She got to her feet.

Hope grimaced, good manners battling with her true feelings.

'No, really,' Katherine said, dealing briskly with the American's inner conflict. 'It would be no trouble at all.'

'Then I'd be a fool to say no. Truth is, I'm absolutely famished. Can I help?'

Katherine was about to object. She was all tuned to serve and refuse help but something stopped her. 'If you like,' she said. 'How are you at vegetables?'

'Not bad, not bad. I mean, I may be a Yank but I can still tell broccoli from baked beans.'

'In that case if you make a salad, I'll do some pasta.'

'Pasta sandwiches? Is this a British thing?'

Katherine grinned. 'No, I thought we could have tuna and pasta, tossed in garlic mayonnaise with sweetcorn and a green salad. How does that sound?'

Hope blew a low appreciative whistle. 'Sounds fine, if you really don't mind. Just point me towards those vegetables.'

Katherine handed her a colander from under the work surface. 'They're still in the garden.'

Hope glanced at the shiny black court shoes abandoned by the sofa.

'There are some wellies in the conservatory you can borrow, but it wouldn't hurt to go out in bare feet. I've laid brick paths round all the beds,' Katherine said, taking the pasta out of the fridge.

Hope grinned and picked up the colander. 'Not a problem,' she said and padded off to Katherine's precious vegetable garden, whistling the *Lullaby of Broadway*.

The airport was full of bright streams of travellers. Carol Ackerman glanced at her watch. Harry was never late. Finally she spotted his distinctive red-gold thatch amongst a tight scrum of businessmen. She lifted a hand in greeting and as a body the men headed towards her.

'Good. You made it then,' said Harry, before she had chance to say anything. He glanced sharply at a plump executive, who was standing no more than a step behind him toting an expensive brief-case.

Carol lifted an eyebrow. Harry pulled his face into a uneasy apologetic grimace as the businessman pushed forward with his hand extended. He spoke in heavily accented English.

'I am very pleased to meet you, Miss Ackerman. How very good of you to give up your weekend for us. These breakfast meetings – pah.' He lifted his thick chubby hand to add an exclamation mark.

Carol opened her mouth to speak again when Harry stepped forward, closing his fingers tightly around her elbow.

'No problem at all, Herr Bader,' he said with false heartiness. He looked at Carol with an expression of appeal. 'No problem at all, was it, Carol?'

'Er, no,' Carol began.

Herr Bader grinned and slapped Harry on the shoulder. 'Harry has already said you are his very best secretary, Carol. Perhaps you could lend her to me when we get to Paris, eh Harry? I have some faxes I desperately need to get off. Oh and then there is the shopping, for my wife –' He turned and headed towards the gate.

Carol glared at Harry, who had turned his attention to shepherding the rest of Herr Bader's entourage through into the departure lounge.

'Not again,' she hissed furiously from the corner of her mouth.

Harry shrugged and followed Herr Bader and his companions towards the plane.

Someone had booked Carol into a seedy little annex room overlooking the kitchen compound at the hotel.

Furiously she dragged her well cut crop into sleekness.

8

'Ten years,' she whispered, snapping on pearl earrings. 'Ten bloody years.' She looked at herself in the pitted mirror. Her expensive little black evening suit was cut well above the knee revealing most of her elegant legs. Not that she could see them. The bedroom mirror was snapped off in a jagged razor edge just above her waist.

She ran her tongue over her teeth. 'Why do I let you do this to me, Harry Bourne?' she said crossly and touched up the vivid scarlet slash of lipstick that set off the rich cream skin she had been blessed with. She picked up her clutch bag and hurried off to meet Harry.

It was an hour before dinner and the corridors of the hotel were being prowled by mistresses reshuffling themselves into the right rooms. Their nonchalance bordered on the neurotic and fooled no one.

Carol glanced over her shoulder before she tapped on the door of his suite.

Harry, wrapped in a thick bath towel, opened it a crack and practically dragged her inside.

'Did anyone see you?' He flicked the TV set onto mute.

Carol snorted. 'For God's sake, everyone is at it. No one takes a blind bit of notice – particularly in Paris.'

Harry looked uncomfortable. 'The Germans don't like it.'

Carol went to the mini-bar and poured herself a glass of wine.

'Bugger the bloody Germans. Herr Bader couldn't keep his hands off me. Did you see him on the plane? He was all over me like a rash. And why, in God's name, did you tell him I was your secretary? Do you realise I've now got six faxes in my brief-case?'

Harry looked up anxiously. 'You have sent them, haven't you?'

Carol downed the wine in one. 'Of course I haven't, I don't know how to use a fax machine, my secretary does all that for me.'

Harry slapped his forehead. 'Well, go back to your room and get them.' He glanced at his watch. 'Maybe there's someone in reception who can do them.'

Carol slammed the wine glass down on the counter. 'When you said a weekend in Paris, Harry, this was not exactly what I had in mind.'

Harry gave her his little lost spaniel expression.

She sighed. 'Oh, all right. Pour me another glass of wine will you?'

Harry grinned. 'Thank you darling,' he said, blowing her a kiss. As she got to the door he flicked the TV remote and the sound came back on. 'You won't mind doing his shopping for him tomorrow then?' he added over his shoulder as he eased himself back into the armchair.

While Carol found Herr Bader's faxes, Katherine Bourne opened another bottle of wine and refilled Hope's glass.

'I'm surprised,' said the American, as she leant forward to light a cigarette from the candles in the centre of the table, 'that a house this big is still a family home. Most of them are converted into nursing homes and hotels round here. I mean, I really love the space, but don't you find it a bit on the big side?'

Katherine rolled her glass around in her capable hands. 'No, not really. And of course there are the children.'

Hope, her eyes bright with wine, laughed. 'I should have guessed.' She paused and looked out of the open French windows onto the terrace beyond. The light was just beginning to fade, kissing the urns of bright summer annuals into perfection. 'You remind me of my mother.'

From anyone else it would have sounded like an insult, from Hope Laughton it sounded like the ultimate accolade. Katherine smiled, feeling infinitely flattered.

'So how old are your kids?'

Katherine pushed her chair back and stretched out her legs. 'Sarah's twenty-three and Peter's twenty-two, there's only fourteen months between them. Quite a handful when they were little but lovely now.'

'I bet. Do they live here too?'

'No, Sarah's just finishing her first year teaching in Norwich and Matthew is still at university in Leicester. He took a year out.'

'Not coming home for the summer?'

Katherine shrugged. 'Who can tell?'

'Indeed, who can tell.' Hope peered around the comfortable dining room. 'It's a great place but don't you ever get bored? I mean, you're a smart cookie – do you work?'

The question was really too close. What was the truth?

Hope looked away, sensing she had strayed into a prickly area. 'What I mean is, my mother went back to teaching when we were off her hands. Three boys and then me, as if that wasn't enough kids for anyone.'

Katherine struggled to regain her composure and shrugged. 'I was a nurse. But I really couldn't imagine going back to that now. The hours, night duty – besides Harry wouldn't like it.'

Hope bent forward, leaning her elbows on the table. 'He's your husband, right?' She blew a slow winding curl of blue hazy cigarette smoke across the table. 'How many bedrooms have you got here, six, eight?'

'Five, we're using one as an office for Harry at the moment.'

Hope nodded thoughtfully. 'It would make a great rest home.'

'Smelling of boiled cabbage and old ladies?'

Hope pinned her with her bright piercing blue eyes. 'And maybe a lot worse, but there's a lot of bucks in it, babe, and you could take in who you want. It's a growing market. And you've got the space here.' She paused. 'Those great buildings you've got around the back, staff rooms, recreational facilities, for Christ's sake you've already got a pool. Go for the upper crust.'

Afterwards, Katherine would say that the idea built slowly, with much thought and infinite planning, but at that second, watching the shrewd American take another long slow pull on her cigarette, Katherine saw the whole thing. 'How would I go about something like that?' she said evenly.

Hope shrugged. 'How the hell should I know? I'm just looking for place to shoot a TV series, but hey – how hard can it be?'

Katherine refilled her own wine glass. 'You're right,' she said softly.

Dinner at the hotel in Paris was grand, wine, six courses. Carol had been seated between someone called Herr Roch and a tiny ginger man with thick glasses, whom everyone referred to as Klaus.

'Have you been to Paris before, Klaus?' Carol said, slowly trying to drag up one of those polite stilted conversations that launched a thousand forgettable encounters.

Klaus leered at her. His eyes rolled behind the lenses. He'd obviously had quite a few aperitifs before they'd sat down for dinner. He said something in a low lecherous purr. Carol did not ask him to repeat it. Although she didn't speak German very well she could understand lust in any language.

Harry, on the far side of Herr Bader, smiled and waved as if she were standing at the far end of a jetty.

Viciously she speared at the tiny collection of shellfish exquisitely arranged amongst fennel and delicate curls of vegetables on her plate and stuffed them into her mouth. As she went for a second forkful she felt Klaus' hand slide stealthily up over her thigh.

She turned to smile at him, he grinned and moved his fingers higher. Without breaking their gaze she lifted her fork and plunged it into the back of Klaus' hand. His eyes shrank to pinpricks behind his thick glasses, she felt his fingers contracting and he made a strange kind of high-pitched wheezing noise in the back of his throat.

'*Gesundheit*,' she said pleasantly and wiped her fork on her napkin. Klaus coughed, tears forming in his eyes. Very slowly he turned to talk to the man on his left and Carol went back to her shellfish.

They got to bed around twelve. A bucket and a half of house wine had made Harry forget to pretend they weren't a couple and he practically dragged her upstairs to his suite.

'One day,' he purred, cupping her breast, while he fumbled for his keys outside the door to his suite, 'you and me, we'll be together. We make a good couple. Herr Bader said you were lovely.'

Carol fished the keys out her clutch bag. 'Well, that's all right then, as long as the Germans approve. You've had rather a lot to drink.'

Harry giggled and tapped the side of his nose. 'Never been a problem has it, Carol? Never been a problem.'

She slid the key into the lock as his hands slid up under her skirt.

'God, you feel so good tonight,' he hissed in her ear. 'And stockings, God, I love stockings.'

Carol pushed the door open. The suite looked as if Harry had been burgled, shirts dropped on the floor, bed rolled back in an unseemly scrum. Harry launched himself towards the bed like an Olympic diver.

'Come to bed my pretty little Kitty-Kat,' he slurred. 'You know, someday me and you, we'll be together. Let me show you what you're missing. Paradise –' He slapped the unmade bed beside him.

Carol closed the door quietly. She had a pretty shrewd idea of what paradise might be, and realistically, this wasn't it.

Afterwards, when Harry was sleeping, snoring in postcoital bliss, Carol lit a cigarette and poured herself another glass of wine. She looked at the tousled soused self-appointed sex-god with a mixture of affection and indulgence. She didn't really want there to be a someday when they would be together. There had been a time, a long time ago, but that had passed – thank God.

They'd met at some promotional beano. He'd looked lush and tidily clipped like a well manicured front lawn, in a perfectly tailored suit and a snowy white shirt. It had taken her two hours to get him into bed – that was back in the days when she thought predatory was a good thing for a woman to be.

There had been a gap then – not a gap from Harry – just a gap where a casual fling and a lot of rumpy pumpy in strange plastic hotel rooms turned to a regular fling with less rumpy pumpy and Harry had started to say things like, 'My God, I wish it was like this all the time. I want to be with you forever.'

He had been now, well, almost – ten years counted as an awfully big slice of forever.

Once upon a time Carol had agonised frequently about the morality of it. Girl friends had told her he would never leave his wife – and of course they were right. But as time had gone on it had become less and less important. What Carol and Harry had was comfortable. She didn't really want him in her life as a resident, just as a visiting alien.

At first he justified his lack of up and leaving because of his children, then the mortgage, an operation, his wife's nervous disposition – how vulnerable and weak that woman was. Recently he'd found it harder to come up with a plausible excuse, until, with a streak of pure genius, Carol had hit on the menopause.

'Oh yes,' he'd said with breathless gratitude. 'I can't leave now, not when she's so vulnerable. I mean it's a big thing for a woman.'

Thoughtfully Carol flicked the ash from the cigarette

and poured herself the last of the wine. Yes, a big thing for a woman. But not quite as big as her arrangement to have safe sex with a comfortable familiar body, while not having to do his washing or clear up after him, just picking the ripest cherries from the top of the tree and leaving the rest for his wife to pip and bottle.

It might not be very commendable but then again what was? At least Carol had no intention whatsoever of snatching Harry away from his wife. Had she? She looked down at him, weighing her feelings against the windblown cherries; there had been a time when she really hoped that he would leave his wife. She took a long pull on the cigarette. Things change, people change. She'd given Harry one last chance to choose her, one last bridgehead and he had retreated.

Carol sighed, thinking about the might-have-beens and then shook her head to clear it. Too much wine, she thought, draining her glass. It didn't do to think too hard. There were a lot of compensations, lots; she had her job, her friends, her family – her sisters had produced six kids between the two of them so if she pined for the whiff of baby puke she could always pop over for a fix, even though sometimes the soft touch of their skin against her cheek and the smell of their tiny tiny bodies made some ancient part of her ache with need. Sweet torture. She sniffed, thrusting the pain firmly back into its box.

When Lactons had offered her a job as one of their top commercial loans team she had been able to smile with quiet confidence at the interview and say, with no guile whatsoever, 'No, I don't anticipate any career breaks.' Executive speak for babies and messy and very expensive maternity leave.

Oh no, she told herself, someday she most definitely didn't want them to be together, not now – and she knew, secretly, Harry was relieved. And now her boss was up for early retirement and she was in line for his job, one more

15

small step and she would be made part of the executive team. Life was almost perfect. Carol slid her glass onto the bedside table and headed off to the bathroom to brush her teeth.

'Bastard things.' A drunken Hope Laughton tried to land a slippery court shoe with her foot from beside the sofa in the kitchen.

Katherine handed Hope another brandy. 'Oh, leave them,' she snorted. 'I'll lend you a pair of my wellies.'

Hope collapsed back among the wealth of cushions braying like a donkey. 'You know, I haven't had this much fun for ages. We really ought to do it again some time.'

Katherine Bourne grinned. 'You're right. Look, I think I ought to call you a cab. You can't drive.'

Hope nodded. 'You're right. Shit, I can hardly see straight.' She straightened herself, trying to scrape together the last vestiges of her dignity. 'But you're on for the series, aren't you?'

Katherine giggled. 'Oh absolutely.'

'Good, good. I'll get the girl to draw up a contract . . .' She leant forward to pick up her handbag, fished a slick little mobile phone out and began to bang in a series of numbers.

'Hang on, hang on, what are you doing?'

Hope struggled to focus. 'Ringing my office, why?'

Katherine blinked and peered at the pine clock above the Aga. 'It's nearly two-thirty.'

Hope swayed dramatically. 'Good, they should all be back from lunch by now.'

'No, no two-thirty in the morning.'

Hope pulled a surprised face. 'Really?'

'I think it might be better if you stayed the night. The only decent taxi firm round here are probably all tucked up in their beds by now. What do you think?'

When she looked across at the sofa Hope Laughton was

sound asleep, still clutching her mobile phone. Katherine didn't mind. Manfully she struggled upstairs and dragged a duvet off one of the spare beds and then very gingerly climbed back downstairs.

In her short absence, Hope had curled up on the sofa and was snoring softly. Katherine folded the duvet over her unexpected and very welcome guest and headed back to bed.

Chapter Two

Herr Bader took the late afternoon plane to Bonn on Saturday. Carol watched Harry embracing the fat little German with a great show of filial affection. As the last hug and wave were complete she slid up beside Harry. At least they would have Sunday together.

'Good-bye, Carol, my dear.' Herr Bader whispered conspiratorially. 'So nice to meet you. You are very good at the shopping.'

Carol extended her hand. 'Very nice to meet you too, Herr Bader. I hope your wife likes her presents.' She pulled a business card from her bag and handed it to him. 'Why don't you look me up when you're next in London.'

Herr Bader peered myopically at the little rectangle of cardboard. Before he had chance to focus, Harry whipped it out of his pudgy little fingers.

'Carol's little joke,' he said, giving her a withering look and slipped it into his jacket. He smiled back at Herr Bader. 'They're calling your flight. We don't want you to miss your plane, do we?'

'No, don't want to keep the little hausfrau away from all that expensive designer knitwear, do we?' she growled in an undertone.

Harry caught hold of her arm. 'For God's sake, you nearly gave the game away.'

'Heaven forbid. What now? Back to the hotel? We've got time to go for a cruise along the Seine if we hurry.'

Harry looked uncomfortable.

'What? Oh, Harry. Look, I'm free until Monday morning.'

He stuffed his hands miserably into his pockets. 'I rang home this morning, and she doesn't sound too good. I thought it would be better if I went home early.'

Carol sighed. 'What is it this time?'

Harry looked non-committal. 'She didn't actually say, but I could tell there was something not quite right. You know what she's like. I'm always worried about leaving her on her own.'

Carol glanced round the airport. 'So when are we leaving?'

'Well, as soon as possible really. You know she's . . .'

Carol nodded. 'I know, vulnerable. Let's get back to the hotel and pick up the luggage.'

Katherine Bourne had a hangover the size of an emerging African nation. It sat like a hot and heavy grumpy toddler in the place her brain should be. Every time she moved, it rolled forward and beat against the front of her skull demanding attention. She closed an eye speculatively to see if it eased, instead too much razor-sharp daylight forced itself through the solitary open eyeball and started up another spasm of pain. It was late afternoon and the house looked – well, rough – almost as rough as she did.

Harry's early morning phone call had woken her from a particularly vivid dream in which she and Hope Laughton had been throwing Harry's limp but immensely unwieldy corpse over a cliff.

Hope, still a little unsteady, had left after coffee and biscuits around ten, with promises to be in touch and exuberant thanks for a good evening well spent.

It was very difficult to understand how two middle-aged women had created so much mess, thought Katherine, as she shovelled the remains of the salad into the bin she kept for composting. She sniffed the pasta and tuna salad and realised, a split second too late, as her stomach registered a violent and very vocal complaint that it had been a mistake. She closed her eyes as it plopped damply into the bin beside the salad. It shouldn't take that long to clear up, assuming she could find a way to jump start her body. The phone rang again.

'Hello, Katherine Bourne speaking.'

'Are you all right, Kitty-Kat?'

Katherine winced. 'Hello, Harry. How's it going in Paris?'

'You still don't sound very well, Kitty-kins.'

Katherine sucked her mouth into shape. 'I'm fine, really,' she said as robustly as she could.

There was a pointed silence.

'Well, maybe a little fluey. I think it's something going around.' Yes, around and around, like her head.

Harry made a strange throaty noise at the other end of the phone line. 'I just called to say I'm on my way home,' he said. 'I really don't like to think of you there all on your own. I'll be back tonight.'

Before she had a chance to say another word he hung up, so she said the other word anyway, 'Bollocks,' and slammed the receiver down into its cradle. The one time she needed a day to recover he decided to play Mr Sensitive Caring Husband. She opened the cabinet above the sink and took out a bottle of paracetamol.

Harry pressed his lips dryly to Katherine's forehead as he dropped his cases on the hall floor.

'What's for supper? I'm absolutely famished.'

Katherine looked up at him from behind eyes which still ached dramatically.

'I'm not well,' she said thickly.

'I know that, Kitty-Kat, that's why I came back early. A sandwich would do.' He dropped his jacket beside the cases. 'Isn't there something in the freezer I could have?' He was already on his way to the kitchen, pulling off his tie, slipping off his shoes.

Katherine sighed. Should anyone ever want to trace Harry they wouldn't have to worry about hiring a native tracker. They could simply follow the trail of discarded clothes, abandoned like little heaps of sloughed skin. She really didn't want to bend down to pick them up. The headache toddler, almost asleep now, but still hanging on tenaciously to a few favourite brain cells, wouldn't be able to cope with being plunged towards the parquet. She opened the hall cupboard and artfully kicked the jacket, tie and shoes inside.

Harry was searching the kitchen units frantically as if he was up against the clock.

Katherine touched his arm. 'Go and sit down, I'll make you an omelette.'

He stepped back, glumly, stuffing his hands in his pockets. 'I don't really fancy an omelette.'

She knew she was meant to be pleased that he'd arrived home early. His undoubted sacrifice, like the robes of the king, was supposed to heal all in its path and render her cured. She pulled a slab of frozen pasta sauce out of the freezer. 'Will spaghetti bolognaise be all right?'

He cheered visibly. 'Fine, yes, that'll do beautifully, any chance of a salad with it?'

Katherine glanced at her Wellingtons by the kitchen door, so recently abandoned by Hope Laughton. Outside it was getting dark; the torch was tucked in the drawer with the string and kitchen scissors.

'I'm sure I can manage that,' she said. 'Why don't you go and watch some TV and I'll call you when it's ready.'

'If you're sure you can manage?' he said as he slipped past her on his way to the sitting room.

'Oh, I'm sure I can,' she whispered, but he was already gone.

Katherine didn't eat with Harry, even the smell of the pasta made her feel nauseous. He chippered on, folding great spirals of spaghetti and sauce into his mouth, splattering his shirt with oozing red gobs of the damned stuff. She poured herself a glass of tonic water, added a slice of lemon, and then glanced at the kitchen sofa.

'Oh, by the way, I had a call from a film company while you were away.'

Harry stopped mid-shovel; a piece of spaghetti flopped damply onto the table-cloth.

'Really? What about?' he said with his mouth full.

'They want to know if they can use the house for a new TV series – just the exterior. They don't want to come inside.'

Harry wiped his lips on a napkin. 'Bet they were pissed off when you said no, eh? Takes them months to find the right place.'

Katherine nodded, poking at the slice of lemon in her glass. 'Actually I've said yes, provisionally. I mean, it can't hurt.'

Harry's face contorted like a fairground mirror. 'What? What in God's name made you agree without asking me first? I mean . . .' he spluttered.

'I didn't think you'd mind. You're not here during the day, most evenings you're not home until eight. They'll be finished shooting by then and it's only for a couple of days.'

Harry snorted. 'Oh well, that's it then, isn't it?' he said huffily. 'I mean, you've obviously made up your mind. And do they pay for this privilege?'

Katherine nodded, careful to disguise the little red hot spark of revolution that she knew gleamed in her eyes. 'Not a huge amount, but it'll help with the new plans I've got for the house.'

Harry tipped his head on one side. 'Plans? What plans?'

Katherine could sense the minefield looming ahead; Harry hated disruption. She smiled her best winning smile, even though her face muscles screamed in complaint.

'Nothing too dramatic, nothing that'll cause a lot of fuss, just a few alterations.'

Harry nodded, sucking a tricky bit of pasta out of his front teeth. 'And this film business will pay for it?'

'Oh yes,' said Katherine confidently. It would certainly pay for an architect to draw up the plans for the conversion she was toying with.

Harry persisted, but she could see the tension had gone out of his face. 'So, what is it you're planning to do with the house, again?'

Katherine got to her feet. 'Would you like some ice cream for dessert?' Nursery food for a nursery mind.

He nodded. 'Yes, now what about the house –'

Katherine peeked round the freezer door. 'Let's say it's a surprise, shall we?'

Harry grinned. 'All right,' he said, 'just as long as there isn't too much mess.'

'Oh, there won't be,' said Katherine, drawing the spoon through the red raw entrails of the raspberry ripple. 'I've been thinking about doing something like this for a very long time.'

No fresh milk and two demented ginger tom cats headbutting her for attention. Carol Ackerman threw her overnight bag and brief-case onto the kitchen table and plugged in the kettle. The kitchen was suffused with a lingering but not unfamiliar odour from the cat litter tray. She barely had time to prise a mug out of the sink before the back door opened.

'Carol, petal, we didn't think you'd be home until Monday night.'

Carol peered at Ray, her next door neighbour. 'Change of plan, do you fancy a coffee?'

Ray rolled his beautifully made up eyes. 'Not instant with that dried muck in it. I'll pop next door and get you a carton.' He stopped mid-pirouette. 'Everything all right, sweetness? You look completely done in. How was Paris?'

'About the same as usual. Oh and cut the high camp, I'm not much in the mood for mincing tonight.'

Ray snorted. 'Ouch, ouch, aren't we the grumpy one? We're off clubbing, got to get in the mood. Hang on. Have you eaten?'

Carol grimaced. 'Warm BR sandwich, carton coffee and a Mars bar.'

Ray scrunched up his nose and vanished.

A few minutes later he re-appeared with his friend, Geoff, in his wake. Between them they carried two trays. On one were two half-eaten meals and on the second a plate of chicken casserole with rice and a coffee pot full to the brim.

'Angels,' said Carol, pouring the mug of instant down the sink.

'Just plain nosy,' said Geoff with a wry grin, as he unpacked their supper onto the kitchen table.

Ray pulled a can of cat food out of one pocket of his chinos and a carton of milk from the other. 'And we didn't forget the ginger boys either, pass me the tin opener will you?'

'*So* what did you think of Le Chunnel?' Geoff was spooning double cream over the cherry crumble he'd just brought round for dessert.

Carol Ackerman shook her head. 'Uh huh, we flew. Harry is claustrophobic.'

Ray pulled a face. 'Amongst other things, darling. The man is a complete shit. You've wasted your youth on him.' As he spoke, he slapped the back of his hand against his forehead.

Carol poked him with her fork. 'I said cut the camp. He suits me, no strings.'

'Good sex?' Ray beaded her with his hypnotic blue-green eyes.

'Don't be so personal,' snapped Geoff, handing Carol

24

her dessert. 'But really, darling, we all know he expects too much.'

'We've got this super chap who's just started using the café at lunch-time. Right up your street.'

Listening to Geoff and Ray was like hearing a single conversation performed by two players.

'Lovely hands,' Geoff.

'Lovely manners,' Ray.

Carol spooned bitter-sweet cherries into her mouth; these conversations could go on all night.

'And he loves animals because we asked him,' Ray.

'Particularly cats,' Geoff.

'Not like Harry with his bloody allergies,' both.

Carol licked the cream off her lips and shook her head. 'I'm spoken for.'

'No you're not,' hissed Geoff.

They began the recitation of this new superman's glowing attributes. She had known the pair of them for years, since she'd first bought the house in Cambridge. Commuting was a real bastard but coming home to a proper house was total bliss. Ray and Geoff, who lived next door, had instantly adopted her, buying her the ginger kittens as a moving-in present, mothering her appallingly until she thought of them as family. Better than family. They'd never met Harry but they knew all about him, in fact there wasn't much they didn't know about her.

Across the table, the fully guaranteed reference for Mr Right was being drawn to its usual conclusion.

'So what do you think, then?' said Geoff, reaching for the coffee pot.

Ray laid his spoon down. 'Well, I think he's absolutely perfect.'

They both looked at her for some sort of reply.

'I've got presents,' she said softly. Two pairs of eyes brightened with avarice. She picked up her brief-case.

'You shouldn't have,' they both purred in unison.

Carol grinned and opened it. 'Ciggies.' They squirrelled them across the table. 'A little aftershave for the men of the house.' She passed them each a bottle of Roget & Galle *Le Homme*, their absolute all-time favourite. 'And finally –' she produced two beautifully wrapped parcels.

Geoff ripped the bow off. 'Black silk boxers, you little vixen,' he giggled.

Ray opened his more carefully. 'Leopard skin, my favourite,' he said, holding them up for Geoff's approval.

'And even more finally –' Carol brought out a small bundle wrapped in a wedge of paper napkins. 'A new coffee pot for the collection in the shop.' She pulled off the paper to reveal a tiny black Art Deco coffee pot rimmed with gold.

Geoff ran a finger over its lid, still stained with a spot or two of coffee. 'Which you stole . . .'

'. . . From a very chic little cafeQ, in a very chic little boulevard, under the nose of a very unchic German businessman,' Carol added.

'While buying his awful wife her awful presents.'

'And masquerading as the shit's secretary.'

Carol nodded. 'The very same.'

Ray and Geoff whistled appreciatively.

'You should have worked for the Resistance,' said Geoff, refilling her coffee cup.

'Or better still, let us fix you up with our new friend.'

'Who is Carol Ackerman?' Katherine was getting ready for bed and taking the oddments out of Harry's jacket before it went into the basket for the dry cleaners.

'Uh?' Harry's voice percolated through from the bathroom.

'Carol Ackerman?'

Harry peered round the door, toothbrush wedged in his mouth. 'Commercial Loans, works at Lactons. Why?' he asked, through rabid mint-flavoured froth.

'Her business card is in your jacket pocket.'

Harry slipped on his dressing gown. 'Oh really? I can't think . . .' he paused thoughtfully. 'I know, Friday. Must be something to do with the Germans. A very shrewd cookie is Carol. I use her a lot. She's nice though, you'd like her.'

Katherine sighed, thinking it was a shame Harry obviously didn't, it would be so much easier if he was having an affair. She looked at the card again: 'Carol Ackerman. Commercial Loans Adviser.' Maybe Carol Ackerman would know something about financing a country house conversion. Katherine slipped the card into the jewellery box in her dressing-table drawer.

'Have you finished in the bathroom?'

Harry mumbled something incomprehensible and then flushed the toilet.

He was already in bed when she came out again.

'Come to bed my pretty little Kitty-Cat,' he purred. 'Let me show you what you've been missing. Paradise –' He slapped the bed beside him. Katherine snapped off the light. There was only so much paradise one woman could take in a lifetime.

Chapter Three

'Wakey wakey, it's bright and early Sunday morning and I've got hot croissants and black cherry confiture.'

'Piss off.' Carol Ackerman rolled back under the duvet, valiantly trying to resist the smell of the coffee Geoff was wafting towards her.

Ray sat down on the end of the bed. 'You said . . .'

'Yes, yes, I know what I said.'

'So get up, you lazy cow. We've got to be down at the café in an hour and you said . . .'

Carol peered out from behind deeply tired eyes at the two grinning men and the two ginger cats.

'Is nowhere sacred?' she protested, scrunching the duvet up to her armpits. Ray and Geoff were both dressed in identical white tee-shirts and faded narrow-legged jeans. They looked drop-dead gorgeous. 'What is this, Marlon Brando week?'

'You said that you would come with us to the café this morning and give Mr Right the once over, you promised.' He handed her the coffee.

'I lied. I wanted you to go home. I was too tired to argue.'

Summer Sundays at their café were a local ritual. Ray and Geoff invited about twenty people, usually regular customers, to an informal running buffet. Everyone helped to serve and clear, everyone got totally blasted and nobody minded paying for what was always a great afternoon.

Carol ran her tongue around her teeth. 'I need another man in my life like I need a boil on my bum.'

Geoff slid the tray up over the bed clothes. 'Your trouble is you never give yourself a chance to peer over the ramparts, darling. The world is full of bright shiny possibilities.'

Ray nodded. 'And no one, but no one goes for a dirty weekend in Paris, comes home a day early after shopping for fat Germans whilst hubby rings home.'

Carol bit the end off the croissant. 'All right, so Paris was a bit of a disaster.'

Ray nodded. 'And so was Hamburg.'

'And Copenhagen,' Geoff.

Carol rolled her eyes heavenwards. 'And?'

Ray began to tick off place names on his fingers. 'Edinburgh, Birmingham – I ask you, who takes his mistress to Birmingham for a dirty weekend – Norwich, that place in Oxfordshire, Geneva . . .'

'Don't forget Brighton,' chipped in Geoff.

Carol groaned. 'All right, I'll come. Just give me ten minutes to get some knickers on.'

They both climbed off the bed, followed by the cats.

At the door Ray turned. 'And don't wear one of those "tough business woman, don't mess with me" bloody power suits half way up your bum.'

Geoff popped his head round to join Ray's. 'Very passé, very eighties, specially with those shoulder pads.'

'What then?'

Ray hesitated and then sprung back into Carol's room. 'Long cream cotton jumper with a boat neck, skirt and those nice leather sandals we brought you back from Morocco.'

Geoff: 'Leather shoulder bag, soft hair and something flowery behind the ears.'

Carol picked up her pillow threateningly. 'Thanks for the make-over, lads.'

They giggled and vanished. A millisecond later, just before she had had the chance to climb out of bed, a muscular sun-tanned arm appeared around the door bearing a loaded coat-hanger.

'Oh, very, very slick,' said Carol, sliding across the room with the duvet still bunched around her. She took the proffered clothes. 'Last time I saw this lot they were on their way to Oxfam in a black bin-bag.'

'I recycled them,' said Ray's voice from behind the door. 'Just because Harry likes to see you dressed up like Joan Collins, there's no need for the rest of us to suffer. And remember, nice soft hair.'

Katherine Bourne didn't worry too much about clothes. She preferred elastic-waisted skirts from Marks and a succession of white blouses and shapeless cardigans. Sensible shoes in the winter, sandals all summer. She dragged her greying wavy brown hair back into order. Harry was still asleep. She glanced at the kitchen clock – ten more minutes. He liked to be woken with tea and two digestives, then All-Bran for breakfast with a tumbler of fresh orange juice – this was the scaffolding that shored up the start of every day, even Sundays.

She'd already hung his golfing clothes out on the bedroom chair. Harry would undoubtedly ring his friend, George, and suggest they play a round before lunch as he was home early from Paris.

The phone burbled, she picked it up before the second ring.

'Hi, Katherine, this is Hope.'

'Hello, how are you?'

The American woman laughed throatily. 'God, so much better today. I just rang to say I'm going back to London this afternoon. You haven't changed your mind about the film shoot have you?'

'No, not at all.'

She could almost hear Hope smiling. 'Great. Look, I've arranged for a guy to come out and photograph the house sometime next week so I can pitch it to the clients. Would you like me to give you his number so you can contact him direct and arrange a day?'

Katherine teased a pen out of the jar near the phone. 'Right, fire away.'

'Okay, well, his name's Ben Morton. You'll like him, he's a real garden freak.'

Katherine scribbled down the number and didn't protest when Hope suggested that as soon as she came down again they went out to dinner.

Just as she laid the receiver back in its cradle, Harry appeared at the top of the stairs. He was not beautiful in the morning. His gingery complexion was livid and his hair peaked into a series of unruly looking knots and swirls. He looked like a bad tempered guinea pig.

He stretched and scratched. 'Who was that on the phone?'

Katherine turned slowly, palming the piece of paper into her tidily curled fist. 'Market research. Wanted to know if we eat cream crackers.'

Harry snorted. 'On a Sunday morning? Good God, is nothing sacred? You'd think they'd have more bloody consideration.' He rolled his wrist around to look at his watch. 'Thought I might give George a ring. See if he'd like a round. You don't mind do you? How are you feeling this morning?'

Katherine smiled bravely as he kissed her forehead. 'Much better, thank you.'

'Good, I knew you would be. I'll just go and get dressed.' He hesitated. 'Got the kettle on?'

Katherine nodded. 'Oh yes,' she said. 'Breakfast will be ready by the time you are.'

He preened, as if he'd pulled off some kind of personal triumph, and headed back upstairs to the bedroom. Katherine slipped the telephone number into her pocket and hurried into the kitchen.

'That's better,' Geoff and Ray said in unison as they posed against the side of their beloved, ancient, open-topped Volkswagen Beetle and surveyed Carol as if she was a lamb chop. She obliged by doing a long slow turn on her walk down the drive.

'You should dress like that more often,' said Ray, opening the car door for her and pulling the seat forward.

Carol climbed in. 'Lactons wouldn't like it. They like their women in suits, preferably something with pearls from the Thatcher years.'

Geoff grimaced. 'Not at home surely?'

Carol grinned. 'I thought you of all people would understand, Geoff, I'm a method actor – I live my role.'

In the front seats the two men looked at each other and shrugged.

'Don't tell me, what I really need is a new man in my life.'

Ray and Geoff's café was in a chic little alleyway off one of the main streets behind the market. On one side was a shop selling ethnic jewellery and African artefacts and on the other a second-hand book shop. Neither used their handkerchief-sized gardens and so Geoff and Ray had gradually 'acquired' them. With mirrors, trompe l'oeil, elegant lattice woodwork and cunningly arranged plants, Ray and Geoff had succeeded in dragging the mythical silk purse out of a very unpromising pig's ear.

Les, a plump bibliophile with a penchant for paisley scarves and Beaujolais, was already stoking the barbecue on the rectangle of paving slabs at the back of his shop. Their other neighbour, Leandra, ethnic-is-us, was happily balanced on a step-ladder, pinning window-panes of sun-faded scarves to the stained pine loggia, whilst listening to some kind of New Age confection on a tape deck.

Ray dispensed glasses of wine like alms and disappeared into the kitchen while Geoff fluffed tables, waiting to take his place behind the barbecue, like a conductor at his podium.

Carol sat under the shade of a tumble of variegated ivy, closed her eyes and tipped her face towards the sun.

'Miss Right, I presume?' A low even voice slipped seamlessly into her consciousness.

Carol's eyes snapped open. 'My God,' she hissed, feeling her colour rise, 'they didn't actually say that to you, did they?'

'I'm afraid so.' The speaker hunkered down beside her. Carol turned to focus on him. Toffee-brown eyes looked back steadily into hers from under the shade of a straw fedora. 'I'm Sam Richardson.' He extended a large sun-tanned hand. 'And you must be the inimitable Ms Carol Ackerman.'

Carol could feel her colour deepening as he continued, 'You like cats, you work in London, you –'

She took his hand and shook it firmly, holding up the other to silence him. 'Please, no more, what are we going to talk about if you already know everything?'

Sam shrugged. 'Maybe we could just get blind drunk.'

'I can see why they thought you and I might get along. Why don't you sit down and humour them?'

He folded himself onto the bench seat opposite her and placed his hat alongside his wine glass, long fingers picking at the brim.

'What I really want to know is why a woman like you is going out with a shit like Harry. Oh and by the way, I'm supposed to tell you, you look much, much better without the power suit.'

Carol glanced towards the open door of the café, wishing she had taken more notice of what Ray and Geoff had said over supper.

She sipped her wine. 'Why don't you tell me about yourself?' she said softly.

Sam Richardson unpeeled a tiny tinfoil parcel to reveal slivers of salmon rolled around butter-sweet vegetables. Carol peered over his shoulder.

'It's a bit like Christmas, what have you got in yours?'

Carol sat down beside him and obligingly unpacked her offering from the barbecue, then tipped it out beside a generous portion of salad. 'Chicken with spring onions, garlic and er . . .' she poked at something greenish and soft, 'and something else.'

'Lovage, darling,' Ray hissed, as he swept past them with a tray of wine glasses.

Carol picked up her fork. Sam wasn't bad, in fact on reflection, he was quite good. Tallish, forty-ish, with a sort of craggy folded smiley face.

She wrinkled up her nose; a little too much wine and it would be all too easy to slip into the trap so carefully baited by Ray and Geoff. It wasn't that they hadn't tried before, but this time she almost found herself being tempted. She sipped her wine and watched Leandra talking to Les over by the loggia. It had to be because she was feeling so raw about the trip to Paris.

When she turned back, Sam was looking at her. She shivered. 'Sorry, what were you saying?'

Sam grinned. 'I wasn't, you were just going to tell me all about your job.'

Carol grimaced. 'Oh no, surely I wasn't, was I? I didn't say that, did I?'

'You've heard about mine.'

Carol slipped off her sandals and let the crisp grass slide up between her toes. 'You don't look much like a lecturer.'

'You don't look much like a banker.'

Ray slipped artfully onto the bench opposite them. 'Come on then, I want to know how it's going?'

'We hate the sight of each other,' said Carol, spearing a sliver of tomato. 'You've got it totally wrong again, Ray.'

34

'I've always preferred blondes –'

'And I've got a phobia about lecturers.'

'Don't be so ridiculous. You pair were made for each other,' Ray snorted, looking at Sam. 'She's gorgeous, isn't she?'

Sam raised his glass in salute. 'Absolutely, in fact before you arrived I was just about to pluck up the courage to ask her out to dinner.'

Ray leant forward. 'She's late home Mondays but she's usually free on Tuesdays or Wednesdays. Thursdays are a bit dicey because of the shit. Fridays are out, she's always a complete cow on Friday nights. Oh, and most weekends are okay because Harry is at home with the lovely wife . . .'

Sam nodded. 'Okay. So how about Tuesday next week then?

Ray fished a diary out of his back pocket. 'What date is that?'

'Oh, please, don't mind me,' said Carol, waving her hand. 'You make me sound like a charity case. I *do* have a social life of my own, you know.'

'Well, I don't,' Sam said. 'I don't really know anyone round here at the moment. Think of this as a philanthropic exercise.'

Carol threw her napkin onto the table. 'Oh right, so *you're* the charity case, that makes it all so much better.'

Ray pulled a shrewish face. 'And you can take her any-where, she's a complete Philistine, she'll eat absolutely anything.'

'Enough, enough,' Carol snapped. 'Tuesday is fine, why don't we just go out for a drink and see how it goes, without the Brando sisters here dipping their fingers into our arrangements?'

Sam grinned. 'Fine by me – about eight?'

Later that day, Carol snuggled down on the sofa, comfortably curled around the ginger cats, watching an old weepy on TV and feeding herself therapeutic chocolate-covered nuts and raisins.

One date, she decided. One date and then a gentle brush-off. It was a new tack for Ray and Geoff to tell the prospective Mr Right straight out, up front, about Harry, but it would make it much easier to get rid of him. Sam hadn't seemed unduly shocked but most men were. At least this way she wouldn't have to be deceitful.

She stroked the cat's head. 'After all, Augustus-mog, I'm spoken for, aren't I?'

What a strange archaic expression that was. Harry had spoken, hadn't he? Well, maybe not spoken, but as good as, and of course she'd spoken too – she must have at some stage, it was just that exactly when escaped her.

There had been a weekend in Somerset when they had first got together. It might have been then. A stolen summer Sunday on a deserted beach, walking arm in arm watching the tide rise in the Bristol Channel, when it felt as if things just couldn't get any better. She popped another half-a-dozen chocolates into her mouth. But they hadn't spoken then; they hadn't needed to. Carol up-ended the paper bag and tipped the remnants of chocolate nuts and raisins into her palm.

The cat mewled softly and rubbed himself up against her fingers in his most appealing, 'Love me, love me, make a great fuss of me' way. It struck her, as she dropped her hand to rub his soft furry ginger belly, that he looked an awful lot like Harry.

'Hello.' On the far end of the telephone line, Ben Morton the photographer's voice was as smooth and inviting as a freshly pressed linen sheet.

Katherine Bourne coughed slightly. 'Hello, this is Katherine Bourne. You don't know me, but –'

'Oh right. Hello, Hope rang me about you first thing

36

this morning. You're the lady with the wonderful house she wants to use.'

Katherine preened. 'How nice of Hope to say so. I was just wondering when you might be coming down. I'd obviously like to be in.'

Ben laughed. 'I hadn't anticipated doing the photos while you were out. I'm really glad you rang. Actually I'm free on Monday morning but I wasn't sure how you'd feel about doing it at such short notice, or how you'd take to being rung on a Sunday morning.'

'Oh, I don't mind at all and Monday morning would be fine.' Katherine took a steadying breath; it didn't do to gush. She leant back against the wall thinking about how Hope would handle it – casually but efficiently. She ran her fingers through her hair as she had seen Hope do.

'Maybe you'd like to stay and have some lunch?' Even as she said it she blushed crimson, what in God's name had made her suggest lunch?

'That sounds wonderful. Hope said you were a nice lady. Would ten be okay? Obviously if it's peeing down with rain we'll have to re-schedule.'

Katherine nodded, then realised that he couldn't see her and said casually, 'Re-schedule? Right, well, that's wonderful, I'll just put you in my diary.'

After she put down the phone she wondered what on earth had come over her. She hadn't even got a diary, just a calendar the milkman had given her that she'd Blu Tacked to the fridge door. She peered around the hall feeling vaguely ridiculous – something was happening – and it was happening to her.

Even as she cooked Sunday dinner she was thinking about Ben Morton's dark humorous voice, and it wasn't until she packed the plates into the dishwasher that she realised she hadn't listened to a word Harry had said to her while they'd been eating.

Maybe there was an alternative to murder after all.

Chapter Four

'Outdoor tomatoes?' It was late Monday morning and Ben Morton was on his knees down amongst Katherine's vegetable garden, cupping the red fruit in his fingers. He looked up appreciatively. 'I've never had any success with mine. You'll have to give me your secret.' He surveyed the neat well-weeded rows all hemmed around by faded redbrick paths. 'It's wonderful here. I wouldn't let the film crew around this side of the house if I were you. Most of them wouldn't know a shallot from a hole in the ground. Traipse all over the place, dragging their leads and cables behind them—'

Alarm bells went off inside Katherine's head.

'Do they usually make a lot of mess, then?' she said anxiously.

Ben shrugged. 'No, not always, but they're not exactly the most sensitive group of people in the universe. They've got tunnel vision – this shot, this light, this angle. You'll need to make it very clear where they can go and where they can't.'

Katherine handed him a colander. 'Maybe you'd like to pick some tomatoes for lunch?'

Ben Morton had been at the house for nearly three hours already, though she'd only discovered how quickly the time had gone when she'd nipped inside to make a pot of coffee. It had quite shaken her. For a few minutes, while the kettle boiled, she had watched him from the kitchen window, walking around the garden. Ben Morton was the sort of man she imagined it would be easy to lose time with. He was easy to talk to. He hadn't minded at all that she had trailed after him, watching him set up his camera – they had talked for most of the morning.

Now, crouched beside her vegetable patch he grinned up at her. She blushed and then felt foolish – after all she was a grown woman, not some gauche little teenager. The cuffs on his shirt were frayed and at the seam just below his shoulder the stitches had given way. As he moved she could see a tantalising sliver of sun-tanned flesh.

She swallowed and took a therapeutic glance at the raspberry canes.

'Actually,' she said very slowly, 'I'm seriously toying with the idea of turning it into a rest home, you know, a retirement home.'

Ben looked up from rolling tomatoes off their stalks.

'Really?' He set a plump tomato gently amongst the others in the stainless steel colander. 'I'd have thought that would be right up your street. You've got a natural talent for making people feel at ease.' Stiffly he pulled himself up. 'If I wanted a place to spend my last days it would be somewhere like this.'

Katherine felt gratified. 'I'm thinking about converting the outbuildings.' She pointed to the row of neat, white painted, brick sheds that sheltered her precious garden. 'I thought they'd make nice self-contained flatlets and then . . . Well, I've got a lot of ideas but first of all I've got to think about raising the money.'

Ben Morton's shadow fell across her and she felt an odd little tingle in her stomach.

'I can tell you about it over lunch if you like, if it's not too boring?'

Ben nodded. 'Not at all, I'd be very interested. I'll bring the tomatoes in. Is there anything else you'd like?'

Katherine hesitated. There was something else she would like, but how did a married, middle-aged woman ask a photographer, whom she barely knew, if he'd take her to bed in the middle of the day? The thought flashed white hot through her mind, it was so completely unexpected that it made her cheeks flare crimson. Hastily, not meeting his eyes, she retrieved the colander and turned away.

'No thanks,' she said, a little unsteadily, 'the tomatoes will be just fine.'

'Hello, Carol Ackerman speaking. How can I help you?' Carol glanced at her watch: Monday afternoon, just before three o'clock. Where the hell was Jeanette? Outside her fish bowl office, Jeanette's empty desk yawned like a tooth socket. Spread over Carol's desk were the latest projections for Danic PLC, big loan, big company, potential for a great big star by her name if she managed to pull it off. Carol glanced at the glossy prospectus while the caller summoned up the courage to speak.

'Er, hello,' said a low voice. 'I'm not sure if I'm talking to the right person.'

In the reception area, Jeanette, clutching a bright scrunch of carrier bags, slid stealthily behind her desk. She didn't even glance into Carol's office. It didn't take a great deal of intuition to guess Jeanette was treading water at Lactons until something more interesting came along. Carol wished she would hurry up and find whatever it was; her time-keeping was an old bone of contention chewed bare. She felt a flicker of annoyance.

'I got your number from er . . . a friend of mine.' The voice broke Carol's chain of thought. She grimaced. Another dinner party connection for some woman wanting to start a home catering company. 'Well, perhaps you could –'

But the woman cut her off, suddenly finding the confidence to say her piece. 'I wonder if I could come and see you to discuss a business loan? I need some advice.'

Carol picked up her pen and pulled a pad closer. 'Of course. If I could have your name.'

'Katherine . . .' The woman hesitated for a split second and then charged on as if she was running downhill, 'Jackson, Katherine Jackson. You see, I have this very large house. I am hoping to convert it into an old people's home, thinking about it anyway, and I need – well, I really need to talk to someone about how to go about it.'

Carol nodded. Although she didn't know that much about the care market she knew who she could pass the enquiry on to. Meanwhile, her caller seemed to have hit her stride.

'The thing is I would need sufficient capital to refurbish and do the conversion and then –' the caller's hesitancy returned, 'I need to buy out my partner.'

'Your partner.' Carol jotted down notes on her pad. 'I may not be the person you need to speak to, Ms Jackson. Perhaps I could get one of my colleagues to give you a call?'

The woman at the far end of the line coughed, confidence faltering. 'At the moment, I'm really in the preliminary stages – I had your name, I just thought –' Her voice faded and died.

Carol, against her better judgement, teased her diary closer. 'Perhaps it might be easier if you came in and discussed your plans face to face. I could certainly point you in the right direction if that's any help?'

The caller took a deep breath. 'Yes, yes, that would be wonderful. Could I see you personally? I've never done anything like this before.'

'No problem, why don't we arrange a meeting? When are you free?'

Katherine Bourne slid the milkman's calendar closer so that she could write in the day and the time she had arranged with Carol Ackerman. She wasn't quite certain what had made her ring, perhaps it had been the after-effects of Ben Morton's stout presence or his jovial good humour over lunch, or the two glasses of wine she had

41

had with it. Whatever, it was done now and Katherine was glad. A bit of a sticky moment over her name. She hadn't really wanted Carol Ackerman to know who she was, just in case Carol and Harry saw a lot of each other. It was too soon to give the game away. If there was a game to give away, she wanted to be the one who did it. Besides, it wouldn't hurt to find out some more information.

Katherine looked at the list of people Carol had suggested might be able to help her: the local council, environmental health, her solicitor. She'd scribbled the list down on a jaunty illustration of a bottle of milk with a Cheshire cat grin. It wouldn't hurt to ring any of them, after all, she only wanted a little more information.

Outside, Ben Morton was finishing the last shots of the house. Rain had started to fall in a damp curtain, bringing out the colour of the old bricks in the garden paths. He waved at her through the French windows as she dropped the phone back in its cradle, his grey hair slicked down like an ageing seal.

'All finished,' he mouthed, folding up his tripod.

Katherine waved him in, unlocking the doors. 'For goodness sake. You can't go home like that, you're completely soaked through. Come in and have a cup of tea. Let me get you a towel.'

Ben stepped inside, dripping puddles onto the red quarry tiles. 'I really don't mind the rain, not summer rain anyway.' Water had soaked his faded blue shirt to navy across the shoulders. 'I've got some wonderful pictures of the house. Would you like me to send you a set?'

Katherine nodded as she dragged a fluffy blue towel out of the ironing basket. 'Please.'

'Maybe you could use them for publicity?'

She paused mid-tug. 'Sorry?'

'Your plans for a retirement home, decent photographs for the brochure. And there'll be the TV connection after Hope's mob have finished. Great selling point.'

'I hadn't thought about that, would you come back and do some more if I decide to have the outbuildings converted?'

'My pleasure. You've got my number.'

As she handed him the towel their fingertips touched for the briefest of moments. Katherine felt the heat rising from somewhere just above her sensible shoes. Everything in the kitchen seemed unnaturally still and bright – and – in the very same instant, just as she thought how ridiculous she was being, Ben Morton leaned forward and kissed her so softly, so gently that she thought she might faint.

On Tuesday evening Carol and Sam walked through the Cathedral grounds at Ely. In the distance the music from the choir seemed to harmonise with the summer sunlight and the remains of the still evening.

'This is where I'm moving next,' said Carol, folding herself down onto a bench overlooking the cathedral meadow, which was full of sleepy bullocks. 'I've found this beautiful house down by the river.'

'Ely? I'm surprised. I thought your job was very firmly in London?'

Sam had leaned close to her – he smelt of wind and sun and cologne.

'Lactons have a five-year relocation plan, it's one of the reasons I took the job in the first place.'

'And they're coming to Ely?'

'No, Cambridge, but I'm addicted to commuting.'

Sam grinned. 'What about Ray and Geoff?'

He was so close now she could see the tiny lines around his eyes and the dark promise of stubble on his chin. She swallowed and looked back at the bullocks. One date, one date and then goodbye – except that he smelt so very tempting. Before she could stop herself she lifted her hand to stroke his chin, almost casually, almost without thought.

He felt warm and . . . and then he kissed her, so softly, so gently that she thought she might faint.

Later in the week, Jeanette showed Katherine Bourne, née Jackson, into Carol's office. As Carol turned to welcome her, she saw Jeanette roll her eyes derisively. Katherine Jackson, sometime Bourne, was dressed rather uncomfortably in a smart navy suit that had obviously once fitted beautifully and now didn't. Katherine held a rather tattered brown brief-case and had quite the nicest eyes Carol had ever seen. She stretched across the table, took Carol's hand and shook it firmly.

'It's very good of you to see me,' Katherine said with a great deal of warmth. 'I'm rather nervous about all this; I'm afraid I'm a bit rusty when it comes to business.'

Carol smiled. 'Not at all, why don't you take a seat. I'll organise some tea.' She buzzed Jeanette, who peered over her shoulder as she picked up the receiver in time to catch Carol's mime of a tea cup.

'Now, how can I help you?'

Katherine unsnapped the brief-case and smiled warily. 'I'm not really used to this kind of thing, I'm afraid. But let me explain. I have a very large, very beautiful house that is far too big for me and my husband. Years ago I used to nurse and I thought – I thought it would do me good to do something for myself at long last.'

Carol nodded, warming to the woman's cheerful honesty. 'It's a big step to turn your home into a business. How does you husband feel about your plans?'

'Part of my plan is to leave him, or rather persuade him to leave.' As she spoke Katherine laid out a great sheaf of photographs of an elegant and obviously well loved Georgian house on Carol's desk. 'I've already rung several of the people you suggested and everyone seemed to think it was a splendid idea,' she paused. 'But, of course, splendid ideas do need money to turn them into reality.'

Carol picked up a photograph of the rear of the house, all neatly laid down to vegetables.

Katherine got to her feet and pointed. 'See, those are the outbuildings I was telling you about. I think I could make four very nice little flatlets out of those, and then in the house itself, there are six bedrooms. There's really far too much room for just the two of us.'

Carol looked at her again. 'The one of us?'

Katherine nodded nervously. 'Well yes, but I really need to know what you think my chances are of getting some sort of business loan.'

They talked about it over tea, Katherine would need a valuation, a proper business plan but Carol knew there shouldn't be too many problems. Once tea was over she introduced Katherine to Dougie in sales, who would hold her hand through the process. Watching the woman walk away, clutching her brief-case like a shield, deep in conversation with her new financial mentor, Carol realised she rather liked Katherine Jackson in her strange ill-fitting suit.

That evening, Katherine Bourne's, née Jackson's, eyes were firmly on the driveway as she set the table in the dining room. She'd made spicy chicken casserole.

Under her breath she said, 'Harry, I think the time has come for us to both admit our marriage is over.'

No, that wasn't it, he wouldn't consider it was over until they carried her out in a box.

'Harry, I would like you to go. I . . .' She gritted her teeth. 'I'm sick to death of you and I want you to leave. Do you realise that there isn't a day goes by when I don't think about murdering you, you selfish, ungrateful, manipulative little . . .' Outside, she saw the familiar grey lines of Harry's company car pulling up outside the windows and carefully wiped her hands on her pinafore.

*   *   *

She had been very good with Ben Morton and his kiss – she'd handled it very well. When he'd kissed her, he had pulled away very, very slowly, inviting her to ask for more. But she'd shook her head firmly.

'Oh Ben, I'm so sorry,' she'd said. 'But I'm afraid I can't do this, however much I want to – and believe me I do want to. It's just that things are complicated at the moment. You see I am still married and before I get involved with anyone else I really need to be free of Harry.'

Well, she would have said that, except that he kissed her again, just when she had got to 'Oh Ben,' and after that she really didn't want to say anything else, particularly anything else that had anything to do with Harry. He had asked her if he might take her out to lunch and she had said yes, she would love that, but he had to give her a little time.

In Carol's kitchen, Ray stood a cup of coffee in front of her and said, 'So?'

Carol grinned. 'So what?' She snapped a home-baked biscuit into tiny fragments.

She thought she'd actually handled Sam Richardson very well. When he'd kissed her, he had pulled away very, very slowly, inviting her to ask for more. But she'd shook her head firmly.

'Oh Sam, I'm so sorry,' she'd said. 'But I'm afraid I can't do this, however much I want to, and believe me I do want to. It's just that things are complicated at the moment, before I get involved with anyone else I really need to be free of Harry.'

Well, she would have said that, except that he kissed her again, just when she had got to 'Oh Sam,' and after that she really didn't want to say anything else, particularly anything else that had anything to do with Harry. He had asked if he could see her again and she had said yes, she would love that, but he had to give her a little time.

*   *   *

'Bloody lousy day at the office, sodding computer went down and lost half my files. Benson's off sick, *again* – and who do you think they asked to cover the presentation to the Japanese? All that bloody grinning and bowing –' Harry threw his jacket onto the sofa. 'Something's going on, I can feel it in my bones. That bastard Phelps is playing his cards very close to his chest at the moment, everyone is so tight lipped – there's talk of a general staff meeting next week.' His voice droned on, a steady counter-point to Katherine's thoughts.

Katherine Bourne stood the casserole dish on the centre of the table, neatly, between the salad and the new potatoes. Too many calories really.

'And Paterson, you remember Paterson? Well, he's been in God's office all afternoon talking about lord knows what . . .'

Two pale pink linen napkins tucked into silver rings, Katherine preferred real napkins. 'Harry?'

'You must remember Paterson. Little bald chap, looks like a threadbare weasel.'

Katherine couldn't hold it in much longer. She felt like a child with a particularly special secret. 'Harry?'

He looked up from behind his pale creamy lashes. 'Yes? Are you feeling all right, you look a bit flushed?'

'I'm fine –' she began.

'Well, as I was saying. God came out around four, looking like the cat who got the cream, then Paterson . . .'

'Harry, I want a divorce.'

He looked ridiculous with his mouth open, lips still formed into the word Paterson.

'What did you say?' he hissed breathlessly.

Katherine pulled out her chair and started to dish up supper. 'A divorce, and I've been thinking, I'd really much prefer it if you left fairly soon. I understand we're entitled to half of the assets each, though my solicitor did say that I ought to hold out for more. Could you possibly find somewhere else to stay over the weekend? I would have thought George might put you up for a day or two.'

Harry was still frozen to the spot.

Katherine carefully arranged his salad beside the chicken and picked out a stray slice of cucumber – Harry hated cucumber.

'I'm trying to negotiate a loan at the moment to buy out your half of the house.'

His face gradually went scarlet. It was quite interesting to watch the colour creep up from his collar over his throat, chin.

'What?' he snorted, clambering away from the table as though it was on fire. 'What in God's name are you talking about? Are you serious?' He was magenta now, even his ears were livid.

It felt a bit like watching a TV soap opera, not that Katherine watched a lot of them. 'Sit down and eat your supper,' she said softly, 'and don't make such a fuss.'

'A fuss?' He balled the napkin from beside his plate into a missile and threw it across the room. 'A bloody sodding fuss?' He looked at her in disbelief, as she calmly began to eat her supper. 'Well, that's it then, is it?' he fumed, stamping his feet like an angry little boy. 'That's bloody sodding it? Right, well, in that case I'm not hanging around where I'm not wanted. Thought I wouldn't call your bluff, did you? Eh? Well, I'm going. And I'm going now – so there.'

He stormed towards the dining-room door.

'Your clean shirts are in the linen basket,' she said, as he hurtled into the hall, all arms, legs and red, red face.

Carol Ackerman picked up the phone in the kitchen and cradled the receiver between her neck and shoulder as she spooned tuna chunks into the cat dishes.

'Hello, Carol Ackerman.'

'Hello, Carol, it's me, Harry.' He sounded breathless.

'Oh hello, it's not like you to ring me at home. Are you all right?'

'Well, Kitty-Kat, I've finally done it.'

'Done what?' Carol stooped to give the ginger boys their treat and was rewarded with the pointed indifference spoilt cats perfected before their eyes were open.

'I've finally left Katherine. Well, it had to be done, didn't it? I mean, we just couldn't carry on living a lie, could we? Damn, there's the pips, hang on I'll give you my numb . . .' the phone went dead.

Carol stood very still and looked at the two sleek ginger bodies beside her, purring their greed into the tuna bowls. She hung the phone back onto its hook and put on the kettle. It couldn't possibly be true, she reassured herself. A row, something like that – except that in all the years she'd known Harry, he and his wife had never argued.

The phone rang again, it was extremely tempting not to answer it. She rested her hand on its treacherous plastic casing for a few seconds and then finally snatched it up.

'Hello,' she snapped.

'Ouch, Ray warned me you were a real cow on Fridays.'

'Sam? Oh, hello. I'm so sorry, I thought it was someone else.'

She heard Sam's amusement from the far end of the line. 'God, I'd hate to be on the wrong side of you. I wondered if you were doing anything tonight.'

Carol leant against the wall – only possibly changing her whole life beyond all recognition. 'No, not really, why?'

'Well, I wondered if you'd like to come out for a drink, there's a folk band playing down at the Ox.'

Carol glanced up at the clock. 'Sounds wonderful, what time?'

'An hour too soon?'

'No,' she said quickly. Not soon enough really.

'Would you like me to come over and pick you up?'

Carol shook her head vigorously. 'No, no, I'd rather

meet you there. I've got one or two things I need to do here.' She tried to keep the hysterical note out of her voice.

'Great, well. See you in about an hour then.'

'Look forward to it,' said Carol. When he rang off she laid the phone down on the kitchen unit, off the hook, and went to have a bath.

Katherine Bourne carefully picked the salad off Harry's plate and put the casserole in the fridge. She might have it for lunch. She packed the dishwasher and thought how quiet the house seemed without him. She felt a little bit sick and shivery, aware that she had carried the thought of divorcing Harry for so long that it seemed almost impossible she had finally said it aloud. The sense of relief was totally overwhelming.

Of course, she would have to ring the children soon, go and clear up the bedroom – Harry's packing had been very violent and more than a little disruptive. But it was only temper, it wouldn't take an awful lot to put right. Although she might change the bed linen, it didn't seem right beginning a new life in sheets that still smelt of Harry.

Carol heard the doorbell from the bedroom. She pulled on a long tee-shirt over her leggings, and quickly dragged a brush through her tangled wet hair.

'Hang on. I'm coming. I said I'd meet you there.' Laughing, she jerked open the front door.

Harry Bourne was standing in the porch, surrounded by suitcases. Some of them had things hanging out: sleeves and something knitted.

'Well,' he said cheerfully. 'Here I am. Thought I'd come straight over, no need to mess around now, is there, eh?'

'I didn't realise you were coming here,' said Carol slowly.

Harry walked past her. 'I rang from a service station.' He inspected left and right. 'I never knew you lived so far out of town. Maybe we ought to think about getting somewhere closer to London – I've always hated commuting now – that we're finally together.'

From the kitchen door two ginger heads pressed imperiously through the cat flap. Harry looked at them nervously and took a step back.

'Cats?' he hissed, in the same tone a doctor might mumble bubonic plague.

Carol swept them up in her arms, defensively, like a shield. 'Augustus and Tosca,' she said. 'Why on earth didn't you tell me you were –' she paused, mid-thought. What exactly was it Harry was doing?

'I've given this a lot of thought, I decided –' he sneezed, 'it was only fair. I wanted to be fair to you, after all the years we've been together. These last few months I've heard your biological clock ticking away.'

'What?'

'Babies, you know, children, well, perhaps not children, that's something we'll have to talk about, but a life with – well, a family. Me.'

Carol pushed open the kitchen door. 'Why don't you come in and have a cup of tea?'

Harry eyed the cats suspiciously. Carol shooed them out of the front door into the garden and then looked at the suitcases, still piled up high on the doorstep. She closed the door quickly and followed Harry into the kitchen.

There was a plate of chicken curry on the table, more accurately, a plate half full of half-eaten chicken curry and beside it, in the colander, the little plastic bags Carol had boiled it in and the scissors she'd used to open it. Friday night Ray and Geoff stayed open late and she didn't always wait for them to suprise her with something yummy. She plugged in the kettle and fished two mugs out of the dishwasher.

Harry peered out of the kitchen window and sneezed again.

'Cats,' he said unhappily. 'Allergic. It's the dander they leave around the place.'

Carol didn't say anything, for the first time in her life she was utterly speechless. On the kitchen unit beside the sink the phone still lay off the hook, buzzing accusingly. She had to take control.

'So,' she said, swinging around with a bright unnatural smile on her face. 'What are your plans?'

Harry looked uncomfortable. 'My plans? I don't really have any plans at the moment, not as such. I thought I'd stay here.' He crept closer, trying hard to look seductive. His eyes had started to run and redden. 'I mean, we've always said we don't get enough time together.'

Carol skilfully sidestepped his lustful advance. 'I don't remember saying that. What about Katherine, I mean, isn't she upset? You always said –'

Harry flushed scarlet, mouth tightening into a narrow pleat. 'I really don't want to talk about Katherine,' he snapped and yanked open the fridge. 'I'm famished, have you got anything to eat?' He glanced speculatively at the half-eaten curry.

Carol made tea, thinking, thinking, thinking. She really couldn't have Harry in her life full time. She hung the phone back on its cradle. When she turned back he was putting the curry into the microwave. She didn't like to tell him that Augustus-mog had already picked the remains of the chicken out of it.

While he ate, she dragged his suitcases into the hall and tried to work out what the hell she was going to do. The doorbell interrupted her thoughts.

She clambered over the heap of luggage and jerked the front door open.

'Hi, I wondered where you'd got to?' Sam Richardson, leaning against the porch, beamed at her. He was wearing a white collarless shirt, unbuttoned at the neck to reveal a tempting V of hairy chest, and a pair of well worn Levis. He looked almost edible. 'Everything all right?'

Carol glanced nervously towards the kitchen. 'Now is really not a good time.'

Sam stepped into the hall followed by the cats who rubbed gently against his long legs. He stooped to pick up Augustus-mog.

'Hi boss,' he muttered, rubbing the cat under the chin. Tosca complained bitterly at being overlooked. Sam looked around the scrimmage of cases and then back at Carol. 'Unexpected guests? Do you want me to come back later?'

At that moment Harry's voice hurried out to join them in the hall. 'Who is that?'

Carol took a deep breath and looked appealingly at Sam. 'It's Harry.'

Sam set Augustus down on the sideboard. 'Sorry, I didn't realise he came here,' he said thickly, suddenly looking terribly uncomfortable.

'He doesn't,' Carol hissed in a voice barely above a whisper. 'He's . . . well . . . he says he's left his wife.'

But Sam was already heading back towards the door.

She hurried after him. 'Please don't go,' she said softly, so softly she wasn't sure whether he'd heard her or not.

'It must be nice for you,' he murmured, as if he was struggling to find the right words. 'I'm sorry. I wouldn't have come round if I'd known –' his voice faded.

'But it isn't what I want,' she said unhappily. It felt as if something bright and fragile had slipped through her fingers and smashed on the hall floor.

As she spoke Harry appeared behind her, pale blue eyes streaming, face florid. In his hand he was carrying the half eaten chicken curry. He was not beautiful. Carol groaned but Sam was still heading across the gravel.

'Who was that?' said Harry, through a mouthful of rice.

Carol turned her back on Sam, closed the door and guided Harry back towards the kitchen.

'A friend. Or at least he *was*,' she murmured.

Chapter Five

All in all it was not an easy weekend.

There was a moment, as Katherine Bourne switched on the kettle on Saturday morning, when she realised she hadn't taken Harry's tea and digestives up to him. She glanced anxiously at the kitchen clock, he would be late if she didn't . . . the thought flared crimson and then burnt itself out. Harry had gone, no more Harry, no more tea and digestives.

She wasn't certain whether she wanted to cry or laugh and instead took a deep breath. It happened again when she set the breakfast table. Without thinking, on automatic pilot, she took two cereal bowls out of the cupboard, two side plates, two spoons and two knives and arranged them on a tray.

She stared down at the crockery and as she did an empty day opened up in front of her, threatening to swallow her whole. She hadn't really considered how much of her day was hitched to Harry's plans. What was she going to do? All the freedom she had ever dreamed of seemed to draw itself up into a great inky blackness. And it wasn't just today, there would be tomorrow and next week, years ahead when Harry wouldn't be drinking tea while she made breakfast.

A single tear trickled down over her cheek. Abandoning the tray, Katherine scrubbed off the tear with the back of her hand and pulled a notebook out of the kitchen drawer; there were people she ought to tell. She'd make a list.

Wrapped snugly in her dressing-gown, Katherine settled herself on the sofa under the kitchen window with a mug of tea, feeling as if she had just come out of hospital and needed time to convalesce. She glanced down at the list, tucked the phone under her chin and dialled the first number.

'I've left your father,' Katherine said calmly, after the social niceties had been exchanged and her daughter, Sarah, asked imperiously why her mother had called. There seemed no other way to explain it. The words hung in the air, suspended on the ether for a second or two.

'Or rather,' Katherine said quickly, staring out into the bright sunshine at the little bay trees that stood sentinel to the garden path. 'I asked him to leave.'

The silence from the other end of the line was unbearable, a heavy impenetrable blanket. Katherine ran a finger down over the curled phone cable. It needed untwisting.

'And he went. Last night. I'm not sure where he's gone exactly. Not yet. But I'm sure he's all right. I suggested he went to stay with George. I'll ring later to find out –'

Nothing.

'– I thought you ought to know before anyone else calls you, not that anyone else knows at the moment, but they will. I've already made a list – I . . .'

There was a low rumbling sound from the far end of the line, like a train approaching. Her daughter, Sarah, when she finally spoke, said crisply, 'Look Mum, I really haven't got time to talk about this now. I'm due at a hockey match in ten minutes. I'll call you back.' And hung up.

Katherine stared at the receiver for a full minute and then tapped in her son, Peter's, number. She was relieved when nobody answered. On the kitchen unit the second cereal bowl, with its cutlery tucked neatly inside it, glinted malevolently in the summer sunlight.

It ought to be easier to do this, Katherine thought, and looked at the other names on her list. The children had to know before anyone else and have their chance to say whatever it was they wanted to say. How long did a hockey match take?

Katherine refilled the kettle and resigned herself to wait for Sarah to ring back.

Carol Ackerman rolled over, opened her eyes and was disconcerted to find that there was someone asleep in her bed. The movement disturbed Harry, who snorted and farted, and then dragged the duvet over his shoulders. Carol slipped out of bed feeling as if she had run a marathon. A four hour twenty minute marathon, a marathon where she was in the also-ran pack, struggling to prove a point, struggling to catch up with the front runners. She pulled on her dressing-gown and crept downstairs into the kitchen, barking her shins on Harry's suitcases in the hall.

The cats, furious at being shut in the kitchen all night, mugged her, yowling their disapproval. Carol yawned and plugged in the kettle. Outside, the bright new day made her feel worse.

The kitchen looked as if she had been burgled by a frustrated gourmet or perhaps the guests from the Mad Hatter's tea party. She opened the dishwasher, flipped the bin lid and began to shovel the debris out of sight while Augustus and Tosca pressed their petition for breakfast. Carol opened a can and then set about attacking the kitchen units with a cloth and a bottle of bleach.

After Sam had left, Harry, completely oblivious to her state of mind, had suggested they go out for dinner. After all, they'd got a lot to celebrate, hadn't they? And besides that there wasn't much in the fridge and he hadn't eaten since breakfast. They went to Fernados, an over-priced Italian restaurant near the market square, which was the only place they could find a table at such short notice, and for which Carol felt decidedly underdressed.

It should have been romantic, except that she had a sense of unreality as the obsequious waiter pulled out the chair for her. In fact, she glanced back over her shoulder to ensure he hadn't removed it completely.

Between breadsticks and aperitifs, Harry enthusiastically set out his plans for their future.

'Maybe we ought to think about getting a *pied-à-terre*, somewhere in town. I know this chap who runs an estate agents in Highgate. The market's still fairly sluggish at the moment but it's on the up so we oughtn't wait too long. Buy now on the start of the curve. We could always think about getting a little place in the country too, for weekends. Near a golf course.' He grinned and snapped another breadstick in two. 'What do you think your place will fetch?'

Bemused thoughts froze Carol's features into a mask, tidying her reactions away behind a fixed smile.

'Not straight away of course,' he added quickly in a reassuring tone. 'We can take our time. No need to rush anything.' He smiled again and patted her hand. 'After all the years we've had to wait for this, Kitty-Kat, we want it to be just perfect, don't we?' He leaned back in his chair and smiled. 'You know, on the way down here I thought we should really have done this years ago.'

'Champagne, a bottle of your best,' said Harry to the waiter, as he approached their table with the wine list. Harry winked at Carol. 'I reckon we can afford to put this one on the entertainment budget, don't you? Put it all down to expenses.' He waved towards her copy of the menu. 'What are you going to have? Order what you like.'

Carol stared across at him. Harry was behaving as if she had never eaten out before, as if she might be uncertain or not confident enough to order what she liked. He seemed to have forgotten the remains of the chicken curry, surely he could guess she had already eaten? Was she supposed to be flattered that he was charging his celebratory supper to business expenses, or grin conspiratorially and order the most expensive thing on the menu to prove a point?

'Actually, I'm not that hungry.' She pushed the menu away.

'Oh, come on,' said Harry, running his finger down the list. 'The veal looks good.'

'Really, I'm not hungry.'

Harry shrugged.

The waiter, pad and pencil in hand, smiled. 'We have a light supper menu if madam would prefer.'

Carol conceded defeat.

The mozzarella and tomato salad was limp. The cannelloni was undercooked, not so much *al dente* as crunchy. At the table next to them a group of foreign businessmen engaged in a lengthy monotone debate, punctuated by angry mumbling from a man wearing an enormous handlebar moustache. Carol found herself struggling to pick out words she understood.

Dessert; the zabaglione made up for the rest of the meal, but by now Harry had had most of the champagne and a bottle of house wine, and was waxing lyrical about the rosy future he had arranged for them both. Carol realised, as she took her final spoonful of dessert, that she had barely listened to Harry all evening. Her mind had flittered back and forth, first to Sam, and then to Sam again and finally to Sam, his face, his soft voice and sad eyes as he had excused himself from her hall.

After Harry settled the bill she drove them home, while Harry stared out into the urban landscape.

'At last,' he murmured as they threaded their way in and out of the late night traffic. 'A new beginning, eh, my pretty little Kitty-Kat? A new beginning for both of us. It's quite exciting really, isn't it?' He yawned and settled himself down into the bucket seat of her sporty little hatchback.

Carol had glanced across at him at the traffic lights. Surely there ought to be some sense of elation, some joy at having finally won, instead it felt as if she had just been convicted of a crime she didn't commit.

The feeling had still been there when she woke up the following morning. Harry banging around upstairs in the bedroom brought her back to reality. A few seconds later he peered round the kitchen door.

'Shirts?' he said pleasantly, pulling his dressing-gown a little tighter.

Carol frowned. 'Sorry?'

Harry's attention rested momentarily on the cats, engaged in consuming their breakfast, and then he pulled out a chair from under the kitchen table. 'I've just been looking in your wardrobe.' He paused as Augustus shot him a disapproving glance. 'Couldn't they go outside and do that?'

Carol took the teapot off the dresser and made tea. 'I'll put them out when they've eaten,' she said flatly.

Harry sniffed and then sneezed.

'What were you saying about shirts?'

He sneezed again. 'I'll need somewhere to hang my clothes. I can hardly live out of a suitcase, can I?'

By the dishwasher Augustus arched his back and shivered, marking his territory. Harry sneezed again, while the cat with calculated insouciance made his way across the black and white tiled floor towards the hall. When the cat got within striking distance, Harry turned and pushed the door shut with his foot. Augustus froze and then they both looked up at Carol – appealing to the umpire for a decision.

Impasse. Carol picked up Augustus and scratched his wedge-shaped head. He purred, confident that he had won. She stared down at Harry, who smiled, assuming that he had won and that the cat would now be dumped outside the back door.

'There's another wardrobe in the spare room,' she said. 'You can hang your things in there for the time being.'

Harry nodded but did not move.

'In fact,' she continued with forced cheeriness, 'why

60

don't you go and do that now while I get us some breakfast? Take your tea up there with you. It will give me a chance to get myself organised.'

Still he didn't move.

She sighed. 'Or had you got something else in mind?'

Harry nodded towards Tosca, the second cat, who was making his way to the cat litter tray. 'Doesn't that disturb you? I mean, it must be terribly unhygienic.'

Carol bit her lip. 'Why don't you go and sort your clothes out. The cats will be out on the prowl by the time you get down again.'

Harry nodded as Tosca began to scrape a suitable hole. 'I was rather hoping you'd give me a hand. Help me get everything organised. Female touch and all that. Have you got some sort of system that I ought to know about?'

Carol shook her head.

So Harry continued, 'You know, socks here, shirts there, so you can sort out the laundry more easily? I don't want to mess up your game plan.'

Carol caught an unnerving little glimpse of the big picture.

'My system? I don't actually have a system, I've never needed one.'

Harry got to his feet. 'Right,' he said. 'Liberty hall it is then. I've got one or two things that need washing, where exactly *is* the laundry basket?'

By midday, Katherine Bourne felt she couldn't wait for her daughter Sarah any longer. She had spent the whole morning, in her dressing-gown, in the kitchen, waiting by the phone, which didn't seem a very positive way to start a whole new way of life. Waiting had made her thoughtful and then weepy, then frustrated, resentful and finally angry. When the hands on the kitchen clock reached high noon she snatched up the receiver and banged in Sarah's telephone number.

'Oh, it's you,' said Sarah flatly when she answered after the sixth ring.

Katherine felt her anger harden up. 'What do you mean, "oh, it's me"? I've been waiting all morning for you to call back, Sarah. I've been waiting here for, for –' she stopped. 'You said you would ring me.'

Sarah sighed. 'I know, but I assumed it would have all blown over by now. How are you feeling anyway?'

Katherine sat down heavily on the edge of the sofa. 'What?'

'I read an article in one of the Sunday supplements, last weekend, I think it was,' Sarah continued. 'Women in crisis. I'll see if I can find it and send you a copy. Dad said you were having a rough time with the change. You really ought to go and see a specialist, you know. They can do wonderful things with HRT these days. Don't be fobbed off by the local quack saying it's all only natural. Do you still go and see old Ferguson? These new drugs they've developed control hot flushes, mood swings, weepiness, the lot – all that sort of thing is a thing of the past, this article said. You ought to ask him about putting you on something, and if he doesn't know about it, try someone under pensionable age. Ferguson is like something out of the dark ages. Probably be happier prescribing leeches and regular purges. I suppose Dad's gone to play golf until the storm blows over. Are you there on your own?'

Katherine's anger trickled away, leaving behind an acute sense of betrayal.

'Sarah,' she said slowly, enunciating every syllable. 'This is not some sort of menopausal mood swing. I have asked your father to leave and he has. He left last night. I wanted to tell you first.'

The silence at the end of the phone opened up again. After a few seconds Sarah snapped, 'For God's sake, Mother. I thought you were exaggerating. You're serious, aren't you?'

'Yes.'

'Oh my God,' muttered Sarah, voice cracking. 'What the hell do you think you're playing at? I don't believe it. How on earth could you throw Dad out? It's crazy. What on earth are you thinking about?'

Katherine waited, using the time to arrange her thoughts into a defensive circle. Sarah's thoughts tumbled out unfiltered, untamed, like a flood tide.

'It's something I've thought about for a long –'

Sarah, voice tight with tears, cut her short. 'How could you? After all these years. For God's sake. It's totally ridiculous. It's sick. Where's Dad? I want to speak to my father.'

Katherine began to explain that she wasn't certain where Harry was, but it was obvious Sarah wasn't listening. This time it was Katherine who hung up, and then – hands still shaking – rang her son's number. She had already known Sarah's reaction would be the worse of the two. Daddy's little girl.

Peter answered on the second ring. His voice sounded deep and comforting.

'Peter, love,' she said softly, wondering if her courage might fail. 'I've just rung to tell you that your dad and I have separated. I've asked him to leave –' she stopped. The silence was there too, but it was softer, gentler, almost like an embrace. 'And he has. It's something I've been thinking about for a long time.'

Peter coughed. 'I know. Well, I guessed. How are you? Are you okay?' he said quietly.

'A bit shaky at the moment. I thought you ought to know before anyone else.'

There was a second's stillness before he spoke again. 'I'm glad you rang. Do you want me to come home? I can be there in an hour or so if you need me. I don't mind.'

She smiled. 'No, no, that's all right. I'm fine. I've just rung Sarah, so you can expect a phone call from her as soon as I've hung up. How's everything with you?'

Peter snorted. 'Much the same as usual. Look, I really don't mind coming home if you want me to. Is there anything you need?'

Katherine caught herself shaking her head before she realised he couldn't see her.

'No, really. I'm sure there'll probably be lots of things I'll want to say or you'll want to ask later, but I don't think I'm up to it at the moment.'

Peter made a noise of agreement then added, 'I'll call you tonight.' There was a pause. 'It'll be all right, Mum. Just don't rush into anything. I'll speak to you later. Love you,' and then he was gone.

Katherine looked around the familiar kitchen and wondered what to do next. The old order had gone, now she had to decide what to put in its place. From where she was sitting she could see into the sunlit utility room. There were still one or two shirts to be ironed, sheets in the wash basket. She stretched. First she could get dressed and then she would systematically remove Harry's things, unravel his thread from her life, box everything up and put them in the office. His golf clubs, his squash racquets, his clothes, all those other things she had regularly had to find for him, so when he sent for them or rang or whatever it was he intended to do, she would be ready.

For a few seconds she wondered where Harry was and then the phone rang and the thought vanished.

'Hi, Katherine?' said a soft transatlantic voice. 'It's Hope Laughton here. Sorry to ring you on the weekend. I just called to say I'm back in London and wondered if we might be able to get together? I could bring the draft contract down for you to have a look through if you think we need an excuse.'

'Hope, how nice to hear from you. Things are a bit –' she stopped herself and said in a low voice, ' – that would be wonderful. It would nice to see you again.'

She could hear the American was smiling when she

replied, 'Great. I owe you a dinner. Do you know anywhere round your neck of the woods or would you rather come up to town? We could do a show, catch a movie, have a real girls' night out? It'd be fun.'

Katherine glanced at the dairy calendar stuck on the fridge. 'That sounds like a wonderful idea. When had you got in mind?'

'How about Wednesday?'

Katherine teased a pencil out of the jar. 'Sounds fine.'

'Good, look I've got to go and eat. I've just checked in and my stomach can't work out whether we're in LA, London, or somewhere in between. What about if I pick up some tickets for a show?'

Katherine scribbled down the address and time while Hope carried on talking, 'And I've seen the photos of the house. They're great. You and Ben seemed to really hit it off, his fax was full of Katherine this and Katherine that.'

Katherine blushed crimson. Perhaps she ought to ring Ben next. It was tempting but it was too soon. She debated whether to tell Hope about Harry leaving, but before she had the chance, Hope giggled. 'Look. Gotta go, room service just arrived and he's real cute. I hope the steak is half as good looking. See you Wednesday.'

Unpicking Harry from the house, like the alterations she had once made to a knitted suit, was not as simple as Katherine had anticipated. It was very difficult not to lose the thread or accidentally unravel a piece you meant to keep untouched.

In their bedroom, armed with a roll of black bags, three cardboard boxes and two suitcases, Katherine began with a single-minded determination. The first half of the wardrobe was easy. Out went Harry's business suits, his Burberry mac, his good winter coat, endless crisp white shirts – those were easy things, anonymous things that vanished without trace. It got harder as she got further along the rails, further back in time.

Her hands hesitated over the grey wool jacket that she was certain had been sent to Oxfam years ago. Instead of seeing the jacket empty, her head filled with jerky home movie memories. It was hard to imagine that the man who had left and the man who had worn the grey jacket were the same person. As her fingers brushed the rough knobbly tweed she could see another Harry, a different Harry, grinning over his shoulder as he pushed Peter in a baby buggy up a hill on a holiday that she had completely forgotten about.

He was wearing a thick claret-coloured scarf, though that couldn't be right, she couldn't remember Harry ever wearing red. The image faded and she almost wished she could rewind it. This Harry looked as if he might love her. She wouldn't have asked that Harry to leave.

And it got worse. Glancing along the rail, she rediscovered a Harry who made her laugh, a Harry who brought her a single battered sunflower rescued from a roadside verge. A Harry who hurried out from their first tiny town terrace house to get fish and chips because she was too tired and too pregnant to face cooking, and a Harry who whistled in the mornings, who never forgot her birthday or their wedding anniversary. As she stared along the rail all the Harrys ganged up and clamoured for her attention.

Katherine Bourne leapt back from the wardrobe, sweating in terror. What had she done? As if she was searching for an escaped snake, she poked at the clothes with a wooden coat hanger, standing well back to see what else might slither out. Then she spotted Harry's old dinner suit, a polythene bag pulled down tight over the shoulders – and everything was all right again.

This Harry had stood in the bedroom door on the eve of some long distant Christmas party, tugging at his lapels. 'You're not going out in that, are you?' he said as she pinned a corsage the company had sent her onto a fuchsia pink evening dress.

He had been up for his first big promotion and insisted on her buying something new. She had bought a dress, a long forgotten dress, in the sales because she knew they couldn't afford to spend a lot. Standing in the doorway he had sighed, looked her up and down and then shaken his head. Nothing more.

'I'll tell them one of the children is sick,' he said.

Katherine Bourne marched into the bathroom, pulled on rubber gloves and then strode back to the wardrobe. Memories, like germs, couldn't breach rubber and without looking, without hesitating, she gathered the hangers up off the rails and flung Harry's clothes into the boxes and bags, sealing the tops tight with thick brown tape. When she'd finished, Katherine dragged everything into the office, piling the boxes and bags inside, then locked the door just in case the other Harrys decided to regroup and stage another break-out.

It was getting dark when she finished. With a strange sense of emptiness that wasn't altogether unpleasant, Katherine stripped off her clothes on the landing, leaving them where they fell, and, naked as a new baby, walked back into the bedroom to run a shower.

Chapter Six

While Katherine Bourne spent her Saturday trying to disentangle Harry from her life, Ray stared at Carol and wordlessly poured a mug of coffee from the jug on the counter of his café. Carol arranged a pile of shopping bags around the stool, eased off her shoes and looked up at Ray for solace, silent or otherwise. It was Saturday afternoon and the café was in the comfortable lull after lunch-time. Two old ladies were eating eclairs in the window seats; outside in the garden a few other customers were enjoying the sunshine. Carol felt hot, headachy and totally exhausted.

Ray sucked his teeth. 'Talk?'

Carol shook her head and took another pull on the coffee. 'I'd like a cigarette.'

'I thought you gave up smoking.'

She extended her hand. 'Now.'

Ray pursed his lips and took a Marlborough out of the top pocket of his waistcoat. 'You'll regret it.'

'Undoubtedly,' she said, taking the cigarette. 'Have you got a light?'

The first puff made her head spin but she persevered.

'It's not any of the family, is it?'

Carol shook her head. Ray paled. 'Oh, my God, not one of the cats?'

'Worse.'

Geoff came in from the kitchen, drying his hands on his apron. Ray shot him a warning glance and continued. 'So what is it?'

Carol rubbed her hands over her face. 'Harry. It's Harry. Harry has left his wife.'

'Jesus-H-Christ,' muttered Geoff.

Carol looked up, acknowledging his presence. 'And he turned up at my place last night. You must have seen the car in the drive.'

Ray and Geoff exchanged glances.

'We thought it might have been Sam. That's why we didn't come round – we thought . . .'

Carol groaned. Sam, Sam. Where was he today?

Geoff looked out into the street. '*Is Harry here?* Now? I mean are we finally, at long last, going to come eyeball to eyeball with the little shit?'

Carol shook her head. 'No, I left him at home watching the sport on the TV. I told him I'd have to do some shopping if he was staying for a while. He said he had some calls he wanted to make.' She stared at them, feeling a rising sense of panic.

'What the hell am I going to do now?' she hissed. 'I never thought he'd leave her. It's ridiculous. He can't stay with me. He hates the cats.' She hesitated. Surely there ought to be some sense of triumph – after all he'd left his wife, she finally had him after all these years.

'He's talking about us buying a house together.'

Ray and Geoff looked at each other before they looked at her. 'Has he said what his plans are?' Geoff began tentatively.

Carol groaned from behind a cloud of tobacco smoke. 'Shirts, laundry, wardrobe space, biological clocks tick-tick-ticking away. I really don't think I can handle this. The whole point of Harry is that he's spoken for, absent, away – a distant, impossible thing. I don't think I want him to be real.'

She stared up at the array of decorative coffee pots on the shelves behind the counter. A lot of them were there as the result of her forays in Harry's company. Souvenirs, scalps snatched from under the noses of maître d's, concierges, waiters, butlers and innkeepers all over Europe.

They were a record of past infidelity and maybe they were the only souvenirs she truly wanted, the brass ring had never been on the agenda.

She looked back at Ray and Geoff without focusing on their faces. 'I have got to go home and tell him, haven't I?'

Both men nodded. Carol pulled a pound coin out of her purse and laid it on the counter alongside her coffee mug, stubbed out the cigarette and, without another word, gathered up her shopping and left.

Ray flipped the coin into the air off his thumbnail. 'Heads she tells him, tails she doesn't. You call. Heads or tails?'

Geoff didn't call, instead he caught the coin mid-flight and dropped it noiselessly into the till.

Harry was still watching TV when Carol carried in the shopping. He did acknowledge her arrival but only by muting the golf for a second or two and lifting a hand in salute. While she stood in the doorway, laden down like a donkey, he grinned at her from the sofa.

'Great to be together at last, eh?' he said, patting the cushions beside him. 'Why don't you leave all that and come and sit here with me?' His voice lowered a fraction. 'We could snuggle up and watch this –'

Apparently golf was one aphrodisiac she knew nothing about.

Harry's eyes glittered. 'Or,' he said with feigned lightness, 'maybe we could slip upstairs if you'd prefer. I've been thinking about you all morning.'

Carol puffed out her cheeks. 'I bought ice cream,' she said lamely, holding out a Sainsbury's carrier bag like a chastity belt. 'I really need to get it into the freezer before it melts.'

Harry shrugged and turned the sound back up. Carol hoisted up the bags manfully and headed for the kitchen.

They had to talk, she had to say something. All the way home she had been constructing a carefully worded speech. Dropping the shopping onto the kitchen table before she lost the imperative she hurried back into the sitting room. 'Harry?'

He looked up from a particularly long and tricky putt that would birdie the eleventh.

'Changed your mind?' he said with a wistful grin.

Carol shook her head and switched off the golfer, mid-crouch. 'We need to talk.'

Harry stared at the blank screen. 'I was watching that,' he said miserably. 'Couldn't it wait until he's at least taken that shot?'

'No, I really need to talk to you. Now. We have to get some things straight.'

Harry gathered himself back up into a tidy heap, bright-eyed, like a respectful schoolboy. 'If it's about the cats, I thought –'

Carol held up a hand to silence him. 'It's not about the cats, Harry, it's about this, about you, about us – about me.' She took a breath, the carefully rehearsed logical speech evaporating as he stared up at her expectantly. 'And yes,' she added as an afterthought, 'about the cats too.'

Harry smiled winsomely. 'I thought we could build them a run out in the garden, wire netting, a proper little house and everything. I've been such a fool for so long. Hanging on to a marriage that was already dead, really. And all the time you've been here patiently waiting for me.'

Carol felt her stomach contract sharply. If only she could make Harry shut up, she could launch into the carefully scripted monologue, this was going seriously wrong – he wasn't supposed to speak. She started to pace, careful to avoid his eyes. Eyes, she suddenly remembered, that had once made her go weak at the knees. She stamped on the thought to extinguish it. This wasn't that Harry but another one who had mysteriously taken his place when she wasn't looking. How could that have happened? She swallowed hard; it wasn't the time to fill her head up with old snapshots of who they used to be.

'I really feel –' she began hesitantly, willing him to be quiet, 'that we need to take this new development one step at a time.'

'I couldn't agree more.' He glanced around the cheerful, untidy sitting room. 'I'll get onto my friend, Charlie, on Monday to come and do a valuation, stick the house on the market, start to look round for somewhere of our own. A fresh start for both of us.' He seemed to have swollen to fill the entire sofa. 'I'll get the rest of my things sent down – have to hire a van probably. I thought I could use the spare room as an office in the meantime, if you've got no objections. I mean you've got all your things down here. I'll get my desk sent down. Which reminds me, have you got a tape measure? I'm not sure if it'll fit in that alcove, but maybe if we took the wardrobe out. And I've got a nice set of oak bookshelves that –'

Open-mouthed, Carol stared at him. 'Harry?' she snapped, her tone as sharp and effective as a pistol shot over a riot. He paused mid-flow, his mouth the mirror of her own.

'This is not one step at a time. This is not what I wanted to talk about.'

Harry's face contorted, eyes suddenly bright with tears. 'I know, love, these are all practicalities, but at the moment I'm really not ready to think about the other things.' He glanced nervously at the phone. 'I ought to ring the children and let them know what's going on but I just can't do it. And then there's Katherine . . .' He winced as if her name was a stomach cramp.

Carol felt a wave of tenderness that she hadn't planned for and in the same instant felt her speech finally curl up and die. 'Why don't I go and fix us something to eat?'

Harry cheered visibly. 'Good idea,' he said. 'I don't suppose you've bought any sausages, have you? I usually have sausage and mash on Saturday, with beans – I like beans. Bit of a ritual really, but –' he lifted his hands in an apology. 'You know how these things are.'

And so, half-an-hour later, Carol Ackerman found herself grilling sausages, and in doing so realised that she had chosen to perpetuate a ritual that had no place in her life. From the kitchen door she could heard muted cheers from the golf course and tried to convince herself that after they had eaten she would say something. It didn't happen. After lunch, Harry went to sleep on the sofa surrounded by the Saturday papers which he had disembowelled into tented chaos, lulled into dreamland by a full stomach and an illusionary sense of wellbeing.

Carol camped out in the kitchen, willing him to stay unconscious while she re-read the notes she had made on the Danic loan project, trying very hard to be businesslike. Faded images of the original Harry kept surfacing, fragmentary images: a passionate kiss stolen at a tube station, a single red rose delivered by courier with a note that said, 'I love you, H.' What had happened to that other Harry? Without her noticing he had changed somewhere along the way, passion and novelty slowly transformed into something else, something constant but incomplete and unsatisfying. She rubbed her eyes, concentrating her thoughts on the computer projections, not letting her mind slip through her fingers and rush headlong into the confusion that beckoned.

Carol hadn't given any thought to Geoff and Ray and so when she heard their familiar voices coming up the path in the early evening, she instinctively got up, switched on the kettle and opened up the back door.

Geoff peered in expectantly. 'Can we come in? Is he still here?'

Carol waved them inside. 'Asleep in the sitting room last time I looked.'

Ray shouldered past him. 'How did he take it? What did you say to him? We were half expecting to find blood-stains and a whole mess of feathers.'

The expression on her face told them everything they needed to know and in unison they looked heavenward.

'You have got to say something,' whispered Geoff, 'this is ridiculous.'

'Do we get to meet him?' said Ray.

On cue Harry appeared through the hall doorway, untidy from sleep, face flushed, crumpled polo shirt half tucked in half tucked out. He nodded an acknowledgement to the two men and then looked at Carol. 'Hello. I thought I heard voices. What's going on?'

Carol lifted her hand. 'Harry, I'd like you to meet my next door neighbours and very good friends, Ray and Geoff. They run a café in town.'

Ray pouted provocatively. 'Not *a* café, darling, *the* café.'

Carol saw something flash across Harry's face, and then watched in surprise as he retreated into himself, shrinking back into the woodwork. The hand he had extended to greet Ray and Geoff dropped like a stone. Mouth open he stared fixedly at the two men, then after what seemed like an eternity he pulled himself together and mumbled a brief greeting. Carol stared at him; he looked completely undone.

Geoff grinned wolfishly. 'Nice to meet you at long last. Carol has told us *so* much about you, Harry, and all of it bad. Don't mind us. We usually have a coffee here when we get home from work. Oh, and we've brought back salmon mousse and salad if you're interested in supper.' He glanced at Carol. 'Do you mind us eating here with you? We can head on home to the old hacienda if you'd rather, if you two love birds have plans for an intimate little dinner *à deux*. Nothing worse than playing gooseberry.'

Harry coughed uncomfortably, eyes glued to the tray Geoff was carrying. When he spoke again his voice sounded forced as if he was purposely trying to make it sound deeper.

'Actually,' he said with measured casualness, 'I'd more or less decided that Carol and I were going to eat out tonight. Bit of a celebration. Me moving in and everything.'

That was news to Carol.

Geoff held up his hand. 'Not a problem. We quite understand if you two need time alone to talk.' He said the last four words with his gaze firmly fixed on Carol.

She caught hold of Ray's arm, expression full of appeal as she stopped him from backing out of the door. 'Wait – hang on a minute, you two. I want salmon mousse,' she said with forced cheerfulness. 'I've been looking forward to it all week. Here. Sit down, I'll get some knives and forks.' Hastily she pulled out a chair at the kitchen table. 'I'll just finish making the coffee. Why don't you unpack the tray?'

She busied herself rinsing out the cafetiere, finding cutlery, while all the time she could feel Harry's eyes burning into the back of her head like branding irons willing her to look up. When she finally did he was wearing a peculiar inane lopsided grin.

'Er, do we have any wine to go with this?' he asked lamely.

Ray who had been serving up the salad, nodded. 'We most definitely do. She's probably got a bottle or two squirrelled away in the cupboard under the stairs. Do you want me to go and take a look?'

Harry nodded and for some reason both Ray and Geoff glided noiselessly towards the hall. Harry sprang backwards out of their way.

Carol stared at him. 'What on earth is the matter with you?'

Harry indicated the hall door. 'Those two,' he murmured. 'They're your friends?'

Carol nodded, pouring boiling water onto the coffee

grounds. 'Yes, we've been friends for years, since I moved in. Have you got a problem with that?'

'You know what they are, don't you?'

Carol felt comprehension clatter down through her mind like a slate falling; she chose to be obtuse. 'Great friends,' she said lightly and motioned towards the supper tray. 'Great cooks.'

Harry crept up beside her, so close that his lips were no more than a fraction of an inch away from her ear. 'Great pansies,' he hissed. 'They're gay. Queer. Bent as a box of frogs, the pair of them.'

Carol couldn't resist the urge to giggle. 'I do know that.'

'Doesn't it worry you?'

Carol looked up at him. 'No, why? Should it?'

Harry puffed and tugged at his shirt front. 'They make me nervous, that's all.'

Carol sighed. 'Relax, Harry, you're not their type.'

She might as well have slapped him, he leapt away from her, face glowing scarlet. He looked as if he might choke and at that moment Ray and Geoff returned triumphantly bearing a bottle of their house white.

The impromptu supper party was not easy. Harry's tension spread like smallpox. The salmon mousse turned to cardboard in Carol's mouth. Harry sat very upright, reluctant to speak, with the air of a condemned man and meanwhile, as if on cue, Ray and Geoff camped it up most horribly, until Carol had to call a halt by insisting she had work to get on with. She had barely finished her sentence before Harry scrambled to his feet, scooping up crockery, cutlery and meals barely finished, throwing plates into the sink with reckless abandon.

'Bit nervous, isn't he?' said Ray with a grin, as Carol shooed them out of the back door.

Carol growled.

Geoff nodded towards the two cats who were manning

a picket line on the back fence. 'Seems like the ginger ninjas don't much care for your house guest either.'

Carol sighed. 'What the hell am I going to do?'

Geoff leant forward and pecked her on the cheek. 'Nip it in the bud, darling, and quickly before he gets himself dug in.'

Carol sighed; if it was only that easy.

Inside Harry was gamely attacking the washing up. The sink was awash with an explosion of bubbles and hot water. He smiled as she closed the door.

'I'll ring Charlie first thing Monday morning. Don't worry, it'll all be sorted out once we've moved,' he said with a joyful grin. 'It'll be much better.'

Better for who? Carol caught hold of the edge of the table and forced her expression into neutral. 'Harry, we ought to talk about this before it goes any further.' She carefully avoided his eyes, her attention rooted on a cracked tile a few inches to the left of his head. 'It really worries me that you've assumed you can just come here and set up home. You didn't ask me. You didn't think to discuss it before you made the decision.'

He started to speak but she held up a hand to silence him.

'Whatever it is we have said in the past about eventually being together, it was never really part of the plan, was it? And if you're honest you know that. Surely I have some say in this? I really don't think I'm ready to play house with you.'

Had she said enough? She took a long slow deep breath, offering Harry an opening to speak. She arranged her thoughts for a counterattack. Mentally up on her toes she considered she was ready for any parry he might offer. Elbow deep in suds, Harry seemed to be frozen to the spot and then to her horror one huge tear rose up like a spectre from under his sandy eyelashes and rolled slowly, without mercy, down over his florid pink face.

'But I thought . . .' he began.

Desperately she tore her attention away from following the shiny path of the teardrop.

'No,' she said in an undertone, struggling to keep a rein on the emotion in her voice, 'you didn't think at all, Harry, you just assumed. That's the problem.'

Harry sniffed. It was a majestic throbbing sniff that seemed to roll through him like a thunder clap. 'But I thought you loved me,' he whined. 'If it's the cats or those . . . those,' he motioned towards the door through which Geoff and Ray has so recently disappeared.

Carol shook her head. 'Harry, it's you and me – it's us. I don't think I'm ready to have you in my life full time. I'm not ready to make a commitment to you.' There, it was said, all out in the open and up for grabs.

The monumental sniff found a partner. 'But what am I going to do? I thought – I thought –' his shoulders folded forward. 'I've burnt my boats for you, Carol. I thought you'd be really glad that I'd finally made the break. Where can I go? – I mean, I've got nowhere else. I love you.'

Carol glanced down; her knuckles were as white as alabaster where she was clutching the table top.

She took a deep breath. 'I'm not saying you have to leave now. At least, not straight away. Take some time to sort yourself out. I'm just saying that it would be a mistake to rush into this.' The words dried up in her throat. What exactly was she saying? How could she offer Harry a lifeline without finding herself getting all tangled up in it, or promising something she didn't want to deliver?

He crept over towards her and gently kissed her on the cheek. He smelt of Fairy Liquid.

'I know what this is about,' he said with a grin. 'You know, you don't fool me. It's about having children. It is, isn't it? I thought yesterday I shouldn't have said anything. I mean children would be nice but I'm really not that desperate to have a second family if you don't want to. If you want to have a career that's fine by me. In the baby department I'll be happy for you to set the agenda.'

Carol couldn't find anything to say.

Harry had hit his stride. He slipped his arms around her waist and before she could protest or resist, he pulled her close up against him.

'You're just afraid, that's why you're saying all these things – that's what this is about, isn't it? All those years you've spent being a spinster of this parish. I can understand that. It's a big thing finally getting together after all this time – I can understand you being defensive – but don't worry. I'm here for you.'

Open-mouthed, Carol stared up at him. Surely he had to have been listening to a different conversation? He kissed her gently on the top of the head. 'Why don't we just leave the clearing up until tomorrow and go to bed?'

Carol finally found her voice. 'It's early—'

Harry grinned. 'I know.'

Chapter Seven

Katherine Bourne was very surprised that Harry didn't ring her over the weekend. She had expected, imagined, rehearsed and resigned herself to a difficult phone call sometime over those first long forty-eight hours. In fact, on Sunday she had barely moved from the phone all day. So when it rang and woke her first thing on Monday morning – she had switched off the alarm, after all she need no longer get up at five-thirty to make Harry's tea or make sure he had clean socks – she gritted her teeth before she picked up the receiver.

Peter's voice rolled cheerfully down the phone. 'Morning, Mum, I'd expected to hear from you. Are you all right?'

The tension trickled slowly out of her spine. 'I'm fine. You caught me having a lie-in.' She knew she sounded defensive.

Peter laughed. 'Why not. Start as you mean to go on, eh? I just rang to say I'll be coming home later in the week, maybe stay the weekend, if that's okay? I thought you might be grateful for a bit of moral support. Sarah has been on the phone all weekend giving me the benefit of her opinion. I think she's using me as a sounding board, honing her argument to do battle with you.'

Katherine grimaced, grateful that Sarah had seen fit to keep her views to herself for a while longer – the silence wouldn't last long. She forced herself not to ask what Sarah had said.

'It will be nice to see you.' She felt around inside her head for things to tell him that didn't involve Harry and came up with very few. 'I'm going out to lunch today.' How brave and fearless that sounded. It had taken almost all her courage to ring Ben Morton and ask if he was serious about taking her for a meal. 'And then on Wednesday I'm off up to London to meet Hope Laughton. You know, I told you about her?'

There was a pause while her son caught hold of his thoughts. 'The American film woman?'

'Yes, that's right, she invited me down to discuss the contract. And another thing I think you ought to know, I'm seriously considering buying your father out and converting the house into a retirement home. Maybe we can talk about all that when you get home?'

There was another silence. She could imagine his face; like Harry he didn't like upheaval.

Finally Peter spoke again; his tone was still warm but not so confident. 'It sounds as if you've been thinking about all this for a long time.'

Katherine caught a fleeting glimpse of herself in the dressing-table mirror. With the phone cradled against her ear, head tipped to one side, she looked younger, her hair – which needed cutting – had a wild tousled look about it. She smiled at her reflection. Yes, she had been thinking for a long time but Peter didn't need to know that.

'I suppose I just realised that if I didn't do something soon I might miss my chance.'

'God forbid. Have you heard anything from Dad?'

'No, not a word. How about you?'

'No, nothing. I did think he might ring me. Do you know where he is?'

Katherine coughed uncomfortably. She had assumed Harry would go and stay with his friend, George, drink, moan, phone – but he had done none of those things and when she had rung George he seemed surprised to hear from her.

'No, haven't seen him, m' dear. Not hide nor hair,'

George had said a little testily. 'He rang me Saturday afternoon to say he didn't think he'd be up for golf. I thought perhaps he'd got the flu. He told me the other week you'd had a run in with it. Is everything all right between you two?'

'So who are you going out to lunch with?' Peter's voice snapped Katherine out of her mental meanderings.

She took a fraction too long to compose herself. Before she could speak, Peter said, 'Oh no, Mother, don't tell me, not a man?'

Katherine started to protest and then gave in gracefully; after all, did it matter now?

'Yes, actually it is a man. He's a friend, nothing else.' Yet, whispered her rogue mind. 'He's the chap who took the photographs of the house for the film company.'

She could hear amusement masking the uncertainty in Peter's voice when he spoke. 'Well, just behave yourself.'

She stretched and then glanced at the clock. The little demon voice in her head said that she had already behaved herself for far too long but she didn't argue. There were still nearly fours hours until she met Ben, perhaps she would begin the day with a long leisurely bath, and maybe the hairdressers might be able to fit her in for a quick trim – and then of course she had to think about what to wear.

Peter continued, 'Anyway, look, I've really got to go, I've got an early lecture. I'll see you later in the week – if you can fit me into your busy social calendar that is.'

Katherine felt a rush of affection for him. 'I'll look forward to it, thanks for ringing.' She paused. 'It will be all right, love.'

Peter didn't reply, which made something ache inside. While Sarah had grown up and flown the coop, Peter had found it so much harder to let go. He'd hung on at home an extra year, teetering on the brink of independence, waiting for a sign that it was all right to fly away. In an odd way she realised Peter's approval was more important to her than Sarah's.

She climbed slowly out of bed, eyes fixed on her reflection. There was a graceful almost sensual elegance about the way her body moved, one that she had quite forgotten was there. It occurred to her that she had survived two whole days without Harry and the weight of him, the weight that she had barely realised she had carried all those years was finally beginning to lift. It showed in her face, in her posture – she grinned and the mirror cheerfully followed suit.

Jeanette, Carol Ackerman's secretary, was genuinely surprised when she rolled into work half-an-hour late, as usual, and found that Carol wasn't already there. As she dropped her shopping into the bottom drawer of the filing cabinet the shimmering glass office behind her work station was as empty and silent as the tomb. A few minutes after switching on the coffee machine, taking a desultory glance at the post, answering the first of the morning's calls and eating half a Mars bar, the doors to the lift opened to reveal Carol Ackerman as Jeanette had never seen her before.

Her boss's eyes were ringed with shadow and her normally calm facade rippled like a stormy lake. Her expression, habitually composed, was as sharp as fingernails raked over a blackboard. Jeanette glanced down at the diary; she was due to meet the big-wigs at eleven-thirty for a final presentation of the Danic Project. Last minute nerves? It seemed unlikely.

Jeanette, not normally known for her shows of fidelity or compassion, sensed something dark and unusual was brewing, poured a mug of coffee and handed it wordlessly to Carol as she reached the desk. Carol stared at her blankly then nodded her thanks, taking a long pull on the tepid liquid.

'Have you got any tights in your drawer?' she asked.

Jeanette glanced down at Carol's normally immaculately black silk-clad legs – a ladder stretched from below the knee to mid-thigh revealing the plump creamy white flesh beneath.

Jeanette shook her head. 'No, but I'll send someone out to get a pair, it won't take more than five minutes.' She paused, curiosity alight. 'Rough weekend?'

Carol drained the rest of the mug in one long gulp. 'Something like that.' Her voice dripped with irony and exhaustion.

Jeanette suppressed a grin. 'Don't forget you've got Danic at eleven-thirty.'

Carol groaned and waved her cup towards the filter machine. 'More please, tights, and could you bring me two paracetamol when you've got a minute.'

From the corner of her eye Jeanette saw her friend arriving at the desk opposite. For a split second their gaze met; there was something going on and Jeanette had every intention of finding out what it was.

In her office Carol threw her brief-case onto the desk and ground the heels of her hands up under her eye sockets to try and relieve the headache that threatened. The entire weekend had been a complete disaster and there was a good chance that she was in for more of the same – and this morning . . . She stared out at the Thames, eyes glazing over. Her little lecture had done no good whatsoever.

'Where have you put my clean shirts, Kitty-Kat?' Harry's voice insinuated itself into her head, waking her from a dream.

She rolled over, struggling to focus. 'Sorry.'

Harry had been standing in his underpants and socks by the open wardrobe door clutching a crumpled sweaty shirt in one fist. 'I put this in the laundry basket on Saturday. The ones I hung up in the spare room are still all creased, I can hardly wear one of those to work, now can I?'

Carol licked her lips. 'I'm not with you?'

Harry slumped down onto the side of the bed, making her teeth crunch. He was trying to sound jovial and jokey; neither of them was convinced.

'It's really quite simple, darling. I just need to know what you've done with the ironing?' He spoke slowly as if she was an imbecile.

Carol crawled off the bed, pulled down her tee-shirt and opened the other wardrobe door. Sleeping with Harry had been a big mistake. Inside the wardrobe were the blouses and shirts she wore for work, hanging alongside a series of expensive business suits, all immaculately pressed.

Harry glared at them accusingly. 'When did you do those?'

Mornings were not Carol's best time. She sucked speculatively at the inside of her mouth, resisting the temptation to swear at him and contented herself with an icy stare instead.

'I didn't do them,' she said slowly, enunciating the words with equal care. 'A woman at the laundrette does them for me. I drop off a laundry bag on a Friday evening and pick up the clean things from last week. One bag in, one out, I've done it for years.'

Harry waved the dirty shirt at her like a red flag. 'So what exactly am I supposed to wear for work?'

He was quite obviously expecting an answer.

'I don't know. You could always iron one of the creased ones, there's an ironing board in the utility room.'

Harry forced another humourless smile. 'Oh, so you do iron, then?'

Carol could feel her temper rising. 'Not if I can possibly avoid it, that's why I pay someone else to do it for me.' She glanced at the clock. 'Shit, it's nearly seven. Why didn't you call me? I'll miss my train.'

'There's no need to swear, I didn't want to disturb you so I turned the alarm off. That mattress isn't very comfortable, is it? I barely slept a wink all night.'

Carol couldn't bring herself to speak and instead hurried off into the bathroom. Even there with the door locked she didn't feel alone. The pale cream sink was splashed with shaving foam in which nestled tufts of bright gingery stubble, the tiled floor was littered with damp discarded towels and the water in the shower was tepid. Outside the bathroom door, even above the sound of the running water, she could hear Harry prowling up and down the landing like a night stalker. Presumably, she thought, turning the tap full on so that the water ran like iced Perrier, still clutching his bloody shirt.

He had insisted on driving her in to work. Leaving later than usual they had hit the worst of the traffic, and then, as she had got to her office he had dragged her brief-case out from between the seats and in doing so managed to ladder her tights. It was not the best Monday morning on record.

She snapped open her brief-case and looked at the crisp navy blue Danic dossier she had spent months helping to compile. Clinging to her cuff was a clutch of ginger cats' hairs. She brushed them away and staring down at the subtly embossed file cover felt a rush of panic. All the things she knew about Danic, their aims, their objectives, their business plan and their management structure, seemed to have fallen through the newly formed holes in her mind. She had planned to spend the weekend reading through her notes until all the information, already well fixed in her mind, had become like an extension of herself so that the presentation would be painless, seamless.

A bead of sweat lifted on her top lip as she opened the first page. The words of the introduction swam in front of her eyes; her carefully worded proposal was the writing of a stranger, lost somewhere in the previous forty-eight hours.

Sanctuary to war zone in two days. A heavy weight seemed to have settled itself between her shoulders, a millstone, a burden, and its name was Harry Bourne. She pulled her chair out and sat down. Concentrate, stay calm. Carol took a long deep breath. She could do this, this was important, this was . . .

There was a knock at the door and Jeanette, looking uncharacteristically solicitous, came in bearing a tray on which was another mug of coffee, two pairs of tights, a bottle of paracetamol and a glass of iced water.

She smiled. 'Here you go. You look awful.'

Carol sighed. 'Thanks.'

Instead of leaving Jeanette hovered by her desk. 'Do you want to talk about it?'.

Carol had always had a copper-bottomed rule about not mixing her social life with business. It had been so easy when Harry had flitted in and out of her schedule, a regular visitor with no complications. Her rise up through the ranks at Lactons had been too hard won to compromise with a messy personal life. She stared up at Jeanette's face. The girl had composed her sharp features into the benevolent countenance of a confessor. Carol shut the Danic file.

'I'll close the door,' Jeanette said.

When Carol had done, Jeanette made them both another cup of coffee. 'Do you want me to ring the board and tell them you're sick?'

Carol felt her colour drain. 'No, no I can't do that. No, I'll be fine. Really.'

'You don't look fine to me.'

Carol sniffed and rubbed her hands over her skirt. 'No, you're right, but given half-an-hour and another coffee I'll be back on the case.' She hesitated, looking at the retreating form of her secretary with an unnerving sense of foreboding that came from breaking her own rules.

'Jeanette, I'm trusting you to keep this to yourself.'

The girl's face was as impassive as a china mask. 'Goes without saying. I'll hold your calls until you've had a chance to get your head together. Oh, by the way, that

Jackson woman, the one with the country house, rang up first thing this morning, and asked if she could come and see you on Wednesday.'

Carol remembered Katherine Jackson and her warm friendly eyes.

'I thought we'd already set her up with Dougie?'

Jeanette shrugged. 'Me too, but she said if you'd got the time she'd like to come in and talk to you. If you could fit her in. I said we'd contact her later today.'

Carol glanced at her diary. Katherine Jackson, stolid calm Katherine Jackson, with her ill-fitting suit and sensible shoes, all excited about her bright shiny new start without a man in her life. 'Okay, ring her back and arrange an appointment.' She paused for a split second. 'Actually, would you ask her if she'd like to talk over lunch?'

Jeanette pouted. 'Lunch? Are you sure?'

Carol nodded. Maybe Katherine Jackson had some practical tips on getting rid of an unwanted man.

'Have you ever thought about having a colour?'

Katherine Bourne, swathed in a hairdresser's shroud, glanced up into the salon mirror and from there into the reflected eyes of the girl standing behind her. The girl, pale and slim as a stick-insect, had a mop of sleek blonde hair and looked as if she was barely out of puberty. Her nose-ring glinted in the downlighters as her fingers moved speculatively through Katherine's thick grey-brown hair with intense professional interest.

Katherine's usual woman was off having her veins done, but they had said Kerry could give her a trim, no trouble.

'A colour?'

The girl nodded. 'Yeah, it would get rid of all this grey. And the new vegetable dyes we're using are really good, they just enhance yer natural colour. And they fade rather than grow out so you don't have to worry about the roots showing.' She gathered Katherine's hair up in her fingers

88

and lifted it to frame her face. 'And if I put in a few layers, cut it a bit shorter, sort of soft and wispy around the jaw line, it'd take years off you. What d'you reckon?'

Katherine stared at her in astonishment, her usual woman normally said things like, 'How much would you like me to take off?' and 'How's the family?'

She nodded. 'Sounds okay. Would it take very long?'

The girl grinned. 'No, 'bout twenty minutes for the colour to take, half-an-hour to do the cut.' She slid the watch round on her wrist. 'I've got no one else in till half past, so we've got plenty of time. I'll just nip and get the colour chart, shall I?'

Katherine examined her new haircut with interest. It felt a little like meeting an old friend and being surprised how well they looked. Kerry, the little blonde hairdresser, was busy performing the dance of the rear-view mirror behind her.

'What do you reckon then?' she said, tipping the mirror back and forth to reveal the soft wisps of layered brown hair that curled into Katherine's neck.

Katherine smiled. 'Wonderful,' she said breathlessly, almost sad that she had had to choose an adjective.

Kerry made approving noises. 'I knew you'd like it. What you want now is some long earrings to set it off, dangly jobs.' She tugged gently at the hair behind Katherine's ears, as proud as any mother hen. 'I reckon it really suits you, and it's so easy to do with that gel. Just scrunch the top up, run yer fingers through the rest, like I showed you. Only takes a few minutes.'

Katherine nodded dumbly. Taking off the shroud she looked coolly at the sensible floral skirt and white blouse that appeared from underneath it.

Kerry grinned. 'I reckon you could do with something to go with yer new image.'

Katherine reddened a little at the girl's completely unselfconscious and uncanny ability to read her thoughts.

'I'm not sure if I'm ready for all this change.'

'It's as good as a rest they tell me,' Kerry said, whisking a broom through the crow's nest of hair around the chair. 'There's a new shop over in Talbot Street that does factory seconds, good stuff, ends of lines and things. You want to go and have a look, the woman in there is really nice.'

Katherine took the cheque book out of her handbag and wrote Kerry a handsome tip to go along with the price of the haircut. After all it wasn't everyday someone helped you to find something you didn't realise you'd lost.

An hour later, laden down with new clothes and not a shred of guilt, Katherine Bourne, née Jackson, headed home to get ready for her lunch date with Ben Morton, a pair of dangly earrings carefully secreted in her handbag along with a growing sense of adventure.

In her office Carol tucked the mobile phone under her chin. In front of her, spread out on the desk, like a royal flush, were the duplicate pages of the Danic report. The pristine, bound copy still nestled in her brief-case. This was her working copy, notes neatly made in her crisp square handwriting in the margins, notes that she had now loaded into her lap-top, notes she already knew by heart. Another half-an-hour and she would be at the flip-chart, in front of the board and the partners, making her pitch. The biggest pitch of her career. She was calmer now and the words that had seemed like gibberish first thing had reformed themselves neatly back into familiar thoughts and arguments; she was ready and feeling more charitable.

'I wanted to apologise about this morning.' Harry, at the far end of the line, sounded contrite. 'I'm a bit tense that's all. You know, leaving Katherine, moving in, the cats – the shirts, you know, everything – I just wanted you to know that.'

'It's all right, don't worry about it,' she said without any side. 'I just never gave your shirts a second thought. Are you okay?'

He laughed. 'A little crumpled around the back but not bad. The thing is I've got a meeting this afternoon. I was wondering what you'd got organised for dinner?'

Carol felt her charity cooling. 'Dinner?'

'Yes, tonight when we get home, you see I'm not sure what time I'll be finished and I didn't want whatever you were going to cook to spoil. I wonder whether you'd mind taking the train home, or do you want to hang around the office and I'll come by and pick you up? I could give you a ring to let you know when I'm on my way, if you like.'

Carol laid the opening page of the Danic report back on the desk. 'Don't worry about me,' she said very carefully.

Harry made a strange noise in the back of this throat. 'So what are you going to do about dinner –'

Carol hung up and switched her phone off; she would ring him later, after Danic, after lunch, after she had time to reflect on what it might be like to be a wife and a mother, some time before hell froze over.

The buzzer flashed on the intercom. Carol looked out beyond the glass walls of her office, straight into Jeanette's bright eyes.

'Are you all right?' the girl mouthed.

Carol nodded and picked up the receiver.

'I've got Lee Fenman from Danic on line three,' Jeanette said over the phone. 'He says he'd like a word with you.'

'Okay, put him on.'

Lee Fenman was slick, businesslike, the frontman for Danic's pirate trade in business take-overs. He was a good looking privateer.

'Hi, Carol, just rung up to see if there's anything you need.'

'No, I'm fine, Lee. All ready. The figures are here in front of me. I really think we are in business. I thought I was going to see you in the meeting.'

Lee laughed. 'You will, you will, I just wanted to make sure my rep was up to snuff.'

Carol unconsciously checked the front of her blouse. Lee Fenman, without ever making a single advance, always made her feel as if he was looking at her naked. She ran a well manicured fingertip down over her notes.

'All the preliminaries are done. There's really no need to worry.' Not that Lee sounded as if worry had any place on his agenda. 'I'm certain we're fine – almost home and dry.'

'A mere formality?' Lee suggested.

Carol framed her next sentence carefully. 'When we're talking about a loan of this size, there is really no such thing as a formality. And Lactons, as you are aware, have always been a very conservative company. I think it's safe to say though that everyone is very very keen to get this project off the ground.'

Her project. Danic had approached her direct to raise the finances for a major buy-out, and once the deal was done, the money guaranteed, then they would crack the nut, strip off the outside shell to reveal the soft flesh inside, break it up and sell it off in small sweet chunks. The structures were already in place, buyers already waiting.

Danic had perfected their act in the eighties, honed down their operation to a streamlined athletic shape during the recession, vultures cheerfully feeding on a failing economy, and now they were amongst the best in their field. Pirates who promised corporate salvation for harassed CEOs with cash-flow problems. Carol wasn't the only one who felt Lee Fenman stripped people naked.

'See you in the bull ring.'

Carol hung up, all thoughts of Harry and dinner drowned out by a rush of adrenaline.

Lee Fenman took her out for a champagne lunch afterwards, while the ink was drying on the agreement. Before they took their seats in a fashionable brasserie, tucked up at tiny tables under the insane eyes of a Michelin starred chef, Lee made a single phone call and then he was hers and hers alone.

'You know,' he said, waving the waiter to pour the first of the Krug. 'We could use a brain like yours at Danic. Lots of travel, great perks, fast car, health care package, prestige offices. Hong Kong, the States, all over Europe – if you joined up with Danic the world could be your oyster.'

Carol shook the napkin over her lap. 'I've got a feeling you've used this speech before.'

Lee leant forward, eyes alight with mischief as he touched his glass against hers. 'Yeah, but I don't always mean it. This time I'm deadly serious. You're wasted in Lactons. Why not think about it? There's an opening coming up in our New York branch in the autumn. You'd be a natural. Maybe we could get together over dinner some time and talk about it?'

Dinner. Carol's face froze. She noticed that Lee Fenman's expensive white silk shirt had razor-sharp creases running in single unsullied lines down from the centre of the sleeve head to the cuff, on each arm. It looked as if the distance between them had been calculated with a micrometer. They were as close to perfect as you could get. They were the mark of a wife, no laundry on earth would care that much.

Lee registered the lapse of concentration. 'What is it? Worried about leaving the little man at home?'

Carol shook her head, struggling to regain her composure. 'No, not at all, there is no little man. I'm a free agent,' she said with a cheeriness that didn't quite ring true.

Lee waved the waiter over with the menus. 'Good, well in that case, think about it. I'm serious. Chances like this don't come along every day, nor do they hang around for ever. Tell you what, just to let you know I'm on the level, why not fly over for a couple of weeks to see what you think – on me, on the company?'

Chapter Eight

Katherine Bourne took one last look at her reflection in the rear-view mirror of her little car, gave her new haircut a final fluff, and then climbed out into the sunshine. There was a small, not altogether unpleasant, knot in the place where her stomach should have been, and she wondered whether she would be able to eat anything.

She glanced down at her watch; Ben had said he'd meet her at around one, at the Victory in Huntingdon, did she know it? He wasn't sure of the name of the road but it was a nice place, near a river, a comfortable old-fashioned place where they did wonderful food. She'd nodded. Of course she knew the Victory, or at least was certain she could find it. She had only had to ask directions twice.

She tugged her new skirt straight, her change of image. And so here she was, out on her first date in years, all dressed up in a comfortable jersey granddad shirt in bitter orange, over a long cream print cotton skirt with matching suede pumps. She looked good, felt confident – or at least she had done when she'd left the house.

It was a quarter to one. Katherine surreptitiously glanced left and right, trying to pick out Ben Morton's silver Volvo amongst all the other cars in the car park. He had been so easy to talk to when he'd been at her house. She hoped it would be as easy today. Her scalp prickled. Gardens, photos – they could surely find some common ground.

Across a belt of weedless gravel the Victory Hotel lay ready and waiting for her grand entrance, all gift wrapped in Virginia creeper and summer sunshine. A couple of the patrons had taken up residence in the sunlight on the benches outside, and the sound of soft music and cheerful voices meandered across to comfort her.

Katherine took a deep breath and glanced into the side window of her car; foreshortened by the curve of the glass she looked dumpy and the new earrings disproportionately large. Should she wait for a little longer in the car? Would she look too eager if she arrived there before him? What if she'd misunderstood him and got the wrong day? What if it had been a cruel joke and he didn't turn up, at all. What was it he thought he might get from her? A voice, not unlike her mother's, asked if she thought his intentions were honourable – whatever that might mean. A little phalanx of fears and doubts forced their way up from inside the knot in her stomach, vying for attention alongside the sense of expectation and excitement.

She opened her bag and took out a mint; this was crazy. She was a grown woman not a twelve-year-old. Whether he showed up or not there was nothing to stop her having a quiet drink and a spot of lunch. Before she had time to change her mind she headed off across the gravel towards the main door, shoulders squared, new handbag tucked up under her arm.

Inside it took a second or two for her eyes to adjust to the gloom. When her vision cleared she could see she was in a reception area. A boy in a suit was sorting file cards at the desk. She smiled at him and headed for the loo to gather her thoughts around her.

Even in the vanity mirror, under the unforgiving fluorescent light above the sink, she still looked good – handsome, intelligent, humorous. She smiled encouragingly at her reflection. Here's to a new beginning, a Harry-free life, and the hair looked great.

'Hello,' she said to the young man behind the reception desk. 'My name is Katherine Bourne. I'm meeting Mr Morton here for lunch.'

The boy smiled an acknowledgement and turned his

attention to a large diary on the desk. After a few seconds he looked up, face impassive. 'Morton, you said? Is that M-O-R-T-O-N?'

Katherine shifted her weight. 'Yes, that's right. Ben Morton, one o'clock. Table for two.' The boy's gaze dropped back to the book and Katherine felt the knot in her stomach pull tight, a noose now.

'I'm very sorry.' He shook his head. 'I'm afraid there's no one called Morton on my list, are you sure he's booked? We do an awful lot of bar meals here, maybe –' he stopped, smiling inanely, apparently not wanting to waste words on further explanation.

'Right,' Katherine said, just a shade too brightly, glancing over her shoulder to see who might be listening. She was absolutely certain Ben had said he was going to book a table.

'You know, this sort of thing happens all the time,' the boy added pleasantly. 'Have you got any idea when Mr Morton booked the table?'

Katherine shook her head, not trusting herself to speak.

'Well, I'm really sorry, we haven't got a booking in that name.' The boy lifted his hand, a gesture of both consolation and invitation. 'Why don't you go through into the bar, madam, and have an aperitif. When Mr Morton arrives I can tell him you're here?'

Katherine nodded again and mumbled her thanks. She glanced again at her watch; it was barely one, plenty of time yet, a strange hearty voice in her head said. She didn't believe it.

In the quiet shadows of the bar, at a table by the window chosen for its place in the wings not the spotlight, Katherine cradled a bitter lemon and tried very hard not to look too conspicuous or too desperate. Her confidence had begun to ebb the moment the receptionist looked puzzled.

Above the double doors that led into the foyer an antique clock meticulously ticked off the seconds of her discomfort:

one o'clock, quarter past, half past. She wished that she had had the sense to bring a magazine. As cars crunched across the gravel outside the bay window she forced herself not to look up to see if Ben was at the wheel, but found it impossible.

Couples moved in and out of the little bar, engaged in conversation, laughing, talking, all apparently totally at ease, dancing the familiar steps of their own personal fault-less gavotte. She felt as if they were all looking at her, that they knew – and then she dismissed the idea as ridiculous – who'd want to look at her, a middle-aged woman done up to the nines, out on a date, who had quite obviously been stood up? Pity would make them do the decent thing and ignore her. Maybe this was what Ben Morton did, perhaps it had been his intention all along. What on earth did she think he might see in her? She reddened at her own thoughts and took another mouthful of bitter lemon, wishing she had ordered something alcoholic instead.

Self-pity washed over her like an incoming tide and she stared fixedly out of the windows, out towards a stand of ancient oaks, swallowing down a great wave of tears. So this was what it felt like on the other side of the fence.

Ben wasn't going to turn up, she and the receptionist already knew that. He should have said *if* Mr Morton turns up, not when. She stared down at her large capable hands where they folded around the glass. Nail varnish, a soft orange blush, completely out of character, and now look-ing quite ridiculous, glinted back at her. She was so foolish. A single tear threatened to roll down her face. She sniffed it away.

False hope, a new haircut, new clothes – the pain, the sense of humiliation, was like nothing Katherine had ever experienced. She had always considered herself robust and strong and here she was struggling not to weep over a fragmentary might-have-been.

A tiny indignant blue flame ignited in her belly and burnt

off the last of the self-pity. She drained her glass. Waiting around any longer would accomplish nothing other than rubbing her misery in. Squaring her shoulders she got to her feet: it was nearly twenty to two, he wouldn't be coming now. She'd go home, have a sandwich, change her clothes, wash off all this make-up, take off the nail polish and get out in the garden.

Eyes still fixed on the window, Katherine turned to pick up her handbag and as she did someone called her name.

She swung round and there was Ben Morton, red-faced, shaking his head. She stared at him without really focusing. She didn't trust herself to speak.

'Thank God you're here. I'm so glad I found you. This was my last-ditch attempt. I've already rung your house twice.'

She bit her lip and glanced down at the single empty glass on the table; wondering whether to believe him.

'I didn't think you were coming,' she said in a voice that didn't sound anything like her own. 'They said you hadn't booked a table.'

He shook his head. 'No, you're right. I hadn't, not here, but I did, at the *Fig Tree*, not the Victory. I said the Fig Tree. I should have been more specific about where it was and then this wouldn't have –' he stopped and extended a hand. 'I'm really so sorry, you must think I'm a total bastard.' He smiled.

Katherine stared at him, the colour lifting in her cheeks. 'I do. The Fig Tree?'

'That's right, down by the river. I've been waiting for you since one, I thought you'd stood me up. And then the penny dropped, some sort of flash of inspiration, I suppose. I remembered you saying you weren't quite sure where it was but that you'd able to find it. And then I wondered if you'd come here by mistake – it was a shot in the dark, really. I'm so sorry.' He spoke with an endearing lopsided grin, rubbing his hands down over faded Levis. She opened her mouth to say something but nothing came out.

'I don't know about you but I could really use a drink. Are they still serving lunches? I'm starving.'

Katherine nodded.

He stopped mid-stride and then turned back and looked at her. The tension was easing out of his face. He leant forward, caught hold of her arms and pulled her towards him, and as he did, he kissed her oh-so-gently on the side of the cheek.

'You look absolutely gorgeous,' he whispered. 'And I love the hair.'

Katherine blushed. Whatever his motives it was a long time since any one had flirted with her. The knot in her stomach was rapidly melting away into a soft warm glow.

Jeanette normally left Lactons the instant the second hand hit the crosswires of five-thirty, and emotionally was getting ready to leave from lunch-time onwards. But today was different.

Carol Ackerman had left the office just before one, arm in arm with Lee Fenman. The smell of her success at the meeting was as all pervading as an expensive perfume, and then she returned, looking particularly sparkly at around three. She literally breezed in, picked up her brief-case and breezed out again, with barely a backward glance.

Harry Bourne had rung around four, while Jeanette was off somewhere – maybe in the canteen, maybe in the post room, maybe playing with the new fax machine in dispatch – she had a well developed habit of wandering, whether the cat was away or not.

Harry had left a peculiar message on Carol's answering machine.

'Oh, damn, I hadn't expected – look, this is really difficult to talk about on the phone, I'll be round at about five to pick you up and we'll talk then. I . . . I'll see you then.'

His tone was so crackly it almost sounded as if he was choking, and, after the events of the morning, it made Jeanette's curiosity sit up and beg for more. Of course she should have rung Harry back and told him that Carol had already left the office but she couldn't bring herself to dial the number.

Instead she tidied her desk, shredded some old envelopes she had been saving for a moment of emotional crisis, touched up her lipstick and sprayed on a fatal dose of the perfume she had bought in the duty free on her way back from Spain.

Jeanette was wasted as a secretary, she should have been a detective or a spy, she thought as she shaped her large mouth into an exaggerated O for the benefit of the mirror. Lip gloss gleaming she arranged herself artfully behind her desk, sitting slightly sideways so the first view anyone got from the lift was of her long, long legs and high black stilettos, and then she settled herself to wait for Harry Bourne.

He arrived as the second hand scratched five. She knew who he was instantly. He looked terrible. He stared blankly at Jeanette though she did notice that he took in the view of her legs.

'Hello, I'm Harry Bourne, I'm looking for Carol Acker-man, they directed me up here from reception. She is expecting me,' he said, looking over her shoulder towards Carol's office.

Jeanette got to her feet. 'You look as if you could use a coffee,' she purred in a low, carefully measured tone.

Harry blinked myopically.

Jeanette didn't wait for him to make a decision, she was already pouring a mugful. 'There you are,' she said with a breathy smile.

'Thanks,' Harry mumbled, bemused, hands folding instinctively around the warm china. 'So, is Carol here, then?'

Jeanette sighed. 'I'm afraid not, she's already left. Maybe I can help?'

Harry looked as if he might cry. 'But I left a message on her machine.'

Jeanette shrugged. She had to carefully insert the wedges that when driven home would open him up.

'Perhaps she had got something else arranged. She's always got something on.' Jeanette glanced down at the diary on her desk, moving her whole head so that Harry's eyes were compelled to follow. Before his arrival she had Tipp-Exed out 'Lunch: Danic' and replaced it with 'Lunch with Lee Fenman, Holden's Brasserie' in carefully formed capitals. You could read the words across the office if you squinted.

'She was having lunch with Lee today.' Her tone was contrived to sound casual. 'Maybe they've gone on for dinner or something. They get on really well those two.' She paused and looked wistfully into the middle distance. 'He's a really nice guy.' She flipped through the rest of the diary, careful to avoid letting Harry see anything else.

'In fact,' Jeanette continued, 'Carol's got a lunch date every day this week.' Something in her voice managed to imply, without adding another word, that every date was with a man. Harry stiffened and swallowed the lie whole. If he had seen the other pages he would have known that the only other lunch Carol had booked was with one Ms Katherine Jackson on Wednesday.

'Very popular lady, Carol,' Jeanette added after a suitable pause and then looked squarely at Harry. 'Are you a friend of hers, or is this business?'

Harry, eyes glazing over, sat down heavily on the edge of the desk.

'Er, er, I'm, I'm –' he stopped and then focused sharply on Jeanette's face. 'I know this is a bit of a cheek, but I don't suppose you fancy going for a drink somewhere do you?'

Jeanette allowed herself a small triumphant smile. 'You stay there. I'll just get my coat.' As she turned she shot Harry a final concerned glance. 'Did you borrow that shirt?'

Harry groaned softly.

Katherine Bourne and Ben finally found their way down to the river after lunch at the Victory. They walked along the tow path. It was late afternoon by the time they got back to Ben's car. Sunlight dappled through the overhanging trees and seemed to crystallise in the water amongst the reeds. Here and there ducks fractured the shimmering surface.

'I used to think I was quite a brave person, self-confident, but now I'm not so sure. I'm making plans though.'

'Converting your house?'

Katherine, hands in pockets, nodded. 'That's part of it, I'm going down to London to see Hope on Wednesday – she doesn't know about any of this business with Harry yet – and then I'm going to talk to the woman who's helping me organise the loan to buy Harry out.' She looked across at him. 'Why did you ask me out to lunch, Ben?'

'Company, a challenge?' He grinned. 'I don't know really. I suppose I thought you looked –' he paused.

For one awful moment Katherine wondered if he had asked her out of pity; it would be more than she could bear.

'Leaving your husband, it had nothing to do with me, did it? I mean, I'm not –' he reddened. 'What I suppose I'm saying is that I don't want to be responsible for you leaving him. Although I don't want you to think that I habitually make passes at married women . . .'

'I've been thinking about leaving Harry for years. In some ways it does have everything to do with you, but not personally, if that makes any sense. It was the final weight on the scale just enough to tip me over the edge. I'd got no idea I had any passion left in me. When I saw you in the garden I had this odd feeling, like a pain. It's very hard to describe; I suddenly caught a glimpse of this great undiscovered country, this huge part of me that I hadn't realised still existed, it was like seeing a place I had come to believe was only a myth. I hadn't realised how much of me I've pruned away to keep Harry happy. And then there was meeting Hope too. We had such a good time together, but I knew, if Harry had come in and found us, he would have been quietly furious and so disgusted and so disapproving. Surely I'm old enough to do what I like now? Do I really need to have my life approved of? What Harry really needs is a mother, not a partner ... not me.' She looked out over the river. 'So why did you ask me out?'

Ben grinned. 'Is it too crass to say that I fancied you?'

Katherine coloured. 'Not at all, it's very flattering.'

'And I thought I'd like to get to know you better. Talk, walk –' he lifted a hand to encompass the view. 'This sort of thing really. I've been on my own a long time and made a mess of a lot of things on the way.'

She turned back towards Ben, knowing that the sun would catch in her hair, knowing that Ben was looking at her with eyes that reflected the light on the water, aware of every breath in her body, every pulse, every sound on the gentle breeze. He was standing so close that she could smell him and pick out the path of every grey hair nestling in the neck of his shirt. It didn't matter what he wanted, she relished the feeling of closeness.

'Maybe I ought to ask what do you want from me?' he said in an undertone.

She looked up at him and smiled. 'Nothing, to be honest I think you've given me everything I need already.'

As she spoke he moved a fraction closer and she tilted her face up to meet his. His kiss lit a thousand tiny spiral flares in her mind, the sensation was deliciously intense. When she pulled away he was grinning.

'Want to reconsider your demands?'

Katherine Bourne laughed, a laugh that rolled up through her like a summer storm.

'I'll write a list,' she said and caught hold of his hand. 'But first I really need to get home and water my tomatoes.'

Hand in hand they walked back to the car.

Chapter Nine

Once they were out of the Lactons office, Jeanette took Harry to a nice quiet pub well away from the financial district. She'd only been there twice before, both times in the company of Lee Fenman from Danic, who had offered her a really good job in New York and then in almost the same breath suggested she might like to go back to his hotel for a little light sexual entertainment. They had both known he hadn't been terribly serious about one of the suggestions, but the thought was nice none the less.

Safely tucked up in the quiet of the lounge bar, she ordered a club soda for herself and a double brandy for Harry, who had seemed quite happy to be guided into a taxi, guided into a pub, over to a table and then arranged under a particularly purple rendering of an ageing Queen Victoria. Balancing both glasses and a bag of crisps, Jeanette slid onto the bench seat alongside Harry and put the drinks down.

'That's twelve quid you owe me,' she said when he looked up.

He pulled a face.

'Taxi fare, and this round.'

He nodded. 'Right.'

Jeanette sighed, maybe this wasn't such a good idea after all. Harry Bourne was obviously in a state of shock. She leant closer, edging the drink towards his fingers. 'So, now we're here, what is it you wanted to talk about, then?'

Harry, eyes still not really focused, took a long pull on the glass. 'Work. Or rather, lack of work. I've been made redundant, just like that. Fifteen years up in smoke.' He glanced up towards the nicotine-stained beams as if there might be a tell-tale plume spiralling away above his head. 'Mind you they have said they could probably find me something else if I'd consider a sideways move – into bloody handling and transport. Bastards. Same salary for a year and then – shit – jump or get pushed, what a bloody choice.'

Jeanette sucked her teeth. 'I'm so sorry.' She paused, eyeing him thoughtfully, well-oiled cogs turning in her mind which, despite appearances, was remarkably sharp. 'After all that time you'll get a decent golden handshake, though, surely?'

Harry sank another mouthful of brandy. 'Oh yes, they're offering very generous terms, they really know how to sugar-coat the bullet. But what the hell am I going to do, now? I'm nearly fifty, do you know what that means? I'll never get another bloody job, not at my age. Who the hell will want me? Down-sizing they call it. Some little git with acne, barely out of puberty, not shaving, had set himself up in the board room. I *knew* there was something going on, I've known for weeks, but couldn't put my finger on it. Those bastards on the board played it very very close to their devious backstabbing little chests. Then they called us all in, and, this – this child – steps up to his big slice of the pie chart and calls us all colleagues and co-workers, gets on with his jolly little slide show about the new corporate identity, and within five minutes he's onto down-sizing, rationalisation and cutting out the deadwood. Bastards.'

Harry's fingers tightened around the glass. 'I'd give my eye teeth to get my hands on the bastards who financed the take-over. It's like selling your own grandmother – it's tantamount to treason – that's what it was, you know. A betrayal. It was a great British company, British owned, British managed, market leader – and now some shitty little Japanese firm are going to end up running it. I should have guessed – they've been bowing all over the office and my turf for months. Meanwhile the guys who made the buy-out are planning to streamline the operation, make it cost efficient. They've brought in their own management team. "Think of me as a surgeon," this little git said, "trained and ready to painlessly cut away the things that no longer work as well as they did. When I'm done, the patient, our company, will be leaner, fitter, more competitive. Ready to take its place in the global market." Bastards.' Harry took another belt of brandy.

Jeanette had a peculiar feeling somewhere in the area behind her designer belt buckle. 'Your company has been bought out?'

Harry nodded. 'Oh yes, apparently everything was all primed up and ready to go, they just needed the ink to dry on the financial agreement. Signed just before lunch time today apparently. Champagne all round for everyone in the boardroom no doubt. All those little creeps who've been screwing me for years now retire with shed loads of money to the Bahamas – and by half-past-fucking-three I'm out of a job. Bastards.'

Jeanette topped up her club soda and poked the slice of lemon down amongst the backwash of bubbles. 'Do you know who bought you out?' she asked with feigned non-chalance. Company take-overs were ten a penny, it would be too much of a coincidence, surely?

Harry looked across at her in surprise as if he had only just realised she was still there. 'Danic Enterprises PLC,' he said. 'Some flash international gang of corporate raiders, all Armani suits and lap-tops. I thought all those bastards had crashed and burned after Thatcher went.'

Jeanette went up to the bar and bought herself a brandy. She felt she needed one. Harry was slumped forward, elbows on the table looking dejectedly into the top of his almost empty glass. Jeanette waved the barman closer. 'A single for me and another double for my friend.'

The man behind the bar had one of those heavily lined, laconic faces that encouraged you to pour your heart out. Perhaps, thought Jeanette, on reflection she ought to have left Harry to have found him single-handed. She wasn't sure what she had hoped to find out about Harry and Carol, mostly she thought, a little dirt about her boss, a little tantalising glimpse of the staid Ms Ackerman's bedroom antics. What she had got for her pains was a diatribe on un-ironed shirts and untimely redundancy.

Manfully she made her way back to Harry who looked up with doleful eyes. He couldn't have eaten all day; the first brandy had already scored a double top.

'You know,' he said, sliding his hand onto her knee, 'you really are a very nice person. What did you say your name was, again?'

Jeanette smiled, ignoring his hot sweaty palm, and handed him his drink. 'Jeanette, and I've put this one on your bill along with the others.'

Harry snorted. 'Don't worry, I'll pay you out of their thirty dirty pieces of silver. Did I ever tell you about my wife?'

Jeanette shook her head. 'No, I don't think you did.'

Harry rolled his eyes. 'Do you know what she did to me? Eh? There's another prize bitch. It's been one helluva a week so far. But what a cook, and iron – Jesus, no worry about clean shirts with her, my boy, no no – I gave her everything, everything. Paradise.' He glanced at his watch nervously. 'Maybe I ought to ring her and let her know I'm going to be late home.'

'Who? Carol or your wife?'

Harry downed the second brandy in one long swallow. 'Who gives a shit? Maybe both, maybe neither. They don't deserve a man like me. Deadwood, the bastards.' He pulled his wallet out of his inside pocket. 'Why don't you get another round in while I go to the loo.' He glanced at the brown calf notefold and then handed it to Jeanette. 'Take

what I owe you out of that. I'm trusting you, you know.'
As he clambered unsteadily to his feet he patted his pockets.
'Do you smoke?'

Jeanette shook her head.

'No, me neither, no one does these days, do they. I could
murder a fag.'

It had taken under an hour for Carol to get from her office
in London to the gym in Cambridge. She wasn't a regular
gym freak like a lot of her colleagues at Lactons or some
of her friends. She certainly wouldn't think of going to the
company gym, but in her home town she kept a bag and
a change of clothes at Raouls in Leven Street as a mute
gesture towards healthy living. As she had travelled home
on the train, watching the fenland landscape unfold, she
had felt this wild skein of physical energy winding itself
back and forth, demanding her attention.

Opening her locker at the gym she tried not to breathe
too deeply. It had been a long time since her leotard had
seen the light of day, the navy tracksuit smelt of mildew
and the hand towel looked stiff and unwholesome. The
only thing that looked relatively inviting was a new swim-
suit she had bought on impulse and left in its packaging
on the top of the shoe locker. She picked it up and turned
it over thoughtfully; she could hire a towel at reception
after she'd finished working out in the gym.

On the step machine, sweating hard, she thought about
Lee Fenman. He had asked her to ring him about New
York at the end of the week, and then – after the champagne had taken hold – there had been several other more
covert offers. He was very cute, very handsome, but those
crisp creases in his shirt had told her everything she needed
to know about him. It had given her the greatest pleasure
to decline the offer of his body, diplomatically of course.
He had bowed, waved a hand, taken it in his stride,
unoffended and still as convivial as ever.

Nice buns though, she thought, sliding down onto the rowing machine.

Picking up a mammoth soft pink towel from the girl behind the reception desk, Carol strode downstairs to the pool and slipped, without so much as a ripple, into the warm azure blue water. It was tea time and the pool was empty. She rolled over onto her back and let the water ease away the last of the nervous tension in her spine and shoulders.

Danic was done, over, finished, complete – a cheerful shiny gold star on her chart and maybe, if she took Lee's offer seriously, and there was no reason why she shouldn't, it might augur a mercurial move onwards and upwards. There would be no harm going to New York to take a look at what he had to offer. She was due a holiday, Geoff and Ray would be happy to cat sit, and Harry . . .

Mid-stroke, Carol suddenly jack-knifed and folded up, taking in a great lungful of warm water as she slithered gracelessly down towards the bottom of the pool. Harry – Harry Bourne. It was madness but in her euphoria, since the shirt incident at lunch, she hadn't given him another thought. Wiping the water off her face, she looked up at the clock above the pool.

He would be on his way home or on his way to her office. He would be busy thinking about dinner and ironing. Still coughing and spluttering she made her way to the side and clung on. Hooking her bag off the lounger she switched on her mobile and rang home. Her machine told her she couldn't come to the phone – which hardly came as a surprise. She couldn't think of anything she wanted to tell herself when invited to leave a cheery message so she hung up. Next she pressed the button that would recall her messages from the answering machine at work.

'Oh, damn, I hadn't expected – look, this is really difficult to talk about on the phone, I'll be round at about five to pick you up and we'll talk then. I . . . I'll see you then.'

His tone was so crackly it almost sounded as if Harry was choking, and, after the events of the morning, it made Carol's guilt sit up and beg. Something was terribly wrong.

She wrapped the towel around her shoulders and tried his mobile. It was a number she seldom rang, conditioned as a mistress to leave his real life well alone. It was switched off anyway.

With no make-up, damp hair, swathed in the mildewed tracksuit, working clothes stuffed in a hold-all she hurried through the back streets of Cambridge to Ray and Geoff's café. They would rescue her, provide a take-out supper, they were bound to have something wholesome in the freezer that she could microwave. They would soothe her fevered brow. They were terribly good at that sort of thing.

She shoulder barged the café door open; it was ten minutes to weekday closing time. Ray and Geoff sat either side of the counter, sharing a cigarette and a cup of coffee, and beside them cradling a cappuccino, as suntanned and gorgeous as she remembered him, was Sam Richardson.

Ray grinned and waved her over. 'Hi, come in, we've just been talking about you.'

Katherine Bourne sang all the way home from Huntingdon. She had had the most wonderful afternoon after a very shaky start. She had also resisted the temptation to ask Ben to come home with her. And it had been a temptation. They had parted in the car park of the Victory, reluctantly.

'May I see you again?' he had asked, almost coyly, as she unlocked her car.

She smiled. 'That would be wonderful, but this time please make sure I know exactly where I'm going.'

'I've got tickets for a summer concert at the weekend. Saturday night. I get them for doing the orchestra's publicity shots. It's an open air thing at Tollman Abbey, would you like to go? We could take a picnic. It's the most beautiful setting.'

Katherine nodded. 'It sounds lovely.'

'Wonderful, I could come over and pick you up about seven?'

'I'll look forward to it. Do you want me to bring the food?'

'We'll share the load, I'll bring the wine and the dessert, and you can bring, what? Salad and chicken legs? That sounds about right, doesn't it?'

There was a brief weighted pause when they stood a little too close, but not quite close enough. She smiled and stepped boldly into his space, brushing her lips against his. 'I really have had the most lovely time.'

'Me too.'

Driving home, radio on, early evening sunlight ricocheting off the windscreen, Katherine Bourne felt great. This was the way new beginnings ought to be. She slowed the car, waiting for traffic to pass so that she could turn into the lane that led down to her house.

She knew she didn't love Ben, she didn't even want to love him, but was grateful to have the opportunity to play with all those emotions she thought had vanished long ago. It would be therapeutic to have nice things to look forward to. Little shrines to pleasure on the long slow road away from her marriage to Harry, places to leave flowers and little supplications to the gods of delectation and desire.

She turned the radio up another notch, they were playing something inspiring. It was something by Brian Ferry – she laughed aloud, amused that she could still recognise the singer after all these years – how very strange.

Her house, set at the end of a carefully tended gravel drive, looked wholesome and inviting against its backdrop of horse chestnuts and copper beech. Home. Something caught her eye as she swung in through the gates. Squatting malevolently behind the walled borders, filled with old fashioned lavender and framed by white lilac, was a black car. A small black beetly car, its carapace glinting in the sunshine: her daughter Sarah's snappy little GTI.

Katherine felt as if the breath was being driven out of her chest. The knot she thought had dissolved in her stomach tightened back up into a clenched fist. She made an effort to hang onto the glorious sense of wellbeing and pulled up outside the garage.

Sarah's car was empty which meant she was already in the house. A treacherous voice in Katherine's head cursed for not having had the sense to change the locks. With enforced calm, Katherine opened the garage doors, drove inside, slowly, slowly, savouring the seconds before she had to face her daughter's raw indignation. She could almost feel Sarah's disapproval – a rolling grey-green cloud – creeping out towards her through the ether.

She didn't get the chance to prepare her entrance speech.

'Where on earth have you been? I've been waiting for hours,' snapped a petulant voice from behind her on the driveway. Sarah was quite small but her presence was enormous. She tracked Katherine down into the shadows of the garage.

'I drove here straight from school. I had to miss a staff meeting.'

Katherine carried on locking up her car, checking each of the doors in turn.

'Well?' insisted Sarah.

Katherine fought the urge to leap forward and slap her daughter's face and instead smiled. 'I've been out. You should have rung first, darling. Peter did.'

'Don't talk to me about Peter. You know what he's like – treating the whole thing like some sort of enormous joke. I haven't been able to get a sensible word out of him. I've been thinking about you and Dad all weekend. I've asked my headteacher for a few days off so that we can get this thing sorted out.'

Katherine concentrated on trying to hold herself erect. 'Thing, dear? What thing?'

The years that had peeled away since Harry left seemed to drop back on her shoulders, a vampire weight that, if she wasn't careful, would pucker up and suck her dry. Did Sarah really think by the application of the right adhesive she could reform and repair what had been broken for so long?

Sarah stared at Katherine as if seeing her for the first time. 'You've dyed your hair.'

Katherine hefted her bag up onto her shoulders. 'The hairdresser assured me it was no longer a capital offence. Now, are you planning to stay out here or shall we go in and have some tea?'

Sarah sniffed, confidence wavering. 'Where is my father?'

Katherine shrugged. 'I really have no idea, darling, but I'm sure he'll be in touch when he wants something. Hasn't he rung you?' As she spoke she circumnavigated the car, with some difficulty as it was parked quite close to the end wall, and in doing so avoided Sarah's ambush. Heading towards the house, Sarah had to hurry to catch her up.

'You can't do this.'

Katherine, sorting through her keys, glanced back over her shoulder. 'Dye my hair? Oh, I'm sure I can.'

'Don't be so bloody obtuse. You know exactly what I'm talking about.'

The front door was already open. By the bottom of the stairs, standing side by side on the old gold parquet, was a large blue suitcase and matching handbag.

'You are avoiding looking at me,' growled Sarah.

Katherine carefully hung her bag on the hall stand. 'No, no, I'm not, dear, I'm just trying very hard to avoid saying things that I might regret. I've had a lovely day and I don't want to spoil it.'

It was too much. Sarah stamped her feet like a six-year-old, her pretty classic English face contorting like a carnival mirror, and then a huge explosion of tears of frustration and fury coursed down her face.

'You really are a cow,' she roared between sobs, 'you're not supposed to be out having lovely days. How dare you be so – so – so *fucking* composed about all this.'

In a blinding rush of revelation, Katherine realised that Sarah would be much happier – and perhaps even expected – to find her crawling around the kitchen floor, weeping and agonising over the terrible thing she'd done. She wondered fleetingly if those days would come, and then extinguished the thought before it had a chance to catch. She started to tremble and caught hold of the banister.

'Sarah,' she said in a gentle voice, not altogether certain what she intended to say after she had her daughter's attention.

Sarah glared at her from behind the torrent of tears. 'You're so bloody selfish. Dad worked all these years so you could have all the things you wanted.' She lifted her hands to encompass the house. 'He's slaved away for years for you, for us – and now – and now . . . you've taken all that away from him, from us –' Her argument exploded into another wracking sob.

Katherine looked on in amazement, quite astonished that her grown-up, successful, self-assured daughter could be so hurt, so hysterical and so lacking in understanding. Was it so black and white after all? Hadn't she willingly given up everything to be the wife Harry wanted? Hadn't she catered and cooked and nurtured them all, quietly, selflessly without a shred of martyrdom, without any real thought about what it was she truly wanted? Never complaining when he was late, putting her own life on hold to make his all the smoother?

She had read somewhere that implicit in the meaning of the word sacrifice was an element of co-operation by the victim. The sacrifice walked cheerfully to the block. And yes, she had been willing to give up all sorts of things to be a wife and a mother, but something had happened, she had given Harry so much – and now all she wanted to do was change her mind before it was too late. Surely it was time then to climb down off the block? What was the truth? Or was truth as nebulous as opinion?

She wanted desperately to put her arms around Sarah and make it all right, hold her close and wipe away the rising tide of hot snotty tears, but something held her back.

'I'll go and put the kettle on,' she said, above the noise of rolling sobs. 'Or would you rather have a brandy?'

Sarah froze. 'You're drinking as well? Oh, my God, this has gone further than I thought. Oh, my God.'

Katherine poured them both a small tot. Sarah tailed behind her and dragged out a kitchen chair. With the rivulets of mascara running down her pale face, slumped miserably over the kitchen table she looked about twelve.

Katherine handed her a tumbler. 'Here we are, darling,' she said gently. 'Drink this.'

Sarah scrubbed her eyes on her sleeve.

Katherine pulled out the chair opposite her and sat down. 'I really had no idea you would react like this.'

Sarah's bottom lip rolled out like a moist shelf but Katherine pressed on. 'I want you to understand, this is really not about you, this is about me and your father. You're all grown up now, you have a life of your own. And I am an adult too. I've made a decision about my life and even if you don't understand it, or approve of it, please, you have to respect it. It was my decision to make and live with, not yours.'

Sarah made a strange choking sound way back in her throat. 'So exactly how long have you been drinking?' Sarah asked. Katherine drained her glass and went in search of the rest of the bottle.

Chapter Ten

Frozen in the doorway of Ray and Geoff's Café, Carol instinctively covered her eyes with a hand. It was a gesture that said both, 'Oh my God,' and also, 'Please don't look at me.'

Sam Richardson was already getting to his feet, tidying his clothes, draining the last dregs of the coffee. 'I'd better be getting off,' he said, nodding a farewell to the two other men. He looked so uncomfortable.

Carol did too, and at the same time was aware of the miasma rising from her elderly tracksuit.

'Sam,' she said softly, in a tone she hoped would convey everything she wanted to say and anything else she might have forgotten, 'I'm really sorry about last Friday night. I had no idea Harry was going to turn up.'

He looked up, sucking his lips in, rolling them nervously over his teeth. For a split second their eyes met and Carol felt a horrible stabbing pain somewhere under her ribs.

'I shouldn't feel like this,' he said flatly, looking away. 'After all, they did tell me all about Harry, I just thought –' he glanced uneasily back over his shoulder towards Ray and Geoff. 'I thought from what they said, and the way that you were with me that the relationship was more or less over. I thought you wanted out – I thought you wanted to be with me.'

Carol tightened her fingers around the handle of her sports bag. 'I did, I do,' she babbled. 'It was, I mean, it is – I had no idea he would ever leave his wife.' She felt a flurry of tears bubbling up. 'Please give me the chance to try and sort this out.'

Sam nodded. 'Okay. Let me know what happens. I'll see you around sometime.' He looked down, stuffing his hands into the pockets of his chinos, discomfort oozing from every pore. 'Look, I really do have to go. I hope everything works out.' He bumbled past her.

There was a great ragged silence in the seconds after he closed the door. Carol sniffed once, twice, finally losing the battle against the tears.

'Oh shit, balls and arseholes!!!' She shrieked with frustration and slammed the sports bag down onto the floor. When she looked up Ray and Geoff seemed to have been trapped, unmoving, in a frame of film. She smiled grimly, wiping the back of her hand across her hot, red, wet face.

Ray lifted the coffee pot. 'Could I interest you in a mug of hemlock?'

Jeanette couldn't remember the exact chain of events that led up to her finding herself in bed with Harry Bourne at the Strand Palace Hotel, nor precisely why they had chosen such a prestigious venue for what had – if her memory served her correctly – been a fairly mediocre sexual encounter.

Maybe it had been all that talk, over an ocean of brandy, about how so very few real women there were left in the world. Real women who wanted to be nurtured by real men who wanted to put them on a pedestal and worship them. That was all Harry wanted. He had told her so.

Carefully, Jeanette lifted Harry's warm damp hand off her hip and rolled over into the cool space on the outside edge of the bed.

If she was honest – and Jeanette was almost always painfully honest with herself if no one else – there were several things she saw in Harry Bourne that really attracted her. It was not the fact that he had managed to keep two women reasonably well satisfied for so long, nor his looks, nor his personality. No, what Jeanette saw with blinding clarity as she stared down at the sleeping man curled in the middle of the bed, was the size of his golden handshake, precise details of which were now safely filed away in her memory.

But there was something else, something even more compelling. In Harry Bourne, Jeanette had inadvertently stumbled across the very thing she had been looking for: a man who wouldn't expect her to work for a living. No more earning her share of the rent, no more going Dutch. Harry Bourne was the Holy Grail.

What Harry Bourne pined for was an old-fashioned dependent woman, who was prepared to hand over her aspirations in exchange for a meal ticket. The man was a dinosaur, but, at last she could finally see a way to pay off her credit cards. Finally a way to have more time for all the important things in life like TV, step classes, manicures, and lunches with friends.

She grinned, as in the gloom, the fantasy took on a life of its own. Harry was tired of women who wanted more than he was prepared to offer, tired of women who wanted an independent existence. What he wanted was a childlike companion not an adult. She imagined a life where she waved Harry goodbye at the door of a stylish executive house and while the cleaning lady whipped the Hoover round, she slipped into a leotard and headed off to the gym or to the hairdresser or went out to lunch. Maybe she could get him to buy her a Volvo or a cherry-red BMW.

She couldn't imagine a man of Harry's calibre would be out of work for long. Someone was bound to snap him up – and there was always the golden handshake to tide them over. All those foreign trips and weekends away that he had wasted on Carol Ackerman. If Jeanette was his wife she wouldn't let him out of her sight, she'd have a bag packed and ready so she could fly away with him at the drop of a hat.

Rubbing her hands together so they were nice and warm

Jeanette rolled back under the covers and insinuated a hand down into the warm junction between Harry's thighs.

'Oh God, Harry, that was so good,' she purred, even though the event had taken place hours before. 'No one has ever made me feel like that before. Why don't you come over here and let me show you just how grateful I am.'

Harry Bourne opened one eye, reluctantly. She caught a glimpse of a furred tongue darting out around what she guessed were very dry lips. For an instant he reminded Jeanette of a scaly sunbaked lizard. He groaned, tensing slightly, as if he might resist, but under her fingertips Jeanette had already found the answer she wanted. Very, very, slowly, making sure her heavy breasts brushed against his arms and chest, she slithered down under the bedclothes to get more closely acquainted with the key to her meal ticket.

'Can I beg a lift home, as well?' Carol asked, finishing off the last of the coffee.

Geoff, who was busy wrapping tinfoil around a casserole dish, nodded. 'Not a problem. Five more minutes and then we'll be off home. Ray's just taking one final walk round the family estate. Have you got any rice to go with this?'

'Basmati.'

Geoff grinned. 'You're learning. What time are you expecting the shit home?'

Carol winced. 'I really don't know. He sounded terrible on the answer machine. I'm really grateful for supper.'

Geoff pulled a face. 'I'm doing this for you not Harry, you know.'

Ray, who had appeared at the kitchen door, dropped his apron onto the counter. 'The path of true love never runs smooth.'

Carol lifted an eyebrow. 'I've noticed, so are you going to tell me what Sam said?'

'Nope, the coffee shop, like the Catholic Church, has sworn to keep the confessional sacred. All I will say is that he's a really nice guy and you are a total idiot. Here.' Geoff handed her the dish. 'Roghan Gosht, make sure you warm it right through, but it's one of those things that improve with cooking so it won't hurt if it sits in the oven for an hour or so until your lord and master appears. I cooked it this afternoon, you can road test it for me.'

Carol ignored the lord and master crack. 'I'm really grateful.'

'So you should be, but I'd wait until you see the bill if I were you. Our take-out dinner menus are very expensive.'

At home, later, alone, feeling calmer, Carol slid the dish into the oven, had a shower, rinsed the uncooked rice and settled down on the sofa in the sitting room with a cup of coffee, a wild-life video and the cats for company, and waited for Harry to come home. She lay back and closed her eyes; five minutes nap was what her body needed, just five minutes.

It was very, very dark when she was woken up by the phone ringing. Carol was on her feet in an instant, scattering the cats like buckshot. She blinked, not quite certain exactly where she was. The TV screen, the only light in the sitting room, was peppered with white noise. Stumbling over the coffee table and a pile of magazines she picked up the phone, struggling to find a voice and ignore the pins and needles anaesthetising her left leg.

'Hello?' she murmured, trying to shake some life back into the senseless limb.

'Hello, is that you, Carol?' She was astonished to hear Jeanette's voice.

'Yes, it is, what's the matter? It's, it's –' she screwed up her eyes and peered at the blurry little red numbers on the video. 'Good God, it's nearly two o'clock in the morning.' She couldn't keep the surprise out of her voice.

'I know, I'm sorry to ring you so late,' Jeanette hissed in a stage whisper, 'but I thought you might still be waiting up for Harry.'

'Harry?' Where was Harry? Had he come in and slipped upstairs without waking her?

Jeanette already had the answer. 'I just rang to tell you that he's all right and not to worry, he's here with me. I've just put him to bed.'

The statement posed far more questions than it answered.

'With you?'

'Yes, he turned up at the office after you left. He was in one hell of a state. I think he must have been drinking before he got there. Anyway, I made him some coffee, talked – you know the kind of thing. And to cut a long story short he's had quite a lot more to drink. I stayed with him because he was in no condition to be alone. You never know what they'll do when they're in that state, do you? I've just booked him into a hotel.'

'A hotel.' Carol wondered if she was doomed to echo Jeanette's comments all the way through this unexpected conversation.

'That's right.'

'Do you know why was he so upset?' She wondered if the events of the last few days had caught up on him. It couldn't have been easy to have left his wife, and Carol had hardly offered the sympathetic joyful response he might reasonably have expected. She winced, thinking about the cats, the food – and then there were the shirts.

'He found out this afternoon that he's been made redundant.'

Carol felt a totally inappropriate sense of relief followed by a rush of guilt.

'And,' continued Jeanette, 'although I haven't said anything to him, because I didn't think you'd want him to know, in a funny kind of way, it's your fault.'

'My fault?' Carol choked.

'Yeah. Danic bought his company. I think his firm was part of the package Lee Fenman had got lined up to snip and strip. They barely waited for the ink to dry before the heavy mob moved in.'

'Oh, my God,' whispered Carol, thinking about Lee Fenman's one brief phone call before lunch. He must have been lighting the blue touch paper on a dozen similar schemes that were part of the latest package. She stared down at the handset. Why was it she hadn't noticed Harry's firm on the list of acquisitions?

'Why exactly are you ringing to tell me this?'

'I thought you might be worried when he didn't come home,' Jeanette whispered defensively. 'After this morning with the shirts and everything.'

'Well, thank you,' Carol murmured. 'Thank you very much.'

Before Jeanette had a chance to reply Carol hung up and stumbled into the kitchen. She never normally fell asleep on the sofa, it must have been the combination of the gym and the swim. She plugged in the kettle and looked out of the kitchen windows to see if Ray and Geoff were still up – outside everywhere was in darkness. Her stomach rumbled ominously. She sniffed; the cooker was still on.

Geoff was right, Roghan Gosht did improve with cooking. She made a real effort not to think about Harry, or Danic, or Lee Fenman or Jeanette as she hungrily shovelled curry and rice into her mouth. She'd go to bed, maybe everything would look better in the morning.

It was nice to have the bed to herself. Carol woke bright and early the next morning. She was just reversing her car out onto the drive when a taxi drew up in the road outside her house, blocking her exit. She stared at in the rear-view mirror, willing it to move on. Her eyes were slightly blood-shot but otherwise she looked fine. Once she got into work she'd talk to Jeanette and find out exactly what had happened to Harry. Track him down and make sure he was all right.

She drummed her fingers impatiently on the steering wheel. Maybe Harry would take the opportunity to go home to his wife. It seemed very likely, after all in a crisis a broad familiar pair of shoulders was surely the best place to cry? What was that cabby doing?

As she looked back again the driver caught her eye and beckoned her over. He was probably lost – just what she needed. She'd given herself plenty of time to get to the railway station but really didn't need to spend ten minutes crouched on the kerbside trying to drag up directions to some obscure backwater. Slowly, she climbed out of the driver's seat. Rounding the hedge she spotted Harry kneeling on the floor in the back of the cab sifting through a handful of change. The cabby leant across and slid the window down.

'Morning, Missus, that'll be eleven quid,' he said without emotion, nodding towards the huddled figure in the rear seat. 'I picked him up out on the ring road. He reckons he can't find his wallet, he told me you'd pay.'

Carol nodded and opened her handbag. She only had a twenty pound note but didn't wait for the change.

Harry slithered out of the door and caught hold of her arms.

'My angel, my saviour, my darling Kitty-Kat,' he whispered on breath that would cut sheet steel, and was then promptly sick all over her shiny black court shoes.

The driver revved the engine. 'Glad he saved that till he got out. He said he'd hitched home. Best of luck, darling.' He lifted a hand in farewell and pulled away, while Harry gently slid to his knees on the pavement, Carol looked heavenwards.

'I don't feel very well,' Harry spluttered miserably.

'You surprise me. Why don't we get you inside and get you cleaned up?'

'I knew you'd be here waiting for me. God, I feel so bloody terrible.'

Carol pulled him to his feet and taking the bulk of his weight guided him back into the house. On the front door-step she kicked off her shoes and juggling Harry and her handbag unlocked the front door. The clock at the end of the hall announced that, short of a miracle, she would miss her train. She left Harry slumped on the sofa while she ran a bath, made coffee and then rang the office – no one would be in that early except for perhaps the cleaners – but she could leave Jeanette a message: 'Hello, Jeanette. Harry's just turned up at my house, so I'll be late in. If anyone asks I've gone off to meet a client. I'll try and get back as soon as I can.'

She manhandled him up the stairs and sat alongside the tub while he berated his job, his life and the Danic take-over. It did not make for easy listening. Finally, twenty minutes later, all buffed up, warm-water pink, dry and wrapped in one of her spare bathrobes Carol propelled Harry into her bed, pulled the curtains closed and sloped off downstairs. Other than let Harry sleep it off there was very little she could do to help – except perhaps combing the house for any trace of documents relating to the Danic project and hiding the sharp knives.

The sound of the doorbell broke into her thoughts. Geoff, face folded into a mask of curiosity and concern, was leaning against the door frame. Glowing with good health, lightly suntanned, hair swept back and dressed in navy sweat pants and matching muscle vest, he looked beautiful. Carol sighed. Not for the first time in their friend-ship she wished that at least one of her neighbours was straight.

'Is everything okay?' he said, looking past her into the

hall. 'We were just out partaking of our customary morning bout of masochism and saw your car was still in the drive. I tried the back door but it's locked. Is something up?'

Carol shook her head in frustration. 'How long have you got?'

Geoff grinned and looked down at his watch. 'A lifetime, darling, let me just tell his nibs that there's trouble at mill. Shall I put the coffee on or will you?'

Carol waved him inside. 'I'll do it.'

'By the way, how was the curry?'

Carol smiled thinly. 'Oh, absolutely wonderful.'

Ray, towel wrapped around his broad shoulders, still jogging, had joined Geoff on the step. 'Did Harry enjoy it?'

'Why don't you both just come inside?'

'I reckon he'll be flat out for hours yet,' said Ray rounding the bottom of the stairs and stepping into Carol's kitchen. The whole of her extended family seemed to have called an impromptu council of war around the kitchen table. Geoff sat on one side, the two cats, Augustus and Tosca, crouched amongst the papers beside the tea-pot and Ray took his place beside Carol, smelling of the aftershave she had brought home from the trip to Paris.

'You look like shit,' he added as an afterthought.

Carol groaned. 'I have got to get into work.'

'Go on then, you can catch the later train,' Geoff said. 'Your secretary will cover for you, won't she?'

Carol lifted an eyebrow. 'In a perfect world. Trouble is it was she who booked Harry into a hotel last night. God knows what he told her.' She ran her fingers through her hair. As if Jeanette wasn't enough trouble already. 'What am I going to do?'

Ray got up again, looking businesslike. 'Get changed, go to work, Geoff and I will keep an eye on the dreadful Harry.'

Carol stared up at him. 'What about the café?'

He shrugged. 'Your little ginger friend isn't going to surface much before lunch-time by the look of him. One of us can nip back after the rush and make sure he hasn't died in his sleep, soothe the savage brow, and then if he's up to it we'll take him into town and prop him up in the staff room at work.'

Carol looked up at their handsome, kind faces. She couldn't think of any way to soften the truth. 'Harry hates gays.'

Geoff aped astonishment. 'You really surprise me,' he said in a voice dripping with sarcasm. 'You mean he really meant all that two step, now-you-can-shake-my-hand, now-you-can't stuff the other night when we dropped in for coffee?'

'The man's a complete Philistine,' Ray continued, camping it up most effectively as he tugged his tee-shirt straight. 'Anyway, we're big boys now. I'm sure we can manage to cope with Harry. We've got to go, duty and a large box of Dublin Bay prawns call. Don't worry, poppet. He looks too sick to fight us off. We'll keep an eye on him for you. Now, off to the ball, Cinderella.'

Carol picked up her brief-case, immeasurably grateful to be relieved of the responsibility. As they reached the door, she said, 'Be gentle with him, boys. He's just lost his job.'

'And his wife,' Ray added

'And you?' concluded Geoff.

Carol winced. 'Be kind.'

They both grinned. 'We will be discretion itself. Now, hurry up or you'll miss your train.'

The cats, sensing the meeting had been officially adjourned, leapt down from the table and struck body-building poses on the lino before slithering out through the cat flap. Alone at the table Carol surveyed the kitchen with new eyes. By the breadbin, propping up the post, was a Danic mug, in stylish navy blue china – part of a promotional package Lee Fenman had had delivered to her office. Getting to her feet Carol picked it up and dropped it into the swing-bin on her way upstairs to check on Harry before she left.

Chapter Eleven

Katherine Bourne woke at just after seven, with a hangover. She groaned and rolled gently out of bed feeling as if she had been beaten up. She headed for the bathroom and prayed that the noise of the water running wouldn't wake Sarah. Their evening together had been a disaster. Every gentle, kind, rational thought she had conjured to try and explain what she had done had been parried, ignored or ground mercilessly into the carpet. And although Katherine hadn't mentioned Ben Morton, the memories of the lunch date made her feel guilty – in fact she couldn't have felt more guilty about Ben if she had spent the whole afternoon in bed with him. She also regretted feeding her daughter brandy – despite Sarah's fears, neither of them drank regularly – and it had been obvious after the second glass that Sarah wouldn't be in any fit state to drive home.

Katherine looked at the new clothes she had hung in the wardrobe. Like armour they seemed to offer protection against slipping back into the mire. She pulled on a pair of caramel cords and an oatmeal shirt, raking her fingers through the new haircut. She didn't normally wear make-up but this morning she felt she needed a mask to hide behind. Glancing in the mirror she added the new earrings, and convinced herself she was ready to face the fray.

Downstairs everywhere was deathly quiet, like a battle-field waiting for the artillery to begin again. In the sitting room the curtains had been drawn shut to block out the summer sunlight, and in the kitchen two mugs and two glasses stood on the draining board, still on watch from the night before. The tidiness surprised her, in some part of her mind she had expected the house to be a ragged war-torn mess. She unpacked the supper dishes from the dishwasher, watered the plants. It was like doing a rosary – and the mindless familiarity soothed her, her day painlessly unfolding safe in the arms of the routine that had guided her through countless years.

She didn't hear Sarah padding up behind her as she rinsed the sink out. Once the pattern had caught hold she had been so absorbed she had almost forgotten Sarah was in the house and time had passed unnoticed.

'Has Dad rung yet?'

Katherine jumped and then struggled to compose her thoughts. 'No, Sarah, you know he hasn't. And if he had rung you at home you wouldn't know because you're here. And while we're talking about home –'

Sarah made a throaty miserable sound. 'My God, it's nearly ten o'clock. Why did you let me sleep so long? You ought to ring the hospitals or the police or something. When was the last time you spoke to Dad? Anything could have happened.'

Katherine plugged in the kettle. 'Don't be so melodramatic. He's only been gone since Friday. We would have heard if there was a problem. I'd imagine he's staying with a friend from work, or booked himself into a hotel somewhere. Would you like a cup of tea?'

She glanced over her shoulder. Sarah was caught in a shaft of sunlight, wrapped up in a bright pink candlewick dressing-gown, eyes half closed, hair tussled into clumps. She was scratching and yawning. For the first time in years Katherine realised just how much Sarah looked like her father.

'You really ought to go home, darling, there's nothing you can do here,' she said in a voice that offered as little threat or aggression as she could muster. 'There's really no point your staying. I'm all right.'

Sarah snorted. '*You're* all right? You really take the biscuit, Mother. My life is falling apart round my ears and you don't want to know.'

Katherine stared at her. '*Your* life? What has this got to do with your life? This is my life,' she said slowly, surprised to hear how strident she sounded.

Sarah glared at her and threw herself onto the sofa under the kitchen window. 'Self, self, self, you've always been the same,' she snapped. 'I don't know why Dad didn't leave you years ago.'

Before Katherine could reply, the phone rang. She wondered fleetingly if it was Ben. Picking up the receiver before Sarah had time to move she heard a vaguely familiar female voice wish her good morning.

'Is that Mrs Bourne?' the woman continued.

'It is.'

'It's Diane here, your husband's secretary at Kestrel? I wondered if I could have a word with him, please.'

Katherine took a deep breath. Sarah was watching her, sleepy eyes coal-bright.

'I'm afraid he's not here at the moment, Diane. Can I help?'

The woman at the far end of the line made a small surprised sound. 'Oh, well that's thrown me completely. I assumed – I wonder where he is, then? The thing is he was scheduled for a breakfast meeting first thing and it's not like him to be late, let alone not show up at all. I know he was upset after yesterday – well, we all were after the takeover was announced officially. He didn't say very much, but that chap from Danic did say it would be business as usual.'

Katherine felt the ground slipping silently out from beneath her. She coughed and then said slowly, 'Harry didn't come home last night. He sometimes stays in town if he's got an early start, so we haven't had a chance to talk,' she lied.

Across the kitchen, Sarah's attention was now fully on Katherine and the phone cradled under her chin.

'Oh, my goodness,' said the woman, 'so you don't know anything about the buy-out then?'

'No, no I don't.'

Katherine remembered Diane from endless Christmas parties and corporate get-togethers – as a good company wife Katherine was supposed to know everything about everyone, including their spouses' names, their children, and be able to organise a four-course dinner party for twelve at the drop of a memo. She had never let Harry down in that department. Her lasting impression of Diane was of a faithful mongrel dog, grey haired, slightly grizzled around the maw. At one time Katherine had hoped Harry would employ a siren who would inveigle herself into Harry's heart and then run away with him. Diane was most definitely not siren material but was a perfect secretary, in fact she had probably been born clutching a shorthand pad and an appointments diary in one tiny fist.

'I'm not certain if I ought to say anything really,' Diane said in a tone that suggested she was being watched. 'I'm sure Mr Bourne would be much more comfortable telling you himself.'

Katherine cursed the faithful Diane under her breath and then in her most unctuous tone said, 'As he hasn't come in to work today I think perhaps you ought to tell me, Diane, in case there's some sort of problem.'

Sarah was on her feet now and closing fast.

'You're probably right. The thing is he was made redundant yesterday. They had a meeting – they gave him a month. Well, him and a lot of the other managerial staff too. They were all supposed to meet this morning to discuss some sort of programme that Danic have set up to help them relocate – you know, retraining and all that.'

Katherine sat down heavily on the stool beside the work bench. She had to hang on to the phone; Sarah was trying to prise it out of her fingers.

'Thank you,' she said evenly, firmly pushing Sarah away. 'I'll get Harry to ring in as soon as he gets home.'

'Well?' demanded Sarah, after she hung up.

Katherine looked up at her. 'Your father was made redundant yesterday.'

Sarah made a grab at the phone. 'We have to ring the police. He could have thrown himself off a bridge or anything. Here.'

Katherine shook her head. 'Calm down and make the tea. I'll go through the address book, someone is bound to know where your father is.'

Sarah glared at her. 'You should have done this over the weekend, not now, now it might be too late.'

Katherine took a deep breath, wondering if in some previous life Sarah had been part of a Greek chorus. When the phone rang again she stared at it for a second or two as if it might leap off the work surface and bite her. She picked it up very cautiously.

Ben Morton's calm deep voice filled her head. 'Hi, I just rang to say I really enjoyed yesterday and wondered – I know I asked you to the concert on Saturday night – but I'm going out to the abbey sometime today to do some background shots and wondered if you fancied coming along for the ride?'

Katherine looked across at Sarah, hunched, wound tight, just inches from her face, and the address book beside the phone. 'I'd love to,' she heard herself say.

'Good,' said Ben. 'We can have a spot of lunch at this lovely little place I know. I'll be there in half-an-hour. Is that okay?'

'Absolutely. I'll look forward to it,' said Katherine and laid the phone back in its cradle. She looked up at Sarah. 'I'm going out,' she said carefully, enunciating every word.

'I think it might be better if you've gone by the time I get back.'

Sarah reeled as if Katherine had hit her. 'Leave?' she hissed. 'What now? You can't be serious. I thought you were going to ring round and try to find Dad.'

Katherine nodded. 'So did I, but he's a big boy now and I've spent years chasing around after him. Now if you'll excuse me I have to get ready to go out. Would you please lock the door when you leave. I've got my keys.'

As she walked away Katherine started to tremble but she refused to look back, if she once saw the outrage and pain in her daughter's eyes she knew she would waver. Her daughter already thought she was selfish and who was she to disabuse Sarah of her long-held beliefs. At the top of the stairs the trembling got so bad that Katherine had to run into her bedroom. Under the shower she permitted herself the tears that she'd held in check since Sarah's arrival. Such a cocktail of emotions, pain, hurt, frustration and loss all came pouring out on a raging flow of bubbling hot water.

When Katherine re-appeared at the bottom of the stairs, dressed, totally composed and ready for her trip out with Ben Morton, Sarah was hunched over the phone, gnawing at her thumb nail.

'So you haven't seen him, then?' she was saying into the receiver. 'Well, if you do, please can you ask him to ring his daughter straightaway. Yes, that's right. He has got my number, only we are all terribly worried about him. Yes – yes, of course I'll give your regards to my mother. Thank you.' As Sarah dropped the phone back into its cradle she looked up at Katherine and reddened furiously. 'Well, somebody has got to do it,' she snapped defensively.

Katherine sighed. 'So who was that?'

'You really care?'

Katherine stared at her. Sarah sniffed and then looked away, withdrawing from the confrontation. 'It was some-

134

one called Walford, he was terribly nice and seemed very concerned about Dad.'

Katherine tugged her new jacket straight. 'He's the fishmonger in town, he runs the place next to the shoe shop.'

Sarah's colour deepened. 'I wondered why you'd got him down on the F page.'

'How many people have you rung so far?'

'Everybody in your phone book from A to F.' Sarah's eyes brightened, as she flicked the pages back and forth through her fingers. 'I was just about to make a start on the Gs.'

Above her, pinned to the notice board, was Katherine's list of people she felt needed to know Harry had left. It contained half a dozen names, Sarah and Peter's being the first and then below them, a long way below them in importance if not position, were a clutch of other names: Harry's older sisters, Katherine's sister, one or two others. Now, thanks to Sarah the whole neighbourhood knew, or at least those unlucky disparate souls in the first quarter of the alphabet.

Gently, Katherine prised the book from Sarah's fingers. 'Why don't you go upstairs, get dressed and go home, darling,' she said as evenly as she could manage. 'You can't do anything here and if your dad rings here I'll ask him to call you. I promise.'

Sarah rubbed her mouth. 'But you're going out.'

'I'll leave the machine on.'

'Some solace that's going to be when he rings up. "Leave a message after the tone and I'll get back to you." What if he needs to talk to someone? What if he's suicidal?'

'Sarah, if he had wanted to phone home he could have done it any time over the last few days. And if he wanted to phone you he could have, but he hasn't, and I'm damned if I'm going to spend the rest of my life hanging round here waiting to see if he changes his mind. Now go and have a shower.'

'We're not talking about the rest of your life, Mother, we're talking about a few hours, maybe a few days, just until he gets in contact, just until he lets us know that he's all right.'

Katherine said nothing, silently counting up the years she had already spent waiting at home for Harry to ring.

'You're trying to get rid of me, aren't you?'

Katherine nodded. 'Yes, I am.'

Sarah beaded her with her sharp little eyes, so much like Harry's. 'So where are you going anyway?'

Katherine picked up her handbag. 'Out for a drive with a friend.'

'Do I know them?'

Katherine tidied the telephone book back onto the shelf with the recipe books. 'Not unless you made it through to M. Now, are you going to be all right, only I thought I might wait outside?'

Sarah's expression hardened. 'It's a man, isn't it? You've found someone else.'

Katherine, with a growing sense of exhaustion, lifted a hand to wave a brief goodbye. 'Don't forget to lock up, will you?' Her impression of Sarah was of a harridan, hair still muzzy from sleep, face pink, shoulders hunched, fists clenched. It was a great relief to be out in the sunlight. She barely had the chance to close the front door before Ben's silver-grey Volvo drew onto the gravel. He grinned and waved a welcome.

'Hi,' he said, hopping out of the car to greet her. He caught hold of her elbow and pressed a kiss to each cheek. 'God, you look gorgeous and smell even better. Are you all set? Got everything?'

Katherine nodded. 'Absolutely, it was nice of you to think of me.'

Ben laughed as he opened the car door for her. 'I've barely thought about anything else since yesterday. You make quite an impression, Mrs Bourne.'

As they drove away Katherine caught sight of Sarah framed in the sitting room window. She was wearing an 'I knew it' expression on her face, the colour of which almost exactly matched her livid pink dressing-gown.

'. . . It's a bit of hike out to the abbey,' Ben was saying. 'But there's not much to do once we get there, the trustees want something for the front cover of their new book. So I thought we'd have some lunch first and then drive on afterwards. Catch the best of the afternoon light.'

Katherine was thinking about Sarah, who in her mind was already shrinking like the dot in the centre of a TV screen. 'Do you think I'm selfish, Ben?'

He glanced across at her looking puzzled. 'I hardly know you well enough to pass judgement,' he said pleasantly. 'But I wouldn't have thought so, no, not at all. Why do you ask?'

She settled herself down into the passenger seat, eyes fixed on the passing hedgerows. 'My daughter thinks I am.'

'Children always do. They think you've got nothing better to do than sit around and wait for them to call, or ring. Surely you must know by now we exist purely for their convenience. It's a stage of growing up; when you least expect it they suddenly transmogrify into your parents. My daughter is the same. I kept hoping when she left home she'd grow up. She's got a family of her own now, two boys, nice house, but it hasn't worked. She still wants to know what time I get in, where I've been, how much I drink, if I'm eating properly. She disapproves of my friends, my clothes, my taste in music.' He laughed. 'Actually I quite enjoy it, it feels like being a teenager all over again. Fortunately she doesn't live too close but even so when she rings or comes over to visit she starts to lecture me on responsibility and I feel like a rebel taking on the establishment all over again.'

Katherine sighed. 'I don't think I like my daughter very much.'

Ben reached across and patted her arm. 'It's all right, no law on earth says we have to like our children, loving them sometimes has to be enough.'

Katherine felt a little phalanx of tears creep up unexpectedly behind her eyes. Ben slowed the car and looked at her anxiously. 'Are you all right?'

Katherine pulled out a tissue from her bag. 'No, not really, but I fully intend to be. Just give me a year or two. I'll be fine.'

Ben smiled. 'My cottage is only about half-an-hour from here, you'll feel much better after we've eaten.'

Katherine stared at him. 'We're having lunch at your cottage?'

'Didn't I mention that was part of the plan? You don't mind, do you?'

Katherine didn't trust herself to speak.

Ben's cottage was set well back from the main road, amongst a broad stand of woodland. It was built of flint, with tiny windows in the ground floor and larger ones above set into the roof. Hollyhocks, wallflowers and an explosion of riotous cottage garden colours ran like a river down towards a white picket fence. It was breathtakingly beautiful. She stared at it.

'This is your place?'

He nodded. 'Of course my daughter doesn't approve, she thinks I should sell up and buy a nice little bungalow on a main road somewhere, somewhere easy to clean, preferably on a bus route for when I get too frail to drive myself down to the off-licence. Why don't we go inside and I'll show you around?'

Inside, every wall was painted in the palest cream and hung with paintings, prints and curios. In the sitting room French windows opened up onto a long sun-dappled terrace. The room was furnished with an odd mismatch of furniture which was strangely easy on the eye and the soul.

Katherine dropped her handbag onto a huge jade-green sofa and headed towards the terrace, drawn unconsciously by the vista of trees and the random carpet of flowers. After Sarah the whole place was balm to her soul.

Ben pushed the French windows open and handed her a glass of red wine. She took it without a word. He stood beside her. Shoulder to shoulder they looked out over the rolling flower-beds and the tumble of climbers where they clung to low stone walls.

'Oh, Ben, it's beautiful,' she murmured.

He smiled across at her and leaning forward kissed her very very gently. She didn't have to tell him she liked it – the house and the kiss.

'Would you like to see the rest?'

She was reluctant to move and break the overwhelming sense of peace. Here, caught in the sunlight she felt totally at ease, as if she had stood on the terrace alongside Ben Morton for a lifetime, but she did turn away. She followed him down through the kitchen, built from reclaimed timber, lovingly constructed to follow the convoluted contours of the ancient walls, and then into the dining room, decked out like a medieval banqueting hall in claret and gold, and then, almost without thinking, upstairs onto the landing, where the sun lay on the shiny stripped boards like tide pools from some glittering distant sea.

At the top of the stairs she hesitated just long enough to make sure she knew exactly what she was doing. Behind a heavy stripped-pine door, the master bedroom had a huge double bed in it. It dominated the centre of the room. Four planed tree trunks supported a canopy of twisted cream muslin, while beside it a great arched window framed the tree tops outside.

She turned to meet Ben's gaze and knew then that she was lost. She could see her need reflected in his pupils. He had brought her back to the cottage to make love to her – although she knew, even as the realisation seeped through her bones, that the final decision was still hers to make.

'This is the most wonderful room,' she said softly. Like the lens of a camera, her mind took in the details: the thick cream carpet which matched the delicate cream throw on the bed. The four claret cushions artfully arranged across the head of the bed. The bathrobe thrown so casually over a high-backed chair in one corner. This was a room designed for seduction. Even though she had absorbed every detail she discovered she hadn't taken her eyes off him.

'I'm really glad you like it,' he said as he took the wine glass out of her hand.

She shivered as their fingertips met. 'Have you brought a lot of women up here?'

'One or two. But none that need worry you – I don't make a habit of it.'

'Aren't we too old for all this nonsense?' she said under her breath.

'I don't think so. As long as we don't listen to our children we'll be just fine.' His eyes darkened like a summer storm and he stepped closer. 'Are you sure you want to do this?'

Katherine smiled nervously. 'Please, don't let's talk about it,' she said in a small uneven voice, watching his hand slide her glass onto the dressing table as if it had eyes of its own. 'Let's just see what happens, shall we?'

He slipped his arms around her waist and pressed his lips to her neck. The sensation of his lips on her skin lit a spiral of tiny lights in her mind. She closed her eyes and watched their path through her thoughts. Real life, Harry, Sarah, the house, even the bright little flare of guilt were drowned out by the sheer pleasure of the sensations.

There was a moment, just after he folded back the cream coverlet and, still holding her hand, pulled her down amongst the bow wave of lace-trimmed linen, that Katherine felt a rush of panic, a momentary surfacing of the

140

woman she had been when she was married to Harry. Her clothes were scattered like flower petals around the bed. The other self, mortified by her nakedness, took a long shuddering breath.

'I'm so afraid,' she whispered, ignoring the hand that was trailing down over her belly.

Ben smiled. 'I know.'

She sighed and slipped under the crisp white sheets, lying back as Ben pulled them up around her shoulders. 'I will probably cry.'

'I really don't mind.'

Carol was extremely relieved to discover that Jeanette was nowhere in sight when she finally arrived at the office – only a coffee mug standing sentinel amongst a sheaf of papers indicated that her secretary was lurking somewhere in the building. Closing her office door, Carol picked up the phone, selected an outside line and tapped in Lee Fenman's office number whilst teasing a business card out of her wallet.

'Hi, Carol,' said Lee. 'You must have read my mind. I was just about to ring you to congratulate you again on how it went yesterday – great job. And I really enjoyed our lunch. We should get together more often. Made your mind up about visiting Danic–New York already?'

Carol smiled. 'No, and yes, it was great yesterday. I'll see that you get a copy of all the paperwork – actually though, that isn't what I'm calling about. I wondered whether you knew anything about Kestrel Enterprises.'

Lee made a noise suggesting lack of comprehension. 'No, nothing, why? Should I know them?'

Carol laid Harry's business card down on her blotter. 'They are involved in specialist computer equipment, scales and calibration, I think.'

Lee grunted. 'Means absolutely nothing to me. Why? Are you thinking about branching out on your own and arranging a buy-out?' He laughed. 'I knew you'd got all the makings of a corporate raider.'

'No, quite the reverse. I really wanted to know if Kestrel were part of the Danic package yesterday.'

'No idea, it doesn't ring a bell, but it could be a subsidiary that crept in under the wire. Would you like me to find out for you?'

'Yes, thanks. I'd be grateful.'

'How grateful?'

She could hear the amusement in Lee's voice as he spoke. 'Not that grateful,' she replied, unable to resist a smile herself.

'Pity. Have you got anything planned for tonight? I'm in town until Wednesday and I've got tickets for something arty at the Barbican. Fancy a little culture?'

Carol shook her head. 'Nice try, Lee, maybe next time you're in town?'

'You just don't know what you're missing. I'll get back to you about Kestrel if I find anything – and remember, I'm expecting you to call me about New York later in the week.'

Carol tucked Harry's business card back into her bag. 'I haven't forgotten. I'll be in touch.'

The slick, weightless patois of business life was like a tennis match, superficial remarks that meant very little glided off the tongue like a well practised forehand. After she hung up she glanced out at Jeanette's desk, it was still empty, but the coffee mug prompted her thirst.

She took a superficial glance at the paperwork in her in-tray and headed instead for the canteen. It seemed that the bush telegraph was on full alert – or was she just imagining that people were looking at her in an odd way? In the lift the conversation between two girls stopped abruptly the second the doors opened and she stepped in. She was being over sensitive. Coffee would cure her paranoia.

On the third floor the doors glided open silently and she was about to step out when she saw Jeanette, standing back to the lift, deep in conversation with another woman she vaguely recognised from somewhere else in the bowels of the Lactons treadmill.

'So, I've got no idea whether Miss Goody Two-Shoes is going to show up today or not, and she's expecting me to cover for her – again. He was in one helluva mess. Drunk? God – you wouldn't believe the state he was in when he rolled in here.'

The words hung in the air, a banner headline above Jeanette's carefully coiffured blonde locks. Jeanette's one-woman audience looked up distractedly as the lift doors hissed closed. The expression of horror on her face as she stood, leaning idly against the wall, cradling a bundle of files, might under other circumstances have made Carol laugh, but today the open jaw and the glazed eyes made her furious.

'Well,' Carol said in a cold icy tone. 'If you're being expected to cover for me, Jeanette, the very least you can do is sit at your desk and answer my bloody phone.'

Jeanette half turned, colour draining fast from behind the mask of blusher and lipstick. 'Ms Ackerman, Carol –' she spluttered.

'Well spotted. Now if you've quite finished here, I need the copies of yesterday's meeting with Danic to be sent out to all the relevant parties, and I'd also like a list of all subsidiary companies involved on my desk by lunch-time.' She paused. Jeanette was caught unmoving under her glacial gaze. 'Now would be a good time,' she added slowly.

Jeanette's colour flooded up through her cheeks like mercury rising in a heat wave.

'Yes,' she stammered. 'Yes, of course.' Her tone dropped to something more conciliatory. 'I didn't think you'd be in today.'

'That is painfully obvious.'

With all the dignity she could muster Carol sailed past the two women and into the staff canteen, bought a cappuccino and then slumped down in a seat by the window, hidden from general view by a large imitation fern.

Chapter Twelve

Safe in Ben's cottage, Katherine lay back amongst a tumble of sheets and pillows watching the movement of the trees outside the bedroom window. The daylight had softened now and was fading slowly into a golden afternoon. Ben had gone to make tea. How civilised that sounded.

For the first time since Harry left she felt a real sense of loss. How lovely it would have been if it had been him, not Ben, who walked in through the door bearing a tray. The thought took her by suprise – not the Harry she had asked to leave, but one of the other Harrys she'd found hiding in the back of the wardrobe. A younger Harry with tousled hair and a grin, a Harry who would look down at her with tenderness and make her feel warm and good and well loved.

She sniffed back a tear. Sarah was right, she really ought to have rung round to try and find the husk of the Harry who had left her. She rolled over, wondering if she could make the pain vanish before Ben reappeared. She could still smell him on the sheets.

She wondered why she had gone to bed with Ben. It was so totally out of character. Perhaps it was some subconscious affirmation that there was life after Harry. She couldn't remember the last time she had thought about another man with any whisper of desire or lust, and certainly in the years she had been married to Harry she had given up all thought of being an object of desire. She had become almost asexual, safe inside a cosy if not altogether comfortable arrangement. Until meeting Ben she had convinced herself love and lust were the exclusive prerogative of the young – except now she didn't have the cosy arrange-ment and this was what life was like out beyond the castle wall. And she suspected even that was a lie – she would be a fool to think that Ben Morton was anything more than a sweet little interlude, a fantasy bridge to ease her passage back into real life.

Katherine closed her eyes and tried to recapture the time before Harry. She'd lived, as a student, in a nurses' home and as the thoughts took hold she was suddenly confronted with an intense image of the brooding Victorian pile where she had trained. It emerged from somewhere deep in her psyche like a wreck bubbling up from the depths, every last brick and corridor, even the smell as crisp and sharp as it had been nearly thirty years before.

People she hadn't thought about for years surfaced along with the buildings. The clarity of the memories stunned her. She could almost hear the rustle of her starched apron. At the same time she remembered what it felt like to be painfully shy. When she'd been away from the ward and the patients, she'd never really been at ease with the other girls, but had been a good nurse none the less.

She had always been a quiet person, unassuming, con-scientious. A good person even when it had not been in her own best interests. Katherine blushed furiously, thinking about failed attempts at romance and a messy but intensely private crush she'd had on one of the housemen. Would it be like that all over again once Ben had melted away or would she decide to settle for the promise of grandchildren and her garden instead?

Growing up inside her marriage with Harry had helped her to find more self-confidence, even if it was not with him. Under his ever critical eye she had hosted endless business dinners, tending to others, making inconsequential small-talk, painting the social graces over her uncertainty.

In some ways living with Harry had given her much, but had taken too much in return. She rolled over and stared up at the pale ceiling, wondering for the second time in as many minutes what exactly she was doing in Ben Morton's bed. His touch had electrified her, making every cell of her glow with delight. It had not been smooth, short or predictable but deeply, deeply exciting.

With Harry she knew every move he would make, everything he would say and do, and had laid back waiting for act two to follow act one – her greatest desire being to get him to the point of no return so that she could roll over and go to sleep. Over the years she realised she had reduced sex to another chore – another job on her mental list – to be completed as efficiently as possible.

With Ben, for all their fumbling and uncertainty she had wanted to share what she felt, relish the touch and exploration, giving pleasure and also longing to receive it in a way that had long since died with Harry. With Harry lovemaking was something he did to her – revelations ricocheted around her mind, fragments surfacing and floating forward for consideration. Would she always compare everything and everyone to the Harry yardstick? The thought unnerved her, would he live on forever as a counterbalance to every experience?

Sarah was wrong, she wasn't selfish – she and Harry had an unwritten bargain. She had unwittingly agreed to be a proper old-fashioned wife, tending and caring for his every need, rearing his children, building them all a home, in return for a bye in the game of adulthood.

Had she seriously expected some pay-off, some time when he would say, 'All right, you've done that now, Kitty-Kat and you've made a bloody good job of it, so now you can get on with being who you really are?'

A tear trickled down her face and sank without trace into the plump white pillows. No, the Harry she had thrown out could never say that, because he had never had any idea that when he wasn't looking, she had grown up into another person.

Ben Morton was standing in the doorway, wrapped in a towelling robe, holding a tea-tray. She had no idea how long he had been there watching her. She blushed but didn't feel uncomfortable, quite the reverse in fact. She jiffled up the bed, taking the sheets with her so they were tucked under her armpits, and wiped away the last remaining tear.

He smiled and stood the tray on the bedside table. Without a shred of embarrassment he slipped his robe off and slid into bed beside her.

'Do you still fancy a drive out to the abbey? I really do have to take those photos.'

She nodded, accepting the mug of tea he handed her. 'Actually I'm still waiting for the lunch you promised me,' she said unsteadily.

'We could grab a meal at a pub on the way back if you like or I could make us a quick chicken salad before we go.'

Katherine smiled. 'Salad sounds fine. What about the light?' She really didn't want to leave the little cottage with its beautiful garden – it felt as if it was outside real time and real life.

He shrugged. 'I'd planned to use afternoon light anyway, it makes the stones glow beautifully. But there's no panic, if we miss it today we can always try again another time.'

They drank tea, curled up side by side in the bed. Afterwards Ben went downstairs, giving her time and space to shower and dress alone. She ran her fingers through her hair before slipping in the new earrings. She stared into the mirror and was surprised to see that her face hadn't changed; there were no outward signs, no lasting traces of Ben's touch or her response. She looked closer, wondering if adultery made a mark that was hard to find. Steady blue eyes looked back at her with open curiosity. She winked at her reflection and then hurried downstairs to help Ben with the food.

The hospital and the smell of carbolic and all the Harrys in her life finally sank back beneath the water, vanishing without a ripple as she stepped into Ben's kitchen and he handed her a crisp Cos lettuce. There was a pleasant intimate glow between them. He grinned as she instinctively pressed her lips to the back of his neck.

'Look at that,' he said waving a finger towards the lettuce, 'completely organic. Wait until you taste the tomatoes. They're magic.'

Katherine nodded and picked up a knife from beside the chopping board. 'Anything you'd like me to do?'

Ben snorted. 'Well, you can put that down and pour us both another glass of wine if you like. And Katherine?' She looked round, reddening under his undisguised interest. 'Thank you for this afternoon.'

She flushed scarlet. He smiled easily and planted a kiss on the tip of her nose. 'It was really special. Has anyone ever told you, you look beautiful with a knife in your hand?'

She shook her head and picked up the glasses from the draining board. 'Ben,' she began haltingly, glancing around the cottage, 'can I talk to you about how I feel?'

He shook his head emphatically. 'Absolutely not. On the whole, I've found that wisdom makes for very poor entertainment. Anyway, I'm your lover not your analyst – and very much a flawed hero. Now, are you going to pour the wine or would you prefer a man die of thirst?'

Carol could not bring herself to talk to Jeanette until just before lunch and then it was only to offer perfunctory thanks for the Danic reports being sent off.

Jeanette, as if eager to make the peace, lingered by Carol's desk. 'I'm still working on the list of subsidiaries.'

Carol nodded, willing her away.

'There are quite a few,' Jeanette continued. 'A lot of the new Danic stock is made up of small companies trading under a larger umbrella. It might take me a while to get a complete list.'

'You know what I'm looking for.' Her tone was icy.

Jeanette glanced down at the notepad she was carrying. 'It's not really my fault, you know,' she said in an undertone.

Carol threw the report she had been reading down onto her desk. She might as well get it over and done with. 'Oh really? Are you trying to tell me I didn't overhear you broadcasting confidential details of my private life to the typing pool?' Carol asked in her most imperious voice.

Jeanette flinched.

'Well?'

Jeanette sighed. 'All right, I know I shouldn't have said anything, but Lorna, that's the girl you saw me talking to, saw Harry staggering up here last night. I thought I owed her some kind of explanation. He was all over the place.'

Carol felt herself slipping off the moral high ground. 'Was he very drunk?'

Jeanette pulled a face. 'I'm afraid he was. I had to bring him in here to quieten him down. I was seriously thinking about calling security. He was so upset.'

Carol sighed. 'Thank you. But I would like to make it quite clear my personal life is not to be the subject of discussion. And I really shouldn't have to say this to you.'

Jeanette looked uncharacteristically contrite. 'Was he all right this morning?'

Carol shuffled the papers on her desk. 'He was fine when I left, thank you. Would you please bring my diary in?'

She noticed that the bounce had returned to Jeanette's step and cursed under her breath; she should have made her suffer a little bit longer.

'The only major thing you've got is the Women in Business conference.'

Carol nodded; she had wanted to get the Danic deal out of the way before she gave her lecture at Baneford College any serious consideration. Her alma mater. She had given the same talk at Keele just before Christmas, it just needed a little fine tuning.

'What about this week?' Carol already knew it was slow. Everything, Harry aside, had for the last few weeks been centred around her plans for Danic. These few days were meant to represent a well-deserved lull after the storm.

'Not much really. Regular monthly staff meeting first thing tomorrow. You've got that Jackson woman tomorrow as well. Lunch. I've booked you a table at Carlottas. Oh, and I've got that man, Blackwood? He wants you to go and take a look at a green field site in Northampton.'

Carol glanced out of the window, Old Father Thames was still rolling on by. Lunch with Katherine Jackson would be light relief.

'I know about Blackwood, can you pull the files and see if he can make it next week? Thursday?'

The rest of the week's schedule was full of anticlimax, Lactons' equivalent of fridge cleaning. Maybe she should think about going to New York, Harry or no Harry. She waved Jeanette away.

'Don't book anyone else in until next Monday, especially not the guy from Northampton.' She glanced at her own personal diary; there were clients she should chase, deals that could be wrestled for, but nothing appealed beyond getting to the weekend with as little aggravation as possible. She looked out towards the bustle of the main office. She had expected to hear something from the partners but it seemed they too were playing a waiting game.

Jeanette hovered, waiting to catch Carol's eye. 'Yes?'

'About Harry.'

Carol wished that Jeanette hadn't used his name with such easy familiarity. 'Yes?' she asked again.

'I don't like to bring this up but I paid the bill for his hotel room.'

Carol sighed. 'How much?'

'I'll go and get the receipt.'

Carol pulled her cheque book out of her handbag. 'Where did you take him?' she asked casually through the open door.

'The Strand Palace. He insisted. He said it was where he spent his honeymoon.'

Carol stiffened.

Harry Bourne couldn't quite remember how he had got back to Carol's house nor, come to that, exactly what circumstances had led to his sitting at the counter in a Cambridge café, run by two poufs, who seemed to be labouring under the misapprehension that he was their friend. He sipped the coffee, reluctantly, much as he had eaten the lunch they had given him – a curried meat thing – which despite his fears had proved to be excellent.

What he did remember with remarkable clarity that was quite disproportionate to any other memory of the previous evening, was waking up in the arms of Carol's secretary, Julie, no, that wasn't right, Jean – no, Jeanette, that was her name. Not that it had been unpleasant, just totally unexpected.

He licked his lips, still dry from the heavy application of brandy, and grinned. There was life in the old dog yet, whatever Katherine thought. Her name surfacing in his head made him wonder whether he ought to ring her. A childish sense of spite had prevented him from calling before to let her know what was going on. He had thought about going home there; she was always so good when he was ill. He really ought to ring her and Peter and Sarah – that's who he'd ring, Sarah would understand.

He patted his jacket pockets, instinctively searching out the wallet which he found it very difficult to believe he had lost. The two poufs had rung up and cancelled his credit cards, which rather spoilt his theory that they had stolen them.

He had had difficulty understanding why Carol had gone off to work and left him with Ray and Geoff. She really ought to have stayed there herself, stayed at home and looked after him. He shook his head and instantly regretted it. No sense of priorities, Carol, but then again she wasn't used to having a man about the place. Katherine wouldn't have thought twice about it. Leaving him to fend for himself wouldn't have occurred to her at all.

Harry didn't dwell long on Katherine, in fact his mind seemed keen to skate over the details of why she might want a divorce. If he was honest he saw his present problem as a temporary disruption to his normal schedule that would sort itself out if given a little time. He saw it from a long way off, a distant abstract thing, down a corridor in his mind. He had no desire whatsoever to look at the situation close up.

It had to be her age, Carol was right. Katherine was menopausal, that was the answer, and every one knew women went strange when that happened. Given a few days, Katherine would calm down and be relieved to see him back. He would be magnanimous but firm; this sort of thing wasn't to happen again. Look what a mess she had got herself into while he was away. He hoped she wasn't going to crack up, that would be awful – after all, if she wasn't there, who would look after him?

He glanced into the top of his cup as if the secrets of his life might be captured in the grounds. Katherine would be fine, he assured himself, a few days to cool off and come to her senses and when he arrived home she would be contrite and so terribly sorry for having caused such a fuss.

He would be cool but understanding and say very little, which he expected and hoped would make her feel worse. And when she found out about him being made redundant on top of everything else – he swilled the last of the coffee round the cup, leaving a tidal wave of divination around the bowl – Katherine would feel dreadful about the way she had treated him.

That's what Harry assumed. He looked for no further explanation of her behaviour, he didn't consider whether or not Katherine would be able to cope on her own, or what she might be doing or thinking or why she might have thrown him out in the first place.

His loyalties were as fickle as shifting sand; when he was with Carol he loved her, or more correctly assumed she would love him, and the same was true with Katherine. To some extent Harry believed that both women only existed in a real sense when he was with them. The rest of their life, though he had never put it into clear thoughts or words, was a grey area where he imagined them moving in slow motion, busy but not quite real, their whole life spent waiting for him to arrive and turn on the spotlight.

Harry had a great capacity to believe the things he told himself. Another week or two, if he continued to live with Carol and Katherine refused to have him back, he would believe, at the very root of his soul, that it had been he who had made the decision to leave. He was very good at reinventing his past, but at the moment it was prickly territory, an unformed block of thoughts that he was uncomfortable with, although the edges were already being eroded away and he was standing back, waiting for the moment when the new, more favourable shape appeared in his memory.

He felt no real sense of pain, just a raw glow of indignation that he had decided to ignore, at least temporarily. The nerve of the woman, but he had always suspected women were like that; all of them were unpredictable alley cats who could turn in an instant and bite the hand that fed them. Harry had developed a way of standing well back from his life, on top of a tall hill, and looking down on those who populated it with a kind of airy detachment.

His thoughts ebbed and flowed, weighing advantages. It

might have been a mistake to have hurried to Carol, it would make going back to Katherine far messier, particularly after all the things he had, in his emotional state, promised Carol. She had been his back-up life, a spare in case the first one ever got dirty. What he should have done on reflection was stayed in a hotel and waited for Katherine to come to her senses.

Across the counter, one of the men – Harry had yet to decide which was Ray and which Geoff – was stacking cups back onto glass-fronted shelves.

'So, have you thought about what you're going to do now?' he said, shuffling saucers into a tidy pile.

Harry looked at him, wondering if he could read minds. 'I'm sorry?' he hedged.

'About your job? Have your company offered you any re-training, any suggestions? I mean, surely they aren't just going to push you over the edge of the nest after fifteen years of faithful service?'

Harry grunted; his redundancy was something else that he had almost instantly tucked away in a far corner of his consciousness. After the initial flash of disbelief and fury he had barely thought about the consequences. He would have to, obviously, but not at the moment, he'd tease the idea out a little at a time. Katherine would know exactly how to deal with it. Perhaps he ought to give her a ring and hold out an olive branch.

'Training course, relocation advice, or a dead-end sideways move,' he said thickly. 'I was supposed to go in today for some sort of assessment.'

The man nodded. 'Don't worry. Geoff rang them to say you'd got a stomach bug.'

Harry stared at him. 'He rang my office?'

Ray – for this must be Ray unless he was talking about himself in the third person – nodded again. 'We thought Carol might not get around to it, she was in such a rush this morning.'

'Who did you tell them you were?' Harry asked apprehensively.

Ray grinned. 'Well, I suggested your new gay friend, or maybe your mistress's first reserve, but Geoff thought that was too inflammatory so we settled on telling them that he was your priest.'

Harry felt his colour draining and to his horror Ray giggled. 'Oh, for Christ's sake, lighten up, man, it was a joke. He told them you'd asked him to ring in, and that's all. Don't fret, Geoff was terribly butch on the phone.'

Harry struggled to find something to say.

Any considered reply was stifled by the sound of a mobile phone ringing. It took Harry a second or two to realise it was his and he slipped hastily off the bar stool, fumbling to pull the receiver out of his inside pocket.

'Hello?' he said, wondering for a few seconds if it might be Katherine ringing up to ask his forgiveness. It would certainly solve a lot of his problems if it was.

'Hallo,' said an unfamiliar voice. 'Is that you, Harry?'

He looked round to see who was listening; no one apparently.

'Yes, it is, who is this?' he hissed, making his way over to an empty corner table.

The reply was punctuated by a high tinkling laugh. 'Oh, you sly old fox, you know exactly who I am. It's Jeanette.'

Harry put his hand up to muffle the receiver. 'How did you get this number?' he whispered.

'You gave it to me last night, along with a few other things.' Her tone was heavily suggestive. Harry reddened as Jeanette continued, 'I just wanted to ring up and make sure you were all right after last night. You looked a bit rough when I left. Oh and I've got your wallet, you gave it to me to look after. I wasn't certain that you'd remember.'

He didn't. 'Oh right. Good. Well, yes I'm – I'm just fine,' he blustered. 'And I'm relieved you've got my things.'

Jeanette laughed again. 'I told Carol that I booked you

into a hotel, no names, no pack drill. I was just wondering how I could get your wallet back to you?'

He was about to suggest she give it to Carol but Jeanette was still speaking, 'The thing is I made it all sound like sort of a Good Samaritan thing to Carol, so I can hardly give it to her, can I? Just in case she gets suspicious and wants to know all the details? I'm not a very good liar, and besides we don't want to let the cat out of the bag, do we?'

The very thought of cats made Harry want to sneeze. 'What exactly are you saying?'

'I thought maybe you and I could get together somewhere.'

He felt a strange little trickle of apprehension finger his spine but didn't dwell on the implications of what it might mean.

'I had a *really* good time last night,' she said. Her voice dropped to an intimate purr. 'Carol doesn't know what a lucky woman she is.'

Harry grinned. Old dog. The sand shifted again. In his mind Jeanette was not another complication but a clean slate that would allow him to avoid resolving the situation with Katherine and Carol; he could begin all over again.

'Perhaps,' he instinctively changed to a more seductive tone, 'we ought to meet up in town somewhere, well away from prying eyes.'

Jeanette giggled. 'Oh, Harry. We could meet up for a drink maybe? I don't like to carry valuable things around in my handbag in case they get lost, so perhaps you could come round to my flat afterwards and pick up your wallet from there?'

Harry preened. 'Very sensible. It sounds like a good idea to me. When do you suggest?'

'How about tomorrow, after work, say six, at the pub we went to last time?'

'I'll see you there, then.'

He was about to ring off when Jeanette said quickly, 'You do remember where it was, don't you?'

'Absolutely,' he lied, 'but maybe it would be a good idea to give me the address anyway, just in case.' Teasing a pen from his pocket he jotted directions down on a paper napkin and then folded it up into his pocket.

Walking back to the counter he felt better, much better. 'May I have another, please?' he asked briskly, pushing his empty cup towards Ray.

Ray picked up the coffee pot. 'You look perkier. Good news, was it?'

Harry straightened his tie. 'Oh yes,' he said. 'Very good news.'

Chapter Thirteen

Ben Morton said the light at the abbey was just perfect for the pictures he had in mind. It was closed to the public on weekdays, so they walked around the crumbling walls in perfect isolation, caught up in the glow of fading sunlight, cosseted by the ancient silence. He declined Katherine's offer to carry one of the bags. While he set up his tripod and centred his attention on the great arched doorway that led into the main hall, Katherine sat down on the carefully manicured lawn and tipped her face up to the sun.

The sound of the wind in the trees and a ruffle of evening bird song lulled her to the very edge of sleep. When she opened her eyes Ben had turned and was pointing the lens at her. Instinctively she began to scramble to her feet.

'Oh no,' she gasped, horribly embarrassed. 'I hate having my photograph taken.'

Ben grinned. 'Too late, my dear, you might as well sit down and relax, the deed is done.' He tapped the film cartridge. 'Recorded for posterity. You looked so peaceful there. It was too good to resist.' He dropped onto the grass beside her. 'So what shall we do now?'

Katherine glanced down at her watch. 'I ought to be getting home.'

'Ought to?'

Katherine nodded. 'My daughter, Sarah, is staying with me at the moment, although I'm hoping she will have left by the time I get back.'

'And?' said Ben.

'I ought to talk to Harry.'

Ben pulled a face.

'No need to look like that,' she said indignantly. 'I don't hate him or want to hurt him. It had gone too far for that. I feel –' she fished around for a suitable word, 'almost indifferent to him, but I found out this morning that he had been made redundant. Harry's job is part of him, like the colour of his eyes, or the size of his feet. I wanted to say – to say . . .'

Ben moved a little closer. 'What? That you're terribly sorry and that he can come home now, all is forgiven?'

Katherine stiffened. 'Good God, no. If you knew how many years it had taken me to work up the courage to be able to say out loud that I wanted him to leave . . . No, it's just that I don't like the idea of him being all on his own. I just wanted to say – oh shit, I don't know what I wanted to say, it seemed like the right thing to do.'

Ben leant forward, his face and shoulders cutting out the sunlight. 'The wifely thing to do? The all-embracing "come home and let me make it all better" thing to do?'

'No,' then she stopped and looked up at him in surprise. 'You're right. I would end up saying that, wouldn't I?'

Ben nodded. 'And he will be expecting you to. After all, what caring person would abandon someone in a crisis? Do it, why not? You can put all your new found wisdom down to a mid-life crisis, an aberration, and live happily ever after if you play it right.'

Katherine's rage flared unbidden in the pit of her stomach. 'No!' she growled, pushing him away furiously.

'And, of course,' Ben continued in a teasing sing-song voice, 'Harry will find it in his heart to forgive you because he understands you didn't really mean it and he really needs you to look after him.'

Katherine stared at him, something shifting into place inside her head. 'Are we talking about me or you, Ben?'

He grinned. 'A little bit of both, I think. I've learnt a lot since it happened to me. I was barely out of my thirties, still running on nervous energy. I was a complete and utter bastard and deserved to be treated like one, but what I got instead was love and I thought that there was this bottomless reserve of tolerance, and of course I was convinced I deserved it, so I used it all up, a bucketful at a time. It took me years to work it all out. Here –' he got to his feet and offered her his hand. 'I told you wisdom didn't make for good entertainment, didn't I?'

'What should I do, then? If I don't contact Harry?'

He gave her a wry look. 'For God's sake, don't ask me, do whatever it is you want to do. But don't do whatever it is just because you think it's the right thing to do, or because it's the thing you're expected to do – there is a huge difference between what you want and what is expected.'

'I'm going to see Hope in London tomorrow,' Katherine began.

Ben snorted. 'And for God's sake, whatever you do, don't ask her either. She's been married four times so far and is still looking for the answer. One thing though, if Harry hadn't been made redundant would you have rung him?'

Katherine considered for a few minutes while he stroked stray tendrils of hair back off her face. 'Eventually, I suppose so, there are all sorts of practicalities to be sorted out. So, yes – and I would have expected him to ring me.'

'And has he rung?'

Katherine shook her head.

'So what's changed? The timing's lousy but he could have been made redundant a month from now, two years – any time. Just thank your lucky stars it wasn't just before you decided to ask him to leave.'

'But it's all come at once.'

Ben nodded. 'Always does, I've always considered that God has a very, very sick sense of humour. Fancy a drink?'

'I wouldn't mind.'

'I know a wonderful little place in the woods where they

161

serve a cracking good Australian red, it's not that far from here.'

Katherine grinned. 'Is that the place with the nice terrace and the huge four-poster bed?'

Ben, eyes alight, slipped his arm through hers. 'You know it?'

Carol rang Ray and Geoff before she left the office for home. She had been putting the phone call off all day. Geoff answered, though she could hear Ray in the background adding a line or two.

'We wondered where you'd got to. Harry's fine, we've just sent him down into town to pick up a box of croissants from the deli. You know he thinks we stole his wallet.'

Somewhere close by she heard Ray shriek, 'He thinks *you* stole his wallet. He thinks I'm after his body.'

Carol groaned. 'I'm so sorry about this.'

Geoff laughed. 'Don't be, it's been quite entertaining really and he's cheered up no end since you left him this morning. I think he's going to be okay. We've persuaded him to go into work tomorrow – so the sisters of mercy have pulled it off again. Do you want us to bring something home for dinner?'

'That would be great. What have you got?'

'Quiche and salad all right?'

Out beyond the fish bowl Jeanette was still working at the computer, which was a little disconcerting. 'That'll be just fine. I'll see you when I get there,' she said, tucking folders back into her brief-case. As she put the phone down Jeanette looked back over her shoulder, smiled and got to her feet. Something was wrong.

'I've just finished going through the Blackwood Northampton file,' Jeanette said, opening the office door. 'Do you want me to run you off a copy of the new figures before I go home? Oh and I can't find anything on Kestrel. I thought I'd try Companies House tomorrow.'

Carol glanced suspiciously at her watch. 'It's nearly six.'

Jeanette's expression changed to surprise a few seconds too late for it to be completely genuine. 'Really? I'll just finish up and then I'll be away, it shouldn't take me more than ten minutes.'

Carol looked her up and down, wondering whether this was some attempt to make amends. 'Fine, in that case, I'll see you in the morning.'

Jeanette smiled. 'Right-oh, and don't forget Katherine Jackson. I've got her file out in my tray if you want to take it home?'

Carol shook her head; she really didn't want to know Katherine Jackson's business, just how she had managed to snatch her life back.

'I'll take a look at it first thing tomorrow, she's really Dougie's baby.'

Jeanette counted to fifty after the lift doors closed behind Carol Ackerman and then tapped in Harry Bourne's mobile phone number.

'Hi,' she whispered breathlessly when he answered. 'I just had to ring, I hope you don't mind but I've been thinking about you all day. And about last night – I just can't think about anything else. The way you made me feel, I'm still humming – all over.'

Harry's reply was a guttural groan.

It was nearly dark when Katherine Bourne arrived back with Ben at her house. She wanted to ask him in, but the sight of Sarah's little black car still hunched miserably under the lilacs quickly changed her plans. They lingered in the front seats, neither wanting to leave the other, but it had to be done. Katherine was the first to pull away and open the car door.

'I'll ring you, soon,' Ben promised, as she slithered across the seat.

She leant in to retrieve handbag and one last kiss. 'Good,' she said with a grin, wondering what unlikely miracle had brought Ben into her life when she needed him most. 'You know I'm going down to London tomorrow?'

'All day?'

'I think so.'

'And night?' There was an element of appeal in his voice.

Katherine shrugged. 'I've got no idea what Hope has in mind.'

'Have a good time. I'll ring you Thursday if I can't get you tomorrow – you're still on for the concert at the weekend?'

'Chicken legs and salad, sevenish. You'll pick me up.'

He smiled.

'You know you're really a nice man.'

His face hardened momentarily. 'You're kind – but you don't know anything about me. These days I just try harder.'

Katherine didn't go back into the house straight away, but watched the tail lights of Ben's car moving away, watched them make their way down the lane and out onto the main road. After he had gone the night seemed so still that she could pick out the smell of every flower, every shrub, and clung to the perfumes like a blanket. It did seem strange that a man so whole and so kind hadn't already found someone else to share his life. With a peculiar sense of disconnection she wondered what he was hiding.

'I thought I heard a car.' A square of light splashed out over the gravel from the front door. Katherine looked over her shoulder. Sarah was framed in the doorway. 'Do you have any idea what the time is?'

Ben was right; Sarah had turned into her mother, arms crossed over her chest, face set in a stern mask. 'I cooked dinner,' she snapped. 'I should think it's ruined now – and Peter is here.'

Katherine wheeled round, the heavy scent of honeysuckle

still filling her senses. 'Really? I thought he said he was going to come down later in the week.'

'I rang him after you left. I rang everyone – and no one has got any idea where Dad is. No one's seen him. I think we ought to ring the police. Is alcoholism inherited?'

Katherine looked up. 'I've got no idea, why?'

Sarah sucked her teeth. 'Peter arrived and made straight for the drinks cabinet.'

Katherine sighed; she might join him.

'Hi, Mum,' Peter said as she walked into the kitchen followed by Sarah. He was sitting at the table cradling a bottle of beer. A momentary flash of camaraderie passed between them as their eyes met. 'Have a good day?'

'Wonderful. How about you?'

Peter up-ended the bottle. 'Mine's been shit.' He cast an accusing glance towards his sister who was riding shotgun on them both. 'So what's your new man like?'

Katherine pulled out a chair and sat down opposite him. 'Nice, I think you'd like him. He's a photographer.'

Peter nodded and shook the bottle speculatively. It was empty. 'Fancy a beer?'

Katherine grinned and was rewarded by the slightest twinkle in her son's eyes.

'If you're having one.'

Peter unfolded himself from the table. His limbs were still long and rangy as if he had yet to fill out into a man. He hunkered down in front of the fridge, pulled two bottles out of the cooler and wrung their necks. A hiss of froth lifted in Katherine's bottle as he slid it across the table towards her. 'So where did you go then, anywhere good?'

It was all too much for Sarah. She made an unpleasant sound in the back of her throat.

'We need to talk,' she growled, 'and I don't mean about your bloody fancy man. I'm going to ring the police, and then we'll eat, and then we're going to talk, whether you two like it or not.'

As she turned towards the telephone, Peter raised his beer bottle and without thinking Katherine followed suit.

'Cheers,' he said, tapping the neck of the bottle against hers.

'Cheers,' she said with a wry smile. 'Here's to fewer shitty days.'

'Amen,' murmured Peter.

The police it seemed weren't that interested in Harry's disappearance, despite Sarah's increasingly hysterical pleas. It seemed that adults vanished all the time and most of them turned up eventually. If Sarah would like to come down and file a report. When she had done Sarah hunched over the table beside Peter, while Katherine ladled out a casserole of undistinguished pedigree.

'I don't understand how you can be so calm about all this,' Sarah said staring at her plate. She sounded exhausted.

Katherine sighed. 'Because it's happening to me. I'm at the sharp end. I was the one who asked your father to leave.'

Sarah pushed her food away. 'But what I don't understand is why?'

'Oh, for God's sake, Sarah, it happens all the time, surely you must have seen it coming,' Peter said.

Sarah glared at him. 'No, I didn't. I thought they were happy.'

'Happy? So when was that then?' His voice had dropped to a childish whine. 'All Dad ever thinks about is work and golf.'

Sarah snorted. 'So *she* can have a nice house. Some one had to pay for it you know, it doesn't just happen.'

'You always think you know everything,' snapped Peter. 'He was never here – never – not for Mum, not for any of us. He was always away on business trips or locked upstairs in his bloody office. Or out with that idiot George banging a ball around a field. You just want to find him a nice comfortable excuse for years of ignoring the fact that we existed.'

Sarah's face contorted into a snarl, voice lifting in fury. 'He didn't ignore me. You're just jealous that he always liked me the best. You're so bloody childish. You never could stand on your own two feet.'

Katherine looked from one to the other, feeling as if she had suddenly become invisible. All pretence at adulthood had slithered away, they were back in the nursery.

'Oh right,' growled Peter. 'Childish, am I? So who's down here trying to patch it all up. Let's all play happy families and make pretend this isn't happening.'

Katherine took a forkful of casserole – it wasn't as bad as it looked.

The phone rang and before anyone else could move Katherine was on her feet, fork in hand, and answered it. She listened silently to the caller and then held the phone out towards Sarah. 'It's your father, perhaps you'd like to speak to him.'

Sarah took the phone into the hall and talked while Peter and Katherine picked over their supper in silence.

Sarah had squared her shoulders and pulled herself upright by the time she came back in. 'He just rang to let me know that he's all right. He didn't say where he was staying but he wants to come and pick his things up at the weekend. He rang my flat first. I left a message on the machine telling him he could get me here.' She looked unpleasantly triumphant.

Katherine had a fork halfway to her mouth and was aware that it was still there, caught in midair. 'Did he say anything else?'

Sarah shook her head. 'No. He told me not to be too upset and that he had got no idea that you drank. Though he didn't sound that surprised.'

*   *   *

Harry had phoned home while Carol was in the shower, surreptitiously, watching the stairwell while he dialled the number. He wasn't sure what was making him feel so furtive, but it struck him it had much more to do with Jeanette's unexpected second phone call than Carol or Katherine. He'd been frustrated to find Sarah not at home; he had seen her as his staunchest potential ally. She had sounded as if she was upset but holding it all back.

It came as a surprise to hear that Katherine had a drink problem but then again that would explain her erratic behaviour. For the first time since leaving he wondered if it was wise to go home; perhaps he ought to see a solicitor first. He had an image of Katherine huddled up in a grey plastic institutional chair, drooling, as he signed the papers that would put her away. He would have to get a house-keeper. He wondered if Jeanette might be interested in the position.

Carol was quite surprised how easily the evening had gone. Ray and Geoff had delivered Harry home, after she got back from work, together with supper on a tray. Harry had seemed preoccupied and she had resisted the temptation to ask him about the night he spent in London and his redundancy. Consequently the conversation had been very stilted over the quiche but he didn't seem to have been that worried.

Showered and wrapped up in a robe, Carol settled herself down in the armchair alongside where Harry had unfurled himself onto the sofa. He was watching a film on ITV.

'So did you have a good day then?' she ventured during the commercial break. It was a stupid thing to say but she felt she had to say something.

He looked up, eyes unfocused for a few seconds. 'Uh?'

Carol sighed. 'I wonder how it went today? At the café?'

Harry stretched. 'Not bad, not bad, I should probably have gone into work though. I'll go in tomorrow. I mean, what does it amount to other than cleaning my desk out? I'd better get it over and done with. Bastards.'

She'd opened Pandora's box. 'What sort of deal have they offered you?' she asked as casually as she could. Now the box was open, she could hardly ignore the contents.

Harry shifted position. 'Golden handshake, retraining – access to some sort of executive vacancy hot line thing – usual greasy pole package. I suppose I've got to do it, though. Jumping through their fur-lined hoops will mean another month's money, and it'll give me another month up in town.'

She really wanted him to tell her that he had been ringing round all day trying to pull in old favours, searching out a new job, sniffing his way doggedly back towards employment and a bright shiny new future, but realised it was early days, he had hardly had time to stop reeling from the news.

'Do you think there might be a position for you on the new management team? These companies often hire back once the dust has settled.'

Harry's face hardened. 'That was one of the options but I wouldn't work for those bastards for a bloody –' his voice faded – presumably he had had a pension.

Thin ice. Carol nodded and retreated gingerly toward the shore-line. 'So have you got any plans for what else you might do?' She didn't want to shake the jar of wasps but felt seeing him so comfortable on her sofa obligated her to do something.

Harry's concentration was being drawn back to the TV screen where the opening credits were being flashed up for part three. He eased off his shoes with his toes.

'Something will turn up,' he said grimly, retrieving a can of beer from under the sofa. 'Oh and I've arranged to go and collect my things at the weekend. Could you see about hiring a van?'

'A van?' Carol repeated.

Harry nodded, eyes now firmly fixed on the muscular torso of a young Clint Eastwood. 'Yes, nothing too big, a Transit should do. Oh and I might be home late tomorrow night so maybe you could cook a casserole or something?' He turned the sound up another notch and took a hefty pull on the can. 'Then again I think maybe I'll eat out; one last crack at the expense account. Serves the bastards right.' Without looking he fumbled the can back down onto the floor amongst a pile of newspapers. 'Oh and Ray showed me where you drop your laundry off, they're going to iron those shirts for me. I've arranged to pick one up on the way in to work tomorrow.'

He was digging in. Carol picked up the newspaper to see what time the film finished.

Chapter Fourteen

Katherine Bourne went to bed well before midnight, leaving her children engaged in what amounted to a dog fight. She would have liked the chance to talk to Peter alone, but Sarah had seen that possibility coming and so hung on, refusing to go upstairs, crouched on the sofa with her feet curled up under her, heavy-eyed but not missing a trick. Katherine had finally conceded defeat and gone to bed with a headache. It felt as if a lifetime had passed since her glorious afternoon in bed with Ben Morton.

Peter said he understood her reasons for finally wanting to leave Harry. She had the right to make the choice and he seemed relieved that she had. But as he and Sarah squared up to each other Katherine realised that Peter didn't really see it so clearly at all, he was just using the situation to score points off his sister. Though at least he was trying to make the right noises.

Sarah, by contrast, refused to listen to anything except for her own voice and snapped off every sentence that she didn't initiate. She saw no sense in it at all; after all Katherine and Harry had been together so long, why should they want to change things now? What was the point? What was so wrong with what they had? What was it that Katherine wanted that her father didn't already provide? Although it was the nub of the argument and Katherine recognised that, it was such a nebulous thing that Katherine couldn't find an answer that satisfied herself, let alone Sarah.

Like a word repeated over and over again until it loses its meaning, Katherine saw that at the heart of Sarah's argument was the fact that her daughter believed that eventually any marriage, any long-term relationship, was much the same as another. Two people, a home, shared responsibility. Wasn't one man really much the same as the next? Katherine shook her head, her reasons lost in a maze of semantics. Nothing was that simple. Listening to her, Katherine knew that Sarah had never been in love, if she had she would already know all the answers.

Sarah, talking in a strident classroom voice, still seemed to believe that if she argued Harry's case long enough, the status quo would be miraculously restored and her father would reappear, unbidden, at the door, and everything would be exactly as it had been before.

Katherine dropped her clothes into the linen basket in the bathroom and crawled into bed, feeling immeasurably old. There was a life after Harry, she just couldn't make up her mind what shape it was going to be. One thing she did know was that she couldn't begin to make sense of it all until Sarah and Peter went away and got on with their own lives.

Katherine dreamt she was running alone along an isolated beach looking for a dog. Sometimes she caught a glimpse of it, no more than a tousled grey snout, pushing up from amongst the rocks, but every time she got too close the dog vanished – so quickly that she couldn't really see what it was she was chasing. Although frustrating the game was really quite pleasant. She laughed as a furry head popped up from behind a breakwater and beaded her with one large brown eye.

Barefoot, gulls mewling overhead, she rounded a promontory and realised the dog was playing hide and seek, and if she could only stop herself from running after him he would come to her. She stood still, fighting the compulsion to give chase. Slowly from amongst the boulders a huge hairy mongrel sloped towards her, eyes bright, tail wagging. He looked remarkably like Ben Morton.

He settled by her feet and without thinking she bent

down to catch hold of him. The moment her fingers brushed his collar, he made a run for the open ocean. At the water's edge he changed effortlessly into a seal and slid beneath the surf – and she knew as the waves broke over his slick, wet body, that she would never see him again.

She woke with a start; the dream convinced her that whatever shape her new life grew into it wouldn't include Ben Morton.

Tucked up in Cambridge, Carol dreamt of going away for the weekend to York. It stunned her as she walked into the foyer of a long forgotten hotel to realise that she was with Harry Bourne – and that he looked quite beautiful. He slipped his arms around her waist as they signed the register.

'God, you look almost edible, it seems as if I've been waiting so long for this,' he whispered in her ear. 'I can't wait to get you upstairs.'

She had smiled and rubbed up against him. What was more stunning was that somewhere deep inside she felt a great flame of desire ignite and catch hold. The dream was so vivid that she could hear the tick-tick-tick of the clock on the wall behind the reception desk.

As she looked up into Harry's eyes she realised with surprise that she had wanted this Harry. Some part of her, some part long hidden, long forgotten, had imagined building a life with him. Close by the clock picked out the rhythm of her heart and she wondered briefly if it was the echo of the biological clock Harry said he had heard.

Her eyes snapped open and she found herself in her bedroom, sitting bolt upright in the gloom. The tick-tick-tick that followed her out of the dream was the sound of her alarm clock echoing in the hollow space beneath her bed, where she had hidden it to keep it out of Harry's clutches.

Beside her, arms locked around his pillow, Harry was

snoring softly – except that this wasn't the Harry in her dream. In her dream she had felt something far more potent than resignation – much more. She shuffled down beside him, pulling the tangle of sheets up over her shoulders, and wondered what on earth could have happened since that distant weekend in York.

Somewhere in the spaces that filled up the last ten years they had started to take each other for granted; Harry had come to assume that she would always be waiting for him, just a phone call away, and she had assumed that he would always ring – and assumption kills passion.

Once, she had almost let herself fall hopelessly in love with the old Harry Bourne, not this Harry, but the one who had pulled her down into bed, eyes alight with desire and love. The Harry who had surprised her with flowers and tickets for a show, a strong, handsome, reckless laughing Harry who had lifted her into his arms, begging her to stay just a little longer. The Harry that had promised her so much.

Something must have made her pull back from the edge. Memories trickled down her spine like iced water. There had been a time when she had wanted to be with him all the time, when she resented his leaving, when every time the phone rang she hoped it would be him, when even the sight of him had made her stomach flutter.

When had she taught herself to suppress those feelings or had they just worn thin under the slow dripping tap of familiarity? While her emotional life was on hold the clock had tick-tick-ticked away.

She had a vivid recollection of acute biting broodiness, terrible lonely times when she had struggled to ignore the beat of a primeval drum. What she had been left with instead was an abstract sense of loss and betrayal.

So why was it when Harry had run out of excuses for leaving his wife, she had found him one? Carol closed her eyes, squeezing a phalanx of tears into submission. Wasn't this their last chance? Perhaps Harry was right after all, perhaps she was afraid of commitment.

She had no sense of joy that he had finally left his wife, just a nagging resentment. The time for joy had passed, neatly tidied away with all those other intense distant dreams. She glanced across at his tumble of gingery hair.

Carol swallowed hard; maybe they had just left it too late.

She had stopped herself from falling hopelessly in love and settled for convenience instead. Stopped herself from demanding anything important from Harry and in doing so, the possibility of real love and a real life with a real man had melted away almost unnoticed. What they had built between them, although she had never seen it in quite that light before, had slowly changed into not much more than a business arrangement. And by turning up at her house Harry Bourne was in breach of contract.

In London while the other two women slept, Jeanette was busy consigning a clutch of polystyrene cartons, some still complete with the remains of the burgers in them, into the black polythene bag at her feet. She stopped for a few seconds and glanced around the flat. It was nearly one o'clock in the morning and finally everywhere looked spotless.

Her flatmate, Carly, yawned. 'So what's he like then, this new bloke of yours?'

Jeanette picked up the Hoover and headed out towards the hall. 'None of your business.'

The sound of Carly grunting followed her. 'Oh, come on, Jen. I've just spent the whole bloody night clearing the place up to impress him – and I've already said I'll make myself scarce tomorrow night. I deserve a bit of background info – don't be so bloody mean.'

Jeanette prised a gobbet of gum off the table near the telephone. 'Distinguished,' she said, over her shoulder.

Carly, leaning against the doorpost, pulled a face. 'Old, you mean. I didn't have you down as the sugar-daddy type. What about Bas? I thought that was getting serious.'

Jeanette opened the hall cupboard and shuffled the Hoover and the rubbish bag inside. Bas, whom she had been going out with for almost a year, had a good job in accounts, and had started to talk seriously about them living together. He'd gone on, over a Chinese take-away, to talk about the amount of money they would be able to borrow to buy a flat. His big mistake had been including her salary in the equation.

They saw each other at the weekends and sometimes on a Wednesday – if he wasn't playing squash – she'd already rung to tell him that this week she was having a night out with the girls.

Carly yawned again. 'I don't know about you but I'm totally and utterly whacked. I just hope this guy's worth all the effort. I'm off to bed. Let me know how it goes tomorrow night.'

Jeanette bundled up dusters and spray polish, and threw then in behind the Hoover. 'Where are you going to stay?'

Carly tapped the side of her nose. 'Never you mind, you aren't the only one with a bit of married fluff on her sleeve.'

Jeanette reddened. 'I didn't say he was married.'

Carly turned on her heel. 'You didn't have to. Mine's got a dinky little *pied-à-terre* that he uses during the week. I'm sure he wouldn't mind a bit of unexpected company.'

Jeanette stared at her. 'What about that new bloke you've been seeing?'

Carly peered round her bedroom door and winked conspiratorially. 'You aren't the only one who can keep a secret, you know. Enjoy –'

Jeanette took another look round the hall. She'd put flowers in a bowl on the coat stand and bundled all the old shoes and boots into the cupboard underneath. Above, casting a reflection onto the freshly Hoovered carpet, was a new pink tasselled lampshade, hiding the bare bulb in the hall that had shared her life since she moved in. Slowly she moved from room to room, viewing everything with a critical eye, checking that everywhere looked, if not completely tidy, then at least under control.

The final touch was a clothes horse in the bathroom on which she hung a row of immaculately laundered fluffy white towels, bought from Debenhams on the way home from work, and recently collected from the service wash at the laundrette on the corner. Alongside them she unfolded two white cotton blouses, a lacy slip and a pair of perfectly pressed trousers. They all shared the same origin. The woman had made a great job. Worth every penny. Jeanette looked at them thoughtfully and then threw a crumpled sheet out of the airing cupboard over the whole ensemble in case Carly made the mistake of using the towels first thing in the morning – couldn't be too careful.

Next to the boiler, still in their cellophane wrappers, was a new pair of sheets, new pillow cases and a matching white lace duvet cover. Jeanette brushed her teeth, set the alarm an hour early so she would have the chance to strip her bed and shave her legs before work, snapped off the light and curled up under the covers. She was asleep in seconds. What remained of her night was completely dreamless.

The following morning Carol didn't wait for Harry to offer to take her to the station or to drive her into work. She planned to catch the early train and was all ready to leave before he was even out of the bathroom.

'What's up?' he said, still stripped to the waist, chin covered in a swirl of shaving foam.

Carol snapped her brief-case closed. 'I've got a breakfast meeting. You'll have to get a taxi to the station or if you nip next door I'm sure Ray or Geoff will run you down there.'

Harry sniffed. 'You didn't mention it last night. You know I might be late home?' He flicked his razor through the ice floes of foam in the sink. 'There is a very remote possibility that I may not get home at all.'

Carol noticed that he had lowered his eyes and wondered if perhaps he intended to go home to Katherine after all.

'Whatever,' she said airily. 'I'm off. See you later. Have a good day.' She hovered for a second, wondering if she ought to kiss him goodbye, a Judas kiss. She shivered and smiled instead. 'So, I'm off then.'

Harry caught her eye in the mirror. 'I've been meaning to ask if you've got a spare key.'

Carol stopped mid-stride. 'Er, no, I'm afraid I haven't,' she said as casually as she could.

Harry, who had returned his attention to scything another swathe through the foam on his chin, said, 'It might be a good idea to get another one cut on the way home.'

Carol said nothing, just hoisted her bag and her brief-case up under her arm and headed downstairs. She really needed to talk to Katherine Jackson. Downstairs the cats were sitting on the outside windowsill and caught her attention with an ugly stare.

'I'm doing the best I can,' she snapped.

She arrived in the office before the last of the cleaners had left.

Katherine Bourne, née Jackson, stared at the contents of her wardrobe, running a thoughtful finger along the hangers, trying to work out what to wear for her trip to London. Perhaps she ought to take a bag with a change of clothes in it for her evening with Hope. Her old clothes looked dull and safe – chrysalis clothes. She looked at the bedside clock, wondering if she had time to go into town and buy something new before her train left – until recently clothes had played so little part in her everyday life.

A navy cardigan slithered gracelessly onto the floor. Frumpy, she thought and then allowed herself a wry smile. She picked up the outfit she had worn to meet Ben for lunch.

'Mum?' Peter's voice percolated up the stairs and through into her bedroom. 'Have we got any muesli anywhere?'

'Top shelf, in the pantry, in a glass jar, on the right,' she replied without having to think about the answer. She pulled the hanger out and decided, even though it really was too casual for a business meeting, the outfit said more about the woman she was discovering she was than anything else that was in the wardrobe.

Downstairs Sarah and Peter appeared to have agreed a breakfast truce. Katherine wished them both good morning without meeting their eye and then poured herself a glass of orange juice.

'So what time will you be home?' said Sarah, tipping cornflakes into a bowl.

Katherine shrugged. 'No idea. There's really nothing either of you can do here.' She braced herself, wondering if she had said enough to inadvertently light the blue touch paper.

Peter was the one who looked up indignantly. 'Are you planning to stay out all night?' he said, from amongst a mouthful of muesli.

Katherine sighed. 'No, I'm just saying that I've got no idea what time I'll be back – I've got one appointment at lunch-time and another later today and –' she stopped. She didn't need to justify her actions or her movements to either of them. 'So don't wait up, if you're still here.'

She didn't take the old brief-case that Harry had discarded, just the folder of Ben's photos tucked inside her handbag alongside the figures that the man at Lactons had already drawn up for her.

During the train ride to London she pretended she commuted into the city every day, and that she was heading to her office, which was so familiar that she knew every face, every file, every shelf.

When the train went through a tunnel she caught sight of her reflection in the dusty windows; she looked like someone who worked in something creative, an established artist or a designer, or maybe, she thought with a small private smile, a social worker. She tugged at a stray wisp of hair that curled under her jaw. What exactly did she want to be when she grew up?

King's Cross was busy, all those people streaming away from the platforms to their jobs, all with families, mortgages and cars, bills and worries of their own. She had arrived far too early for her lunch date with Carol Ackerman, so she took the tube to Covent Garden and wandered in and out of the shops and street performers in the old market, feeling horribly alien and contentedly alone by turns. She wandered down Neal Street and then turned and walked back out onto the Strand; a sentimental journey down past the hotel where she and Harry had spent the first night of their honeymoon.

Every view looked like a potential picture postcard, bright and sharp in the summer sunshine.

She glanced inside the hotel lobby, wondering whether she ought to go in and have a coffee there, a supplication to the gods of the past, a final act of atonement – instead she crossed the road and headed towards the Savoy.

In the heart of the city she could have been anyone she wanted, and one thing was certain: she wasn't the nervous little creature, totally overawed by the idea of staying in a hotel, let alone one in London, who had walked into the Strand Palace on Harry's arm all those years ago.

It had been Harry had who had taken on the imperious receptionist, Harry who had arranged for champagne to be delivered to their room. But then Harry had seemed like a friend then, a lover, an equal, a co-conspirator, someone whom she wanted to be with – a man she loved.

She remembered they had stood at the desk, she a little behind him, blushing furiously, feeling terribly self-conscious in her going away suit. He had signed the register and then slipped an arm around her.

'God, you look almost edible, it seems as if I've been waiting so long for this,' he whispered in her ear. 'I can't wait to get you upstairs.'

Upstairs in an anonymous room, she had giggled as the champagne eased its way mischievously into her blood-stream. Drunk on high spirits, standing by the window with the afternoon sunlight splashing the carpet gold, Harry had toasted them both.

'To paradise, Kitty-Kat, to you and I, and bloody para-dise. This is how it should be, me and you in a place like this.' He had patted the bed, eyes alight with tenderness and desire. 'God, I love you so much, Kitty-Kat.'

She shivered, old images walking without heed across her grave. She looked at the doors into the Savoy and decided it would be better to stay out in the sunshine after all. She really didn't need to be locked away from the sunlight, not with a head full of ghosts. She bought a sand-wich and a take-away coffee and headed for St James's Park – much better to stay out in the open where she could see things creeping up on her.

Chapter Fifteen

Katherine arrived ten minutes early for her appointment with Carol Ackerman, and hovered about in the foyer wondering whether to go up or not. The receptionist made her mind up for her.

'Ms Ackerman says she will see you now,' she said, indicating the lift. Katherine nodded and headed upstairs.

Carol Ackerman seemed genuinely pleased to see her as she got up from her desk to shake hands. 'Why don't you take a seat. How are you plans coming along?'

'. . . I thought we could talk more comfortably over an early lunch, I've booked a table at a nice place – it's just round the corner,' Carol said, fifteen minutes later.

Katherine had been watching Carol with great interest since the secretary had showed her into the office. The financial expert did not look well. There were dark hollow circles under her eyes. Katherine had spread the documents she brought to London all over the desk, and they had talked about what she had planned, but she sensed that Carol didn't really want to talk business. It seemed to Katherine that Carol Ackerman was feeling her way tentatively towards the edges of another very different conversation. She was relieved because in some ways she didn't want to talk shop either.

Across the table Carol lifted her hand to embrace the photographs and the financial projections. 'Well, as far as I'm concerned, this all looks fine. Dougie is a good man, he'll lead you step by step through the whole process. There really shouldn't be any problems as long as the valuation works out. That has to be your next step. We can organise that for you, if you'd like –' She paused, gnawing at her bottom lip, and when she spoke again the tone was uncertain. 'So other than your plans for the house, how's life going? I assume by the fact that you're here on your own, you've managed to persuade your partner to leave?'

Katherine shuffled uncomfortably under Carol's scrutiny. 'Yes, yes, I have.'

Carol reddened. 'Right. Well, in that case time for lunch then –' She stopped.

Katherine gathered up the paperwork and photos. 'Is there something the matter? You don't look well.'

Carol took a breath as if she was about to speak and then swallowed the words down. For one moment Katherine thought the other woman was going to cry and reached out to touch her. Carol leapt back, as if struggling to retain her composure.

'No, really, it doesn't matter,' she said decisively. 'Did you bring a coat?' Carol painted on an unconvincing professional smile and waved her towards the door. 'Shall we go?'

'What is it you *really* want to talk about?' said Katherine, realising she was crossing an invisible frontier.

Carol shivered, her shoulders dropping, the last vestiges of restraint slipping away.

'Men,' she said in an undertone.

Over the entrée in Carlotta's restaurant, two streets away from Lactons' office, Carol topped up Katherine's glass. The wine had helped loosen Carol's tongue. 'This is so unprofessional, but I need to talk to someone, and I thought – well, I thought that you might understand. I hope you don't mind. I could do with some impartial advice,' Carol said slowly, reaching round to find the right words.

'I may not be the one to talk to, I'm really not very

experienced with relationships. Honestly. My own life is far from crystal clear – but I'd be happy to listen.'

With no names, no pack drill, Carol began to tell Katherine about Harry. She tried to keep it brief. Katherine said nothing, watching Carol, eyes bright.

'The thing is,' Carol concluded, draining the last of her wine, 'I feel incredibly guilty. For years I suppose we have had an unspoken agreement – now he's finally left his wife and I realise I don't want him.'

Katherine looked pained. 'He just assumed he could come and live with you. Did he ask? Talk about it? It seems a very arrogant thing to do.'

Carol refilled their glasses. 'God, if only you knew him. He's like that with everything. He's driving me crazy.'

'You've got to tell him to leave.'

'It's that easy?'

Katherine worked her knife down through a plump lamb chop. 'No. I'm afraid not. It took me years to get around to saying it out loud. You have to be really clear about what you want.'

'Yes,' said Carol, leaning forward. 'But you know that you've done the right thing, don't you?' Her expression was intense; she so wanted to feel Katherine Jackson had made the right decision.

To her relief Katherine nodded. 'Oh yes, it was the right thing to do, but that doesn't make it any easier. I still feel as if I'm walking around inside some sort of dream. I keep expecting real life to begin any moment now.' She smiled. 'The worst thing is that since he left I keep coming across all these terrible stray memories. People have said it before, but the man I asked to leave really wasn't the same man I married. He had changed so much, though I suppose to be fair, we both have. That was the problem.'

Carol sighed, running her fingers through her hair. 'God, I know exactly what you mean. Harry used to be such a wonderful guy, great fun to be with, good company – or at least I always thought so. I'm not sure now whether he really was or whether I just imagined it. It's hard to see anything clearly.'

Katherine swallowed hard. 'Harry?'

'Yes, that's right, Harry. That's his name.'

Katherine laughed nervously.

'Why, what's the matter?'

'Nothing, just someone walking over my grave. My husband's name was Harry – is Harry.'

Both women looked down at their lunches.

'I know you're right though,' said Carol, quickly glossing over the uncomfortable coincidence. 'I've got to ask him to go. I do know that – I've tried, but I don't think he's heard a single word I've said. Maybe I'm being too subtle. He's got a skin like a rhino.'

Katherine snorted. 'Mine too.'

'The other problem is that I'm not sure I can ask him at the moment. He's going through a rough time at work. It seems so cruel to do this to him as well.'

'My Harry is having problems too. I planned to ring him but I'm so afraid of finding myself inviting him back. The words might come out before I have had a chance to think.' Katherine smiled. 'So, you see, I'm not exactly in control either. What happened to your Harry?'

'He was made redundant on Monday. After fifteen years with the same –' Carol looked up; Katherine Jackson's face was very still. She had her mouth open just a fraction too wide. Slowly she defrosted and laid down her fork beside her plate.

'Redundant?'

Carol nodded. 'That's right. He's completely gutted. That's why I feel I can't –'

'What is your Harry's other name?' Katherine enunciated the words carefully, before Carol could finish her sentence.

'Bourne,' said Carol, feeling something contract in her

185

stomach. 'Harry Bourne. He worked for Kestrel, it's a computer –' she stopped.

Across the table the last shred of colour had drained from Katherine's Jackson's face.

'My God,' Katherine hissed, her eyes not leaving Carol's. 'I had no idea.'

'No idea?' Carol repeated carefully.

'No idea at all. Why didn't I see it? All those years?' She looked into Carol's face and answered her mute enquiry. 'I'm Harry's wife,' she said slowly. 'I'm Katherine Bourne.'

There was a strange hungry pause when both women considered the implications of what they had just discovered – and then – as often happens when two minds bite down on a single thought, they began to speak as one – and then both fell silent.

Katherine lifted a hand in a magnanimous gesture of invitation, after all she was rid of Harry. 'After you,' she said.

Carol opened her mouth to speak and, finding no words, only total astonishment, left it open.

Katherine shook her head in disbelief. 'The sly miserable little bastard.'

'But he told me he had left you,' Carol spluttered. 'He said he'd finally worked up the courage, after all these years – he said . . .' her voice faded.

Katherine picked up her handbag and began rooting through the contents. A second or two later she triumphantly produced a business card from her purse. 'Here we are, Carol Ackerman, Loans Adviser.' She waved it under Carol's nose. 'I contacted you because of this. I rang you and made an appointment because of Harry. I found your card in his suit pocket – after he had been away for the weekend with his firm.'

Carol struggled to find something to say. 'He went to Paris.'

Katherine nodded. 'That's right. He flew home early because he thought I was ill.'

Carol sighed. 'Were you?'

'No, just terribly hungover.' Katherine laughed and turned to track down the waiter. 'You were with him, weren't you? In Paris?'

Carol reddened. 'It was a conference with some Germans, he told them I was his secretary – I was so angry –' She paused trying to gather her thoughts back up into a neat pile. 'When we got to the airport I tried to give my business card to their CEO and Harry pocketed it.'

Katherine waved the waiter over to their table. Carol watched her, quite dumbfounded.

'Champagne,' Katherine said in a clear crisp voice.

Carol stared at her. 'Champagne?'

'Why not? I think we ought to celebrate. You are quite the best thing Harry has given me in years. What shall we drink to?' asked Katherine, as the waiter uncorked the bottle.

'Murder?' suggested Carol.

Katherine grinned. 'Don't be so ridiculous, death is far too good for Harry.'

In a chic little boutique just off Oxford Street, Jeanette, who had taken an early lunch, craned round trying to look at the back of the dress in the cubicle mirror and then pouted. It was exactly the sort of outfit she had in mind for her date, but was a lot more expensive than she'd planned. She tugged unconsciously at the hem, weighing whether or not Harry Bourne was worth the investment.

The shop assistant, tucked away behind a glass and chrome counter, gave her a condescending glance and carried on reading her magazine.

Jeanette didn't invite her approval. She turned again, still considering. It was important that the dress wasn't too obvious, chic, subtle but sexy was what she had in mind.

The little black wool number clung to every curve, covering every inch right up to her neck, not a smidgen of flesh showed but it groaned with sexual promise. She studied her reflection thoughtfully. The dress reminded her of gift wrapping.

It took a few more minutes for her to decide. 'Okay. I'll take it.'

'On your lunch hour?' asked the assistant conversationally, as Jeanette flashed her plastic.

Jeanette laughed, wanting to score points. 'No, actually we're over from Paris. I'm on a photo shoot for one of the Parisian magazines. *Street Fashions*.'

The girl lifted an eyebrow. 'Oh, I'm sorry, are you a model?'

Jeanette tucked her credit card back into her wallet. 'Who me? Good God, no,' she said dismissively but without emotion. 'I've got more brains. No, I'm the artistic director, but we decided to stay on for an extra night, so I thought I'd pick up something cheap and cheerful to wear for dinner.'

The girl sniffed.

It wasn't quite a unanimous decision but Jeanette felt she had won on points and sashayed back out into the summer sunshine. She really ought to be heading back to Lactons; time perhaps though to find a pair of shoes.

Meanwhile, Harry Bourne had spent most of the morning in the staff canteen at Kestrel listening to some woman in a caftan talking about the healing power of seeing yourself in a positive light. In bright blue block capitals on a white board above a stack of crockery, their guru had written: 'This is your new beginning, a chance to redefine your life. Embrace change.'

Harry's stomach rumbled dramatically. He'd had to leave without breakfast. With all this moving around and upheaval his whole constitution was out of sorts. He really needed All-Bran and orange juice. A belch crept up uninvited from under his pristine white shirt.

He glanced down at the photocopied schedule that his secretary had handed him when he arrived. Apparently in the afternoon they were to be subjected to a lecture from someone who called himself Alvin P. Woodruff Junior, on the compilation of a CV that reflected your present life goals.

Harry swallowed down the taste of bile that filled his mouth. His present life goal was to get his arse down to the pub and sink a couple of pints and a pie. It hadn't escaped his notice that Paterson, little threadbare arse-licking weasel, was still at work in the corner office. Apparently Paterson had already had his life goals defined for him – a job with Danic's new management team. He'd probably been put in charge of backstabbing and brown-nosing.

Harry wondered if Carol had finished her early meeting, perhaps he ought to give her a ring and see if he could persuade her to buy him lunch. After all, she still had an expense account.

He tapped his pockets thoughtfully. Ray and Geoff had lent him the train fare and a tenner on top. His secretary had said, after pointing out that she wasn't strictly his any more, that she would chase up his new bank cards, but until they arrived he was high and dry.

'So, are there any questions?' asked the woman in the caftan. Harry blinked; it seemed that he had missed the end of her talk. There was no applause, no one moved or lifted a hand in reply to her bright invitation. She smiled as if it was exactly the response she had expected.

'Well, in that case I think it's high time we all had some lunch. I'd like to remind you all that my office door is always open. Please come in and see me if you feel the need to talk. Remember my name is Cassius.' Harry wondered if he had misheard.

Her head bobbed up and down as she tried to strike up eye contact with the men huddled miserably around the Formica tables. 'Letitia Cassius, and I am here for you, if you need me.'

Behind her, the doors to the kitchen were slowly opening and plump women in hairnets were pushing out trolleys with buffet food arranged on them. It appeared that Danic believed in taking good care of the men they had condemned to the scaffold.

Harry got to his feet, picked up the self-help pack that Letitia had given them all as they arrived and headed smartly for the door. He glanced up at the clock – his reasons for wanting to ring Carol were manyfold – and not least among them was the fact that to talk to Carol he would first have to talk to Jeanette.

He hurried downstairs and then across the car park to the main office block. It appeared that his secretary had already scuttled off to whichever shadowy corner of the building it was she ate her egg sandwiches. Everywhere around him things were being shifted; there was the most disturbing sense of restlessness and an all-pervading smell of gloss paint.

He leant over her desk and pressed the button on the phone that would give him an outside line. As he pushed open his office door, he was surprised to find two men inside, dressed in smart new overalls with the Kestrel logo embroidered on the pocket. They were measuring up his floor. Harry froze.

The taller of the two men pushed his cap further back on his head. 'New carpet,' he said philosophically. 'It'll look real nice in here when we've done.'

Instinctively Harry stepped back – the name plate had gone off his desk, and as he glanced down at the door, he pulled his hand away as if it was red hot – they had removed his name from there too. He had already vanished and nobody had bothered to tell him.

A hand dropped onto his shoulder. 'Hi there. How can I help you?' said a voice with the slightest trace of an American accent.

Harry swung round, beads of sweat breaking out on his top lip.

'My office,' he mumbled, looking across into the bright eyes of a young man in an expensive suit. Beside the man was a security guard. Harry instinctively took another step back.

The man smiled pleasantly. 'Mine now actually. I think you'll find you're all based in the canteen for the time being.'

Harry choked. 'My phone, my things –'

The man nodded. 'Not a problem, Amanda in personnel will have had them all bagged up and ready for you to collect.'

Harry struggled to take another breath. 'That is not how it's done.'

The man, who had still got his hand on Harry's shoulder and was far too close for comfort, smiled again with his perfect set of lily-white caps.

'We've found it's a far more efficient system.'

'Efficient?' Harry whispered.

'Oh yes,' said the man, guiding him away from the office door, accompanied by his uniformed attendant. 'In the past we've observed that at the point of changeover, when a company is radically down-sized, we typically lose between three and seven per cent of short-term consumables, and almost as much hardware. Laptops, phones, even whole computer systems. By the way have you handed over your company car yet?' The man was propelling him gently but firmly towards the lift. 'We're talking large-scale theft here.'

Harry stiffened. 'You little bastard – I wasn't going to steal anything, if you are implying –'

The man lifted a hand to silence him. 'Not you, not

you at all, but people, people walking by, people passing through – other people.' His tone was conciliatory, pitched just a notch or two above patronising.

Harry clenched his fists, fighting the temptation to chin the smug little bastard.

His things were in the canteen, at the back, on a long trestle table, packed neatly inside two red plastic storage boxes, alongside everybody else's. On top in an envelope marked private and personal, were his new credit cards. He conceded gracelessly and ate their buffet lunch. Just as they were about to be served with coffee Alvin P. Woodruff Junior arrived clutching his clipboard.

Harry glanced down at the bulge in his jacket pocket, he'd completely forgotten about the mobile phone. It was too late to ring Carol now. He slumped down into the nearest plastic chair. On the little dais Alvin P. Woodruff Junior, who had an awful lot of hair, smiled benignly.

'Well, hello,' he purred. Like the boy in the main office block, Alvin had a soft nasal American accent and spoke at a level that meant his audience had to crane forward to pick up what he was saying. 'Now, what we're going to do this afternoon is go round the room and one at a time we are going to tell everyone a little bit about ourselves. Now, who wants to start?'

Harry looked heavenwards and slid lower in his seat. It seemed that Alvin had chosen the man in the chair next door to Harry as his first victim. The man made an unpleasant growling sound in the back of his throat. Harry sympathised.

Alvin, who had composed his face into an impassive mask, nodded sagely. 'It's good to get all the aggression out, but why don't we think of something more positive to focus on now. Tell me exactly what it is that you're thinking.'

The man, who Harry seemed to remember was something in product planning, was on his feet in an instant.

'Fuck off,' he barked and headed for the door.

Alvin smiled benignly as the door slammed shut. 'Action is power,' he said and then waved a hand towards Harry. 'Now, what would you like to share with the group?'

Harry glanced around the room, his eyes finally settling on the trestle table. He couldn't think of anything weighty to share and instead said the first thing that came into his head.

'I wanted to empty my own desk,' he whined in a petulant voice straight from the playground.

There was a murmur of assent from the rest of the men.

Alvin smiled. 'That's good, that's really good. I think everyone here can relate to those feelings of having your personal space violated. Would you like to tell about those feelings, Harry – it is Harry, isn't it?'

Chapter Sixteen

Katherine pushed away her dessert plate, scraped clean of the remains of the pavlova. She dipped the last plump strawberry, a succulent garnish, into her champagne flute and then dropped it into her mouth.

'God, that was absolutely wonderful,' she said throwing her napkin onto the table.

'What am I going to say to Harry when he gets home?' Carol said. She licked a stray drip of chocolate sauce off her lip. Her face was still unnaturally pale which accentuated the dark circles under her eyes.

Katherine stretched. 'I know what I'd like to say to him.'

Carol looked down at her last profiterole as if it might be the very oracle she needed. 'Please, Katherine, I know you've got rid of him, but I would really appreciate your help. I can't believe it – he's got such a bloody nerve.'

'And a skin like a bull rhino. It won't matter what you say to him, he won't hear you. You could move house, change all the locks.'

'He hasn't got a key.'

'Keep it that way.' Katherine paused, her attention fixed in the middle distance. Although she had had no idea about Carol, for some reason it didn't really surprise her. It confirmed everything she had always thought about Harry. 'Maybe we both ought to wait awhile. They do say revenge is a dish best served cold.'

'Are you saying I shouldn't say anything to him?'

Katherine nodded thoughtfully. 'Maybe we should bide our time. Why don't you go home and ring that chap up and tell him it's him you want, not Harry.'

'Sam?'

'That's right. I mean – you don't really want Harry, do you?'

Carol grimaced and shook her head. 'No, but I've got to get rid of him first.'

The restaurant was almost empty. Katherine started to collect her things together. 'I've really got to go. I've got another appointment this afternoon.' She reached across the table and caught hold of Carol's hand, reluctant to leave with so much still unsaid. 'We ought to keep in touch.'

Carol flinched. 'Please don't go yet.'

'I'll ring you soon.' She had already fished Hope's address out of her bag and, looking down at the folded paper, hesitated for a few seconds. 'You could always come with me?'

Carol stared at her. 'Come with you?' she repeated.

'Why not? The film contract thing really is only an excuse for a girls' night out. It would be fun. What do you think?'

Carol hesitated and then after a few seconds hooked the mobile phone out her bag. 'Lactons could be a useful contact when it comes to raising the finances for a TV series.'

Katherine nodded. 'I'll order some coffee, shall I?'

Carol was already tapping in her office number. She wasn't altogether surprised when she got the machine, even though it was well after two. Jeanette was no doubt out somewhere, shopping or gossiping. Carol left a curt message to tell her she was off to talk to a client and didn't anticipate returning to the office in the afternoon.

Jeanette, who was relaxing at her desk enjoying an after-lunch mug of coffee, pressed the button on the switchboard to transfer the incoming call to the handset, just in case it was Harry ringing up to find out how she was. She tucked the receiver under her chin and picked up a pen and pad

– it made her look as if she was doing something – while Carol's familiar voice informed her that she wouldn't be back. Before she hung up Jeanette glanced down at the bags tucked under her desk; Carol's absence would give her plenty of time to get ready for her date with Harry Bourne.

Katherine had quite a job finding the place where Hope Laughton was staying, her search not helped by the combination of wine and champagne they had consumed over lunch. She had expected an ostentatious hotel, so was surprised when, after half-an-hour's fruitless searching through the A–Z, the taxi they had hailed in desperation dropped them off in a side street in Kensington. The address turned out to be an anonymous red brick frontage behind which were six service flats, rented by the day, by those who wanted the luxury of a hotel suite combined with all the comforts of a real home.

After checking they were expected, a uniformed security man in the lobby showed them to the lift. Upstairs on the first floor in a magnificent drawing room, Hope Laughton laid out Katherine's film contract on the coffee table and swept an arm over it inviting her to take a look, while a boy dressed in a white jacket and scarlet bow tie delivered tea on a silver tray.

'There we are, my dear, all above board. Why don't you take a look?'

Katherine smiled and picked up a copy. 'You didn't mind me bringing Carol?'

Hope snorted. 'Naw, not at all, more the merrier, any friend of yours, etc. etc. And if she's in finance I'd get her to read through the paperwork for you – it's a foreign country to me all that legal stuff.'

Katherine opened up the booklet and flicked through the photocopied pages, past pages of addresses and titles, to the section that described, in detail, what she had agreed to do and how much she was going to be paid for the privilege.

Hope tapped the edge of the cover. 'No access to the rear gardens,' she said emphatically. 'Page five, last para. Your friend Ben Morton rang up and insisted we put that in. He said you might not get around to remembering.' Hope grinned. 'You've had a real good effect on that guy. He's sounded great. And I'd like to know what you have been up to – you've changed.'

Katherine blushed.

Meanwhile, Carol Ackerman was making her way, a little unsteadily, towards one of the armchairs that flanked the Adams fireplace.

'So,' said Hope, handing out teacups. 'You hired Carol to look after all your hard-earned money, huh?'

Katherine had just got to the part of the agreement where the film company were explaining how long they planned to take to shoot the front of her house and then why it would inevitably take far longer.

She looked up distractedly. 'Sorry?'

Hope laughed. 'I wish you'd invited me to that lunch of yours, it's been a real slow day here. I could have done with the company.' She glanced at Carol. 'You've really got your act together if you've hired a financial consultant already.'

Carol coloured slightly as Katherine caught her eye. Katherine grinned mischievously. 'Oh no, Carol doesn't work for me. No, she's my husband's mistress.' Her tone was absolutely and faultlessly neutral.

Hope's jaw dropped. 'Gee, you're real up front about it – I didn't think the British –'

She stopped as Carol burst into laughter.

'Former mistress,' she added between strangled breaths.

Katherine handed the document over to Carol. 'You can't say former, not yet anyway. Here, take a look at these, will you, and see what you think.'

Carol blinked myopically and then stared down at the pages. 'What's this?'

'It's the way I'm going to finance the first stage of my plans for the house.'

'Does Harry know?' Carol began to laugh again.

Hope glanced at the tea-tray and then up at the boy waiting for her to dismiss him. 'I think maybe you better bring me something stronger – I've got some catching up to do.'

Jeanette had ensured that Carol had left her the set of keys that opened the female executives' washroom. She could have used the showers in the company gym but it wasn't the same as luxuriating amongst the pink marble and blonde wood on the fourth floor. Behind one set of louvre doors was a pile of freshly laundered bath sheets that smelt of sandalwood. She pulled one out and headed to a cubicle, where someone had left a new bar of old English rose and lavender soap. She had been considering how she would handle Harry when she met him again. She had settled on one of two approaches: one involved the application of a great deal of alcohol and she wasn't certain that she could manage it on the new high heels she'd bought at lunch-time. The other was far more subtle, and as her nostrils filled with the delicate perfume of the expensive soap, she decided that this was the ploy that would serve her best.

When, at just after six, a cab drew up outside the Victoria Arms, a demure vision in black floated inside for her assignation, a lingering aroma of old English roses left behind on the evening air.

Harry was waiting in the lounge bar cradling a large brandy. He looked up as she opened the door and smiled. Her response was to lower her eyelids and look coyly in his direction.

'Hello, Harry,' she murmured. 'How are you?'

She wasn't sure what Harry had been expecting but was certain St Jeanette the Almost Virginal hadn't been on the agenda. Hastily he stood up and offered her his bar stool.

'Jeanette, how nice to see you again,' he blustered. 'Let me get you a drink. Brandy?'

'Just an orange juice, please, with a splash of lemonade,' she said to the barman.

Harry lifted an eyebrow. 'Are you sure?'

She nodded and slipped onto the stool beside him, making sure her thigh momentarily brushed his as she reached over to retrieve her drink.

'Oh yes,' she said in a low breathy voice. 'I don't usually drink, it always goes straight to my head.' For a second she lifted her eyes, making sure that Harry's gaze met hers. She had always been able to make herself blush at the drop of a hat – and to her delight as she felt her own colour rising, Harry went scarlet.

She bit her lip. 'I feel so terrible about . . .' she paused as if unable to talk about their late night liaison in the Strand Palace. 'I don't want you to think . . .' she stopped again and leant forward, brushing her lips against his cheek. 'You're so kind, Harry. You made me feel so special. I wanted you to know that. It's just that since Jordan was killed in the accident, there really hasn't been anyone else in my life.' She blushed again and sipped her drink, refusing now to meet Harry's eye. 'He was the only one, you know – until you that is.'

Harry stared down at her. 'Oh God, I'd got no idea. What happened to Jordan?' he said thickly.

Jeanette wiped away an imaginary tear. 'He was killed in a car accident, two years ago. It was so awful. We were going to get married.' She paused for effect. 'I haven't been out much since then. It's so hard to begin again.' She painted on a bright happy face that implied she was being terribly brave in spite of the fictitious Jordan's early demise, and was delighted to see that she had Harry's undivided attention.

'I'm really sorry,' he murmured. 'It must have been awful for you.'

She reached out and gently touched his hand. 'It's all right. People keep telling me I should let it go, that it's time to move on. But you don't want to hear about me, tell me about you. I've been really worried. How's it going?'

Harry took a slug of his brandy. 'Bloody terrible.'

Jeanette arranged her beautifully painted lips into a little moue of concern. 'Really?' she said, feigning surprise. 'I thought things were getting better. Carol told me you were fine this morning. In fact she said that she thought it was all a storm in a teacup.'

Harry made an odd noise. Jeanette wondered if she had pushed it too far and added hastily, 'But I'm sure she was just putting on a brave face.'

Harry waved the barman over and indicated his glass. 'Same again,' he said briskly. 'And another orange juice for the lady.'

Jeanette caught hold of his arm. 'Harry, don't let's have another drink. Why don't we go somewhere and eat? It'll give us the chance to talk.'

Harry focused thoughtfully on her face. 'Have you got my wallet with you?

Jeanette shook her head. 'It's back at my flat. We can go back and pick it up later. If you don't mind, that is?' Her tone was conspiratorial, with a slightly seductive edge.

Harry drained his glass. 'Do you know anywhere around here where we can eat?'

'There's a lovely little Italian restaurant just across the road. The food there is wonderful. Everything's home-made. I prefer home-made things, don't you?' She smiled and tightened her grip on his arm as she climbed down off the stool, adding a piquant touch of vulnerability. 'We have to keep your strength up, don't we?'

Harry straightened his shoulders manfully, a brave knight to her winsome maiden, and wrapped her fingers around his forearm.

Outside on the pavement, right on cue, the heady smell of garlic and peppers wafted across the road.

'God, that smells wonderful,' said Harry. 'Have you eaten there before?'

'I've been here once or twice with friends from work.'

She'd eaten there with Lee Fenman on the two occasions he'd taken her out; they'd both felt the need for sustenance before going back to his hotel.

Hope's plans for their girls' night out were eclectic to say the least. Katherine had had no idea that life could be so *Live*. After tea they had meandered down to an afternoon performance by a string quartet in the park, sat in the sunshine on a bench and shared a bottle of Chardonnay, while the sounds of violins floated up into a cloudless blue city sky. Before the closing bars had had time to fade inside Katherine's head, Hope had hailed a taxi and they'd headed off to have an early supper in Chinatown, before walking down into Soho to a packed pub, where three astonishingly beautiful boys in drag performed their own personal tribute to Diana Ross and the Supremes.

Katherine's face ached from smiling – and she had a peculiar sense of unreality, as if she might still wake up and find herself back at home. Their last port of call was a jazz club deep below stairs in a back street. Carol found them the tab end of a table by the door and went off to order a round of drinks while Katherine took the opportunity to catch her breath.

Hope lit up a cigarette. 'Good time?'

'You really need me to answer that?'

Hope's grin widened. 'It's late, maybe it would be better if you and Carol stayed over tonight. There's plenty of room at my place.'

Carol, balancing a tray of drinks, squeezed herself into the remaining chair. 'The band is about to start another set, do you think we ought to have this and then head home?'

It seemed that all minds were walking over the same turf.

Katherine looked across the smoky room; the band were just settling themselves onto the stage. 'I'd really like to hear them play before we go.'

On cue the band started to pick its way through the opening bars of an old dance number, the name of it teased around the edge of Katherine's mind. It had been years since she wanted to dance, but as the rhythm rolled over, she yearned to get up and move.

Carol shuffled the drinks off the tray. 'Okay.'

'I've already told Katherine you can stay at my place, what's to go home for?' said Hope.

Sarah, Peter, the third degree, and an empty bed, thought Katherine ruefully as she took her Cinzano.

Carol lifted her beer in salute. 'Harry.'

Katherine grimaced and then tapped the neck of Carol's bottle with her glass. 'We'll stay.'

Across the bar, she was surprised to catch sight of a familiar face and then realised it was the boy who had been serving tea at Hope's apartment. The American had already spotted him. He lifted a hand in greeting and then headed towards them, pushing his way between the out-crops of drinkers and jazz freaks on the edge of the dance floor. He was dressed in faded blue Levis and an open-neck shirt – as were his two friends at the table near the edge of the stage.

'Marco, darling,' said Hope, in the few seconds before the band really let loose. 'How lovely to see you.'

The houseboy leant over and kissed her gently on top of her head. 'I thought you'd be here sooner,' he said, vowels slick with Latin lubrication. 'We've saved you a table.'

Hope got to her feet and scooped up her glass. 'Come along, ladies, the fleet's in.'

Katherine coloured. 'I'm really not sure –' she began.

Hope got hold of her arm. 'Think of England, darling,' she said and propelled Katherine across the little dance floor, followed by Carol.

They finally got to bed at around four – alone.

Harry had had other plans and so he was a bit bemused to find himself on Carol's Cambridge doorstep at just after midnight, knocking frantically to try and wake her up. He was bitterly cold. Summer nights weren't what they used to be.

'Carol!' he hissed, throwing a handful of gravel up at the bedroom window. Close by a cat hissed malevolently.

'Carol, it's me, Harry. Open the door, CAROL! Please, let me in.'

A light flickered on in a first-floor window away to his left. He took no notice and picked up another handful of stones. His sense of frustration was steadily rising to boiling point.

'CAROL!!' he roared and let rip with a fusillade of pebbles. There was an ominous cracking sound followed an instant later by a tinkle of broken glass.

Harry threw the contents of his other hand down into the flower bed. 'Shit,' he snorted. 'Shit, shit, shit.'

'Harry? Is that you?' said a male voice from somewhere in the gloom. Harry swung round. Geoff, dressed in white tee-shirt and white boxers, tip-toed his way across the gravel. 'What's the matter?'

Harry retreated. 'Nothing, I was just trying to wake Carol up. Mind, there's broken glass down there.'

Geoff looked warily at the driveway. 'She's not back yet, mate.'

'What do you mean, not back?'

'She's still up in town as far as we know. We brought

supper round earlier. Don't worry, she'd have rung if there was a problem.'

Harry stuffed his hand into his pockets. 'I can't get in,' he said thickly. 'I don't suppose you've got a spare key, have you?'

Geoff considered for a second. 'Why don't you come in and have a coffee while I try and find it?'

Harry said nothing.

'You look all in, come on, it's bloody freezing out here.'

Reluctantly Harry conceded defeat – he *was* all in – and Carol not being there when he got home was the final straw. It had been going so well with Jeanette. They had had a good meal, good wine, great service. She had been giving him the eye over two cannelloni verdi and a bottle of house red – nothing too obvious, just a little suggestion of the goodies that might be on offer later. Once or twice her knee had brushed his under the table, lightly, so they could both pretend it had been an accident.

While the waiter cleared away the remains of the dessert, Harry had suggested they go back to her flat for coffee. That's when it had started to go wrong. She seemed a bit surprised that he suggested it.

At the door to her flat, she had suddenly said, 'I'm not sure that I ought to let you in, really, Harry.'

There had been a very awkward few minutes out on the landing. Jeanette had settled herself in the half-open doorway. God, and she had looked great, in that body, in that dress.

He'd smiled winsomely. 'Oh, come on. What about the coffee you promised me?'

She'd softened a little, looking nervous, and then nodded, and he'd thought he was in with a good chance of recovering the lost ground.

'All right,' she said moving to one side. 'But not for long. I don't usually ask men back here.'

Her flat wasn't at all what he expected – it was extremely

tidy, with fresh flowers and a subtle smell of perfume and pine disinfectant. In the bathroom she'd got one of those things that turned the water in the toilet blue. It reminded him to put the seat down. There were thick white towels hanging by the bath, fluffy white towels trimmed with pink ribbon. He had thought then that maybe he'd misjudged Jeanette. The knitting, tucked neatly away in a basket beside the sofa, was what finally convinced him – that and the smell of real coffee wafting out from the open kitchen door. She reappeared carrying a tray and his wallet.

'Here we are,' she said with a nervous smile.

While he had been in the bathroom, Jeanette had untied her hair and taken off her shoes. As she padded towards him, so tiny, so very blonde, and so shapely, Harry had felt a not all together unpleasant tightening in his groin. She knelt on the floor beside him, flicked a bow wave of blonde hair over her shoulder and handed him a mug.

'How do you like it?' she had said in a throaty little voice. It was almost more than Harry could bear.

He had coughed and, ignoring the coffee, leant forward to kiss her. To his surprise she pulled away, though he noticed that her eyes were bright and expectant.

'Harry,' she said, 'please, don't spoil it. I'm not like that, not really. The other night I was so drunk – you must think I'm awful.'

He didn't think she was awful, not awful at all, all he could think of was burying his head between those perky plump breasts and sliding his hands down over that shapely little arse. No, he certainly didn't think Jeanette was awful. She moved across the floor out of his clutches.

'I think you ought to go after we've drunk our coffee,' she said softly.

'Go?' mumbled Harry, his mind still firmly on the ripe curve of those delectable breasts. 'What do you mean go?'

She licked her lips.

He shivered.

'Out of the door,' she said in an even tone. 'Home, to Carol. To Cambridge.'

He groaned while she arranged herself into an erotic tableau just two feet away from his fingertips. 'The thing is Harry, it's not that I don't like you – not that at all, quite the opposite, but I'm not the sort of girl who takes someone else's man.'

'But Jeanette –' he began to protest.

She leant forward on all fours and pressed a perfectly painted fingertip to his lips. Her breasts strained beneath the little black dress, making his mouth water.

'Sssh,' she said. 'Let's have this coffee.'

He could smell her perfume. Her finger lingered on his mouth for an instant and he couldn't control the urge to kiss it. He caught hold of her wrist and held it tight. She made a soft mewling sound way back in her throat as if she was struggling to control herself and then closed her eyes. Harry swallowed hard. God, this was the most exquisite torture.

He slipped down onto the floor beside her, ignoring the unpleasant popping in his knees, and tried to kiss her again. He could sense she was having real problems trying to control herself.

He kissed her just the once, a long kiss that started off awkwardly as his lips weren't quite in the right place, but with a little jiggling about it worked up to a long, breathy exercise in mouth music and she only put up token resistance as he tried to push his tongue between her lips. He slipped his hands around her, sliding one palm down to squeeze that glorious backside, pulling her closer, relishing the sensation of her breasts pressed up tight against him. She moaned softly as his fingers eased up towards the neck of the dress and then, just as the zip growled his intentions, she leapt to her feet. Reddening furiously she rubbed her hands down over her dress to straighten it.

'No,' she said hastily. 'No, we can't, Harry. I can't. It's not right.'

Groaning, Harry rolled over onto his back. There was a cream cracker glued to the fluff on the mat under the sofa. Above him Jeanette was still tidying herself.

'Oh God,' she murmured unhappily. 'This is just so hard. Don't get me wrong, Harry. You've got to go. I really want to –'

Harry sighed. 'Me too. Come on, who would know? We could keep it to ourselves.'

Jeanette slumped down onto the sofa. 'I would know, I feel guilty about the other night as it is.' She paused, eyes working hungrily over his prone body. 'You know you're the first man that I've felt anything for since – since Jordan.'

Harry got to his knees. He thought the little blonde might be about to cry. Bravely she sniffed back a tear, bosom heaving. The image was so compelling that he couldn't take his eyes off it.

'I think you ought to go now, Harry, before we both do something we regret.'

He had an erection all the way home on the train.

Geoff cut a large piece of cream sponge and laid it next the half-eaten ham and tomato sandwich on Harry's plate.

'There you go, that should stay the worms. You know, you can stay here if you want,' he said, pouring himself a mug of coffee. 'It wouldn't be any trouble.'

Harry stiffened. 'What about the spare key for Carol's place?'

Geoff sighed and glanced around the kitchen. 'I just don't know where it could have got to. I know it's here some-where. Carol always leaves us a key for when she goes away. Ray had an early night, or I'd ask him. Sleeping like a baby he is.'

Harry moved his supper closer, circling it protectively with his arm, and looked around the confines of the kitchen. It was warm, homely, spotlessly clean, and made him feel as if he was about to get mugged – or worse.

Geoff snorted. 'Relax, for God's sake.'

Harry reddened. 'I'd really rather go back to Carol's.'

'Oh right. You can sleep in the shed. Look, there's a spare bed made up in the back bedroom.' He sipped his coffee, eyes fixed on Harry. 'Don't worry, the sheets are clean and you can lock the door if you're worried.'

Harry woke at just before six, unviolated, after a wonderful night's sleep on what Ray assured him over breakfast was a very expensive orthopaedic mattress. He had one last fruitless attempt at waking Carol before Geoff and Ray ran him down to the station to catch his train.

Chapter Seventeen

Near the railway station, a few miles from home, Katherine Bourne fiddled in her purse for change to pay the excess charge for overnight parking. She tried not to read anything into the knowing expression on the face of the car park attendant when she finally slapped a tenner into his sticky little paw.

'Have a nice day,' he said grimly as she closed the car window and edged forward towards the junction with the main road. It was early morning, the verges still decked out in dew. A steady stream of cars heading off to work or turning into the station pinned her firmly behind the white lines.

Her head ached although she didn't think it was a hangover, just sheer exhaustion. Her legs ached; she and a student prince from Denmark had danced the night away to the strains of the jazz band, and then when they had called a halt, carried on to the piped music.

She groaned and laid her forehead on the steering wheel. Life without Harry was far bigger than she had ever imagined. Harry, his name was like a lightning strike. She glanced at her reflection in the rear-view mirror. Harry and Carol. How could she have been so blind for so many years? How many times had she prayed that he would find someone else – and now it seemed that her prayers had been answered all along.

Finally there was a break in the traffic, she eased forward. Maybe she hadn't been specific enough in her supplications to the old fool who was bumbling around trying to keep the universe tidy. She should have asked that Harry had not just found someone else but was so enamoured, so ensnared that he couldn't keep away from her. Katherine wondered if it was too late to change her request.

As she drove down through the industrial estate a bright red company car roared past her on unbroken white lines. A young go-getter destined for something important, who drove like he lived the rest of his life – push, push, push – that had been Harry always chasing the next prize, the next promotion, the next pay rise, self-assured, with a clear vision of where he intended to go and the quickest and dirtiest way to get there. She wondered, pulling over so that the on-coming car didn't hit one of them head-on, why she had never seen that Harry's precocious self-assurance would one day harden up into arrogance. When had his carefully-argued opinions on everything turned pompous? And to some extent, hadn't she been complicit in his trans-formation? Taking her lead from him she had always taken him so seriously. Could she have laughed aloud one day when he was holding court at the tea-table and changed their lives forever?

Perhaps she ought not to be so hard on herself though – after all he'd fooled Carol too.

Carol Ackerman. It struck her as odd that she felt no anger or jealously, only a strange sense of empathy towards the woman who had inadvertently inherited her husband. Her anger was directed firmly towards Harry, who had, despite all the odds, somehow managed to manipulate them both. That did disturb her; Harry had been lying all those years and using them both. Like the hankies in her childhood. One for show and one for blow.

While she had been struggling to make his life easier, placate his moods, listen to his drivel, bring up his children, wash and iron, clean and cook for him, he had been sharing all the special things, the nights out, the weekends away, with someone else. They should have been her reward for long service not Carol's. She had got the work and Carol had all the perks. But then again, by doing so, Harry had denied Carol a real family life, with children and a home – maybe the devil's deal had worked out evenly after all. They had each had a half life and Harry had carefully arranged it so they were both denied the rest.

She felt an odd and unexpected ache in her chest for Carol. He had lied to Carol too, lies that had edited his life into an acceptable shape so that Carol would stay with him. And now, because of Harry, Carol had probably lost Sam as well and had nothing to show for all those years except a few coffee pots.

Outside Katherine's house, furred with droplets of water, Sarah's car was still crouched under the lilacs. If it stayed much longer it would take root in the fertile soil. She pulled up beside it and clambered unsteadily out onto the gravel.

She barely had the chance to get into the hall door before Sarah appeared from the kitchen. Behind her, Katherine could see a nest of sleeping bags and pillows on the sofa under the window.

'I've been up all night,' Sarah said coldly. 'Where the hell do you think you've been? Couldn't you have at least rung? We've both been worried sick.'

Peter appeared behind his sister, dressed in a mis-match of Harry's old pyjamas. He yawned. 'We rang the hospitals.'

Katherine dropped her shoulder bag onto the floor. 'I want you both out of this house by lunch-time,' she said in an icy tone and hurried upstairs to her bedroom to get changed.

Jeanette hummed all the way to work on the tube. Hook line and sinker. She bade the doorman at Lactons a genuinely warm good morning, couldn't be bothered to wait for the lift, and took the stairs two at a time up to the office.

Harry's face had been a picture as she had gently but

firmly guided him out of her flat. Bemused, befuddled, besotted. And somewhere in amongst all that confusion and stifled passion he had forgotten to take his wallet. Perfect. Now she had to try and be patient, wait and see if her plan really had caught hold.

As she reached the first fire door she glanced down into her bag. Harry's wallet was snuggled up comfortably against the knitting she had borrowed from the temp in reception.

She glanced into Carol's office. Ms Ackerman was already safely entrenched. She knocked on the glass door and walked in without waiting for Carol's invitation. 'Morning. How are you this morning?' she said brightly.

Carol looked up, eyes unfocused. 'Oh, hello, Jeanette.'

Jeanette smiled warmly. 'Better this morning?'

Carol pulled a face.

'Harry. You know, the shirts and everything?'

Carol slid the papers she was reading across her desk. 'Yes, fine thank you, and I'd be most grateful if we kept my private life out of the conversation. I've been going through my notes for Baneford College. Would you run me off another copy of the schedule, please?'

Jeanette nodded.

'And would you see if there are any spare places left?' Carol continued.

'What, for another delegate?'

'I thought it would be nice to invite Katherine B –' Carol paused for an instant as if she was trying to find the name in her mental Rolodex. '– Katherine Jackson, the woman I had lunch with yesterday. She's just starting out in business. It will give her the opportunity to network, make some good contacts, food for thought, that kind of thing.'

'I thought Dougie was already dealing with her loan.'

'He is,' said Carol briskly. 'Now what about Kestrel, any luck with that yet?'

Jeanette composed her face carefully. 'Nothing.'

Carol sighed. 'All right. Any word from the board about the Danic deal?'

'Not a murmur, but then again they don't meet until Friday, maybe you'll hear something then. Do you want me to ring this Jackson woman if there's a spare place?'

'No, I'd like to invite her myself. And see if you can get them to accept her as my guest.'

Jeanette pouted. 'You mean for free?'

'If they'll wear it.' Carol's attention dropped back to the documents on her desk. Jeanette went off to replenish the coffee machine before she settled down to wait for Harry Bourne's call.

They met at ten o'clock in the canteen, Kestrel's condemned men. Harry noticed as he took his place at the table that their numbers were thinning and wondered if Danic was picking them off one by one during the night. The man next to him hadn't shaved. As Harry jiffled his seat closer, the man said, 'I wish I'd stayed in bed.'

Harry felt much the same, except that he didn't fancy staying there alone and certainly not in Geoff and Ray's single bed.

Since he had woken up his mind was dragged back again and again to an image of Jeanette crouched in front of him on all fours, mouth slightly open, eyes alight with a mixture of desire and reserve – a heady combination.

Generally speaking though, despite a nagging little burr of frustration, he felt much, much better. Ray had cooked him dippy eggs for breakfast with crisp golden toast soldiers, orange juice and freshly ground coffee and Geoff had lent him a clean shirt and a disposable razor. Other than one tiny nick on his chin he looked great.

The man next to him leant closer. 'That little American shit is going to give us a pep talk this morning.'

For a few moments Harry felt his spirits sink and then he smiled – he could use the time profitably, rerun a few

favourite fantasies, substituting Jeanette for his usual leading lady.

From behind the closed servery he could already smell
the preparations for the midday buffet. This time he would
be much quicker off the mark. If he rang Jeanette when
they broke for mid-morning coffee he could ask if she'd
like to join him for a spot of lunch. He grinned and settled
back in his chair. Behind him the doors to the canteen
swung opened and the boy who, earlier in the week, had
told Harry his life was about to change forever, strode into
the room with a sheaf of papers tucked under the arm of
his Armani suit.

'Good morning, gentlemen,' he said briskly, stepping
onto the dais and dropping his notes onto the lectern. 'This
morning I want to talk to you about success – and how
we can each harness the experience that's inside us. In
1981, Danic –'

Harry closed his eyes and waited patiently for Jeanette
to swing in on a vine, dressed in a leopardskin loin-cloth.
He didn't have to wait too long.

Carol found it hard to concentrate on work. She looked
up from her desk and stared out over the Thames. She
had an icy shard of fury wedged up somewhere under her
solar plexus. That bastard. All that, 'Well, I've finally
done it. I've finally left Katherine. Well, it had to be done,
didn't it? I mean, we just couldn't carry on living a lie,
could we?'

She could hear Harry's voice as clearly as if he was
standing beside her:

'Thought I'd come straight down, no need to mess
around now, is there, eh? I've given this a lot of thought,
I decided it was only fair. I wanted to be fair to you, after
all the years we've been together. These last few months
I've heard your biological clock ticking away. Babies, you
know, children, well, perhaps not children, that's some-

thing we'll have to talk about, but a life with – well, a family. Me.'

She threw the folder she had been reading down onto the desk and clenched her fists, she'd give him biological-bloody-clocks, bastard.

There was a place at the Baneford weekend conference. Carol took the slip of paper Katherine had given her and tapped in her phone number.

'Hello, Katherine, this is Carol Ackerman here, I wonder if you are free the weekend of the twelfth? I know it's short notice but there's a conference I thought you might be interested in.'

Katherine seemed surprised to hear from her. She listened to the details without comment, there was a weighed pause and then she said, 'Yes, all right, I'd love to go.'

When Carol had made all the arrangements she flicked though her diary to find Sam Richardson's home number. He'd be teaching at the moment, but it was still reassuring to see his name. Harry hadn't managed to make Sam disappear, he was still there in black and white, still within reach. She snapped the phone book shut and turned her attention to her in-tray.

Out beyond the walls of her fish tank Jeanette had the phone cradled under her chin; still chasing Kestrel no doubt. Carol wondered if she should buzz through and tell her not to bother.

Jeanette glanced nervously over her shoulder.

'Harry,' she whispered, 'you really shouldn't have rung me at work.'

Harry mumbled an apology. 'I know, but I really wanted to talk to you,' he said. 'I just wanted to – I wondered if I could see you again? I thought maybe if you're free for lunch . . .' His voice tailed off.

Jeanette could smell the rich perfume of victory.

'I'm not sure,' she said. 'What if anyone sees us together?'

Harry groaned.

'You know you left your wallet behind at my place?' she added in case her refusal really did daunt him. 'So I suppose we do have to meet. I'm just not sure I trust myself to be alone with you. After all, you are married and then there is Carol to think about.' By parading his dirty linen in public she hoped it would emphasise that his track record hardly suggested he was the kind of company a virtuous woman ought to be eager to share. Good God, she was practically a widow.

Harry coughed. 'You know I've already left my wife, and Carol and I . . .' he stopped as if sorting through his words. 'We live separate lives. We're more friends than anything else. I just needed somewhere to stay, you know how it is.'

Jeanette made a little noise of doubt. 'What if she found out about us?' She emphasised the word *us* as if they already had a history worth discovering.

'Trust me, it wouldn't be a problem, really.'

'If you're sure, Harry. You wouldn't lie to me, would you?'

'No, never, what shall we say then? One o'clock?'

Jeanette looked down at her outfit; she had chosen a tight-fitting black ribbed sweater and a hound's-tooth check mini-skirt in anticipation of Harry's call. She lay back in her swivel chair admiring the way her legs looked in their sheer black tights.

'We could meet at my flat if you like,' she said softly. 'I've got a dental appointment at lunch-time, so they're not expecting me to be back this afternoon. That would give us plenty of time to talk. I could make you an omelette or something. You remember where I live don't you?'

She could practically hear Harry purring down the phone.

'Yes, and don't worry about cooking anything,' he said. 'I'll pick something up on the way over.'

'See you soon, then.' She dropped the phone back into its cradle. A second or two later she knocked on Carol Ackerman's door, her face contorted into a tortured grimace.

Carol looked up in surprise. 'What's the matter?'

Jeanette flinched. 'I've got the most terrible toothache. I was just drinking my coffee –' she winced sharply as another imaginary wave of pain ricocheted through her jaw.

Carol was already on her feet. 'Have you got any para-cetamol?'

Jeanette shook her head. 'I don't think that'll be enough, I'm going to ring my dentist, he might be able to fit me in as an emergency.'

Carol nodded sympathetically.

'The thing is, if I can get in I'll have to sit and wait in the surgery until he gets time to see me.'

Carol waved her away. 'That's all right. Don't worry, there's nothing I can't handle here. Would you like me to ring him for you.'

Jeanette smiled bravely in spite of the pain. 'No, it's all right, I can manage. God, it hurts. I'll call him straight away.'

Ten minutes later, Jeanette was tip-tapping down the high street towards the tube station. She was glad she hadn't had time to return the knitting. She wondered what Harry would bring them for lunch.

Katherine Bourne sat at the kitchen table and re-read the copy of the contract Hope had given her, alongside it were the plans she had talked through with Carol Ackerman's colleague, Dougie, all neatly tucked back inside their folder. She glanced round the kitchen, quiet now after Sarah's departure.

Peter was still upstairs packing, though she did wonder what was taking him so much time, he normally travelled in the clothes he stood up in. Logic would have suggested that he and Sarah left together but Sarah wasn't hot on logic at the best of times. She hadn't really wanted to leave and it was only after Katherine had insisted, in a tone that brooked no contradiction, that she reluctantly agreed to go.

Katherine turned the page; she was getting good at throwing people out. She hadn't told either of them about Carol Ackerman. It had been odd to hear the other woman's voice on the phone. She looked at the scribbled note she had made on the telephone pad about the Women in Business conference; surprised that she actually wanted to go, perhaps this was part of the shape her new life was going to be.

Peter appeared in the doorway, kit-bag slung over one shoulder. 'I don't suppose there's any chance of a lift down to the station, is there, Mum? And about Dad,' Peter went on, 'I just want you to be happy, you know that, don't you? Only all this other stuff, the man, the staying out all night – it's just happening too quickly for me to get my head round. I'm sorry if I overreacted but Sarah was practically hysterical about it.'

Katherine pushed herself away from the table. 'I know. I should have rung. What time is your train?'

'There's one at quarter past one.'

'Time for a cup of tea before you go,' she gently.

Peter didn't make a move towards the table but hung back in the doorway, shifting uncomfortably from foot to foot. 'So did you have a good time last night, then?'

Katherine nodded. 'I had a great time. Now, while I'm up would you like a sandwich as well?'

Peter nodded and headed for the table, pulling a chair noisily over the tiles. 'Got any ham?'

'I think so.'

Ben Morton rang ten minutes after Katherine got back from taking Peter to the station. 'Hi, how was your day in the big city?'

Katherine smiled at the sound of his voice. 'Illuminating, I'm really glad you rang. I need to talk to someone.'

She heard him snort. 'Is this heavy adult "why don't I make the coffee, here's a box of tissues" kind of talk?'

Katherine laughed. 'Not really, maybe – could be. Are you busy?'

'Nope. What about if I drive over? I could pick up a couple of boxes of Kleenex on the way.'

Chapter Eighteen

Harry woke up slowly, blinked and rubbed his eyes. Afternoon sunlight, as sharp as a sword blade, sliced between thin cotton curtains and lay, molten, across a tangle of white sheets. Beside him, Jeanette, with the bed clothes arranged so that they just covered her ample breasts, was propped up on one elbow looking down at him. Leaning over, eyes bright, she brushed the hair back off his face and kissed his forehead.

'Hello, Harry,' she whispered. 'Sleep well?'

He blinked again. It had been quite an odd afternoon.

On the way over from Kestrel's offices he had bought fish and chips from a little shop in the precinct near Jeanette's, and with the bundle tucked inside a carrier bag headed up the steps to the block of flats. When he reached the landing Jeanette had thrown open the door and grabbed him.

'God, I'm so glad you came. I've been dreaming about you all night,' she murmured, plastering him with big wet kisses. 'I can't cope with this, Harry. Thinking about you is driving me mad.'

He had barely had time to get in the door before she was trying to drag his jacket off. Gamely he had dropped the fish and chips onto the sofa and begun an enthusiastic exploration of the curves he had been fantasising about all morning. She moaned under his touch, thrusting herself against him. She guided his hands to the waistband of her sweater, encouraging him to take it off. He obliged and her breasts appeared like magic, two ripe grapefruit barely contained in a skimpy black lace bra.

'Oh Harry,' she had squealed as he fumbled with her bra strap. 'Yes, yes, please touch me. Oh, my God. I can't stop thinking about you.'

Her throaty little moans confirmed what he had always known; he was a god. A sex machine. Eagerly she pulled him down onto the sofa, shimmying out of her skirt, scrabbling with the buttons of his shirt, thrusting herself towards him, clambering over his hips. Her knickers seemed to have vanished along with her skirt. Well, what could a chap do?

The first time it had all been over a trifle too quickly, but that just seemed to make Jeanette even more eager. She clung to him like a bush baby, rubbing those compelling breasts across his chest way out beyond the moment of no return. He shuddered with after-shocks, convulsing, and gently but firmly pushed her away before the sensation became too intense. She pouted and then grinned, curling up into the crook of his arm. He must have dozed for a few minutes, because the next thing he was aware of was a clammy wet patch hugging his thigh. He had rolled from under her and pulled out the bag of fish and chips, now squashed beyond all recognition.

'I brought us some lunch,' he began, holding up the carrier like a trophy.

Jeanette had moaned and snuggled down against his chest. 'Oh my God, Harry. How can you think about food now,' she whispered. 'You make me feel so good. Why don't we go into the bedroom?'

He had followed her quite mindlessly. From behind her backside looked so plump, so rounded; two pale pink bouncing beach balls.

The second time it had been better.

Beside him Jeanette ran an exploratory hand down over his belly. It rumbled. It must be tea-time. He rolled away from her attentions and picked up his watch from the bedside table.

'My God, it's nearly six o'clock.'

Jeanette smiled. 'Hungry?'

He blinked and glanced around the bedroom. There was no sign of his clothes. 'I really ought to be getting home.'

Jeanette pulled a face. 'Why? I thought you were just lodging with Carol? Besides, I've got strawberries and cream in the fridge and a bottle of white wine.' She paused and ran her tongue over her lips. 'We could have a little picnic, if you like.'

She pulled the sheet lower and slipped effortlessly out of bed. Her nipples were as pink as puppies' noses.

'Have you ever had strawberries and cream in bed?'

Caught in relief against the sword blade of sunshine her body curved in and out like a well-loved Stradivarius.

Harry groaned and watched her sashay towards the kitchen.

It started to rain just after Carol Ackerman left the office around six. It was summer rain; huge crystal raindrops falling recklessly out of a bright sunny sky. She turned up the collar of her mac and hailed a taxi as the droplets began to explode like mortar shells on the pavement around her. She was trying to script her first meeting with Harry since talking to Katherine Bourne. It was pointless. Harry would never stay quiet long enough for her to say her piece.

The train home was full of faces she recognised from other journeys on other days, but this time instead of dwelling on work her mind was full of mutiny. She had found a way to rid herself of Harry, a perfectly legitimate excuse; he had lied to her. She toyed with the handle of her briefcase, perhaps Katherine was right, perhaps she ought to bide her time and make him suffer. Quick and painless or long and tortuous? She weighed the merits of them both as the countryside rolled unnoticed past the carriage windows.

It seemed to take hardly any time at all before the train pulled into Cambridge. As she stepped into the flow of commuters heading down the platform, she grinned. The answer was quite obvious. She got into her car and headed for the supermarket.

Harry arrived home at just before nine; he looked completely exhausted.

'Hello, darling,' she said, as he opened the back door. He barely looked up. 'How was your day?'

He sighed. 'Intense. God, I'm shattered, I think I'll have an early night.'

Carol aped disappointment. 'But Harry, I've been looking forward to this all day. Why don't you sit down and relax. I've put the cats outside and cooked us a special dinner.' From out of the oven, fingers protected by a fold of tea towel, she produced a single plate. A glassy caul of gravy clung to something unrecognisable. He looked up in surprise as she slid the plate in front of him and handed him a knife and fork.

'What's this?'

She uncurled herself onto the chair beside him. 'There we are, nice and hot. I've been thinking about what you said, maybe you're right. Maybe we ought to think about having a family after all.' She indicated the plate. 'Eat up. I've already had mine.'

Harry picked up the fork. 'What is it?'

'Something I cooked myself. Try it, you'll love it. It's one of my specialities.'

Gamely he poked at the gravy. Something rolled ominously under the greasy shroud, as Carol continued, 'I thought, really, we ought to start trying straight away, after all there's no time like the present. What had you got in mind, two children, three? I've always been set on four. We would have to be fairly quick though. As you said, my biological clock is tick-tick-ticking away.'

Harry glanced up. He was wrestling to skewer whatever it was that was lurking under the gravy. He had gone quite pale.

'You mean give up your job?' he said, chewing hard on the lump of grey something that he had wrestled from the amorphous mass.

Carol laughed. 'Oh no, we couldn't both be out of work. No, I thought as you were so keen to set up a new home with me, you could look on this as a chance to take early retirement.' She paused. 'We'd need to buy a bigger house, of course, somewhere with a nice big garden. And I'd need to stay on at Lactons to pay the mortgage. I'll talk to Dougie about it tomorrow.' She waited a second or two before adding, 'You could stay at home. Look after the children.'

Harry swallowed the contents of his mouth with some difficulty. 'Me?' he said with surprise.

Carol nodded. 'Why not? It seems like the ideal solution. What do you think of my speciality?'

Harry grimaced. 'Oh, fine,' he said, poking at the plate with his fork. 'I should have rung you, I'm not really that hungry. I and some of the chaps from work stopped off for a pint on the way to the station, that's why I'm a bit late.'

'Never mind. I've put the rest of it in the fridge, I thought we could have it tomorrow, cold, with salad.'

Harry took one more stab at the meal. 'What exactly is this?'

Carol smiled and handed him a glass of wine. 'Heart.' she said. 'Boiled heart.'

Harry's face contorted. She saw him retch and then swallow hard.

'Oh, by the way, when do you finish with Kestrel?'

Harry took a long hard pull on the wine. 'They've offered us a month's retraining package. Waste of time really. I'd do better ringing round old contacts and going through the papers.' He looked up, waving his fork like a sergeant major's baton. 'About this baby thing –'

Carol snapped the words off quickly.

'I thought if Kestrel had finished with you, you might

like to stay home instead of tearing round to get into town every morning. You just said yourself it was a waste of time. You've got the phone here.' She pulled a diary out of her handbag. 'I've got late meetings most of next week.' She smiled at him over the corpse of his supper. 'You could make yourself useful about the place, Hoover, wash up, that sort of thing – and the garden is a real mess. It'll give you the chance to think about where you're going.' She paused for effect. 'And it would save on the train fares, after all, you've got a potential ex-wife and family to think about. And let's be frank, if I was your wife I'd be looking for a hefty settlement as you walked out on her – does she know about your golden handshake?'

Harry blanched. 'I don't think so, why?'

'If she gets herself a decent solicitor you'll find yourself waving half of that bye bye. And she'll probably get the house. Cast her aside, grown tired of her once she started to fade, part exchanged her for a younger model – they'll make mincemeat of you. Oh, the weekend after next I'm away. I've got a lecture at Baneford College.'

'What, all weekend?' he said, incredulously.

He got up abruptly and dropped his napkin onto the table. 'I think I'm going to go out for a walk,' he announced.

Carol smiled. 'Why not, it's a lovely night. Shall I save your dinner until you get back? I can always microwave it.'

Harry shook his head.

As the door closed behind him Carol picked up the phone and tapped in Katherine Bourne's home number. She was surprised to hear Harry's voice on the answering machine and wondered whether to speak or not, finally she said, 'This is Carol here, I need to talk to you urgently. Please ring me tonight, on my mobile – it doesn't matter what time it is. We have to talk.'

Katherine Bourne rang after midnight. Carol picked up the phone from beside the bed. Harry stirred.

'Go back to sleep,' she said firmly, 'it's a call from Japan.' Padding out onto the landing she whispered, 'Have you and Harry got joint bank accounts?'

Katherine sounded confused. 'Yes, everything is in both names, why?'

Carol glanced over her shoulder towards the open bedroom door. 'I can't talk very loudly, please just listen carefully. Can either of you sign on the account?'

'Yes, it made it easier when Harry was away. I've always handled the finances.'

Carol smiled ruefully. 'Good. Does the bank know you and Harry have split up?'

'I haven't told them, should I?'

'No, don't say a word. Tomorrow morning, first thing, go down to the bank and take out every penny you and Harry have got –'

Katherine made a startled noise.

Carol continued. 'You don't have to take it very far, open another account somewhere and put it in, you don't have to spend any of it – and then tell them that his new credit cards and cheque book have been stolen and that you want a stop put on them, effective immediately. They should be able to put it straight onto the computer. Ask for the new ones to be delivered to your house – and when they arrive, hide them.'

'What if they won't let me have the money?' said Katherine nervously.

'They can't stop you. It's your money, just don't close any accounts and if they say anything –' Carol paused, sifting through her memory for things Harry had told her about Katherine and his family – 'say that one of your children is buying a house and they're borrowing the money for the deposit, once their mortgage comes through you'll put it all back – but they shouldn't ask. Have you got an overdraft facility?'

'No, Harry doesn't believe in them.'

'Good.' From the bedroom Carol could hear Harry moving.

'What is this about?' hissed Katherine anxiously.

Carol grinned. 'A dish of ice-cold revenge. I'm planning to frighten Harry into leaving. Will you do it?'

There was a pregnant pause at the far end of the line and then Katherine said very slowly, 'Yes. And I won't need to open another account. I've already got one at the post-office, I'll put the money in there.'

'Great,' said Carol. 'I'll ring you tomorrow,' and hung up.

Jeanette spent the remains of the evening at home soaking her new sheets in a sink full of diluted bleach trying to get the strawberry stains out. Harry's wallet was still in her handbag. He had had other things on his mind.

'What's this?' said her flatmate, Carly, cradling a mug of tea and poking at the bundle of white greaseproof on the kitchen unit beside the cooker.

'Fish and chips,' said Jeanette, sniffing. The bleach made her eyes and nose run.

'I haven't had any supper yet, do want me to microwave them?' Carly asked.

Jeanette grinned. 'They're a bit mangled.'

But Carly was already unwrapping them. 'You owe me a supper, at the very least. I hung about for ages outside waiting for your fella to leave. What the hell were you doing up here?' She glanced at the stains on the sheets. 'I expect every last detail.'

Jeanette's boyfriend Bas rang at just after nine and offered to come round with a video, as they had missed their regular Wednesday night out. She told him she thought she was coming down with a stomach bug. It had to be something unpleasant or he might have offered to come round and mop her fevered brow. Bas was like that.

Jeanette plugged the kettle in, while Carly scraped the remains of their fish and chip supper into the bin.

'So come on then,' said Carly. 'No more holding out on me. Let's have all the juicy details.'

Jeanette glanced into the sink – it looked as if the stains were finally shifting.

The girl in the bank on the high street couldn't have been more helpful. Katherine transferred the contents of their joint savings account into their current account, leaving ten pounds in each one, which the girl said was the minimum amount needed to keep both open, and then gave Katherine a pink tab of paper with the balance written on it so Katherine would know exactly how much to write her cheque for.

'So where's Peter buying his new house then?' the girl said, sliding the transfer slip under the glass screen for Katherine to sign.

Katherine smiled evenly. 'Cambridge.'

'Oooh lovely,' said her unsuspecting accomplice. 'I've always liked Cambridge. Does Peter come home much these days? Only we were at school together – he was a bit older than me.' She made a valiant attempt to sound casual.

Katherine folded the receipt into her handbag and glanced at the name on the cashier's window.

'Funnily enough he was home this week. I'll mention I saw you, if you like, next time he rings?'

The girl giggled, cheeks flushing. 'I'm not sure he'd remember me.'

Katherine smiled. 'Oh, I'm sure he would.' She turned to leave, the next customer was already hot on her heels clutching a paying-in book and a pile of bills. At the door Katherine held up a hand in farewell and the girl responded with a cheery wave.

Ben Morton was waiting for her outside the bank. Katherine hadn't intended to let him stay the night, but he had, and now as they drew away from the kerb in his Volvo and headed for the post office she was glad he had. She felt like Bonny Parker.

'All done?' he said cheerfully, easing his way back into the market-day traffic.

Katherine nodded. 'Fine.' She was relieved that he hadn't asked her what she had been doing. She trusted Carol but didn't trust herself to explain why.

After he rang, Ben had arrived in the middle of the afternoon and suggested they go for a drive. They had eaten supper at a little restaurant he knew, and then they had driven home in the very last light of day.

It had been her suggestion he come in for coffee, and after coffee they had opened a bottle of wine, and then they had talked and talked – about children, and art and love, and life, and Harry and mistresses and wives and photography and growing outdoor tomatoes, feeling their way around each other's lives.

He looked remarkably like the dog in her dream, comfortably curled up on her sofa – and then slowly, almost imperceivably Katherine had felt desire settle with the falling night, as compelling as the darkness itself.

She had smiled and said as lightly as she could, 'Why don't we go to bed, the wine's finished and there's nothing on the TV.'

He stood his glass down on the hearth. 'Are you sure you don't mind? I really don't want to impose.'

She'd shaken her head. On the way up to bed she had seen the light flashing on the answer machine and had almost ignored it, but old habits die hard. After she talked to Carol she dropped the phone back in its cradle; Ben had gone into the kitchen to stack the cups and glasses in the dishwasher. Katherine waited for him to turn round and then smiled an invitation. Even the machinations of her husband's mistress hadn't been enough to stop her climbing the stairs hand in hand with Ben Morton.

Chapter Nineteen

Friday morning began quietly enough: Carol went off to work early, leaving Harry to catch a later train. Ray and Geoff had already offered to drop him off at the station if he needed it.

Harry Bourne sat at the kitchen table in Geoff and Ray's house waiting for his lift. In front of him Ray had arranged a full breakfast and a fresh pot of Earl Grey.

'We have all the national papers delivered to the café if they'd be any help,' said Geoff, packing the grill pan into the dishwasher. 'Local ones too, there are lots of companies based in Cambridge.'

Ray snorted. 'I really can't see why they expect you to go in at all, unless of course they enjoy prolonging the agony.' He glanced at Harry. 'Do you want me to pick up those other shirts from the laundry? They're only at the end of the road.'

Harry had taken another stab at ironing one himself; it had not been a great success. He poured himself a cup of tea. 'I thought I might not go in after today. The only thing is I've got a lot of contacts in town – shame to let all those go.'

Small blonde contacts with breasts that jiggled like puppies under a blanket; last time he had seen them they had been smeared with fresh strawberry juice. The thought had haunted his dreams all night long, along with a far less attractive image of Katherine chasing him with a carving knife, followed by Carol clutching a screaming baby – as the night progressed the women had cheerfully exchanged roles.

He shuddered and turned his attention back to the problem in hand. 'Without the company car life is more complicated –' He sucked a stray tomato pip out of his teeth. 'Carol thinks I ought to stay at home. Maybe think about early retirement. You know, be a househusband.'

Geoff pulled a face. 'She must be completely mad,' he hissed.

Harry looked up, feeling he had missed something. 'Sorry?'

Geoff continued quickly. 'What I mean to say is you're a city boy. A go-getter. You don't want to be stuck at home. No, no –' he paused, 'I don't think it'd be any good for you at all. Something will turn up.'

Harry saw Geoff look pointedly at Ray, who coughed. 'No, no good for you at all.'

Harry stirred another spoonful of sugar into his cup. For the first time the gravity of his situation was beginning to sink in. The anxious faces of the two other men weighed the scales.

'I've been working on my CV, and they've given us details of an executive employment agency. Lots of contacts and numbers to ring. Today they're going to have someone come in from the DSS to talk about benefits.'

Ray whisked Harry's empty plate off the table. 'Surely you've got everything going for you, qualifications, experience.'

Harry didn't want to think about it, realistically he was no longer thirty, and he hadn't got a degree like most of the younger men who would be up for the same jobs. The odds on him walking into a nice cosy middle management position with as much leeway and clout as he had at Kestrel were not good. He might be determined but he had never had the gumption to be brilliant – his successes had always been earned doggedly, through perseverance, so instead of giving his inquisitor a reply, he made what he hoped was an optimistic noise somewhere in the back of his throat.

Ray lifted an eyebrow. 'That good, eh? Maybe until you get yourself sorted out we could find you something down at the café. Washing up, odd jobs – that sort of thing.'

Geoff stared at Ray, as Ray continued. 'Temporarily of course. Just until you get yourself fixed up.'

Geoff picked up his jacket. 'Time we were off, I think.'

Harry smiled. They weren't such bad chaps after all, shame about the other stuff though.

Carol was safely tucked behind her desk at Lactons, Katherine Bourne was well on her way to draining Harry's bank account dry, and at around the same time, Jeanette was putting the sheets, now gleaming white, into her washing-machine before leaving for work, late as usual. Outside the summer sun was shining, the sky was blue. It was a beautiful English summer morning, cliché-ridden, and promising to be more so by lunch-time.

When she got to the post office, Katherine Bourne signed and then posted her copy of Hope's contract off to head office, deposited Harry's life savings in her Girobank account and then suggested she and Ben have a coffee before returning home.

When Jeanette finally arrived at work Carol had just two things on her desk – one was her phone book opened at the page where Sam Richardson's telephone number was written in her strong square hand and the other was a memo from the executive head of commercial loans, inviting her to join him for lunch.

Sam's number was a lucky rabbit's foot, something to keep her strong, an indication that out beyond the battlements there was more to life than Harry Bourne. She glanced down at the phone, wondering whether she ought to call Sam. He would be out at work – but maybe he had a machine, maybe he would invite her to say something after the tone. She hesitated, fighting the temptation.

The memo was a different matter; this was what she had been waiting for.

Jeanette came in with the morning's post.

'How's the tooth now?' said Carol, closing the phone book.

The girl paused mid-stride as if Carol had caught her with her fingers in the till. 'My tooth? Oh fine, no problem at all. Just needed to have a little filling,' she said quickly.

Carol's eyes narrowed, there was something different about Jeanette, something hard to define. She seemed to be more upright, more confident. Jeanette glanced down at her desk. 'So you've heard from the board, then?'

Carol nodded. 'It was on my desk when I got in this morning.'

Jeanette grinned. 'Ever upwards and onwards, eh? I bet Harry's pleased. By the way, Lee Fenman left a message on the machine, said he was expecting to hear from you. He's in Singapore all next week.'

Carol was aware that Jeanette was concentrating hard on her face as if she expected to see some secret message slowly reveal itself. 'Okay. I'll call him later.'

Thwarted, Jeannette continued, 'And Baneford's faxed the confirmation for Katherine Jackson's place on that course.'

At lunch-time, settled back in a chair in a plush restaurant, Carol watched her departmental head refill her glass.

'We really are most impressed with the way you handled the Danic proposal, smooth, tidy – beautifully presented.' He paused. 'You know we plan to relocate to Cambridge?'

Carol nodded, taking the glass he indicated. 'Next year.'

'I pulled your original application this morning. How long have you been with us now, twelve years?' He leant forward, fingertips resting together. 'You're a good team player, Carol, well liked, efficient, you've done very well . . .'

She felt a little tight bubble forming in her chest. From his tone and his body language she couldn't work out whether this was a compliment or a gentle but constructive put down. He smiled and sipped his wine.

'The thing is we are looking for someone to head your team when we move out of the city. Collingwood is taking early retirement in the autumn, and I've seen how much of his work you've been asked to handle over the last few months. Under other circumstances Danic would have been his baby.' He looked Carol straight in the eye. She felt her stomach flutter nervously. 'So I'm going to suggest we move Dougie Halford up into your job and you head up the section as from October.'

Carol realised she had been holding her breath and tried very hard not to let it out in one great burst. Her boss held up his hand to stem any words that she might inadvertently spill.

'The thing is Lactons are a very conservative company – you know that – I don't have to tell you. The one thing that concerns me is that you are – well . . .' he paused, eyes moving over her face like twin spotlights.

She felt herself reddening. Was he going to say a woman? She sincerely hoped not. Lactons had surely crawled that far out of the dark ages. She'd drag him through every court in the land – or maybe run off to join Lee Fenman at Danic after all.

He began to speak again, slicing through her indignation. '. . . still a little on the young side. Most of our department heads are in their mid-forties.' He continued to hold up his hands as if warding off blows. 'But we can hardly hold that against you, now can we?' He paused and held out his hand. 'So if you want the job, Carol, it's yours. Congratulations.'

She was clasping his hand and pumping it up and down before she really had time to think.

He clapped her on the shoulder. 'It couldn't have happened to a nicer person, I really wish you every success, you've earned it. I think we ought to make sure we're both au fait with all the details before this becomes common knowledge – and I understand there may be things you want to sort out before we move Dougie up. After all I came up the same way.'

Carol, still grinning, took a long pull on her wine glass. Oh, there were things she needed to sort out all right.

Harry felt oddly ill at ease on the train ride into London, as if he had missed a joke that was doing the rounds, but he couldn't quite put his finger on where the feeling stemmed from. On the platform at King's Cross he wondered about ringing Jeanette and then decided on sending flowers first. Say it with flowers. Smiling broadly, he headed off to Interflora.

The machine in the flower shop refused to swipe his card, and when the assistant typed the numbers in it came up 'invalid transaction'. Outside, after an embarrassing patting of pockets and much shifting from foot to foot, the cash machine in the bank wouldn't give him any money either, and then it ate his card. His cheque book was in his wallet. His wallet was still lodged with Jeanette.

Harry sniffed and counted his change. Besides his return ticket for Cambridge, he had four pounds thirty-eight pence. He caught the tube to Kestrel's offices and took his place in the tumbrel cart along with the six remaining men in the canteen – his theory about Danic picking men off in the night seemed to hold water. It crossed his mind to get his secretary to see what the problem was with the bank for him, until he remembered that she was no longer his.

Katherine, he'd ring Katherine, she'd know what to do, she'd ring their local branch and sort everything out. He thrust his hands into the pocket of his trousers and fingered the little pile of coins he had left. He'd ring Katherine.

From ten thirty until eleven a man on the dais explained

how to read the situations vacant column and then after-wards they had a relaxation class. Lying on a green rubber mat in the centre of the canteen, with the blinds drawn, reminded Harry of being at nursery school.

Letitia Cassius led the group on an inner journey into a peaceful sunlit garden. Harry closed his eyes and was relieved to discover that not only was his garden full of strawberries but Jeanette was already there waiting for him. He was woken up by the arrival of the buffet trolley.

Jeanette didn't answer the phone at lunch-time, and he couldn't think of anything he wanted to say to Carol's answer machine, so he ate cold meat and salad with the Kestrel six and wondered whether he could catch Jeanette before she left to go home.

He rang Katherine too – she wasn't in either.

Katherine Bourne had gone out into the garden as soon as Ben Morton left for home. He had invited her to join him on a trip to take photographs of some ancient oak trees but she needed time to think, and knew Ben wasn't the ideal com-panion. At least not for the thoughts she wanted to have.

It seemed the world had turned a long way since she and Carol Ackerman had had lunch in London, and she really hadn't had the time to work out what she felt or thought since then. Perhaps life without Harry would always be like this, a rush, a helter skelter journey without pause for consideration. It was as if she had been stuck in a pool alongside the main stream for years until some freak current, some flood tide, had picked her up and carried her into the torrent. Had Harry been like a dam, a buffer, deflecting the strongest waves?

She carried the kneeler out from the shed, tucked a hoe under one arm, a weed basket filled with hand tools over the other and headed for the vegetable garden. The runner beans, a mass of scarlet flowers and infant pods, clung to their watch-towers alongside a row of onions and another of carrots. Katherine settled herself down to thin out a row of pre-school lettuces. The garden was burgeoning with produce. This was nature's big push. Crouched under the shelter of the bean sticks she felt that if she lay down in the rows the garden would absorb her, and for some reason that feeling gave her great comfort.

The thoughts that she had planned to have slipped away unnoticed and her mind was caught up in nipping and tucking the rows into order, pulling weeds and trimming back stray tendrils of chaos. As she worked she filled a trug with the gleanings of the harvest: tomatoes nestled in the leaves of red beet, a hand of tiny butter-sweet carrots with their fronds of fern, a stook of spring onions.

It was mid-afternoon before she went inside for tea. The answer machine blinked its Cyclops eye, but she was too content to want to ruin her tranquil mood with intrusive voices. Cradling a mug she kicked off her shoes, headed into the sitting room and curled up on the sofa. Weary from work and sunshine she closed her eyes; what she really needed now was a cat, a big furry cat to curl up beside her and purr his approval. She smiled, pulled a rug off the back of the sofa, and let sleep claim her.

Harry rehearsed his speech to Jeanette: 'I just dropped by as I was in the area. I thought maybe, when you've finished work we could go somewhere and talk.' He glanced up at the front of Lactons' office building and sighed. He had slipped out of the talk on DSS benefits, frustrated by being referred to as a customer, and the constant sound of Carol's answer machine every time he rang her office number.

He toyed with the idea of going into reception and asking if Jeanette could come down to see him – but that looked too domineering – women didn't like that kind of thing. He stuffed his hands in his pockets. The tube to Lactons had taken the rest of his money and his secretary, his ex-secretary, had refused to let him have a fiver out of petty cash.

He had played and replayed every scenario: Carol and Jeanette were both out; he went home. Carol was in but Jeanette was out; he'd talk to Carol, lie and say they had been let out early and then share the ride home. Carol and Jeanette were both in; he got to exchange pleasantries with Jeanette, maybe getting the chance to have a word or two to arrange another get-together, but would still have to go home with Carol. Or, if God was in his heaven and all was well with the world, Carol would be out and Jeanette would be there all on her own, in which case – a voice cracked the shell on his thoughts.

'Harry?'

He swung round. Jeanette, dressed in a pale blue summer dress and high-heeled sandals, hurried down the pavement towards him. He started to salivate even before she was within striking distance.

She stared at him, standing well back as if he might explode. 'What on earth are you doing here? Have you come to see Carol?'

He shook his head, swallowing hard before he drowned. 'No. No, I came to see you. I've been trying to ring you all morning.'

'Carol's not here,' Jeanette said, glancing nervously over her shoulder as if she hadn't heard him. 'She's gone out to lunch with one of the bigwigs from upstairs.'

Harry glanced at his watch; it was nearly three o'clock. Jeanette meanwhile was backing slowly towards the main doors. He looked up and, seeing her retreat, made a desperate lunge forward and grabbed her elbow. 'Wait, we need to talk.'

Jeanette's eyes seemed to fill her whole face. 'Not here, someone will see us,' she hissed. Her lips were just like Marilyn Monroe's, Harry thought.

'What if Carol sees us?' she said, wriggling free of his grasp.

He hesitated, blowing out a steady stream of air.

Unexpectedly she smiled. 'Missed you,' she said, and leaning forward kissed him on the side of the cheek. Her tongue momentarily brushed his ear at about the same time as her nipples brushed against the front of his shirt. 'Yesterday was absolute heaven, magic, the best picnic I've ever had,' she whispered as she pulled away. 'I'm in now, you could ring me, if you like.'

Before he could protest she slipped through the plate glass doors and vanished into a lift.

He took a deep cleansing breath. There was absolutely nothing on earth to stop him from going up to see Carol, after all they lived together, they were – were – friends. Nothing on earth, expect that he knew that if Carol once saw him look at Jeanette she would instantly know everything. Women were like that. He closed his eyes and leant against the wall, trying to collect his thoughts, and as he did a hand dropped onto his shoulder.

'Harry? What on earth are you doing here?'

He looked up, eyes unfocused. 'Carol?' he said with total surprise.

She smiled. 'Who else do you know who works at Lactons? What's the matter, you look terrible?'

Harry blinked to clear his vision and fumbled around for an excuse. 'They let us out early today, Friday and all that.' He waved vaguely down the road towards the traffic lights, searching for inspiration. 'Some bastard nearly mowed me down on the pelican crossing. Amber flashing light and the bastard revved up and went for me, I swear it.'

Carol took hold of his arm. 'Why don't you come up to my office. I'll get Jeanette to make us some coffee.'

'Jeanette?' said Harry unsteadily.

Carol was already guiding him through the door. 'Yes,

you remember Jeanette,' she said cheerfully, holding the heavy plate glass ajar for him. 'My secretary? You met her the other day.'

Harry stiffened. 'The other day?'

Carol nodded. 'That's right. You came here after the meeting at Kestrel.'

Harry sighed. 'Oh yes, I remember now. Little blonde girl.'

Ahead of him the lift doors slid open silently like the gates of hell.

'That's the one,' said Carol. 'That's always assuming she's got back from lunch yet.'

Harry stepped into the lift, and wondered if it was sulphur he could smell.

Chapter Twenty

Carol noticed that Harry seemed very uneasy when Jeanette brought the tray of coffee in to her office. She wondered just how drunk he had been when he had shown up earlier in the week, how much he'd said and why exactly he was trying to shrink down into the carpet now.

Jeanette, perfectly at ease, set the tray down on the desk.

'Hello, Harry,' she said pleasantly. 'How are you?'

Harry didn't even look up but perched himself on the edge of the sofa, hands clutched in prayer. Carol waved Jeanette away.

'So, how's it been today?' she asked, as Jeanette closed the door behind her.

Harry snorted. 'Not so good. It's all been a bit too complicated really.' He pulled a face. 'And the bloody cash machine ate my card.'

Carol handed him a coffee cup. 'Any luck on the job front yet?'

His face contorted even further. 'No, mind you Ray and Geoff offered me a job at the cafe this morning.' There was less derision in his tone than she would have expected. He looked out of the window and then let his gaze move slowly around the contents of her office. 'What about you?'

Carol uncurled herself into the swivel chair, unable to keep the smile off her face any longer. She didn't think even Harry could dampen her mood. 'You are now talking to the newly appointed head of the loans team, as of October. It's not official until my boss announces it. So . . .' she left a pregnant pause, turning to the next page of her plan, '. . . you won't have to worry too much about getting another job, and as Lactons will be based in Cambridge by next year we can stay where we are. You won't mind staying put, will you?'

Harry looked up distractedly from concentrating on the contents of her bookcases. 'Did you order the van?'

'What?'

'For tomorrow. I told Katherine I was going to go and pick up my things tomorrow.'

Carol shook her head; it was a mistake to underestimate Harry's capacity for dampening. 'No,' she said slowly, 'I never gave it another thought.'

Harry's attention moved back to the bookshelves. 'I don't think we can get all my things in your car – unless the seats drop down, but even then it would be a tight fit. Have you got a roof rack?'

Carol sighed and then said, 'Why don't you go and have a word with Jeanette? I'm sure she'll be only too happy to help you organise something.' She wanted Harry gone. In a single sentence he had managed to whip the gilt off the gingerbread and also sidestepped her baited trap.

'You don't mind?' he asked cheerfully.

Carol waved him away. 'No, not at all. I've still got a few things that need sorting out here and then we can go home.'

He was already on his feet. As he was about to close the door, he added. 'At least you'll be home at a decent time.'

Carol looked up. 'Sorry?' Her mind had moved on.

'If you're working in Cambridge. You'll be able to slip home in the lunch-hour and do things –'

Carol didn't ask him what things, but had a horrible feeling it revolved around washing, shirts and game plans.

She picked up one of the folders from her in-tray and swivelled her chair round so that she could look out over the Thames. When she looked back Harry and Jeanette had vanished. She leant across her desk, picked up the phone, opened her book and tapped in Sam Richardson's home number. The machine cut in after the third ring.

Just the sound of his voice made her stomach flutter.

'Hi,' she said slowly. 'I just rang to see if you were okay. I wanted to let you know I'm nearly there. Nearly –' She paused and took a deep breath, summoning up the courage to ask the other thing that was on her mind. 'I wondered if you'd like to go out to dinner with me tonight, at the café, around eight. I've got something I'd really like to celebrate. I know it's short notice . . .' She left her mobile number.

She rang Katherine next, with one eye firmly fixed on the front office. Harry's recorded voice answered and, knowing he planned to go there, she daren't leave the message she wanted, instead she said quietly, 'Please ring me as soon as you can,' and hung up.

Finally she rang Ray and Geoff, to book a table for two for eight and prayed that her run of luck changed.

'Sure,' said Geoff above the background noise of the café, 'I can let you have your favourite table between the loo and the kitchen door. The thing we both want to know is why the hell you're encouraging Harry to stay home and play house?'

'It's part of my master plan.'

Geoff snorted. 'What if he says yes? He looks pretty desperate to me. Your master plan is all set to crash and burn, babe.'

'I don't think so, I've still got an ace in the hole,' she said.

Geoff made a disapproving noise. 'Oh, really. So shall I tell you what we've got on the menu tonight for you and the lovely Harry?'

Carol glanced down at her desk and the open phone book. 'Actually I've invited Sam Richardson.'

Geoff groaned. 'As if life isn't complicated enough already.'

*　　*　　*

While Carol was on the phone Jeanette was leading Harry down through the labyrinth of Lactons' service stairs.

'You had got me worried,' Jeanette said, eyelashes fluttering. 'I thought perhaps you wouldn't want to talk to me again after yesterday.'

He looked hurt. 'How could you think that? I kept getting that bloody machine so I thought I'd come over and see you instead. Too good an opportunity to miss, really. Has anyone told you you look gorgeous today?'

Jeanette turned, lips puckered into a pout. She was so close that the gesture would be easy to mistake for a kiss.

'It's very dangerous. But I'm glad you did come over. I've been thinking about you.' She shivered, making every centimetre of her gorgeous flesh ripple. 'Not you, really, about us. The thing is, I don't think we can carry on like this, can we? It's not right.'

Harry found it impossible to suppress a groan. 'What do you mean?'

'You just make me feel so ... oh, I don't know. The thing is I'm not a tart, Harry. I don't want you to think that.'

He reddened. 'I never said you were, did I? You don't think that's what I think do you?'

She flounced down another set of stairs. 'I don't know what you think.'

Harry grimaced and hurried after her. He really didn't know *what* he thought, but he did know that being anywhere near Jeanette made him hornier than he'd felt in years.

'Here we are,' she said with a flourish as they rounded yet another corner in the windowless stairwell.

Harry stared at a fire door. 'Here we are where?'

Jeanette pushed it open. 'Tony's little cubby hole. He works in dispatch. He's got a van. He owes me a favour.' She looked back over her shoulder, eyes alight with mischief. 'Maybe we could go for a little ride to try it out.'

The idea was very tempting but Harry remembered just in time that he'd need a hand to lift his desk and the bookcase. He nodded, searching for a compromise. 'What if I came back up to London with him, I could call in and see you when we've finished.'

'I might be busy.'

On Friday evening, Carol ate her celebration dinner at the café alone. Harry made himself comfortable on Carol's sofa, fantasised about Jeanette and watched TV. Katherine Bourne took the phone off the hook and watched a gardening programme on 2, while Jeanette, after calling Bas, to say that she was still throwing up, hired *Thelma and Louise* from the video shop across the road and ironed her sheets.

On Saturday morning Harry was up well before six and made a lot of noise trying to be quiet. Carol groaned and rolled over, woken, finally, by the sound of the wardrobe door squeaking shut. She opened her eyes in time to watch Harry shuffling towards the bedroom door in his pyjama bottoms.

'Where are you going?' she said before she could stop herself.

Harry looked around in surprise. 'Tony is picking me up at seven. I thought you were asleep, I didn't disturb you, did I?'

Events of the night before surfaced unbidden into Carol's head. 'Tony?' she managed through a furred mouth.

'The chap with the van, I said I'd meet him at seven. Good of him to come this far out of London really for –' he paused thoughtfully. 'Have you got any money? Only I promised him a decent drink and I haven't got any cash until I sort this thing out with the bank.'

Carol slithered across the bed and dragged her handbag

up from where she had dropped it the night before. It had been optimistic to think that Sam would turn up just because she asked him to, out of the blue. She winced and wondered. It was too presumptuous to assume that she could summon him up whenever she wanted him. She fished her purse out. 'Ten pounds?'

Harry pulled a face. 'I was thinking more like fifty.'

'I don't usually carry that much cash, won't this Tony take a cheque?'

Harry's expression gave her the answer.

'Look, why don't you give him the tenner and then by the time you get back I'll have had the chance to nip into town and get to the cash machine.'

Harry sniffed. 'What if he needs money for diesel?'

Carol closed her eyes. 'Tell him you'll reimburse him later. Just make sure he gets a receipt.'

She heard Harry pick his way to the bathroom and as he pulled the door to, jerked the covers back up around her shoulders. Sam might have at least rung to say he couldn't make it. Ray and Geoff had been very kind, plying her with champagne and then finding her a taxi to take her home.

'So how did your dinner go last night?' Harry's disembodied voice breached the still, quiet space behind her eyes. 'Lactons have got a bloody cheek to ask you to entertain clients on a Friday night, if you ask me. You ought to say something –'

Carol wrapped the bedclothes around her head.

An hour later, somewhere in the comfortable hazy grey ocean between waking and sleeping she heard the sound of a horn pipping cheerfully. As the last echo faded she felt her shoulders relax and unconsciousness embraced her like an old friend.

Tony's van had once been white but was now bullet-holed with rust. The back bumper was tied on with orange nylon string, the passenger side door was green and the rear windows were obscured by a sun-bleached rebel flag.

Harry, who had shaved very carefully and was dressed in a smart navy polo shirt and cream cotton trousers to prove a point to Katherine, stared first at Tony, and then into the back of the van.

Crouched on a pile of blankets was Jeanette. She was dressed in skin-tight jeans and cream crop-top. Harry knew he had his mouth open. She clambered into the front seats and planted a huge kiss on his lips.

'Hello, Harry,' she purred. 'I thought I'd come along for the ride. You don't mind, do you?'

Harry was speechless. Tony had parked the van on the pavement outside Carol's house and they were on their way to visit the wife he had just left. Harry swallowed hard, scrambling around for something suitable to say.

'No, not at all,' he murmured thickly. 'I'm just a bit surprised, that's all, and er – er . . .'

'Don't worry about me getting in the way,' said Jeanette cheerfully. 'I'll stay in the van when we get to your wife's place. What's she like anyway? Is she like Carol?'

Before Harry could reply, Tony, chewing gum, grinned and waved him aboard. 'You're an old dog,' he said with a conspiratorial wink. 'I'd like a bit of whatever it is you've got. You'll have to give me a few pointers.'

Harry reddened, fastened his safety belt and slipped lower in the seat.

Jeanette curled up against him, delicately tipping her head so that it rested on his shoulder. She made soft throaty noises of contentment and wriggled against him until he was obligated to put his arm around her.

'Oh,' she said suddenly, 'I've bought you a little present.' Rooting in her handbag she produced a bottle of after-shave. She undid the stopper and stroked a little behind each of his ears. 'God,' she said sniffing the air, 'I really love the smell of that.'

A few miles down the road Harry's initial embarrass ment ebbed away and was replaced by something more buccaneer. Strapped into the ageing Transit, one foot up on the dashboard, smelling like a rose, roaring down the ring road, with Jeanette tucked up under his arm, he began to feel like a gypsy prince. He didn't complain when Tony slammed a compilation of rock and roll classics into the tape deck and rolled down the window. Harry grinned, this was the life.

Katherine Bourne was pacing the kitchen, feeling a little fist of discord tightening around her heart. She didn't want Harry to come back home, and if there had been any way she could have carried all his things out onto the front door step she would have done it. What had stopped her – beside the weight – was that she was almost scared to open his office door, afraid of what she might find lurking inside.

On the kitchen table, cooling on a rack, were four large puff pastry cases that she had cooked to take with her to the concert with Ben. She hadn't intended to bake them so early but felt compelled to do something practical to take her mind off Harry's imminent arrival.

She filled the kettle and plugged it in, a nervous gassy bubble exploding in her stomach. She hadn't seen Harry since he left, not seeing him had made her feel strong and fearless. What if he was horrible or rude or worse still begged her to take him back? The thought troubled her like a toothache. She looked at the phone and then, without too much hesitation, rang Carol Ackerman.

Harry's mistress, her new friend, answered the phone with a grunt.

'Carol, is that you?'

She could hear Carol making an effort to rouse herself. 'Katherine?'

Katherine wondered if she had made a mistake in calling

'I didn't mean to disturb you so early. I just need to talk to someone,' she said anxiously. 'You don't mind, do you?'

Carol coughed. 'No, not at all, I was having a lie-in. Harry is already on his way to your house.'

Katherine sat down heavily on the sofa. 'Oh God. What am I going to say to him?'

'You told me not to say anything.'

'No, not about you,' Katherine said, voice trembling slightly. She felt a hot tear break free from the pack and trickle down her face. 'I feel awful. I'm afraid,' she said thickly. 'And I'm angry that Harry can make me feel this way. It's like waiting outside the headmaster's office. My stomach is in knots, I've got the most appalling headache.' She took a deep breath. 'And what if he comes in and I think, "Oh my God, I've made the most terrible mistake?" What then?'

There was a weighty silence and then after a few seconds Carol said, 'Just remember the weekend in Paris.'

Katherine stiffened. 'Paris?'

'Yes, that's right, Paris, and all these other lost, lousy, lying weekends – and all his bloody white shirts.'

Katherine felt her resolve returning. 'And having to boil his underpants,' she said.

There was another pause at the far end of the line. 'What underpants?' asked Carol in a tone that suggested she regretted having to ask.

Katherine felt the tension begin to ease, her attention settling on the four crisp, golden baskets of puff pastry on the kitchen table, all ready to take a cream sauce laced with fresh prawns, cod and a sprinkling of fresh chives. She was going to make a salad to go with them. 'Oh, you'll find out, you just have to prise them off him first,' she said with a giggle of relief. 'Thanks. I feel so much better now.'

She heard the sound of tyres on gravel and took a deep breath. 'Look, I've got to go now. I think he's here. I'll ring you later.'

Before Carol could reply Katherine hung up.

She checked her appearance in the hall mirror. The new earrings glittered like spun silk. Two strides and she opened the front door with a positive flourish.

Outside on the damp gravel stood a battered Transit van, driven by a man with a ponytail. Harry climbed stiffly out of the passenger side. He straightened his shoulders and tidied his clothes before looking at her.

'Good morning,' he said crisply. 'Are all my things ready?'

Katherine nodded and stepped aside. 'They're all upstairs in your office. I've packed your clothes.'

'Good, well in that case, this shouldn't take too long.'

He seemed reluctant to meet her eye and spoke as if she was no more than an acquaintance. As he passed her in the doorway she felt a tiny chill of panic; the shirt he was wearing was the one she had bought him for his birthday but it soon passed. She distinctly remembered that he always liked to take it away with him at weekends.

The man with the ponytail loped in behind him. 'Morning,' he said cheerfully, touching his forelock. 'How's it going? Any chance of a cuppa, only I'm parched?'

Katherine smiled. 'I've just boiled the kettle, I'll bring you one out.'

The man grinned. 'Cheers, missus. Nice gaff you've got here.' His eyes moved appreciatively around the warm homely decor. 'I'd really love a place like this.'

Standing halfway up the stairs Harry glared down at him. 'Come on,' he snapped. 'We've got work to do.'

The man with the ponytail shrugged philosophically. 'Duty calls.'

Katherine suddenly had a stray thought and tapped her pockets. 'You'll need this,' she said and pulled out the key to the office. The man took it, flipped it up off his thumb, caught it within a curled fist and then jogged up the stairs after Harry.

Katherine headed for the kitchen, closed the door behind her, and then let out a huge sigh of relief. She didn't want Harry. There wasn't any magic left, no last tendril of enchantment that bound her to him. She rested her head against the wooden frame and let the last of the tension ebb away. She was safe after all.

Chapter Twenty-one

Harry was vaguely disturbed by the fact that Katherine looked so well. Once everything was loaded up he climbed back in the van and tugged the seat-belt tight around him while Tony closed the back doors. Tony, who was rolling a fag, clambered aboard and cheerfully waved a hand in farewell to his wife.

Until he arrived at the house, Harry had spent very little effort thinking about what kind of reception he might expect when he got home. He'd thought Katherine might cry, might tell him she had made a terrible mistake, might beg him to come back. What he had not expected was what he'd got.

Katherine had been cool and civil but appeared to be completely unmoved by his arrival. He could have been the gas man for all she cared. And she looked different, younger, more upright, more confident – and that had genuinely surprised him. And she'd done something to her hair.

He sniffed, wondering if she was just putting on a good show for his benefit. He wouldn't put it past her; after all she was the one who was in the wrong. He concentrated on the view out over his garden, or was it now strictly speaking, her garden? The stray thought did very little to cheer him.

He realised that some part of him, quite a large part in fact, had assumed that once Katherine saw him she would change her mind. He would walk up to his front door, she would open it for him, her face alight with a mixture of gratitude, contrition and adoration. She would open her arms and embrace him, and with very little effort things would be just as they were. He'd pay Tony and send him on his way, with an apology for a trip wasted.

She should have welcomed him home, he thought angrily, all thoughts of Carol and Jeanette sinking without trace under his indignation. They could put this hiccup down to a mid-life crisis, a minor upset in an otherwise tranquil domestic sea. After all, who could expect life to run smoothly all the time; this was one of those moments, a predictable but brief bad patch like the ones he'd read about in the problem pages of Katherine's magazines. In fact, that may well be where she got the idea from in the first place.

They weren't helpful, those things, but subversive, stirring up trouble where there was none.

It would have been a great relief if she had asked him to come back; life with Katherine was predictable and comfortable, living outside was more complicated than he thought. She must feel that too. He glanced in her direction; she was just hiding how much she really missed him. Well, he wasn't fooled. Taking his things away would make her realise how ridiculous she was being, it would bring home the seriousness of what she'd done. He smiled. Serve her right.

But, if Katherine intended to keep up this farce he really ought to go and see a solicitor, and show her he couldn't be toyed with. Perhaps Carol might know someone who could help.

Beside him, Tony turned the ignition key, wrestled the van into first and with a puff of oily smoke they pulled away.

'We'd better go and pick Jeanette up first,' he said rolling up the window. Harry had completely forgotten about Jeanette.

Tony took a long drag on his roll-up. 'You really know how to pick 'em, don't you.'

Harry pulled a face. 'Pick them?'

Tony nodded. 'Come on. Don't give me all that crap, Harry. Your wife's a right little cracker and then there's Jeanette – and that posh bird up in loans. Christ, you must have the constitution of a bloody donkey. What's the secret?'

Harry reddened. Katherine had already gone back inside and closed the front door. 'What do you mean about my wife?' he said guardedly.

Tony snorted. 'Come off it, she's bloody gorgeous for her age, lovely figure – you're spoilt for choice, mate, that's your trouble.'

Harry closed his eyes and thought about it, maybe Tony was right.

Half a mile down the road, where the country lane joined the bypass, Jeanette was waiting outside a Little Chef, arms wrapped tightly around her chest.

'So how did it go?' she said, as she clambered over Harry to get into her seat.

Tony indicated the anonymous pile, swathed with blankets in the back of the van. 'Sweet as a nut.'

Jeanette glanced at Harry. 'You didn't have to leave me here, you know. I wouldn't have said anything. I wouldn't even have got out of the van.' There was more than a hint of accusation in her tone. She held out her hand and dropped sixty pence and a few coppers into his palm. 'That's the change out of your tenner.'

Harry nodded and pocketed it. It wasn't that he mistrusted Jeanette, or that he thought she might have inadvertently let something slip. What worried him, although he didn't really understand how it worked, was the strange insight and intuition women had about other women. Tony had suggested they pass Jeanette off as Tony's girlfriend, but Harry knew instinctively that that wouldn't have worked. Katherine would have taken one look at Jeanette and had her weighed up in a millisecond. She would have been able to detect the scent of sexual goings-on in the wind. And he didn't want that. No, when it came to it, he wanted everyone to understand he was the innocent, completely blameless party.

He would tell his solicitor, even if he hadn't told Carol, that Katherine had thrown him out without any provocation whatsoever. He glanced back over his shoulder and then at Tony, considering what he had said about Katherine being gorgeous. Maybe Harry could try and convince his legal man that Katherine had found someone else, surely that would strengthen his case however unlikely it was.

Jeanette curled up against him. 'I had a really lovely breakfast,' she said sleepily in a breathy little-girl voice. 'Shame you couldn't stay and have one too. And then cherry waffles.' Her hand settled convivially on his thigh. Her touch was as feather light and warm as a kitten's paw. She eased closer and stroked a finger along the inner leg seam of his trousers.

'Is there a café near Carol's place as well?'

Harry nodded. 'We'll find you another Little Chef.'

Jeanette grinned. 'Tony said he'd take the train back to London if you wanted to drive me home,' she whispered. 'I told him you'd got one or two little jobs to do for me.' Her eyes lit up mischievously, and all thoughts of Katherine trickled painlessly out of Harry's head.

Katherine stood in the open doorway of Harry's study and looked around the small sunlit room. There were no demons left lurking in the shadows, only a sense of emptiness and a lingering odour of upheaval. A few dust bunnies clung to the skirting board where the desk had stood, and a pleated cobweb hung on the wall behind the bookcase. He hadn't taken everything but what was left was either anonymous – an Anglepoise lamp and a waste paper bin stood side by side on the carpet – or insignificant, just fragments of Harry, not enough to re-form into something that might leap out and bite her. Devoid of the piles of clothes, the sports equipment and books the room was blessedly neutral.

She would paint the cream walls with something more cheerful, take down the roller blind and hang curtains. In a day or two and she could completely exorcise any last vestiges of Harry's shade. The sunlight seemed to fill the room like water bubbling up in a crystal vase. She had always wanted a work room, somewhere where she could read, or sew or paint, perhaps it would be fitting to finally nail Harry's ghost by filling the room with her pleasures. She smiled and pulled the door to. She would nip into town before Ben arrived to pick her up for the concert and get some paint charts.

While Harry was collecting his possessions, Carol drove into town and parked near the Grafton Centre. The stroll across the park, Christ's Pieces, always lifted her spirits. As she walked through the arcade near Drummer Street bus station out onto the main road she saw a familiar face ahead of her and without thinking called out.

'Sam?'

Sam Richardson looked up, in surprise and then his features changed and softened as he recognised her. He lifted a hand in greeting and at once began to apologise. 'Carol, I'm really sorry about last night. I was going to give you a ring – unfortunately I'd already made plans.'

Something drew Carol's eyes away from his face. Standing a foot or two away from him was a tall slender blonde girl in a summer dress. They were quite obviously together. Her hair was the colour of clotted cream and caught up in a thick twisted knot. As Carol unconsciously absorbed every detail, the girl glanced down at her watch, eager to be off. Before Sam had time to explain or introduce them, the girl slipped her arm through his and guided him away.

'Come on, Sam, darling. We're already late as it is,' she

said in a low cultured voice. 'If we don't get a bus down to the station soon we're going to miss the train.' She smiled without emotion in Carol's general direction. 'Don't mind us, will you? He's always late for everything.'

Sam shrugged and let the girl drag him off at a brisk trot. 'I'll ring you,' he called back over his shoulder as the shoppers closed around him.

Carol felt as if someone had squeezed all the air out of her lungs. Her shoulders slumped forward; she'd left it too late. It didn't matter that she was nearly there, Sam had got tired of waiting and already moved on.

Carol sniffed and looked heavenwards trying to ignore the little thread of emotion that promised to tease out tears if she didn't get a firm hold of it. She glanced back into the crowd. In the distance amongst the scatterings of people, she could see Sam laughing. The blonde girl poked him playfully and then quite unselfconsciously leant forwards and kissed him on the cheek.

Carol flinched and then took a long slow breath; she had to go to the cash machine, get some money, maybe walk around the market, maybe – she sniffed, losing the battle against a rising sense of loss. Bastard, she thought, not sure whether she meant Harry or Sam, dragged her bag up onto her shoulder and headed towards the café. Before she did anything else she needed a large strong coffee and a piece of cake, so rich that you could hear your arteries hardening with every mouthful. Ray and Geoff would be happy to supply both.

Harry and Carol arrived home within ten minutes of each other. As she indicated to pull into her drive she discovered a Transit van was already parked outside her garage. The back doors were propped open and the gravel was strewn with boxes, bags and odd pieces of furniture. The two cats had taken up residence on top of a filing cabinet. Carol's state of mind was not improved by the chaos.

Harry, red-faced and sweating hard, was crouched over a crumpled pile of papers that had spilt out of a black bin bag. Beside him a chap with a ponytail, presumably Tony, was sliding a bookcase out of the back of the van. Without someone to help him lift it it landed with a unpleasant thud a few inches from Harry's feet. They both looked up as Carol slammed her car door.

Harry rubbed his hands down over his trousers and smiled sheepishly. 'Hello there, Kitty-Kat,' he said, heading across the gravel towards her. 'I wondered where you'd got to. I think I've got everything. Did you remember Tony's money? Oh, and can I have the front door keys?'

Carol shook her head firmly. 'You are not putting any of that in my house.'

Harry's mouth dropped open. 'But . . .'

Carol held up a hand to silence him. 'You can stack it all in the garage. It'll give you a chance to sort it out.' She was in no mood for arguments.

The man with the ponytail loped up behind them.

'Morning,' he said cheerfully, touching his forelock. 'How's it going? Any chance of a cuppa, only I'm parched?'

Carol sighed. 'I'll go and put the kettle on.' She opened her handbag and pulled out five crisp ten pound notes. 'And there's your money.'

Tony smiled. 'Great, oh, and then there's a tenner for diesel, I've got the receipt.' Carol pulled another two fivers out of her bag.

Harry, having abandoned the landslide of papers, followed her into the house. The cats rode shotgun.

'Carol, I thought we'd already agreed that I'd put my desk up in the spare room and the bookcase in the alcove. I've arranged with Tony to help carry it all in.'

Carol swung round, fury erupting like magma from a deep boiling, bubbling pit somewhere in her chest. 'Then you'll just have to bloody well unarrange it, won't you? This is my house, my spare room, my life. And I don't want you camped out in any of it, is that perfectly clear?'

Harry took a step back, 'But you said –'

Carol fixed him with an ice-cold stare.

'If this is about Tony's money,' he began, 'I'll pay you back when I sort –'

Carol's expression dried the words in his throat.

'I'll get him to put all the stuff in the garage,' said Harry, backing out of the hall.

Carol headed for the kitchen, closed the door behind her, and then let out a huge sigh of relief. She didn't want Harry. There wasn't any magic left, no last tendril of enchantment that bound her to him. She rested her head against the wooden frame and let the last of the tension ebb away. She was safe after all.

After a few minutes she took a tray of tea outside. Tony was busy relaying boxes and bags into the garage from a huge heap in the centre of the gravel. Under the hedge was a tide mark of stray papers that had already escaped.

'Thanks, missus,' he said scooping a mug off the tray.

'Where's Harry?' she said, looking around for the van.

Tony paused. 'He's already gone. Things to do, people to see, places to go, you know how it is. D'y reckon when I'm done here you could give me a lift down to the station?'

Carol blinked. 'I don't understand. I thought you would be driving the van back.'

Tony shook his head. 'Nah, he's driving it back to London and I'm gonna grab a train.' He lifted the mug in salute. 'Nice gaff you've got here. I wouldn't mind a place like this, meself.'

Carol tried to sort through the pile of disconnected thoughts that filled her mind; had Harry left, had her refusal to let him move his things in finally driven him away? Had it been that easy? She doubted it.

'How long ago did you arrange to let him take the van?' she asked slowly.

Thoughtfully Tony wrinkled up his nose. 'First thing this

morning. Why? Don't tell me you're missing him already, are you?' He laughed. 'Christ, that man is a real dog.' His voice had an edge that to her surprise Carol realised was admiration.

'What do you mean?'

Tony took a mouthful of tea. 'Nothing, I don't suppose you've got a biscuit have you? Only I'm absolutely bloody starving. We didn't have enough dosh to get any breakfast.'

Dumbly Carol nodded. 'Why don't you come inside and I'll make you a sandwich.'

Out on the M11 Harry slapped the rock and roll album back into the tape deck and then clenched his fists on the steering wheel. He felt ruffled, and even Jeanette, who was so close she might as well be in his lap, couldn't shift the feeling of discomfort. He had had to borrow twenty quid off Tony, which didn't help his frame of mind.

'What's the matter?' she asked gently.

Harry pushed his foot down to the floorboards, straining to get a few more miles per hour out of the ageing engine.

'Women,' he snapped furiously. 'Bloody aggravating, selfish, self-centred, bloody women.'

Jeanette looked hurt. 'Oh Harry,' she said unhappily. 'I didn't think you'd mind me having another breakfast – I'll pay Tony back.'

Harry sighed. 'Not you, no, not you, just my wife and Carol. Jesus, they make me so angry, the pair of them. You know, I've given those two everything and what do I get in return? Sweet bugger all. Not even a civil word, not from either of them. No gratitude at all.' A great engulfing wave of self-pity rose up along with Harry's indignation. He eased back into the slow lane. Despite his ministrations to the accelerator the Transit wouldn't do any more than sixty flat out.

Jeanette rubbed his thigh. 'You've got me, Harry,' she said in a low voice.

He glanced across into her bright glittering eyes and smiled.

She eased even closer. 'Do you know anywhere quiet around here?'

Harry frowned. 'What do you mean?'

Jeanette undid the top button of her crop-top and batted her eyelashes. 'I know just what you need to get rid of all that tension.'

Harry gulped and then braked sharply; another two yards and he'd be parked in the back of a Nissan Micra. 'You mean –' he coughed.

Jeanette grinned. 'Why not? There's loads of blankets in the back, and besides I've always wanted to make love outdoors. You know, in the raw, back to nature.' She shivered, and closed her eyes. Harry wondered what exactly it was she was imagining behind those beautifully painted eyelids.

'It would be dangerous – and exciting. I think of you as dangerous, you know, Harry. Like a pirate, come to steal my virtue.'

'A pirate?' he said, wanting to ensure that he'd heard her correctly.

She giggled. 'You've just got no idea have you, Harry? All these years since Jordan died I've dreamt of a man like you. You could say I've been saving myself.' She sat back and ran her fingers through her hair, her whole body engaged in a provocative little wriggle.

Harry coughed. 'Er, right,' he blustered. 'Hang on a minute, I think there's a turn-off just up here.'

Chapter Twenty-two

Carol had brought two things home from her trip to Cambridge; Tony's money and a huge bar of milk chocolate. Tony liked chocolate and so after she made him a ham sandwich they shared the squares out into two equal heaps over a pot of tea in her kitchen. He liked cats too, and gardening.

Staring out of her kitchen window, he said, 'It's a shame I live so far away really, I could have this place looking shipshape in no time at all. Do all the patio, clean the pond – wouldn't take more than two or three days to get it round. Me and my brother run this little business doing odd jobs, mowing lawns, weeding, that sort of thing. Any outside painting jobs that need doing. It's a real nice garden you've got out there, shame to let it run wild.'

Tony was remarkably good company for a van driver, Carol decided.

'Ah well,' he said, standing his mug back on the sink. 'Better get the rest of Harry's stuff in the garage. Thanks for the food.'

Carol waved the thanks away. 'Not a problem. Just give me a shout when you want that lift to the station.' She felt as if she was in shock, frail, as if she needed tucking up in bed with a comfy blanket and a hot water bottle.

At the door, Tony hesitated. 'Do you mind if I ask you something personal?'

'Why not?'

Tony sniffed. 'It's a bit delicate, really, and you don't have to answer if you don't want to.' He hesitated as if composing the question as subtly as he could. 'Can you tell me what it is women see in that bloke of yours, you know, Harry? What's so special about him?'

Carol dropped her mug into the washing-up water. 'His stunning personality, the man is a lion in bed.' Every word dripped with sarcasm.

Tony nodded. 'Right,' he said and headed back towards the front door.

Harry had parked the Transit van on the edge of a landfill site, screened by a fringe of scraggy dust-laden trees. Overhead seagulls were wheeling, screaming their derision.

Jeanette smiled benignly. 'Don't worry, Harry, it happens to everyone from time to time. I read about it –' She rolled off him gently, her breasts brushing against the hairs on his chest. 'We'll have another go in a few more minutes if you like.' She leant forward and kissed him gently. 'Oh my little pirate. Don't be embarrassed. I don't mind, really.'

Harry glanced down at his sleepy little friend. He was way out beyond embarrassment. It had never happened to him before. Watching her scramble around the van in a tiny pair of bikini briefs was such sweet torture.

'It's probably just nerves,' she said, dragging her jumper back on over her head. 'You've had a funny old day one way and another. Those other two just don't know what they're missing. Why don't we just stay in the back here and snuggle up together under the blankets. I love a cuddle, don't you?' She wriggled back alongside him on the cold metallic floor. He could feel a rivet or something boring into one of the cheeks of his backside. She pulled a grey army blanket up over them both and then giggled. 'You know, this is really exciting, like we're camping out or something. We could be all alone on a desert island. No one else in the world except for you and me.'

Harry nodded. A desert island far away from Carol, away from Katherine and away from Kestrel sounded just perfect. A place where he could truly be a pirate. Maybe they would be able to find a leopardskin loin-cloth after all. He slipped his arm around Jeanette and pulled her closer, her breasts settled on him like warm bread dough, her hair smelt wonderful.

'Oh, what's this,' she said breathlessly as she slid a leg over him. 'You naughty boy, you were having me on all along, weren't you?'

Harry closed his eyes and almost imagined he could hear the sound of bright crystal blue waves lapping against a coral beach while above them the gulls cheered him on.

Katherine Bourne spread the photographs that Ben had taken of the house over the kitchen table, beside the picnic basket she had packed to take to the concert. Although she had looked at them several times, today was the first time she felt as if she was really seeing them.

The garden had grown since he had taken the pictures; the tumble of honeysuckle and old gold roses that crept across the faded red brick garden wall had moved silently towards their grand finale. Pods of lilac had exploded like confetti. She turned a print over and glanced at the stamped date. The photograph had been taken before Harry left. She sat down and picked up another photo, a long shot of the front path, curving up towards the front door, decked out in flags of wisteria. She stared at it, wondering if she could still somehow see the course of his leaving. All the lies he had told her. How could she have been oblivious to all those secrets? Ten years Carol said she had been with Harry.

Where was the evidence, what was it that she had missed? The children were barely in their teens when Harry had found Carol across a crowded room. What day had it been? What had she been doing?

They must have bought the house at around the same time. For Katherine it had truly been love at first sight with its high elegant ceilings and its sweeping lawns. Had her new love made her oblivious to Harry's? She swallowed hard; these were the thoughts she had dreaded, the ones she had expected to have when she had been working in the garden the day before.

She looked up, imagining younger versions of Sarah and Peter, dressed in summer clothes, running from room to room, the smell of new paint and the sound of footsteps on bare floorboards as the removal men carried furniture in. Was it then?

She fingered through the rag-tag collection of photographs in her mind. Had there been a point when Harry had seemed more preoccupied, more furtive? She sighed; Harry had been like that for so long that she couldn't remember a pivotal moment. For years he had had his cake and eaten it. She shuddered; all those years when he had climbed out of Carol's bed and then headed home, carrying some little trinket for them all.

Hurt and angry Katherine swallowed back a wall of tears – how could he have been so bloody callous? He had been making a fool of her for nearly half their married life. Had he assumed that she was so stupid that she wouldn't guess, or worse still, wouldn't mind? The euphoria which had sustained her for days suddenly burst into tiny crystal fragments and she began to sob, wild frantic hysterical sobs that made her chest hurt and shivered through her like the tremors of an earthquake.

She cried for herself, for the children, for all the things that might have been and strangely enough for Carol Ackerman. The noise of her grief seemed so big in the empty kitchen.

When she had done, Katherine scooped up the photographs and dropped them into their folder, working on automatic, hands trembling. It didn't matter that she had been the one to finally throw Harry out, a heavy sense of betrayal clung around her heart like a rusty chain. Harry had even cheated her when he left, even that had been a lie.

Upstairs in the bathroom she ran a sink of cold water and splashed her face, holding a flannel to her red puffy eyes. Bastard, she growled to her reflection. Whatever revenge Carol had planned it wasn't enough.

Through the open window she heard the sound of wheels on gravel and glanced at her watch. Ben Morton was arriving to take her to the concert. She looked terrible and felt worse.

Drying her face she hurried downstairs to let him in. He was carrying a bunch of scarlet peonies.

'Hi,' he said, eyes moving benevolently over her face. She rubbed the back of her hand across her cheeks, struggling to compose herself.

'I think I might just die,' she said, lips trembling uncontrollably. 'Everything inside me is breaking up into little sharp pieces.' A tear trickled down her face. She was afraid if she didn't try to stop the rest they might dissolve her.

Ben's expression didn't change. He stepped over the threshold, laid the flowers down on the hall stand and then got hold of her hand. 'Have you got your half of the picnic done?'

She nodded dumbly, his hand closed around her arm. 'Then we're all set. Let's go –'

She stared at him in surprise. 'But I look as if I've been in a prize fight, what about the flowers you brought –'

He leant forward and kissed her forehead. 'Everyone always cries over classical music in the open air, no one will take a blind bit of notice. I'll stick the peonies in the sink till we get back.' He went into the kitchen and re-emerged a few seconds later with a picnic basket over one arm and her handbag on the other. 'Is this everything?'

'Yes,' her voice sounded crackly.

He guided her out towards the car. 'Good.'

At the doorway she turned towards him. 'Are you being incredibly understanding or just horribly callous?'

He grinned. 'Callous is my middle name, didn't I tell you?'

Carol was annoyed that she felt obligated to wait in for Harry; not that she had any other plans. Not now. It was nearly half-past seven on a glorious sunny Saturday evening. The cats were on the patio stretched out like hearth rugs to absorb the last heat of the day, and she was waiting in. Waiting for Harry.

On countless other Saturday nights she would have popped out for a drink or had supper at the café, gone to the cinema, arranged to meet friends, visited her family, or just stayed in curled up on the sofa and watched a video, or read a book – but this felt different. She could do any of those things, but still some part of her would know that she was waiting for Harry to come home.

And then there was Sam Richardson; she had a vivid image of being politely sidestepped by the girl with the blonde hair, and winced. For years she had lived alone and had been quite self-sufficient and now after barely more than a week, Harry Bourne had managed to throw her whole life into total disarray.

She found herself wandering distractedly from room to room, which annoyed her even more. Outside in the front garden Tony, the van driver, had tidied away the evidence of Harry's exodus from Katherine's but the garage was full of his possessions; suitcases, boxes and bags, a bookcase and a desk. Tony had arranged the furniture against the far wall. It looked quite bizarre standing neatly by an old filing cabinet, as if it had been conjured up, a refugee from some corporate office.

Carol couldn't get her car back inside and so parked it tight up against the doors, a barricade against Harry's influence. Finally at just before nine she microwaved her supper, and then climbed into the bath.

*　　　*　　　*

Harry was woken by the sound of native drums beating out a warning of impending attack. He picked up a spear, strapped on his loin-cloth and then opened his eyes, astonished that the noise followed him out of sleep. He blinked and looked around, muddled, cold, and with pins and needles in his arm. They were still in Tony's van. Beyond the rebel flag fixed to the rear windows he could just make out the red glow of the setting sun, and instantly clambered to his feet. Beside him Jeanette, who had been asleep in the crook of his arm, groaned and rolled over onto her side.

'What-is-it?' she murmured from deep inside another dream.

'Open up, this is the police,' called a voice from outside the van.

Harry, panic-stricken, struggled to find his trousers.

'Just a minute,' he called lamely, 'I won't be a second.' He slipped his feet into the trouser legs, hopping about, hunched over, trying to pull them up.

Jeanette had woken up with a start and was dragging on her crop-top and jeans.

Finally, sweating from the effort, shirt undone, bare-footed, Harry opened the side door of the van a few inches and peered out into the gathering gloom. Outside, standing on a patch of grey grass was a policeman, sucking his teeth, expression impassive. Parked a few yards away on the dirt track was a panda car, with a second officer at the wheel. He had his eyes fixed on Harry too.

'Good evening, sir. Is this your van?' said the first policeman.

Harry shook his head as Jeanette slithered out from beside him. She smiled winsomely up at the police officer. Harry noticed that the top two buttons of her sweater were undone.

'No, officer,' he said. 'I've just borrowed it today to move some furniture.'

The policeman nodded. 'And are you aware you are parked on private property?'

Harry felt his colour rising. 'No, not at all, I'd got no idea. We just thought we'd pull off the road for a . . . for a . . .' his voice faded. The man didn't need to be a Nobel prize-winner to work out exactly what they'd pulled off the road for.

The policeman's expression didn't alter; he extended his hand. 'If you'd both like to get out of the vehicle for a moment, please. What is your name, sir?'

Harry reddened. 'Bourne, Harry Bourne.'

The man sniffed. 'And have you got any identification on you, sir?'

Harry patted his pockets in what he already knew was a fruitless search. To his surprise Jeanette reached into the van, produced his wallet from her handbag and handed it over.

'There we are,' she said brightly. 'Harry Bourne. Just like he said.'

The officer let his eyes wander across Jeanette's cleavage before opening the wallet and glancing down at the contents.

He seemed to spend a long time looking at the photograph in the front pocket; it was of Katherine and the children. Harry closed his eyes, wishing the ground would open up and swallow him whole.

The man allowed himself a wry smile and then handed Harry his wallet: 'Right you are, Mr Bourne, the thing is we had a report of a suspicious vehicle parked in the area. They get a lot of illegal tipping up here, you know.' He indicated the far side of the landfill site. 'Might I suggest that you and your friend get yourselves back onto the main road and we'll say no more about it.'

Harry nodded and began to frantically button his shirt. Jeanette handed him his shoes, while the policeman returned to his car and his companion.

Harry clambered into the driving seat without even

fastening his laces and turned the key in the ignition. To his relief the van fired first time and he pulled away as if the devil himself was on their tail. Behind them the policemen followed at a more sedate pace.

At the first lay-by they came to, Harry pulled up and took a great shuddering sigh of relief. 'Jesus,' he snorted, tidying his clothes. His hands were still shaking.

Jeanette giggled. 'God, that was exciting, wasn't it? You were wonderful, Harry. Masterful.'

He stared down at her in amazement. 'I've got to go home,' he began. 'What time is it, for God's sake?'

Jeanette looked at her watch. 'Nearly nine.'

He groaned. 'What about if I run you back into Cambridge? You could catch the train back to London from there?'

Jeanette pouted and crossed her arms defensively across her chest. 'Is this how you treat your women?' she said, looking hurt. 'Use them and then dump them.'

He thought for one dreadful moment she was about to cry.

'Oh Harry. You're all the same. You don't respect me at all, do you? Not now you've had what you want.'

He tried to put his arm around her but she pushed him away.

'That isn't it at all,' he said in appeal. 'I do respect you – I just thought –' What exactly was it he had been thinking? 'I'm sorry, I just thought it might be easier for you,' he lied glibly. 'It'll be late by the time we get back to London and then I've got to get back.' It was the first time he'd considered how he was going to get home to Carol's – he had barely enough money for the train fare, although if he was lucky there ought to be some money left in the wallet left with Jeanette.

She smiled at him, running her tongue over her top lip. 'You could always stay at my place and go back tomorrow, if you like.'

If he closed his eyes he could visualise the two open buttons on her top.

'And anyway you can't take the van back to Cambridge tonight. Tony needs it tomorrow,' she said.

Harry sighed. 'I'll have to ring Carol.'

Jeanette grinned and reached back over the seat. The silhouette of her backside in the jeans made his mouth water. She handed him his jacket.

'There you go. You can use your mobile,' she said, fishing it out of his pocket. There was something in her other hand. It took him a second or two to realise it was the lacy bikini knickers he had seen earlier.

He didn't trust himself to speak to Carol with Jeanette so close so he climbed out of the van and tapped in the number. She answered on the fourth ring.

'The van's broken down,' he said, leaping in before she could say more than hello. 'I've already rung Tony and he's arranged to come and have me and the van picked up. I've got no idea what time he'll get here, so the chances are I won't be back tonight. I'm going to ask if I can stay at his place, sleep on the floor or something, and come back tomorrow morning, first thing. I thought I'd better ring in case you were worried. No need to wait up.'

As he clicked the phone shut the policemen who had followed them off the landfill site drew alongside the van and the one who'd spoken to them wound down his window. Harry, phone in hand, froze.

The policeman grinned. 'Tell her you'd broken down, did you?' he said with a lazy wink.

Harry blushed crimson.

'Just take it steady,' the policeman said and slowly pulled away.

Chapter Twenty-three

Harry arrived back at Carol's just before eleven on Sunday morning. He looked terrible and said he had hurt his back trying to push the van up onto a trailer. Carol wasn't sure whether it was a rat she smelt or just the stench of diesel. There was a huge greasy stain on the back of his trousers but it was something about his demeanour that disturbed her – and given that she hadn't heard from Katherine, Carol began to wonder if he had spent the night at his old house after he'd left hers.

But she didn't ask him; after all this was a man who had lied to them both for ten years. She watched him as he headed upstairs to get changed, wondering whether they were active lies he told or passive ones, little lies of omission that let his acolytes believe exactly what they wanted.

He seemed a little distant, but oddly content – which made her even more suspicious, and then she was angry at herself for not wanting Harry and yet at the same time feeling this odd sense of possessiveness towards him. Dog in the manger. She had planned to go to Ray and Geoff's Sunday lunch-time bash if he hadn't shown up and in a peculiar way resented his reappearance.

By twelve Harry emerged from the bathroom, clean, buffed bright pink and grinning like a Cheshire cat. 'So what time is this lunch thing then?'

Carol glanced at her watch. 'Any time now. We can go down, have a glass of wine, they usually start serving about one.'

Harry nodded and straightened the collar of his shirt, tugging it square, watching his reflection in the bedroom mirror. He had a peculiar expression on his face. Carol tried to suppress the desire to ask him why he looked so smug.

'You don't have to go if you'd prefer not to. I know Ray and Geoff make you feel uncomfortable. I really don't mind going on my own, I could bring you something back if you like.'

Harry pulled a face. 'Don't be so ridiculous. Actually, I've been thinking about their job offer.'

Carol stared at him. 'Are you serious?'

'Why shouldn't I be? Ray said he thought he could find me something to do until something more suitable comes along.'

'You hate them,' Carol said before she could stop herself.

Harry looked hurt. 'Rubbish. What on earth gave you that idea?'

Lunch was strange. Harry seemed beatific, sociable and spent a great deal of time talking to Ray and then Geoff. The jovial atmosphere did nothing to shift the strange sensation in Carol's stomach.

She wandered across the café garden and took a glass of wine from the tray on a side table. Part of her master plan was to drive Harry away by making it appear that she intended to hold him close – too close, so close that she would shut his happy selfish little world down – and in panic he would go. She looked across at the barbecue; maybe it wasn't the greatest plan of all time. Harry was holding court over a glass of Chardonnay, Geoff and Ray were laughing; it did not augur well.

Perhaps Katherine had capitulated after all. Or worse still perhaps Harry had decided to take Carol up on her offer of becoming a house-husband. She took a healthy pull on the wine and slumped down on a bench in the shade. All she needed now was for Sam Richardson to turn up with Little Miss Blonde-Sylph and her afternoon would be complete.

Harry, wearing a warm smile, brought two plates over. 'I've got it all sorted out, you are now talking to Ray and Geoff's official gopher. I start tomorrow morning. Bright and early.'

Carol stared up at him. 'Bright and early?'

'That's right. Five mornings a week, eight until two, afternoons I'll come home and look for a proper job.' He grinned. 'Ring round, send out my CV. Mind you, I might seriously reconsider your suggestion of early retirement.' He slid a plate across the table towards her. 'Here we are. I'll need to borrow your keys.'

Carol looked down at her lunch. 'Early retirement?' she muttered.

Harry cut a hearty slice from the breast of chicken on his plate. 'Why not? I could invest my settlement from Danic and I've got my savings.' He grinned. 'Which reminds me, I must ring Katherine about the bloody bank. Oh and I've got to pick my things up from Kestrel. If I run you to the station can I borrow your car tomorrow? Then I can drive up to town after I've finished work here.' Carol was about to reply when Harry, mouth full, continued. 'The other thing is, do you think you could lend me a couple of hundred quid just to tide me over until I sort this money thing out?'

Carol tipped her head on one side to see if she could hear God laughing.

On Monday morning Katherine Bourne was up before six, wanting to be ready for the arrival of the film crew. As she opened her bedroom curtains she was surprised to see a travelling circus of trailers parked nose to tail along the verge opposite her driveway. Two men were unrolling a bale of cable across the road, and as she watched, a small crane pulled in behind the rest of the wagon train. She didn't bother with a shower, just dressed quickly and hurried downstairs.

Opening the front door was a mistake; a huge man in an enormous fedora, followed by a tiny woman, dressed in a puffa jacket and carrying a clipboard, respectively strode and scurried down the drive towards her.

'Good morning,' Katherine said.

The man sniffed, the girl smiled.

'Esme Thurman,' said the girl, extending a small limp hand. 'I'm Mr Delaney's assistant.' She looked quickly at the man with the hat; Mr Delaney, Katherine presumed. The girl glanced down at her clipboard. 'Mr Delaney is a little concerned about the excessive amount of wisteria.'

'Not a tendril to be pruned,' said a familiar voice from somewhere behind the two TV people. 'It's there in the contract, sub-section five.'

Katherine felt a rush of gratitude. 'Ben? I didn't know you were coming.'

Ms Thurman and Mr Delaney turned a fraction, Ben Morton, who was heading up the drive, hands stuffed in the pockets of an ageing Barbour, grinned and then extended a hand towards the morose Mr Delaney.

'Tom Delaney, you old dog. I had no idea it would be you here. How's it going?'

Tom Delaney sniffed again. 'So, so,' he said in a thin high-pitched voice that was totally at odds with his bulk. 'Small budget, tight schedule and a trailer full of whiny bloody actors, wasn't it ever thus?'

Ben winked at Katherine, while slipping his arm through Delaney's. 'Got the coffee on in your trailer yet?'

Delaney nodded as Ben skilfully guided him back towards the makeshift caravan park in the lane.

Esme Thurman looked bemused, her fingers tightening on the edges of her board. She swung back to face Katherine, determined not to be totally undermined. 'We'd appreciate if you didn't use the front door while we're filming and stay right away from the windows – and also could you move your car out of the garage? We don't expect to be here at this stage for more than two or three days at the most – if the weather holds.'

Katherine nodded.

'Good. Oh and if you could leave the front door unlocked, we'd like to get a few shots of the various characters coming in and out?' As she spoke Esme handed Katherine the clipboard. 'And if you could just sign here.'

Katherine peered down at a sheet of paper tucked under a bulldog clip. 'What is this?'

The girl smiled indulgently and handed her a pen, 'Standard procedure, just a formality really. If you'd like to pop your name at the bottom where I've marked it and I'll date it for you.'

Katherine scanned the text and then smiled. 'I think not. This says I give you permission to go anywhere you like and don't hold you responsible for any damage.'

The girl aped surprise. 'It's purely a formality I assure you –'

Katherine indicated the receding figures of Ben and Delaney. 'I'm not going to sign anything without Mr Morton's say so, besides which I've already agreed where you can and can't go. It's in the contract.' She slid the pen under the clip and handed it back to the girl.

Esme gave a short Delaney style sniff. 'Fine,' she said with a forced smile. 'Well, no doubt we'll see you later. I have to be getting back. Oh and you'll need this –' She slapped a small laminated plastic card into Katherine's hand. It was a badge with a crocodile clip attached to one edge. The production company's logo was embossed on it beneath an official-looking seal and signature was the word 'Visitor'.

Katherine smiled. 'Thank you.'

Ben reappeared half an hour later through the back gate. 'Morning, I'd lock this gate if I were you, have you got a padlock?'

Katherine was pegging out a row of tea towels. 'In one

of the drawers in the kitchen. I was just thinking I might be better going out for the day.'

Ben pulled a face. 'Good God, no, that's the last thing you want to do. They're like magpies crossed with monkeys – you drive away and they'll see it as an open invitation, they'll be all over the place like a shot, no, you want to stay put until they're done – imagine you're under siege.'

Katherine grinned and didn't resist as he slid an arm around her and tipped her face up towards his.

'Why are you doing this? I didn't know you'd be coming over this morning.'

He kissed her gently. 'No? You didn't think I'd let you face this lot on your own, did you?'

As he slipped away from her she realised it was comforting to think he thought about her. 'How do you know Mr Delaney?'

'Tom? He and I were are at Art School together. Last time I met him he was making educational videos. He's done well for himself. Besides being infested by a film crew how are you today?'

Katherine pushed a stray tendril of hair back behind her ear. 'Much better I think, the concert was wonderful. Any reason why you didn't want to stay the night?'

Ben shrugged and then crouched down to pluck an errant weed from amongst the herb-bed that lined the path. 'Experience – grief is something we all have to go through. If I had stayed you would have thought I could help cure you –' His features hardened. 'And I can't – you have to do that for yourself.' As he spoke he looked up at her; his expression reminded her of the old grizzled dog in her dreams.

Katherine dropped the peg bag back into the linen basket, resisting the temptation to make a grab for his collar. 'I think perhaps you're a very wise man, Mr Morton.'

He grinned. 'For God's sake don't tell anyone else, it'll

completely ruin my image. And don't be taken in. I'm on my own because I never can make relationships work; I'm a great starter, they used to say "shows great promise" on all my school reports, but I'm not so good on the long haul – and after all these years I'm probably too set in my ways to change.'

She stared at him. 'Are you warning me off, Ben?'

He smiled. 'Maybe. What I'm saying is don't depend on me. I'm no good at the commitment thing – run a mile when it looks like it might be getting serious. Now, how about we find that sly little cow Delaney is employing as PA and get ourselves a guided tour of the film set?'

Katherine nodded. In her mind's eye Ben transformed into a seal and slipped silently beneath the waves. She sniffed, trying to ignore the dull ache in her heart. 'Sounds good,' she said with forced good humour. 'Let me go and find my visitor's badge.'

In Cambridge, Ray was leading Harry into the kitchen at the back of the café and waving a hand triumphantly over the range of battered stainless steel worktops. Pans lined the shelves around the walls, knives, *chinois*, and all the other paraphernalia of *la batterie de cuisine* hung from hooks and racks on every available surface.

'And this is my domain. Your vegetable prep sink is over there.' Ever onward they marched through the kitchen to a small cubby hole lined with sinks, an industrial dishwasher and endless draining racks. 'And this will be part of your new kingdom too. Don't look so worried, it's really all quite simple once you get the hang of it.'

'I see myself as more of a people person,' he said lamely. Although Harry had accepted Ray and Geoff's offer of a job he had not actually thought about the reality of what it might entail.

Ray lifted an eyebrow. 'Don't worry, Cinderella. You'll be expected to serve too, coffees, teas, stack the dishwasher

– there's no pot washing, we've got a little woman who comes in and does that.'

'And I finish at –'

'At two,' said Geoff, sweeping past the door with a box of vegetables. 'I'll just show you how to prep the veg –' he paused. 'It's new potatoes, broccoli florets, baby carrots and salad today.'

Harry grimaced as Geoff handed him an apron and a set of kitchen whites. 'I've got to go into work and pick up my things from Kestrel this afternoon.'

'Don't worry,' said Ray. 'We'll have you out of here by two sharp.'

Harry gathered up his face into a philosophical expression. 'The thing is, I don't want to burn my bridges just yet; there could still be a position with the new management team. If my face fits –' His voice lifted optimistically towards the end of the sentence.

Geoff nodded. 'We'll lend you a clean shirt,' he said and then sniffed speculatively. 'You smell very nice this morning.'

Harry blushed. 'Just trying to make a good impression.'

Geoff plucked a knife from the rack behind the preparation bench. 'Right, now, I'll show you what to do and then you had better go and get changed. First of all you wash everything thoroughly and then –'

Harry was not used to manual work, nor having to think on his feet or come to that being on his feet for so many hours. The day wasn't busy but even so he found it hard to try and remember everything he was told. Hard but oddly exhilarating. There was a sense of order being dragged out from under potential chaos. It reminded him of getting ready for a school play, everyone rushing around behind the scenes waiting for the curtains to open. And for all the high camp and melodrama over soggy pie crust and bland salad dressing, Geoff and Ray were patience personified.

'Taste this,' Ray insisted, handing him a spoon.

Harry obliged.

'Well?'

Harry pulled a face. 'What would you like me to say?'

Ray grinned. 'I'd like you to say it's the best fucking thing you've ever tasted, but I'll settle for "Um," or maybe "it needs more salt."'

Harry took another mouthful of the sauce. 'I'd say it's just about right.'

Ray laughed. 'Maybe I've misjudged you, Harry. Here, stir this and whatever you do, for God's sake, don't let it burn.'

Harry had never had a job before where he could actually see where he had been or instantly weigh the fruits of his labours. It was strangely gratifying to see the full pans of beautifully prepared vegetables, under salt water, ready for cooking and bowls of salad neatly stacked in the chiller.

Observing Ray and Geoff at work was like watching some strange well-oiled dance routine. As they swung merrily into the lunch-time rush Harry realised, to his surprise, he was really quite enjoying himself.

At ten past two Harry, dressed in one of Geoff's shirts, headed for the car park and Carol's car. Whistling to himself he climbed into the driver's seat, pushed it back as far as it would go, adjusted the mirror and pulled out into the early afternoon traffic.

Carol spent her Monday morning with clients, and most of the afternoon chasing up figures. Jeanette came into her office at just after three. 'I was wondering if I could go early this afternoon.' Nothing in her tone suggested it was a question.

Carol looked up. 'Early?'

Jeanette nodded. 'About four. I've got to go and have this temporary crown replaced. It cracked again over the weekend. They said they could fit me in straight away.'

Carol stared at her. 'I thought you said it was just a small filling?'

Jeanette blanked her. 'I was lucky to get an appointment at all, they had a cancellation,' she said impassively.

Carol sighed and mentally pulled a page from her women-in-management course. This was an old battle-ground, well scarred with foxholes and weathered bomb craters. When she moved to Cambridge she'd make a point of hiring someone who wasn't camping out in the job and who could tell the time. Perhaps Dougie might be able to do something worthwhile with Jeanette.

'I would appreciate a little more notice, Jeanette. I'm concerned about your timekeeping. We have talked about this before and it hasn't improved. Is there something I should know about?'

Jeanette's eye brightened dramatically. Carol disliked tears, but refused to look away.

'I'm really sorry,' said Jeanette, without a shred of sincerity.

Carol waved her away in frustration.

As soon as Jeanette had left Carol tapped in her home phone number and was surprised to get the machine – surely Harry was supposed to be at home job hunting. She left a message anyway: 'Harry, I thought I'd remind you I'd be late home tonight. I don't know what you've got in mind for supper but if you ring Ray and Geoff they'll bring us something home if you haven't cooked anything.' She paused. 'Oh and don't forget I'm going to Baneford on Friday night. I meant to ask you if you'd like to come along. It'll be a good weekend, excellent food, intelligent company – you might make some useful contacts.'

Next she tapped in Katherine Bourne's number; it seemed as if this round of phone calls was becoming a habit – as was the sound of everyone's answer machine cutting in. When Harry's voice asked her to leave a message after the tone she glanced out at Jeanette's empty desk and wondered again if perhaps Harry had driven over to see Katherine. Just as she was about to hang up she heard a voice at the far end of the line over the recording.

'Hello,' said Katherine breathlessly. She sounded elated.

'Hello, this is Carol. Is Harry with you by any chance?' The words were out before she could stop them.

There was a moment's surprised silence. 'No,' said Katherine guardedly. 'Should he be?'

Carol turned a pen over in her fingers. 'What about Saturday night?'

Katherine made a noise of displeasure. 'No, I went out to a concert with Ben. Once Harry collected his things I didn't see him again. Why? Are you all right? You sound really odd.'

Carol teased around inside her head for what she felt and tried to put a name to it. 'I've just got this peculiar feeling,' she said eventually. 'I think he's up to something.'

Katherine laughed. 'What sort of thing?'

'I don't know.'

'Do you think it's something that affects us?'

Carol was surprised by Katherine's choice of words. 'Us?' she repeated in an undertone. 'I really don't know. I wondered if we needed to talk. Before the weekend.'

There was a weighed pause. 'You've invited him to that conference, haven't you?'

Carol couldn't bring herself to reply.

'Harry always seems to get what Harry wants,' said Katherine slowly. 'Maybe he's taken the hint and moved on to pastures new.'

'You mean, he's found someone else. Already?'

Carol could hear the bitter-sweet humour in Katherine's voice as she replied. 'Well, I wouldn't put it past him. He's got a pretty impressive track record. He's been stringing the two of us along for years. I think he looks at women like insurance policies; take one out just in case of unforeseen emergencies.'

Carol felt an odd little chill in her stomach. 'Who in their right mind would want Harry?' She heard herself saying, and instantly regretted it.

To her relief Katherine burst out laughing. 'Do you seriously want me to answer that?'

Chapter Twenty-four

After picking his things up from Kestrel's offices, Harry drove round to see Jeanette. He had a very strange reception. It was late Monday afternoon and she was sitting on the sofa in her flat, clutching a large snow-white handkerchief to one flushed cheek.

'What do you mean, it's over?' he said in total surprise.

She sniffed and waved him away. 'I really think you ought to leave. Now. I can't see any future in this for either of us. I've been thinking about it since you left on Sunday. I've met men like you before. You're just using me. You only see me as a bit on the side.' She paused, shifting her weight so that he had an uninterrupted view of her long, slim legs. 'I think I'm worth more than that, don't you? I want a proper life, a proper relationship, not some shady sordid little affair. I'm no good at all this hiding and lying, I'm not that sort of person.' A single hot crystal tear rolled effortlessly down her cheek. 'So I think we ought to stop seeing each other.'

Harry moved uneasily from foot to foot. He'd brought flowers. 'It's not like that at all,' he said falteringly. 'I . . .'

'You what?' Jeanette demanded, pouting and leaning forward so that he could see the heavy curve of her breasts beneath the thin summer blouse.

He swallowed with some difficulty. 'I think a lot of you, I really respect you – I . . .'

Jeanette got up and flounced over to the window. The summer sunlight spun her twist of blonde curls into a halo.

'It's sheer torture, this is,' she said miserably. 'We're just prolonging the agony. I want you so much, Harry, you must already know that, but you're not free. It's not right. It makes me feel so dirty – and used. I think it would be much better for everyone concerned if we didn't see each other again.'

Harry felt his jaw drop. 'But I've just driven all the way up from Cambridge to see you. I'm wearing the aftershave you gave me, I've borrowed Carol's – a car and everything. I thought we could go out for a drink and then –'

Jeanette swung round and glared at him, stopping the words in their tracks. 'And what? Come back here for a quickie before you go home to bed with Carol?'

Harry reddened. 'Not necessarily –'

Jeanette snorted and began to unbutton her blouse. 'This is all you really come for, isn't it? This is all you really want,' she said, jerking her blouse out of her skirt. Beneath the thin fabric her breasts were fighting their way out of a tiny cream lace bra.

He watched in amazement as she threw the blouse onto the sofa and began to unfasten her skirt. He had always wanted to say someone was beautiful when they were angry and now seemed like the perfect opportunity. Naked except for a tiny pair of knickers, the lacy bra and high-heeled sandals, Jeanette stood in front of him, hands on hips, legs apart. God, she really *was* gorgeous when she was angry.

He looked down at her, feeling a familiar stirring in his groin.

'Well?' she demanded furiously. 'What have you got to say for yourself?'

Harry licked his lips. Her nipples looked like ripe cherries peeping out over a basket of lace. 'I think I love you,' he murmured thickly.

Jeanette gasped. 'Oh, Harry,' she said, on the climax of a thin high-pitched squeal, and launched herself at him. 'You bastard, you total and utter bastard. I never want to see you again as long as I live.' Her lips closed hungrily on his, choking down his reply, while her fingers ripped at the buttons on his shirt. He had never guessed that breaking up could be so much fun.

It was late when Carol finally got home from work; from outside the house looked deserted which was a relief. Standing sentinel at the front door the two ginger cats meowed a twenty-one gun salute. She hefted her handbag up onto her shoulder and was about fish out the keys when she remembered she had let Harry borrow them.

She banged on the front door, calling Harry's name through the letter box. Nothing; no TV, no voices, no music, nothing. Through the letter box she could see the little red flashing light on the answer machine on the hall table announcing she had a message.

She pulled out her mobile phone and pressed the button to retrieve the calls, perhaps Harry had rung. Instead as she flicked the switch she heard her own voice. A sound track in stereo as she walked around outside the empty house, seething with frustration.

As she completed a second circuit Geoff opened the back door of the house next door. 'Hiya babe. You're late tonight. What's up?'

Carol squared her shoulders, determined to hang on to some last vestige of dignity. 'Nothing. Nothing at all. Have you seen Harry?'

Geoff shook his head. 'Not since he left the café at two, he was heading up to the city to pick up his stuff from his office. Why, isn't he back yet?'

'No, and he's got my keys,' she snapped.

Geoff waved her over. 'We did warn you to get rid of him before he had the chance to dig in. Come on in, I'll get the spare set.'

'Harry said you couldn't find them.'

He grinned and opened the gate that joined their two gardens. 'Gamesmanship, darling, pure gamesmanship. Oh, and by the way, despite all the odds, he did really well n the kitchen today – and I think he enjoyed himself. I warned you about your master plan. You want to watch him. Turn your back and he'll be happily tucked up at home whipping up a quick soufflé, waiting for his mistress to hurry home from the office.'

Carol groaned. 'I don't even want to think about it. I need a drink.'

'What you need is a better plan,' Geoff said, standing aside to let her pass.

'I'm still holding an ace.' She paused, thinking about the odd way Harry had behaved over the weekend. 'Or at least, I thought I was.'

Geoff lifted an eyebrow. 'Red wine be okay?'

Carol nodded wearily. 'Particularly if there's a bowl of pasta to go with it. I'm starving and completely knackered. All I really want to do is wallow in a nice hot bath.'

Geoff slipped his arm through hers, dropping into a passable impression of an old crone. 'Well then why don't you come into the parlour, dearie, and you can tell us all about it. We've been dying to know what's been going on, but it's so hard to gossip with Harry hanging around all the time.'

Behind them the two ginger cats, Augustus and Tosca, sprang onto the garden fence, their tandem landing executed with the precision of synchronised gymnasts.

Geoff rolled his eyes heavenwards. 'More gate-crashers,' he wailed, playing to a non-existent gallery. 'You pair had better come in too, I'll get Ray to break out the emergency can of Whiskas.'

Carol smiled, then leant forward and kissed Geoff gently on the cheek. 'I've really missed you two since Harry arrived,' she said.

From the open kitchen door, Ray's voice piped up in a compelling falsetto, 'And so you should, you wicked, wicked girl, never writing home to your old mother. Didn't we teach you anything afore you left for the city?'

Geoff waved her inside. 'Why don't you go upstairs and have a wallow while we cook the pasta?'

An hour later, wrapped up in one of Ray's spare towelling robes, Carol curled herself up on the chaise-longue in their front room and, in between mouthfuls of spaghetti bolognaise and red wine, told them all about Katherine, Harry and the van, the planned weekend at Baneford, in fact anything she could think of that delayed her having to go home.

She finally left at a little before eleven, just as Harry pulled into the drive in her car. He didn't see her standing in the shadows by the side of the garage but she could see him. He crept across the gravel towards the front door.

'Where the bloody hell have you been?' she growled before she could stop herself.

He stopped dead in his tracks and swung round. She just wished that she could see his face more clearly.

'Nowhere special, Kitty-Kat. Just met a few of the blokes from Kestrel and popped out for a pint. You know how these things go – I think there might be the possibility of an opening, nothing definite at this stage. I didn't think you'd mind.'

Carol straightened up. 'You've got my keys,' she snapped, palming the spare into the pocket of Ray's dressing-gown.

'Shit, I'd forgotten all about that,' he said apologetically. 'I'm really sorry, time just flew by, you know how it is.'

Carol followed him round to the front door. Although she couldn't be certain she was sure she could smell a whisper of perfume in the air.

'New aftershave?' she said, as he slid the key into the door.

He nodded. 'Funnily enough it is. I found it while I was moving my things the other day. What do you think?'

Carol pushed past him. 'Smells cheap to me.'

Harry looked hurt. 'It was a present,' he said and then

288

glanced down at the answer machine. 'Any messages?'

Carol tightened the belt on her dressing-gown before she fingered the replay switch. 'Only mine, you might like to listen to it. I'm going to bed.'

The two cats sashayed through the open door. Harry sneezed violently, once, twice.

It seemed like the perfect end to the day.

'About this thing at Baneford,' said Harry next morning over breakfast.

Carol had been sound asleep when Harry had finally come to bed. She nodded and took a bite out of her toast.

'I'm not sure that I ought to go. Maybe I should stay at home and get my things sorted out in the garage.'

Carol sucked a stray piece of orange peel out of her teeth, trying not to appear too desperate – it would be pointless playing the ace if all the other players weren't at the table.

'Suit yourself,' she said casually. 'I just thought you might like a change of scenery. There will be lots of company reps there.'

Harry smiled indulgently. 'Female reps.'

Carol tried not to rise to the bait. 'No, we've got keynote speakers from all areas of industry and commerce. Male and female. You ought to come along, you might learn something.'

Harry grinned and finished his tea. 'Is it all right if I have the car again today?'

Carol shook her head. 'Afraid not, I've got to meet a client on site in Northampton.' She glanced down at her watch. 'In fact I ought to be on the road by now. Ray and Geoff will run you in to work.'

Harry reddened. 'But I've got things I need to do.'

Carol lifted her eyebrows into an expression that might or might not have been an apology, and smiled. She picked up her brief-case. 'Sorry, duty calls. See you later.'

Harry held up a hand to halt her progress. 'What about the house keys?'

Carol looked at the bunch in her hand. 'What time are you planning to get home?'

'Okay,' said Harry crossly. 'Point taken, don't worry, I'll just hang around in the garden shed until you get home. I've already said I'm sorry about last night.'

Carol dropped the fob down onto the table beside his empty mug. 'I expect to be back around six, and I expect to be able to get in.'

In the kitchen at the café Harry carefully arranged a selection of plump summer fruits into the bottom of a single sugar pastry tartlet and then very, very slowly poured on the glaze.

Geoff looked on and then nodded. 'Perfection,' he said kissing his fingertips in a gesture of approval.

Ray, stirring soup on the stove, grinned. 'You've got a real touch for pastry. At this rate you may be on for an early promotion. There's another four dozen to do, do you reckon you're up to it?'

Harry beamed. 'Not a problem.'

Nothing to this cookery lark. Gently he slid the tart off the baking sheet onto a plate and dropped a fringe of shaved chocolate alongside it. He glanced up at the clock. It was nearly ten thirty. He wiped his hands on a cloth. Time to ring Jeanette. Maybe he would be able to persuade her to spend the weekend with him while Carol was away.

'I've just got to make a phone call.'

Geoff waved him towards the office. 'Help yourself, and if they offer you the job tell them you've already got a position as head pastry chef.'

Harry preened and closed the office door behind him.

Jeanette answered on the second ring. 'Good morning, Carol Ackerman's office, how may I help you?'

She sounded cool, prim and very efficient. Harry settled himself in the swivel chair.

'Hello gorgeous. How are you this morning?'

His enquiry was met with an icy silence.

'Jeanette? Are you there?'

Nothing.

'I know you're there. What's the matter?'

'I can't to talk to you now,' she whispered.

Harry laughed. 'Come on. Don't be silly, I know Carol's out in Northampton all day with a client. What on earth is the matter?'

Silence descended again.

Harry coughed, feeling a little foolish. 'We need to talk. I have to see you.'

'We said everything we needed to say yesterday,' Jeanette murmured, 'I've already told you, Harry, it's over. You know how I feel about you, but I'm not anyone's bit on the side.'

Before he could reply she hung up. Harry stared at the receiver, feeling the breath rush out of his chest. He struggled to inhale; all he could smell was the aftershave Jeanette had bought him. He couldn't believe it. Yesterday afternoon he had been awesome; she'd said so.

The phone line hummed quietly while he made up his mind what to do. The more he thought about it the more certain he was that she couldn't be serious. They'd spent all afternoon in bed; he had the scratches to prove it.

He pressed redial and got the main switchboard. The receptionist tried to put his call through but Carol's extension was engaged. When he tried again all he got was the answer machine.

'No luck?' said Ray, as Harry headed back, deflated and confused, into the kitchen.

Harry made his way back to the sink; besides doing the fruit tarts there were still two boxes of salad for him to wash and trim.

Geoff handed him a mug of coffee. 'Don't look so down in the mouth. Something will turn up. You need to keep your options open at the moment, don't make any hasty decisions. What about old contacts, couldn't they help you out? Surely someone must owe you a favour?'

Harry glanced up and sighed.

Ray looked concerned. 'Is there anything we can do to help?

Harry shook his head; he doubted that when it came to dealing with women Ray and Geoff could be any help at all.

But Geoff was right about old contacts – under the circumstances he'd be a fool to burn his bridges. Perhaps he ought to ring his daughter Sarah. The thought hardened up; the focus shifted. After all he had barely spoken to Sarah since he'd left home.

'Won't be a minute,' he said. 'Just got to make one more call.'

In her house near Huntingdon, Katherine Bourne opened her bedroom window and glanced out at the refugee camp across the road. It was nearly eleven, half way through the second day of filming and the film crew were moving light across the tarmac towards her front door and parking them randomly on the centre of her lawn. Cables snaked back through the hedge to a generator. Fired up and running i suffused the morning air with a tuneless hum on the periphery of her hearing. There was a babble of noise, a human mid-morning chorus. Outside, running along the gravel was a length of narrow track on which they ran a camera mounted on a dolly to get tracking shots of cars and characters arriving.

Esme Thurman, Delaney's assistant, had said they should be finished by the end of the day if the light and weather held, although she had pointed out again that in the contract they reserved the right to return as and when necessary.

Katherine shuffled the curtains apart to a spot which a girl in continuity had marked with green tape on the window sill and then headed for the bathroom.

Ben Morton had left in the middle of the previous afternoon. She glanced back at the newly made bed wondering if he was really so wise to leave her alone with the remnants of her grief. He had already warned her not to depend on him. She shuddered. If she didn't concentrate everything felt fragmented; the chaos on the lawn added to the sense of upheaval.

The phone ringing broke her thought patterns and she picked up the bedroom extension. Perhaps it was Ben.

She hadn't time to say more than good morning, before her daughter Sarah said, 'Dad just rang me, they had to fetch me out of a class. I really can't have this.'

Katherine sat down heavily on the bed. 'Good morning, Sarah,' she said slowly.

Sarah continued as if Katherine hadn't spoken. 'He sounds really depressed. He said you made him take all his things out of the house.'

Katherine reddened, indignation flaring. 'That isn't true, he –'

But Sarah was still ahead of her. 'Did you get those leaflets I sent you? It says there that it's easy to make hasty decisions in crisis, decisions that you regret later and that you shouldn't let pride hold you back from admitting when you are wrong. To be perfectly honest I've had quite enough of all this nonsense. I've got Dad's number. I want you to ring him up straight away and tell him you're sorry. Get it over and done with before this goes any further. He's been talking about solicitors and selling the house – you do realise what you've started, don't you?'

Katherine struggled to draw a breath. She wanted to say

something to stem the flood tide of words, something to stop Sarah dead in her tracks.

'Sarah, I've met someone else, you saw him while you were here, in the Volvo,' she said in a strong clear voice over Sarah's schoolmarmish monologue. It didn't matter that Katherine already knew Ben was a passing pleasure; she hoped it would be enough to hold Sarah at bay long enough for her to gather her thoughts. 'And I think your father has found someone else too.' She couldn't quite bring herself to shoot down Harry's saintliness. Let Harry tell Sarah about Carol himself.

Sarah, caught mid-sentence, took a breath and then snorted derisively. 'Don't be so ridiculous, Mother. Dad's completely shattered, heartbroken. Now have you got a pen? I'll give you this number. You really ought to talk to him.'

It seemed that Sarah, like Harry, had an endless capacity to reinvent the truth to suit herself. Katherine picked up a Biro and dutifully wrote the number down on the fly leaf of one of the books on the bedside table.

'I've really got to get back to my class. Ring him now,' said Sarah emphatically.

Katherine dialled the number without really thinking and waited for someone to answer. A man finally picked the phone up. 'Hold the line, I'll get him for you.'

Katherine stared out of the bedroom window. Sarah was right; they did have to talk.

'Hello,' said Harry. 'Who is this?'

Katherine took a deep breath. 'It's me, Harry, Katherine. Sarah just rang me. She said she was worried about you.'

Harry made a thick unhappy noise on the end of the phone. 'We have to talk,' he said in an undertone. 'Can you come and pick me up from the station?'

Katherine felt a little ripple of shock. He sounded almost conciliatory, perhaps Sarah was right after all.

'Now?' she asked in surprise.

'No,' said Harry. 'I'm busy at the moment. Later this afternoon. I'll ring and let you know what time my train is arriving.'

Outside the bedroom window, Delaney and his merry men were setting up for another shot. Too much chaos and Katherine knew she wouldn't be able to think clearly with Harry added to the cocktail.

'I don't think it would be a very good idea for you to come here,' she said.

'Why ever not?' said Harry, the old Harry.

The sound of his voice shook her. She squared her shoulders.

'Because I think we ought to meet on neutral territory.'

Harry snorted. 'This isn't the cold war, you know. But if you insist on being so melodramatic. I'll ring you later on today.' And then he was gone, with no indication of what time he might phone. Katherine bristled. One short telephone conversation and she was back at Harry's beck and call.

Chapter Twenty-five

Carol was in Northampton and Katherine was at home waiting for Harry to ring. It was mid-morning, just before coffee break, and Jeanette was struggling over the celebrity crossword at her desk outside Carol's office at Lactons. It had been a slow day. She'd already finished the five hundred pound word search and spot the odd one out.

Something broke her concentration and she looked up straight into an impressive bouquet of hothouse flowers and balloons. The temp from reception, who Jeanette had borrowed the knitting from, smiled wryly and handed them over the desk.

'These just arrived for you downstairs. It looks like you made a good impression on someone.'

Jeanette grinned and unpeeled the tiny pale pink envelope from the cellophane wrapper. Inside it read, 'I need to talk to you. Love, H'.

The girl was hanging around, waiting to find out who the flowers were from.

'Business,' Jeanette said archly, dropping the card into her handbag.

The girl lifted her eyebrows. 'You must be very good.'

Jeanette smiled. 'Oh, I am.'

Katherine stood on the platform at the railway station shifting nervously from foot to foot. She glanced at her watch. It was nearly four o'clock and Harry's train had arrived late. Those extra minutes alone with her thoughts had been sheer murder, transforming a light breeze of nervous tension into a roaring gale. Daytime trains were always practically empty. She peered at the smattering of travellers and cheap day shoppers heading down towards the ticket collector, finally spotting Harry's red-gold thatch amongst them and took a deep breath, trying to settle herself.

As he reached the barrier Harry glanced up and held her gaze.

'Well, hello,' he said, smiling warmly as they met face to face. 'You're looking good. You've done something different with your hair. I meant to say something on Saturday, but it was all a bit fraught, wasn't it? Where do you suggest we go to talk?'

He looked tired.

Katherine waved her hand towards one of the benches near the waiting-room. 'Here seems as good a place as any.'

Harry's face contorted. 'We're going to discuss our marriage on a railway platform, are we? You've been reading too many spy stories. Why can't we just go back to the house?'

Katherine bit her lip. 'I thought somewhere neutral would be better. Do you want some tea?' She nodded towards the vending machine. She needed something to do with her hands to stop them winding themselves into a hangman's noose.

He nodded. 'Why not.'

With a polystyrene cup in each hand she guided Harry over to the bench and perched nervously on the edge, waiting for him to begin the conversation.

'Well,' he said, taking the cup from her. 'What was it you wanted to say?'

Katherine looked up in surprise. 'I didn't want to say anything. I just thought we ought to get together to sort out some of the practicalities.'

Harry sipped his tea and smiled. 'Come on, Kitty-Kat, I know this can't be easy for you, but I've already spoken to Sarah. In fact, I wish I had rung her sooner.' He reached out and touched Katherine's hand. 'We have had some good times together, haven't we?'

She stiffened as his fingers brushed hers. 'What exactly was it that Sarah said to you?'

Harry shrugged. 'She told me you were going through some sort of mid-life crisis. She read about it in a magazine, it's quite common apparently.'

Slowly Katherine backed away from him. 'Mid-life crisis?'

Harry nodded. 'I blame myself, all those weekends away, working late. I was doing it for the family, for us, you know that, but I suppose I just didn't notice how much the pressure was affecting you. And once the kids had left – well – Sarah thinks you've lost your sense of purpose. I can understand that. Maybe you ought to think about doing some voluntary work, Red Cross or something or even an evening class.'

Katherine felt her jaw drop. All those weekends he'd been away with Carol Ackerman, all those lies, had been miraculously transformed into a selfless act of good husbandry.

She swallowed hard as Harry continued. 'I really miss you, you know – but I honestly think we can put all this behind us if we try. I really want this marriage to work. What I'm trying to say is, I don't hold any of this against you. I suppose to some extent it's partly my fault. But I've always had you down as a capable woman – I just didn't think.'

Katherine didn't know what to say and sat with her mouth open, fingers strangling the life out of the polystyrene tea cup.

'. . . And then there's been all this nonsense with Kestrel on top of everything else.' He paused, as if struggling to control his emotions. 'I need you, Katherine, you must know that. Change of job, change of lifestyle. I've been thinking maybe this is just the sort of shake-up we both needed. A whole fresh start for both of us.'

Katherine took a sip of tea, waiting for the moment when she felt calm enough to speak. 'So where have you been staying?' she said.

He waved the question away dismissively. 'With a friend from work, on their sofa. No one special. But to be honest I think I've almost outstayed my welcome.' He caught hold of her hand, looking deep into her eyes. She winced as his grip tightened. 'This is ridiculous, what exactly is it we're fighting about? I forgive you, Katherine, I really do. Why don't you just let me come home? I don't really understand what's been going on, but I know we can sort it out, whatever it is. I miss you.'

Katherine stared at his white shirt; what he missed was her ironing, her cooking and mostly, she thought, having a tame woman on call. His shallowness stung. She took a deep breath, mustering the words like a line of infantry inside her head.

'Harry, I don't need you to forgive me,' she said, her eyes boring into his, voice as cool and even as a snow-covered lake. 'And whatever Sarah told you I don't want you back.'

He reeled away from her as if she had punched him. 'What do you mean? Sarah said –'

'Sarah is telling you what she wants to hear, Harry. It's over. I thought you wanted to talk about selling your share of the house.'

His face contorted with fury. 'The house? The bloody house? That's it –' he snarled, hurling his tea down onto the platform. Behind them an old lady, peaceably reading the timetable, backed away in horror.

'Typical of a woman to kick a man when he's bloody down,' Harry continued unabashed. 'I've lost my job, I'm on the bloody scrap heap, all on my own and all you can think about is selling the house. *My* house. Money, money,

money, you're all the same – you – you –' He clenched his fists, leapt to his feet and kicked the rubbish bin beside the bench. The old lady, who had been unashamedly watching the drama unfold, hurried away down the platform towards the ticket office.

'All the things I've done for you, all those weekends I worked, all those bloody conferences and sodding meetings – and all for you, Katherine – all for you – and now when I need you you bloody well throw me out. You knew about this Kestrel thing, didn't you? I wouldn't put it past you.'

Katherine's stomach contracted sharply and she began to shake.

Harry was still ranting. 'This is all your fault. I'll go into a steep decline now, you know. Six months and I'll be drinking meths under a bridge somewhere, sleeping in a cardboard box with all the other no-hopers – and it'll all be your fault.'

She picked up her handbag and got to her feet. 'No, Harry,' she said in a carefully controlled voice. 'Whatever happens to you now is up to you. Your choice. I really don't think we ought to meet again, I'll contact you through my solicitor.' Her knuckles were white where they gripped the shoulder strap of her bag.

Harry was livid. 'This is all your fault,' he roared after her as she hurried down the platform, 'I've done nothing wrong, nothing at all. I'm being extremely reasonable – come back here.'

Katherine hurtled across the car park and dragged open the door of her car, afraid to look back. She roared up to the barrier, threw a handful of change at the attendant, then drove out onto the main road like a thing possessed and didn't stop until she was half a mile from home. Pulling onto the verge she tightened her grip on the steering wheel, leant forward and let out a long shuddering breath. It felt like the first one she had taken since leaving Harry at the station. A second or two later she burst into tears.

Of all the Harrys she had ever known she had never seen that one before.

The film crew were just packing up as Katherine pulled into the lane outside her house. She had forgotten they were there and had to brake sharply to avoid hitting a man carrying a bale of cable. Esme Thurman lifted a hand in greeting and then thought better of it and flagged her down.

'All done,' she said with a cool professional smile. 'I'll authorise payment by fax first thing tomorrow. It's gone really well.'

Katherine nodded. She was in no mood for conversation.

Esme smiled. 'It's a lovely house. Hope said you're thinking about turning it into some sort of hotel or something.'

Katherine sniffed. 'A rest home.'

Esme pulled a face. 'Really? God, rather you than me, running around after people. Mind you, I'd imagine there's a lot of money in it if you can stand being tied down.'

Katherine stared up at her.

'You know,' said Esme, 'always at someone else's beck and call.'

The words stung. Esme was still talking. 'You won't be changing anything on the front will you? Just in case we need to come back?'

Katherine was staring into the middle distance, imagining Harry, white-haired, hunched over a zimmer frame, screaming for tea and a clean shirt. As quickly as Hope Laughton's words had inspired her Esme Thurman's casual remarks painted another picture with a big brush on a broad canvas.

'No,' she said quickly. 'No, I don't imagine I'll be changing anything.'

Esme nodded and slid her outstretched hand through Katherine's car window. 'Good, well, I'll make sure they leave the place nice and tidy, and thanks – it's been nice to meet you. I hope all your plans work out. Look out for your front door on the telly.'

Katherine shook Esme's hand and then slowly drove up to the garage. She was so used to caring for other people that it had never occurred to her that she might want a change, that there might be something else to life. The retirement home had been the idea that had persuaded her she could be independent, that had spurred her on to ask Harry to leave, but perhaps the idea on its own was enough.

She looked up, seeing the old house with new eyes. It was beautiful, and she did love it, but if she stayed and had to make it pay she would be tied forever, forever running backwards and forwards placating staff, placating residents, servicing a huge loan to placate Harry.

A chill trickled down her spine like iced water. She took a deep breath, struggling to sort through the new thoughts that had tumbled into her head. If she stayed at the house she would never be free. Harry would always know where to find her, almost as if she was still there waiting for him. With trembling hands she locked the car and headed towards the front door.

Everywhere inside conspired to look inviting, pristine and warm, a velvet-lined prison. She picked up the phone book, shutting her mind to the view, and dialled a local number.

'Good afternoon,' she said crisply. 'Is that Kirby's the estate agents? I wondered if I could possibly arrange for someone to come out and do a valuation for me.'

The girl at the far end of the line said, 'Certainly madam, if I could take your details. Is this with a view to selling your property?'

Katherine Bourne screwed her eyes tight shut. 'Yes,' she said, 'yes, it is.'

*   *   *

When Carol arrived home from Northampton at half past six that evening, Harry was sitting in the kitchen, hunched over the table cradling a tumbler. Beside him were the remains of a bottle of Scotch. She dropped her brief-case by the fridge. He didn't move. The two cats sat on a kitchen unit trying to stare him out. Harry's face was bright red, his eyes streaming and beside him was a roll of toilet paper, little scrunches of which were arranged around the table like a fall of unseasonal snow.

'Bad day?' she asked gently, trying to gauge just how much of the Scotch he had put away in her absence.

He looked up, eyes unfocused. 'Oh fucking wonderful,' he said thickly. 'Absolutely bloody-ace-shit-hot-couldn't-be-any-better-wonderful – one dumps me, two dump me, nobody wants me, why don't you just go for broke and throw me out. I know you want to.' He sneezed, made a grab for the toilet roll and missed. It bounced across the floor, unravelling as it went.

Carol glanced out of the kitchen window to see if Ray and Geoff were home. 'I think you really ought to go to bed,' she said.

Harry grinned. 'Oh yes, now there's a good idea, best idea I've heard all day. Why don't we go to bed my little, pretty Kitty-Kat? Paradise, eh? Me and you.'

Carol helped him to his feet and guided him gently up the stairs. It wasn't easy, his legs were leaden while his hands had some interesting ideas of their own. Finally, hot, bedraggled and sweating hard she dragged him across the landing, rolled him over onto the bed and bent down to pull off his shoes.

He lifted his head and leered at her. 'You little minx,' he snorted, just before he passed out.

When Ray and Geoff arrived home Carol was waiting for them. 'What happened at work today?' she demanded, meeting them at their back door.

Geoff pulled a face. 'Ouch, not so confrontational,

please. Anyway, what do you mean? You look terrible. What's the matter?'

Carol sighed. 'It's Harry, he's been drinking, I've just had to put him to bed, he's practically paralytic. I wondered if anything had happened to upset him?'

Ray shrugged. 'God only knows. I thought he got on really well today; he did the pastry.' Ray paused. 'He did ring up about a couple of jobs – maybe they turned him down. He looked pretty dejected when he came out of the office, and then some woman rang later. I think it might have been someone from personnel.'

'He was going off somewhere after work, maybe he didn't get much joy there either,' Geoff added. 'Though I think he was pretty hopeful, he ordered flowers before he left.'

Carol stared at him. 'Flowers?'

Geoff nodded. 'He gave us the cash and then ordered them on Ray's credit card. I assumed they must be for you, you know, a thank you or a sorry for locking you out or something, bouquet.'

'I've been out on site with a client all day,' said Carol with surprise. 'Harry knew that, I told him this morning.'

'Probably slipped his mind.'

It was later that evening when Katherine rang Carol at home, praying that Harry wouldn't pick up the phone. To her relief Carol answered straight away, and as soon as they had exchanged hellos, Carol said, 'I was going to ring you. Did Harry send you flowers today?'

Katherine snorted. 'No, he didn't. Why?'

'I don't know, I've just got the horrible feeling we're missing something. He was drunk when I arrived home tonight.'

Katherine sighed. 'That might have had something to do with me. He came to see me today.'

'Today?'

Katherine nodded even though she knew Carol couldn't see her. 'I thought he wanted to talk about the house, but unfortunately he'd got hold of the idea that I wanted him back.'

'My God,' murmured Carol. 'That might explain it. Are you okay?'

Katherine laughed nervously. 'Oh I'm fine now, I think. I rang to say that I've changed my mind about taking out the loan. I've made up my mind to sell up instead.' Carol was quiet, so Katherine continued. 'And about the conference at the weekend. I'm not really sure I should go now, if I'm selling up I won't need to –'

Carol cut her short. 'Why don't you come anyway? It will do you good and you could still get some ideas and some advice on what to do next. We could talk.'

Katherine sighed. 'And Harry will be there too, won't he?'

'I'm not sure, but either way I still think you ought to come. It's always a good weekend. It'll be fun. Do you think it's cold enough yet for revenge?'

'Maybe,' Katherine said slowly. She thought fleetingly about the way Harry had made her feel on the railway station; she never wanted to feel that way again.

On Wednesday morning Carol glanced at her post and then up at Jeanette, who was standing beside her desk. 'Were there any flowers delivered here for me yesterday?' she asked casually.

Jeanette shook her head. 'No, why?'

'I just wondered.' Carol pulled a Dictaphone tape out of her bag. 'Could you get this typed up?'

Jeanette nodded. 'Northampton?'

'That's right, and I wondered if you'd made any headway on the Kestrel thing?'

Jeanette shrugged. 'Not a bean. Do you still want me to carry on looking?'

Carol hesitated. Jeanette still had an air of a cat who had got the cream.

Carol shivered. 'Tooth better?' she said quietly.

Jeanette grinned. 'Oh yes, I've got it all sorted out now.'

'Good.'

'Oh and there was a message from Lee Fenman on the machine. He said he can't wait forever.'

Carol nodded. 'I'll ring him later.' She wondered if he would let her have another week to make up her mind; after the weekend at Baneford she might be glad of a trip to New York.

On Friday morning Lee rang her. 'You've been very quiet,' he said. 'I expected you to chew my hand off to take me up on my offer.' She knew he was grinning.

'I've always played hard to get, Lee. I still need a few more days to think about it.'

'What's to think about? Oh and I took a look at that Kestrel thing for you.'

Carol held her breath. 'Was it part of the package Lactons signed for?'

Lee laughed. 'No, we bought it in the new year but were waiting until we were sure of the Japanese connection before we moved in. Why? It sounds as if you have a vested interest?'

Carol felt a great weight lift from somewhere just above her heart. 'No, not at all. It was –' she stopped, pulling back from the edge. Lee Fenman didn't need to know about her private life. 'Thanks for looking into it. I appreciate it. I'll ring you next week about New York.'

Lee snorted. 'I like a woman who plays her cards close to her chest. I'm surprised you couldn't pull Kestrel up yourself, it was on the files I sent over for you to review. Your secretary must be slipping, it's there in the index.'

Carol wondered why Jeanette hadn't been able to find the file. Thinking she was responsible for Harry's redundancy had stopped Carol throwing him out straight away. The last lingering shreds of guilt lifted like dawn breaking.

'Won't you come in,' said Katherine on Wednesday afternoon to a bright young thing from Kirby's the estate agent clutching a clipboard.

The girl smiled and slipped a tape measure out of her bag. 'The gardens are a picture. I'll make sure we get some really nice photographs of those – big selling point. And the location's excellent. Does your husband commute?'

Katherine nodded. 'Would you like a coffee before we start?'

'That would be lovely. How many bedrooms have you got?'

Katherine plugged in the kettle, wishing there was some way she could have this conversation outside, away from the house, so that the walls couldn't hear. Already she sensed they knew she was betraying them. 'Six,' she said, rinsing out the cafetiere, 'although until recently we used one as an office.'

The girl nodded and scribbled something down on her note pad. 'I normally do the exterior shots myself for the detail sheets, but for a house as big as this we usually sub-contract the work out.' She looked up. 'Would you mind if we sent our photographer round?'

Katherine smiled. It seemed that things had come full circle. Perhaps when the girl had gone she would ring Ben Morton and see if he fancied having lunch.

Harry rang Jeanette at coffee time and after lunch all week. She was canny enough to make it very plain she missed him terribly, canny enough to let him know that it was him that she wanted, and after the second phone call on Wednesday morning, she rang her boyfriend, Bas – after all there was no need for her to wait for Harry alone.

*   *   *

At the café Harry made the pastry, peeled vegetables and kept himself to himself, his mind ticked over quietly. He decided to go to Baneford College with Carol – at least that way he could be certain of getting fed over the weekend.

Chapter Twenty-six

Carol pulled her suitcase out of the boot of the car. Harry, at her shoulder, leant over to rescue his bags. Ahead of them Baneford Ladies College stood amongst acres of rolling parkland and mature trees. Without any conscious thought, Carol had a distinct sensation of coming home. The main building, an Elizabethan pile, glowed red-gold in the early evening sunlight. To the left and right new modern blocks emphasised its pedigree.

Behind them, the main car park was already heaving with delegates arriving early for the welcoming dinner. Carol had a pass for the staff car park, divided from the throng by a low wall and set of steps.

Harry was very quiet, in fact he had been very quiet all week since Carol had found him drunk in her kitchen. She glanced across at him. Tick-tick-tick, she thought, as he straightened up, counterbalancing her bag with his own. It wasn't a biological clock she imagined she could hear, but the sound of an unexploded bomb. She was nervous and glanced around to see if she could see Katherine.

As they headed for the main house one of the organisers, Dr Patricia Duffy, hurried down the steps of a side door to meet them. She was an impressive woman, nearly six feet tall, with a mane of snow-white hair.

'Carol, my dear,' she cried, kissed her effusively on each cheek. 'How very nice to see you again. How was your journey? Everyone's here, I've arranged for all the die-hards to meet up in the Cavell Room for sherry and nibbles before we head downstairs to welcome the throng.

Wonderful turnout this year though – full house . . .' She turned a fraction and peered at Harry. 'And this is?'

Carol smiled nervously. It seemed almost cruel to set the ball in motion, but she said in an even voice, 'Dr Duffy, I'd like you to meet Harry – my secretary.'

Dr Duffy modified her enthusiastic greeting to a polite nod. 'I am very pleased to meet you, Harry. How very good of you to give up your weekend for us. So glad you could come.' She slipped her arm through Carol's. 'I would have thought if you were going to hire a man, darling, you might have picked someone with a little more hair,' she said in what passed for a quiet voice. 'Or is it a case of experience outweighing the glories of youth?'

'Something like that,' Carol said as she glanced across at Harry. She saw him wince and almost changed her mind. She had no desire to humiliate him, just teach him a lesson he would be hard pressed to forget.

Inside the lodge, a uniformed porter came forward to take their luggage. Dr Duffy waved a hand toward Carol. 'Ms Ackerman's in one of the guest suites, number three, I think, and –' she looked across at Harry. 'Could you check where Mr . . .' her voice faded. 'Sorry, I'm afraid I didn't catch your second name.'

'Bourne,' said Harry, looking uncomfortable. 'Harry Bourne.'

'Yes, exactly,' said Dr Duffy, 'I'm not certain exactly where Mr Bourne is staying.'

The porter nodded. 'I'll take a look in the book, Dr Duffy,' and then looked at Carol. 'There's a message for you, Miss Ackerman. Nice to see you back again, Miss,' he said plucking a sheet of paper from the pigeon-hole above his desk.

Carol acknowledged his greeting with a smile and then unfolded the note, it read: 'Won't be there until Saturday morning, K.' She smiled and tucked the note into her handbag.

'Thank you,' she said and waited for the porter to show her to her room.

Someone had booked Harry into a seedy little annex room overlooking the kitchen compound at the back of the college.

Furiously he dragged a comb though his hair.

'I don't believe this,' he whispered, straightening his tie. 'Bloody women.' He looked at himself in the pitted mirror. His expensive grey suit was well cut; one of his favourites. Not that he could see it. The bedroom mirror was snapped off in a jagged razor edge just above his waist. 'How the hell, exactly, did I let myself get in this position?' he said crossly and rubbed a tiny shaving nick on his chin. He picked up his wallet and watch and hurried off to meet Carol.

It was an hour before dinner and the main corridors of the college were being prowled by businesswomen chatting in groups and swapping gossip.

Harry glanced over his shoulder before he tapped on the door of Carol's suite. Carol, wrapped in a thick bath towel, opened it a crack and practically dragged him inside.

'Did anyone see you?' She flicked the TV set onto mute.

Harry snorted. 'For God's sake, what is all this about?'

Carol looked uncomfortable. 'The committee don't like it.'

Harry went to the mini-bar and poured himself a glass of wine. 'Bugger the bloody committee. That woman, Dr whatever-her-name is, couldn't keep her hands off me. Did you see her at the sherry reception? She was all over me like a rash. And why, in God's name, did you tell her I was your secretary? Do you realise I've now got six faxes in my brief-case?'

Carol looked up anxiously. 'You have sent them, haven't you?'

Harry downed the wine in one. 'Of course I haven't, I

don't know how to use a fax machine, my secretary used to do all that for me.'

Carol slapped her forehead. 'Well, go back to your room and get them.' She glanced at her watch. 'Maybe there's still someone in the office who'll do them.'

Harry slammed the wine glass down on the counter. 'When you said a weekend away, Carol, this was not exactly what I had in mind.'

Carol lifted an eyebrow.

He sighed. 'Oh, all right. Pour me another glass of wine, will you?'

Carol grinned. 'Thank you, darling,' she said, blowing him a kiss. As he got to the door she flicked the TV remote and the sound came back on. 'You won't mind helping out on the information desk tomorrow, will you?' she added over her shoulder as she eased herself back into the armchair. 'It was the only way I could get you a free place.'

Katherine Bourne lit the candles on the dining-room table and then stood back to admire the effect. The bright gold flames danced in the slight breeze, the movement echoed in polished mahogany. Standing by the sideboard Ben Morton pulled the cork from the wine bottle, it slid out with a satisfying sound.

Katherine smiled. 'I'm really glad you said you'd come.'

'Who could resist an invitation to celebrate the beginning of a new life?' Ben said.

Katherine took the drink he offered her. 'We ought to make a toast,' she said looking down into the top of the wine glass.

Ben snorted. 'Why, for God's sake? Who needs a toast when you've got good food, good company –' Gently he touched his glass against hers. 'But if you insist, here's to the electric kettle and the advent of a sure-fire cure for aphids.'

Katherine laughed. From the kitchen she could smell

the rich perfume of the chicken casserole. New potatoes, already drained and buttered, waited in a covered serving dish, alongside another filled with summer vegetables; fruits of her last harvest. It seemed deeply appropriate to share them with Ben.

'So, when does the house go on the market?' asked Ben.

'As soon as I've spoken to Harry,' she said, taking a sip from her glass. Katherine opened the kitchen door, carefully framing her thoughts. 'Ben, I want you to know I do understand what you said the other day. I'm really glad you're here – but I don't need you,' she said in an undertone. 'I've just come out of a relationship built on all sorts of commitments and compromises – I don't think I'm ready for any more either. I'd just like it if we could be friends. I've had it up to here with commitment.' She drew a line with a flat palm across her forehead. Her voice cracked by the time she got to the end of the sentence. 'Would you like to help me bring supper in?'

Ben grinned. 'Certainly would, I'm absolutely ravenous, it smells wonderful. And I'm flattered that you passed up a full banquet for a dinner with me.'

'Don't be. I decided that I wanted to face Harry in daylight,' Katherine said with a smile.

Ben laughed. 'You're learning fast, see how powerful wisdom is when you keep it quiet?'

Katherine handed him a pair of oven gloves. 'Come on, let's eat.'

Dinner in the banqueting hall at Baneford was grand, wine, six courses. Harry found himself seated between two female executives from a computer company, one of whom was a tiny ginger woman with thick glasses, whom everyone referred to as Chloe.

'Have you been to Baneford before, Chloe?' Harry said, slowly trying to drag up one of those polite stilted conversations that launched a thousand forgettable encounters.

Chloe leered at him. Her eyes rolled behind the lenses. She'd obviously had quite a few aperitifs before they'd sat down for dinner and said something in a low lecherous purr. Harry did not ask her to repeat it. Although he didn't hear the words he could understand lust in any language.

Carol, on the far side of Dr Duffy, smiled and waved as if he were standing at the far end of a jetty.

Viciously he speared at the tiny collection of shellfish exquisitely arranged amongst fennel and delicate curls of vegetables on his plate and stuffed them into his mouth. As he went for a second forkful he felt Chloe's hand slide stealthily up over his thigh.

He turned to smile at her, she grinned and moved her fingers higher. Her eyes had shrunk to pinpricks behind her thick glasses, and as Harry felt her fingers contracting, he made a strange kind of high-pitched wheezing noise in the back of his throat.

'Which room are you in?' she said in an undertone. Harry coughed, feeling his face flush crimson. 'I'm with someone,' he said thickly, nodding towards the top of the table.

Chloe looked disappointed. 'What a pity, I bet I could teach you a thing or two.'

Harry jiffled his chair away from hers and as he did, he disentangled her fingers, his eyes firmly fixed on his plate. Very slowly he turned to talk to the woman on his left and Chloe went back to her shellfish.

They got to bed around twelve. A bucket and a half of house wine had made Carol forget to pretend they weren't a couple and she practically dragged him upstairs to her suite.

'I'm so glad you decided to come, Harry,' she purred, brushing her breasts against him, while she fumbled for the keys outside the door. 'We make a good couple. Dr Duffy said you were lovely.'

She fished the keys out of her clutch bag.

'Well, that's all right then, as long as Dr Duffy approves. You've had rather a lot to drink. I've never seen you like this.'

Carol giggled and tapped the side of her nose. 'How about you?'

He took the key out of her fingers and slid it into the lock as her hands slid up under his shirt.

'God, you feel so good tonight,' she hissed in his ear.

Harry pushed the door open. The suite looked as if Carol had been burgled, clothes dropped on the floor, bed rolled back in an unseemly scrum. Carol kicked off her shoes and launched herself towards the bed like an Olympic diver.

'Come to bed, my pretty little Harry-Kat,' she slurred. 'You know, it'll be great now we're together. You waiting for me at home, me out at work doing battle on the corporate killing ground. Let me show you what you've been missing. Paradise –' She slapped the unmade bed beside her.

Harry closed the door quietly and hurried back to his room. Once inside he double locked the door and pressed his head against the cold varnished wood.

There had never been a time when he wanted them to be together, not really. A long time ago, he had considered it, but that had passed – thank God.

They'd met at some promotional beano, she'd looked gorgeous, exquisitely finished like a well carved sculpture, in her perfectly tailored suit and snowy white blouse. It had taken him two hours to get her into bed – that was back in the days when he thought predatory was a good thing for a man to be.

There had been a gap then – not a gap from Carol – just a gap where a casual fling and a lot of rumpy pumpy in strange plastic hotel rooms turned in a regular fling with less rumpy pumpy and he remembered saying things like, 'My God, I wish it was like this all the time. I want to be with you forever.' But he'd never really meant it. Carol was part of a life apart, not a part of real life.

Once upon a time he had agonised frequently about the morality of it, but he had never seriously intended to leave Katherine. What he and Carol had had was comfortable. He didn't want her in his life as a resident, just as a visiting alien.

At first he justified his lack of up and leaving because of his children, then the mortgage, an operation, his wife's nervous disposition – how vulnerable and weak Katherine had seemed. When he'd found it harder to come up with a plausible excuse, with a streak of pure genius, Carol had hit on the menopause.

'Oh yes,' he'd said with breathless gratitude. 'I can't leave now, not when she's so vulnerable. I mean it's a big thing for a woman.'

Yes, a big thing for a woman. But not quite as big as his arrangement to have safe sex with a comfortable familiar body, while not having to worry about her or depend on her, or pay for her upkeep, just sharing the ripest cherries from the top of the tree and leaving the rest for his wife to pip and bottle.

He had never really had any intention of leaving Katherine, but somewhere down the line, without lifting a finger, he had managed to lose it all anyway.

Harry dropped his suit jacket over the chair by the bed and picked up his tooth brush. Just as he climbed into the bed his mobile phone rang. Sleepily he pulled it out, wondering who it might be.

'Hello, Harry,' said a soft female voice. 'I've been thinking about you all day. I can't sleep. I miss you so much. I don't think I can go on like this.'

He was instantly awake. 'Jeanette?'

There was the sound of a tight emotional little sob. 'God, Harry, I can't believe I'm doing this, we really need to talk.'

Harry looked nervously around the room, as if they might be overheard.

'I'm away for the weekend,' he said thickly, imagining her pressing the phone to her lips. The thought set loose a cavalcade of other erotic images. He took a deep breath.

'Baneford?' she said. 'With Carol?'

'That's right, what about Monday when I finish work?'

Jeanette made small dark desperate noise in the back of her throat. 'I'd rather see you before then, can't you make your apologies and slip away?'

Harry grimaced, struggling with the decision. 'I've got to help out on the information desk tomorrow morning. What about if I came to your place after lunch?'

'That would be lovely,' whispered Jeanette. 'I'll see you tomorrow.'

After she rang off Harry stared down at the phone wondering if he had been dreaming.

He overslept on Saturday morning; by the time he got downstairs hundreds of delegates were milling around in the foyer, having already had their networking breakfast. He felt completely lost.

'Harry?' He looked up at the sound of his name.

Carol, wearing a bright red name badge, waved him over to a little clique of women. The jaws of the group opened to admit him. 'I've told Harriet all about you,' she said, indicating a thin elderly woman in an unfortunate green suit. 'Harry, this is Dr Belcher. She'll tell you what to do.'

Harry glanced round nervously. The women reminded him of a lynch mob. 'And where are you going to be?'

Carol picked up her brief-case. 'Oh, I'm heading a workshop on financial help for new businesses, tapping into the old girl network. I'll be in lecture hall six if you need me. Catch you at lunch.'

Before he could reply she turned and left him to the ministrations of Harriet Belcher.

'Well, my dear,' the old lady said, peering at him over the top of her half-rimmed glasses. 'Let's go and see if we can find you a little job, shall we?' She slipped her scrawny arm though his. 'How very like Carol to hire male help. You know she used to be a student of mine. Wonderful, wonderful mind.'

Katherine Bourne pulled into a parking space and looked up at Baneford College; she was a little early and very nervous. To compensate she had dressed with great care and taken a lot of trouble over her hair and make-up. She'd left Ben at home. He'd promised to water the garden for her. Picking up the new brief-case, bought especially for the occasion, Katherine headed towards the entrance.

On the front desk a porter tipped his hat. 'Morning, ma'am. May I have your name please?'

'Katherine . . .' she hesitated. 'Jackson.'

The man didn't bat an eyelid as he worked a finger down the list on the desk.

'Here we are. Ms Ackerman has already posted your schedule.' He handed her a printed sheet and then pointed through the foyer. 'Down the corridor, fourth door on the left, "Women Finding a Voice", ten o'clock. Oh, and Ms Ackerman has invited you to join her in the dining room at one for lunch.'

Katherine nodded dumbly. She glanced down at her timetable; perhaps it would be more appropriate to substitute the words 'last supper' for informal buffet lunch. Deep in thought she opened the appointed door and found herself amongst a small circle of women.

One was talking, rolling her programme into a wheatsheaf of anxiety. Katherine slipped quietly into a seat at the back.

'I run three successful shops and yet I always felt as if what I said bore no weight, had no depth.' The speaker was in her late fifties and had a warm open face. 'I come from the generation that still think what men have to say and what they want is more important than anything I wanted.'

Katherine shivered. The woman was walking across her grave.

Another woman with a bright red name-tag, who seemed to be leading the discussion, lifted her hands. 'You say felt and had.'

The woman smiled. 'That's right. I decided if I didn't take what I said seriously, no one else would. So I spent time thinking about what I wanted, and then said it, knowing it was what I truly believed.' Her smile broadened. 'A castle of words, well defended, well thought out – and it worked.' Almost as an afterthought, she added 'I wasted an awful lot of years living up to someone else's expectations of what I should believe and think.'

Katherine let her gaze move around the room; it was full of mature women like herself – tall, thin, plump, dark, fair, all ages, shapes and sizes. The tension began to ease in her stomach. Without knowing it, she'd come home.

Chapter Twenty-seven

Katherine was having such an interesting time that she had almost forgotten about Harry. After the first lecture she moved on to another called 'Starting Out – New Business Opportunities for Women', and then looking down at her schedule realised with a start that it was almost lunch-time.

Out in the foyer everywhere was crowded with women, clutching brochures, schedules and glasses of wine, being handed round by uniformed footmen.

Katherine took a drink from a tray and was about turn and look for the dining hall when a woman caught hold of her arm. 'I saw you in the Voice lecture. I'm sure I recognise your face from somewhere, weren't you at Keele last year?'

Katherine shook her head and then to her horror spotted Harry, laden down with cardboard cartons, being led across the room by a tall thin woman in a green suit.

'Make way, make way,' the woman called cheerfully. The groups parted like the Red Sea.

Katherine swung round to face the panelling. 'I think I've just spotted my friend,' she mumbled to her new would-be companion and hurried off in the opposite direction to Harry. As she rounded the main staircase Carol Ackerman waved to her.

'Hello, I'm so glad you could make it. How's it going?'

Katherine downed the contents of her glass in one. 'I've just seen Harry,' she said, oblivious to the little crowd of hangers-on around Carol.

Carol smiled and caught hold of her arm. 'Don't worry, it will be all right. It's nearly over now. Why don't we go into the refectory and eat before the rush starts. One of the perks of the job is that we get to reserve a table. Come on.'

She waved a waiter over and plucked two more glasses off the tray. 'Here,' she said with warm smile. 'Dutch courage. Why don't you let me introduce you to a few people?'

Side by side they walked into the Elizabethan dining room. Katherine tried very hard to keep control of the nasty sense of unease in her stomach. Tucked in behind Carol, she picked up a plate and moved along the serving line without really thinking about what she was doing. All her attention, all her thoughts, were focused on what might happen when Harry turned up.

'Don't look so worried, we are in this together,' said Carol in an undertone, piling potato salad onto her plate. 'You know in a funny way I can't believe we've managed to get this far.' She lifted her glass in salute. 'Here's to no more pretty little Kitty-Kat.'

Katherine choked on her wine. 'Kitty-Kat?' she snorted through a searing mouthful.

'Yes, it's Harry's pet name for –' Carol stopped, eyes fixed on Katherine's face. 'Oh, my God. Not that as well. Katherine Bourne, pretty little Kitty-Kat?'

Katherine nodded. 'Mark one, no doubt you've had a glimpse of paradise too,' she said, furiously swallowing down her apprehension along with the wine. 'How long do you think he'll be?'

Carol eased up on tiptoe and peered over the heads of the other delegates. 'I can't see him, but he shouldn't be long. Dr Belcher is never late for lunch.' She smiled as she spoke, fingers locked tight around the wine glass.

Katherine guessed she was struggling to retain her composure too.

'What did you think of the lectures?' Carol said after a second or two.

Katherine stared at her. 'Wonderful, but is now the time to talk about them?'

'I can't think of a better time, why should we fill our heads up with trash when we can talk about something important? All those years –' Carol stopped, took a deep breath and carried out hasty repairs on her smile. 'So, what made you decide to sell the house?'

Katherine sighed and began to explain, and as she did was aware that Carol's stance had subtly altered and knew instinctively that Harry was on his way. She didn't turn, didn't hold her breath, just calmly carried on talking. She could feel him getting closer. At the very last second she saw Carol look up and smile.

'Harry,' Carol said in an even voice. 'There you are. I wondered where you'd got to. I'd like you to meet a very dear friend of mine. Funnily enough we were just talking about you –'

Slowly Katherine looked up, straight into Harry's eyes. There was a moment, as their eyes met, when the faces around them, the voices, the noise of the buffet, even Carol Ackerman, faded away into unfocused insignificance.

Harry took a step back, his jaw dropped open and his skin faded to the colour of skimmed milk. He made an odd guttural croak.

Katherine smiled and extended her hand. 'Hello, Harry,' she said, emulating Carol's carefully modulated tone. 'How nice to see you, Kitty-Kat and I were just swopping stories. You know, it's quite amazing how much we've got in common.'

Harry reeled back clutching his chest and then swung round and fought his way through the queue of delegates at the buffet.

Katherine looked across at Carol and lifted her glass in salute. For all the appearance of calmness, her heart was racing in her chest. 'Was it something I said? Do you think we ought to go after him?'

Carol shook her head lazily. 'No, I don't think so. Why don't we sit down and have lunch? I don't know about you but I'm starving.'

Harry staggered out into the foyer, gasping for breath. Katherine and Carol. He caught hold of the banister, struggling to drag some oxygen into his lungs. How long had they known about each other? He felt dizzy and slumped down on the bottom step.

'Harry? Are you all right?'

He looked up. Dr Belcher, cradling two glasses of wine, looked down at him with an anxious expression on her face. 'I do hope we didn't ask you to do too much?' she said. 'You look terrible. Here, why don't you drink this?'

Gratefully he took the proffered glass and drained it in a single gulp. She lifted an eyebrow. 'Perhaps brandy might have been a better idea. Would you like to lie down?'

He shook his head. 'No, no thank you. I'll be fine, really.'

His mind was racing, trying to fit disparate images together into a conspiracy theory. Just as the wine began to ease though into his bloodstream someone else called his name. He didn't know whether to run or look up, and decided on balance to ignore it, perhaps whoever it was would go away – and then realised as his mind processed the sound that it was neither Carol nor Katherine.

Framed in the open doors of the main hall was Jeanette. She was dressed in a cream mini-skirt and tiny black sleeveless top. She looked as if she had been crying and hurried over to him. 'I couldn't wait,' she murmured, gnawing her lips nervously. 'I just had to see you.'

Harry glanced over his shoulder. 'How the hell did you get here?' he said.

'Tony brought me in the van.'

Harry nodded. 'Good, in that case, I'll just go and fetch my things. It won't take me a minute. Just wait here.' He turned but Jeanette was too quick for him.

'Harry,' she said thickly, grabbing hold of his arm. 'I think I might be pregnant.'

Harry groaned. 'Oh, sweet Jesus.'

Chapter Twenty-eight

When Carol arrived home on Sunday evening, Geoff and Ray were waiting for her, along with the two ginger cats.

'So?' said Ray, hurrying into the house behind her. 'How did it go?'

'Mission accomplished,' she said grimly, dropping her suitcase in the hall by the stairs.

Geoff stared at her. 'What on earth is the matter? We thought about hanging bunting. No more Harry. You don't look very pleased for a woman who just got her life back.'

Carol sighed as she headed for the kitchen. 'Really? Are you going to put the kettle on or am I? I've got a blinding headache.'

Ray pouted. 'So why are you so bloody grumpy?'

Carol swung round. 'You're right, I ought to be pleased with myself, but all in all it's turned out to be a pretty hollow victory.'

Ray smiled as he picked three mugs off the dresser. 'Sam came to lunch today.'

Carol groaned and threw her coat over a chair. 'Oh please, don't rub it in. Another Mr Right slips through my fingers, eh? Was he with the blonde nymphet?'

The two men looked at each other and then grinned. 'No. He was on his own. And he said he was sorry his sister was so rude to you the other day,' said Ray.

Carol looked up at him. 'His sister?'

Geoff nodded enthusiastically. 'Yep, that's right. His sister. She's been staying with him for a few days until she moves into a new flat. Oh, and by the way, he said as soon as you're home and dry to give him a ring.'

Carol pushed past him on her way to the hall.

'Jesus,' said Ray. 'Where's the fire?'

Carol glanced back over her shoulder, smiling like a Cheshire cat. 'Sorry, I've just got to make a quick phone call.'

'Oh, and someone called Lee Fenman left a message on your machine – he said he wanted to hear from you when you'd got a minute . . .'

Carol grinned as she picked up the receiver. 'Oh, he will, but I don't think he's going to like what I have to say,' she said and tapped in Sam's home number.

Katherine arrived home feeling elated and exhausted and free – finally. Her new brief-case was full of information, her head full of bright ideas. To her delight Ben Morton's car was still parked in the driveway of the house. She hurried up to the front door. He opened it before she had a chance to put the key in the lock.

'I didn't expect you'd still be here,' she said, slipping off her jacket.

Ben grinned and took her bag. 'You didn't mind, did you? It just seemed easier than driving back to do the watering. Oh and while you were away your daughter rang.'

Katherine grimaced. 'What did you say to her?'

Ben laughed. 'Not much really, I just explained that I was your lover and she hung up.'

Katherine groaned. 'Oh, Ben.' She took a deep breath. 'What's that smell?'

He guided her towards the kitchen. The table was laid; two places set with pink linen napkins and a tiny bowl of summer flowers.

'I didn't think you'd fancy cooking when you got back so I made a lasagne. And I've been thinking, until you sort out the house and everything, maybe you'd like to camp out in a little cottage I know.' He looked up, eyes alight with amusement. 'Always assuming it fits in with your plans. No strings, no commitment.'

Katherine pulled up a chair at the kitchen table. 'I thought you were wary about me getting dependent. Didn't you say you couldn't help with my grief?'

He picked up the oven gloves. 'Everything is always open to negotiation. Now do you want salad with this? I've cooked garlic mushrooms as well.'

She smiled. 'Sounds great. Would you like me to open the wine?'

Harry, comfortably curled up on Jeanette's bed, slipped his arm out from around her shoulders.

'I was going to ring and tell you it was all over with Carol, but I really wanted to tell you face to face,' he said brushing his lips against her hair. She smelt divine. Her breasts brushed his chest making him shiver. 'And I've been thinking, I've really enjoyed working at the café, what about if, once everything is sorted out, we opened a restaurant? I mean I could go to college, take a course. Do it properly. What with the settlement from the house, the golden handshake from Danic and everything, we'd have enough to open a really nice place, you know, up market. Chic. We'd have staff. I wouldn't expect you to work, of course, not with the baby and everything.' He lay back, folded his arms behind his head and closed his eyes, imagining an elegant bistro, the pavement outside lined with bright umbrellas and wrought-iron furniture. A waiter stood in the doorway, with a crisp linen napkin hanging over one arm, waiting to show the patrons to their tables. Inside the sommelier was uncorking a bottle of house red. Harry smiled.

Jeanette ran a finger along his jaw. 'Will there be enough for me to have a little car too?'

Harry, mind still full of the sights and sounds and smells of his imaginary restaurant, nodded. 'Oh yes, I'm sure there would, what sort of thing had you got in mind?'

Jeanette slipped a knee between his thighs. 'I've seen this lovely BMW. It would be perfect.'

Jeanette rolled over so she was on her hands and knees. Striking a pose she ran a hand down over her smooth muscular belly. Harry looked up at her as she climbed aboard; she had his undivided attention.

She was ninety-nine per cent certain she wasn't pregnant, and was equally certain that Harry had so little idea about the workings of the female body that he wouldn't realise it was too soon to tell; but the thought, thrown out like bait, had been enough to snap the line tight. She wondered if he would be disappointed when she told him she had been mistaken. Harry reached up to touch her, eyes alight with desire – maybe not.

Being the wife of a restaurateur was not quite what Jeanette had had in mind when she had set her sights on Harry Bourne, but she could see distinct advantages; after all, she had always loathed cooking.